The Scribe

Peter Kerry

Visit us online at www.authorsonline.co.uk

An Authors OnLine Book

Text Copyright © Peter Kerry 2007

Cover design by Siobhan Smith ©

All rights reserved. No part of this publication may be reproduced, stored in a retrieval system, or transmitted in any form or by any means, electronic, mechanical, photocopy, recording or otherwise, without prior written permission of the copyright owner. Nor can it be circulated in any form of binding or cover other than that in which it is published and without similar condition including this condition being imposed on a subsequent purchaser.

ISBN 978-0-755202-96-6

Authors OnLine Ltd
19 The Cinques
Gamlingay, Sandy
Bedfordshire SG19 3NU
England

This book is also available in e-book format, details of which are available at
www.authorsonline.co.uk

About the Author

Peter Kerry was born in Essex and lived most of his life in the South East until he moved to Manchester in 1988. As a writer he created the situation comedies 'Men Of Intelligence' and 'North East Of Eden' for BBC Radio 4 as well as writing for 'The Archers'. His television work includes co-creating the children's comedy 'Big Meg Little Meg' for Granada TV and being on the writing team for the ITV soap 'Emmerdale'.

He lives near Stockport with his partner and two children.

'The Scribe' is his first novel.

Acknowledgements and Thanks

To Beverley, Louie and Kate. This is for you and it wouldn't be here without you ...

Thanks to Mark Illis and Martin Jameson … for the support and constructive criticism.

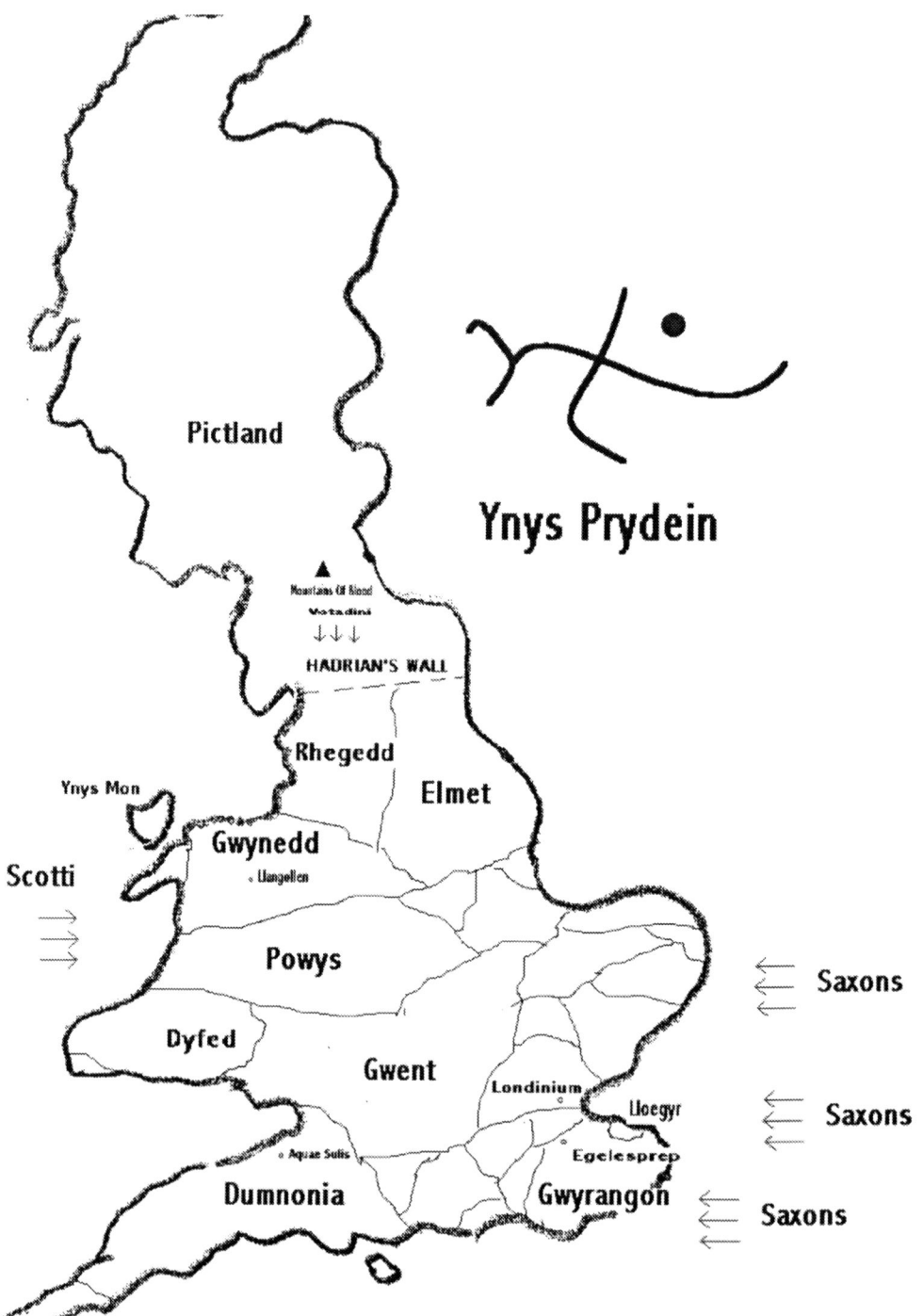

PART ONE

Chapter 1 – The Scribe

It was the warmth that got him.

Llew loved being warm, but had never really understood what it was to feel *cold*, mainly because being cold was the way he had *always* felt. Well, most of the time anyway. It was a natural state of being. Sitting by a fire was warm*er*, but it was never actually *warm*, because there was always a draught at his back unless he sat with his back to it, in which case it was his front that froze. Oh yes, people had told him about the summer from a very young age … 'oh, the days are long and hot in the summer', they said; but when it came round, the days in question never seemed that long or that hot to him. The first summer he was old enough to recognise was all rain and chilly breezes and that year, by the time what people told him was 'Autumn' came round, any long hot days had seemed a far-away memory and he was too busy noticing how cold and damp it was anyway. He decided very early on that the 'warmth of Spring' must be a big fat lie grown-ups told and that the only season that anyone was really truthful about was Winter.

Being really warm, properly warm, became something that Llew knew he must *aspire* to.

And aspire to it he did. As a young boy, any excuse … *any* excuse to sit with his grandmother as she crouched in her hut, stirring a bubbling lamb stew in an iron cauldron over the open fire and he would use it. The other children could splash about barefoot in the snow, or slush, or puddles, but not Llew. He would find a way of getting as close to the fire as he could without it actually burning him and he would sit and listen, because his grandmother would tell stories. Some were made up, some were true – histories of the clan and such like – but she would tell them and he would remember, while he wrapped his cloak around himself tightly and tried, against all odds, to be properly warm.

At which he would then sadly fail.

He only discovered what true warmth was when his father took him to

Aquae Sulis.[1] He was twelve-years-old by then and his father, Gwyddno, the chieftain of a small but not insignificant Cymru clan in the west of the kingdom of Powys,[2] had insisted that he stop skulking about the fire where the women did the cooking and start behaving like a man, because, apparently, now he had turned twelve, he *was* one. He was therefore coming on a trip.

Llew had of course whined and complained as he always did – his father didn't need him to go with him and it was the middle of Winter after all; couldn't he stay behind? He'd come next time. When Llew was like this, his father nearly always lost his temper and started thanking the gods that he had other, older sons to take over running the tribe, because They Only Knew what would happen to Their people if that whining idiot was allowed to take over, before storming off. However, this time Gwyddno had simply thrown a cloak at him and told him to get a pony loaded up. He was coming to Aquae Sulis and there was to be no argument.

He knew the journey would be miserable and in this at least he was not disappointed. The first leg was by pony to the coast. Driving, freezing rain kept him from looking up most of the way, which was probably fortunate because it meant he and his father didn't have to speak to each other (although it didn't feel terribly lucky at the time) and it also meant he didn't have to worry about the wolves and the bears in the forests they travelled through, although the wolves and the bears probably were being sensible – either hibernating or sheltering from the rain. This part of the trip took three days and Llew probably would have been glad when it was over, had he not been told by Gwyddno just before they arrived at the coast that there was to be a *second* leg of the journey.

At sea.

Llew had, of course, never been to sea before, but he was confident it couldn't possibly be worse than the journey by land. In this, he proved to be profoundly wrong. The driving rain did not abate, the wind became a gale and, on top of this, the small and rickety ship that took them across what the Cymru called the Severn Sea moved about in a violent and unnerving way as waves loomed high over the vessel, crashing down on the deck, such that Llew was unable to keep upright, keep dry, or indeed keep his food down.

The third leg of the journey – once again overland by pony – was relatively comfortable in that it didn't involve being thrown about or drowned. It was, however, a *third* leg and Llew had not been told there would be one.

After I get back home, Llew thought to himself, as his pony trudged on and the sleet rained down, I am *never ever* going anywhere else again. Travel is not for me.

---

[1] Bath, as it later became known.
[2] In modern day mid-Wales.

So it was after nine days journeying, Llew and Gwyddno finally entered the city gates.

Aquae Sulis. City of the hot springs.

Llew had to admit he was impressed. The buildings were so … built. Not the ramshackle rock and wood of a Cymru hall. But hard chiselled marble … houses that seemed to tower above him, bridges and roads that seemed to stretch out for miles. There were a lot of soldiers around – there always were in Roman cities, he'd been told – but these were different to the Roman soldiers Llew had come into contact with back home in Powys. For a start, they weren't trying to kill or rob any members of his family. Back home, they were as much bandit as soldier. But here, they were relaxed and not aggressive … well disciplined too.

And then they entered the house of Marcus Artorus and it was *warm*. Not just warm: totally warm, all-around warm and smoke wasn't stinging in his eyes either. It was a big room too. High stone ceilings and lots of statues of strange creatures that he supposed must be old Roman Gods – although he also knew that the Romans had been Christians for hundreds of years now, so the statues must be very old. His father was talking to Marcus in the far corner and he hoped the conversation would go on forever.

People *lived* in places like *this*?

And while he wallowed in this total and absolute feeling of luxury, he became aware that the conversation between Marcus and his father had changed. They were no longer talking about the cattle and sheep Gwyddno was supposed to be providing for the city, they were talking about him.

'Well, what about it, boy?' his father had said, 'How would you like to learn to read and write?'

'You mean stay here?'

'Marcus needs an apprentice scribe and –'

Llew didn't know much about scribes or writing, when it came to it. Almost no one in his village did. It was a practice not trusted.

'You want to leave me here?'

His father had looked uncomfortable, shifting on his feet awkwardly, not looking Llew in the eye.

'Look, I know you'll miss your mother and brothers and sisters, but … well, now your Grandma's passed on … I think it's for the best, don't you?'

Llew's grandmother had died two summers ago. He had been mortified. Not only had she been his teacher and teller of tales, she'd always made sure there was a space by the fire for him. *And* she'd always been able to stop Gwyddno dragging him off in the cold to go hunting, or woodchopping or some such. Llew was, she'd argued, still a baby and Gwyddno was to leave him alone. There'd come a point where he hadn't really liked being called a baby. However, if it was a choice between that or going out to spear some mad wild boar in the snow, Llew decided you could dress him in swaddling clothes any time.

There'd been no reply to his last question, so Gwyddno soldiered on.

'You're a man now and you've some wit about you … although the Gods know what *we* can do with it! You can't hunt, you can't fight … the Druid says you've nothing *he* can use and the priest isn't too enthusiastic either … so maybe this is what you're meant to do. However, if you don't want to stay, I won't make you –'

Llew didn't give his father a chance to finish. He turned to Marcus.

'Which room is mine?'

And Marcus grinned.

Years later, Gwyddno was to confess that he'd rather hoped Llew might put up a bit of a fight. A scribe? It wasn't exactly the noblest of professions. Gwyddno's people, like all of the Cymru, had an oral culture; that is to say, knowledge was passed on by mouth from one generation to another. The idea of writing things down had at one time been thought of as blasphemous and now, although well established since the Romans had come, seemed faintly ridiculous and certainly untrustworthy. The only people who could read and write in your average Cymru settlement was your local Christian priest and he would more often be known in the Celtic tongue as 'a wyr leiaf', literally 'he who knows least', or more accurately 'stupid head'. However, at least, this was at least something the boy *didn't* complain about, so there was a blessing anyhow.

Marcus Artorus was a clerk. Well, a bit more than a clerk – he was one of the counsellors to His Honour Caius Plautus, the governor of Aquae Sulis. Marcus was a kind man, in his middle years, quick witted with sharp, beady, blue eyes. He grew to be quite fond of Llew. Well, fond in his own way. With Marcus, Llew got the impression that he never really let himself get too attached to anything. Or anyone. One day, when Llew had been serving Marcus for some time and had the confidence to ask about this, he said, 'We are none of us here for long boy …'.

He turned out to be, in Llew's case at least, absolutely right.

For five years, Llew trained under Marcus in the beautiful and above all warm palace – the governor's offical residence, in fact – on the high grounds of Aquae Sulis. Llew learned to read and write; he learned all about the way the Roman world worked; he learned several new languages, including Latin, Frankish and Sais[3] – because the governor's house was often host to foreign delegations – and he also learned to sweep. It was amazing how many members of the household, if they came across Llew and he didn't appear to be doing anything at that particular moment, felt the need to pass him a broom and say, 'here, boy, do this floor'. The butler, the steward, the stable hand, the cook … all of them. In the end, Llew took to carrying a broom around with him, so that he could pick it up if he heard anyone coming, and sweep. Then, when they'd gone, he could put it down again and amuse himself instead.

---

[3] Saxon.

It was, in spite of this, an idyllic time. Llew loved Aquae Sulis: he loved the work (or the not doing of it), he liked reading, he liked writing. There was no greater pleasure to the young Llew than making some letters on the page … it somehow made things more *real* if they were written down. He loved using different sorts of quill pens or charcoal to change the style and shape of his writing an awful lot. He loved the … the sheer *cleverness* of sponging the writing on the parchment with vinegar, so that it didn't run or fade and the words would stay there forever. He liked Marcus Artorus an awful lot and above all he liked being warm. And comfortable. And well fed. This Roman life, thought Llew, is the life for me. And if he could have met the inventor of the hypocaust,[4] Llew would have kissed him.

However, this is not to say he was without dreams. One day he was sure Marcus would visit his homeland and Llew was determined that he would accompany him. He had heard so much about the great city of Rome – where it was warm most of the time – and the frescoes on the walls depicting it made it look like a city of wonder. Llew knew he could live in a place like that. He could happily sweep there forever. All right, so he'd vowed he would never travel again … well, Rome was different. Actually, *anywhere* was different as long as the journey and the destination were warm.

This is why it came as something of a shock when, one September, Marcus called him into the office he had just off the Palace's main hall one day to tell him that a few things were about to change. It was good news really. There had been orders from Rome: Marcus and his assistant scribe (Llew) were being posted.

For a few, brief, golden moments, Llew imagined himself on a ship in a very sunny turquoise, Mediterranean sea, looking at white, sun-beaten islands in the distance. There were lemon trees and olive-skinned people laughing on the shoreline. Then Marcus continued to say that the overlord Vortigern needed a new counsellor following the recent tragic death of his last one and Marcus had been hand picked to join him at his court – the hill fortress, Llangollen. This, he hardly needed to add, was a great honour for both himself and Llew.

The little seeds of panic that Marcus had sewn in Llew's mind with the words 'I'm afraid there are going to be a few changes' started to sprout into very tall, very hardy perennials. Not only because Llangollen was in the northern mountains in the kingdom of Gwynedd – which was much like Llew's homeland, only colder and where Llew *seriously* doubted they made use of Roman culture (especially, he noted, his beloved hypocaust) – but also because of Vortigern himself.

---

[4] A system of central heating developed by the Romans. It involved stoking a fire at the base of a house so that heat spread through an empty space of about three feet under the floor boards. The heat would then rise and make the room warm. Those Romans may have had many faults, but they were quite inventive.

Vortigern. King of Gwynedd, overlord of Ynys Prydein.[5]

Vortigern had a reputation that preceded him. Or rather they both did, because there were two. Vortigern Senior was a murderous old tyrant who wanted to kill most people (including his own son) and who lusted after his own daughter. He was what the newly christianised Romans called 'a pagan of the old school' – in that he believed in human sacrifice on a fairly regular basis. Vortigern Junior (also known as Britu) was equally as bloodthirsty and made no secret of the fact that he wanted his father to die sooner rather than later, so that he could have a go at being a bloodthirsty tyrant too. In the court of the Vortigerns, therefore, the intrigue went on in a big way and it was known that advisors from Rome or otherwise did not tend to live very long. And neither did their scribes.

Llew's first reaction was to start crying.

'Oh, come now, boy,' said Marcus testily, 'it's not the end of the world!'

'But you don't know that country like I do, Lord,' sobbed Llew, making no attempt to hold back the tears. 'They're all mad in Gwynedd! I mean, we're *supposed* to be mad in Powys, but even *we* know we're sane compared to those nutters! They say that's why Vortigern set his court up there in Llangollen – so he can just be one mad High king amongst mad subjects. ...'

'Yes, well, he's not High King, for a start! He's just the overlord! Rome will not allow him to be so. Ever.'

'Why?' asked Llew, curiosity overcoming his sorrow for a moment.

'Because, like you say, he's mad ... well, he's a bloodthirsty tyrant, which amounts to the same thing ...,' sighed Marcus wearily, 'but he's managed to keep the alliance in place and while he does that Rome will let him rule.'

This was of course true. Somehow, against all odds, through bribery, corruption skulduggery, jiggery pokery[6] and, sometimes, just plain old murder, intimidation and force, Vortigern had managed to keep all the kingdoms of Ynys Prydein from wiping each other out. From Elmet[7] and Rheged[8] in the north all the way down to Kernow,[9] Dumnonia[10] and Gwyrangon[11] in the south, there was peace – of a kind. Oh, every now and again some feudal chief or client king would try and raise the flag of rebellion – but they never got anywhere. Usually, they'd be brought in chains to Vortigern's court and usually they'd beg for mercy and, even more usually afterwards, their head and intestines would end up in very different public places.

---

[5] The Celtic name for Britain. Translates as 'Island of The Mighty'.
[6] Whatever that is.
[7] Modern-day Yorkshire and Northumberland.
[8] Modern-day Lancashire and Cumbria.
[9] Cornwall.
[10] Somerset, Devon, Dorset.
[11] Kent, Hampshire.

Vortigern also had the advantage of the Roman legions. Although lesser now in number than they had been, they were kept in the main up in the north, guarding Hadrian's wall, keeping back the Pictish tribes. And this was generally what a Roman clerk would be needed for – advice about troop movements throughout the country. It would be a difficult job, because more and more of the empire's legions were being called back to Rome so they could help fight the invaders now regularly encroaching from the East.

'What happened to Pelops?' Llew asked miserably. 'Everyone said the Vortigerns would like him. He was their type!'

'He was; but, apparently, he also fancied the Lord Vortigern's daughter as much as the Lord Vortigern does and there was an … "incident" … a hunting accident or some such thing, and now he is alas their type no longer. …'

Marcus stood up and clapped his hands briskly …

'You'd better go and pack,' he said, 'we'll be leaving at first light.'

Later on, as Llew was miserably stuffing his few possessions into a sack, it occurred to him that Marcus was taking this elevation to higher things awfully well. After all, Marcus knew pretty much everything about those wild lands up in Gwynedd – he'd read enough reports about them and there wasn't a single one that didn't contain the word 'snow' – and he must realise he was giving up what was, after all, a pretty cushy number. Llew inwardly shrugged that Marcus must be secretly pleased at his promotion. And it *was* promotion, not just for Marcus but also for Llew. Vortigern was high king in all but name – and now Marcus was going to be his advisor, a prestigious, if dangerous job. For both of them.

By first light, they were riding north. The first chills of Autumn made Llew shiver and curse the fact that he'd thrown all his old furs away just last year after deciding he was now fully Romanised and wouldn't need them again. The toga, he realised, wasn't going to be of great use in the north. Maybe he could get his hands on some proper Cymru clothing when they called in at Gwyddno's hall on the way. Marcus had insisted that they would visit Llew's family; well, now it might be worth it. Marcus himself, of course, was wearing the purple cloak of Rome. This was not just for warmth. Tradition had it that any Roman citizen could walk freely in any part of the empire and that people would know he was such by the colour of his cloak and that if any harm came to him, the full force of the empire would be dispatched to avenge him.

Thus it was for Marcus, that the colour purple provided protection.

Although not as *much* protection as the ten fully armed legionaries that were also riding with them, because forest bandits are often no respecters of tradition.[12]

Llew twisted round on his pony. The city walls of Aquae Sulis were still

---

[12] It's also worth adding that the definition of 'citizen' only really extended to the Roman nobility and professional classes. Caesar wasn't going to start avenging the death of poor people, was he?

just visible, but disappearing fast. Marcus turned to the soldiers' Captain. He pointed ahead.

'Have they *still* not finished the road up there ...?'

'No, Sir,' came the answer, 'bit of local trouble, I understand. One of the druids has pronounced Badon Hill sacred. Anyone who lays a stone down there, gets an arrow up his arse, begging your pardon, sir.'

Marcus tutted to himself, disapprovingly. The Romans had ruled this island for nearly five hundred years, during which time they had embraced Christianity completely, as had most of the Britons. And yet this old pagan religion still persisted – in the countryside mainly – but also in the court of Vortigern. He turned to Llew.

'You know a bit about these druids, don't you?'

'We had one back in the village. Father used to say "live and let live" as far as religions were concerned.'

'And did it work?'

'Not really – the local Christians kept throwing stones at him.'

'It won't do you any harm, being armed with some knowledge of all that tree and water spirit worshipping nonsense – working for Vortigern.'

'And you, Lord,' said Llew, puzzled.

'Oh yes. And me.'

It was nearly a week later when they arrived at Llew's old village, or what was left of it. Scotti-Irish pirates from across the water had been making raids in the area and Gwyddno's clan had not been left unmolested. Gwyddno himself was in good enough spirits as most of his family had been mercifully spared during the fighting – with the exception of an unpopular uncle – but there was not enough left of the settlement to warrant spending another winter there.

'We're going South and further inland,' he explained to Marcus; 'there's a Silurian clan will let us join them.'

He always spoke to Marcus – hardly a word to his son. It was as if Llew was a bit of an embarrassment.

'I presume the garrison was no help,' Marcus said, gesturing towards the ruin of what had been the settlement's main hall.

'Them? Those bandits left over a year ago,' Gwyddno grunted, 'and with no soldiers here, it's hopeless ...'

Marcus didn't seem surprised. That night, Llew and Marcus ate with his father, mother, brothers and sisters. A lamb stew from the very same cauldron that his grandmother had always used. There was conversation of sorts, but it was nervous and forced. It was polite as well. They didn't make fun of Llew as they always had before and he found himself not really knowing what to say. The stew didn't taste right either. It just wasn't the same.

They left without ceremony the next day. Gwyddno had patted his son on the shoulder and muttered something about making something of his life and not bothering with 'country bumpkins like us' and he'd given Llew some stout clothes and a big fur cloak which Llew almost wept to see. Then they were off again – the country getting more mountainous as they got further north ...

'Master, where did the army go?'

'Recalled to Rome, I expect. Roman soldiers needed in Gaul. The Barbarians are at the gates, they say.'

"But most of the soldiers would have been Cymru men who joined up years ago! Volunteers. They're from *here*! From Ynys Prydein!"

'Ah, well, you join the army and see the world. Besides, no one stays anywhere for long, my young friend ...'

For a good few years now, there had been a small but steady flow of soldiers back across the sea. Not just soldiers either. No one wanted to admit it, but the Roman Empire had been spread a little too thinly for too long. Now someone in a high place had decided it was time to be realistic and, as a result, more and more of the empire's servants were being called home.

The journey north was the closest thing Llew had come to his worst nightmares. The wind howled all the time. Except when it snowed. Actually, sometimes it did both. And on top of that there were the legionaries. Not knowing he spoke their language, they kept making lewd remarks in Latin about Llew, but neither Marcus nor their captain seemed to hear. And all the time, the further north they went the less civilised the country became.

Not just the people, who wore furs in such a way that it seemed they had not bothered to remove the animal, although of course they must have (otherwise where would they have got the skulls to decorate the outside of their huts from?), but the *land* itself, which was becoming more mountainous and impassable with every step. And all Llew could think was *this*? This is to be my *home*?

At last, three days later, they came to Llangollen. Seat of the Overlord Vortigern.

Chapter 2 – Llangollen

Llangollen was as big a settlement as Llew had seen outside the city of Aquae Sulis. It was, or had started as, a hill fortress, built for Vortigern, his family, his warlords and his personal bodyguard of a hundred or so soldiers. However, as is always the case with places such as this, for this fair-sized number of people another fair-sized number of people was needed to cook for them, sew for them, shoe their horses, make their armour, have sex with them and/or generally tend to their various needs (although not necessarily in that order). And initially this second group of people lived outside the stockade's oaken walls. But then, when raiders came, it was these people outside the walls who got taken away to be slaves. Or killed. Which meant less people to cook, sew, shoe, make armour or have sex with. So another wall was built around *them*. And then another group of people then sprouted up outside this second wall – they sold things or hunted things or grew things. And eventually *another* wall was built around them. And then *another* group sprouted up – a group who scavenged and begged, or who behaved in a colourful but insane way – and it was generally felt that this last lot didn't really deserve a wall. Not yet anyway, but time would tell.

At the centre of the three walls was the hall of Vortigern. A huge (by Cymru standards) oaken building with a hole in the thatched roof for the furnace's smoke to escape from.

'See? My lord … they don't even have anything covering the doorways! I mean, that's a draught right off!' Llew said to his master as they looked down from one of the surrounding mountains at what was to be their new home. 'I told you how uncomfortable we were going to find it here.'

'Ah well,' said Marcus, again curiously unperturbed.

Llew also saw that just inside the settlement's outer wall, some construction work appeared to have been going on. The ground had been dug up and about twenty oak trunks had been driven into it, while other planks were nailed across them from one to the other – the first stage of a watch tower, Llew guessed, a big one. However, it looked as if it wasn't the first time a tower, or something like it, had been built there. Much of the area was charred and blackened by fire and there was the wooden debris of a previous structure littered around the place. Whatever had been there before had burned or fallen down.

It wasn't long before they reached the hill on which the fortress stood.

From above, it had looked decrepit and messy – a ragged collection of wooden stakes in giant deformed concentric circles, crows circling its broken battlements and watchtowers. From below, it loomed – dark, forbidding. From neither way did it look welcoming. They trotted their ponies up a well used track, past the scavengers and beggars of the outer wall, to the main gate and, after a few words with the guard there, the gates were pulled open and they rode inside. Actually, the guard should have been a clue to the sort of place Llangollen was. Or rather that the guard was a giant of a man with a vast matted black beard with lice in, wearing ragged bearskins and a sword about the width of Llew's waist. The gates opened and the first thing that greeted the company was the stench. This was, Llew discovered, the kind of settlement where the inhabitants had decided it was much easier just to let the livestock wander around doing what it wanted, where it wanted. And then they'd decided that if some goat could crap on the open ground at will, why the hell shouldn't everybody else?

The next thing Llew noticed was the people. There were basically two types of Llangollen inhabitant. The warriors – who, like the guard, tended to be big, bearded and bearskin-wearing – not lacking in the over-sized weaponry department. And the non-warriors, who tended be small, hungry-looking and ragged – hardly any different from the beggars outside the settlement walls, in fact. Whatever Vortigern was feeding his people, it wasn't enough. Among the non-warriors, he noted with some concern, it was difficult to tell the women from the men – they were all thin, hard faced, dirty and the clothing was by and large strips of cloth worn for coverage rather than style, warmth or even, God forbid, gender definition. No one spoke. They all stopped what they were doing and simply stared at the company as if they had come to Llangollen from another world (which, effectively, they had), while goats, sheep, pigs and dogs fought, defecated and mated with each other noisily.

'Traditional Gwynedd greeting?' asked Marcus as they rode through, nodding occasionally at the staring masses. 'Staring at us, I mean.'

'Actually no, sire,' Llew answered, 'the traditional greeting in this country – for strangers anyway – is generally to disembowel you with a farming implement of some sort. This business of simply staring is a mark of extreme politeness in Gwynedd.'

'Good, Llew, good!' laughed Marcus, 'I can see you're going to get along fine here.'

'You mean *we* are, Sire.'

Llew was getting a very uneasy feeling about this. It was not the first time his master had talked of their new home as if … well, as if it wasn't *his* new home.

By now, they were approaching Vortigern's hall, its great open entrance impossible to see into because of the darkness and the smoke. A dragon's cave, thought Llew. They dismounted and the soldiers were told to stand guard outside, while Llew and Marcus went inside.

A feast was in progress – so some people did get fed round here after all. Warriors mainly, it seemed. Most sat on the floor, biting into great haunches of roast oxen that they cut from spits in the middle of the room, using their daggers as cutlery. They'd also been drinking a fair amount of whatever passed for local ale. This was poured into bowls for them by a ragged-looking servant at one end of the hall from a wooden barrel. Llew noted that, even allowing for the darkness in the hall, the ale seemed to be jet black and apparently had the consistency of treacle. It was certainly having the desired effect, because many of the warriors were either singing, throwing up, fighting to the death on the floor, or had simply passed out. At the far end of the hall was Vortigern's high table, where the old king sat.

The general noise of the feast died down into near silence as they entered and Llew realised they had become the centre of attention. Marcus, who could be an impressive figure when he wanted to, unfurled the official scroll he had been carrying and bellowed as they approached the high table.

'I bring greetings from Rome, Lord Vortigern, in the name of Honorius, true emperor and in the name of the Lord Jesus Christ.'

This caused a muttering among some of the warriors. Vortigern's paganism was well known and he might not like Marcus' greeting – official though it was. Llew peered through the smoke to look at Vortigern. He evidently had once been a warrior – his array of scars and tattoos attested to that, but now he was old and bloated, with whisps of grey hair sticking out of a mainly bald head. He wasn't bearded either, which Llew knew was unusual. Even if the Roman fashion for shaving had reached this god-forsaken place, it was unlikely to have caught on for very practical reasons. This was a country where, if you weren't by a fire on a winter night – you died. A beard was an essential part of your survival kit and Llew realised miserably that he'd probably have to try and grow one – depressing because the few downy hairs that appeared on his chin once in a blue moon meant he hadn't even felt the need to start shaving yet. On one side, behind Vortigern's chair, stood a very frail, scrawny and even older looking man carrying a yew staff. Vortigern's druid, Llew guessed. Actually, he wasn't so much carrying the staff as leaning heavily on it and looked for all the world as if he would fall should he need to point it dramatically at anyone – which druids quite often did. It was part of the job, after all – point the staff dramatically and scream an incantation and/or hiss at the offending party. It was a bit like it was a warrior's job to throw a table laden with food and drink over and go 'grooooaaaaaaha ha ha ha!!!' heartily. It went with the territory.

Next to the druid, behind the king, was just such a warrior. Again, all beard, bearskin and bloody great sword and he looked as if he could heartily roar 'grooooaaaaaaha ha ha ha!!!' with the best of them. Llew guessed he must be Vortigern's champion.

Meanwhile, Vortigern was staring at Marcus and he wasn't looking pleased.

'Who dares to invoke the one-god in my hall!?' he yelled in what was, for such a warrior-like and feared man, an embarrassingly high voice.

'It is the God of Rome now,' said Marcus, 'and it is Rome I represent.'

Vortigern growled slightly, muttered with the druid to his right and turned back to Marcus.

'You're the new advisor?'

'Not quite, my Lord. Allow me to introduce myself. My name is Marcus Artorus. This …'

And here he gestured to Llew.

'… this is Llewellyn my scribe, Llewellyn ap Gwyddno, chieftain of –'

Suddenly, the king's champion launched himself across Vortigern's table and in one bound grabbed a warrior who had, just as suddenly, drawn and aimed a throwing dagger directly at the king. The champion hurled the assailant to the ground and there was a brief and violent struggle, not three feet away from where Llew was actually standing. This ended as quickly as it had begun with the champion cutting the assassin's throat and then having him ejected, gurgling, from the hall by two other warriors.

'Yes, well …,' said Marcus lightly, after what he judged was a respectful pause.

Vortigern gestured to his bodyguard, who was taking his rightful place behind his king.

'Griffith. My champion,' explained Vortigern, 'and this …'

Here he grabbed the druid's beard and pulled the old man's head onto the table …

'This is Cadoc. And Cadoc is *supposed* to have the gift of prophecy! So he's *supposed* to know when one of my trusted lieutenants decides he's going to try and kill me. And. I. Wonder. Druid …'

He was now banging the druid's head on the table in time to the rhythm of his words …

'…I. **Wonder.** If. Your. Gift. Tells. You. Whether. You're. Going. To. Make. It. To. The End! Of!! **This!!!! Particular!!!! Feast!!!!!!**'

'Leave him be!'

The voice had come from the other end of the hall. A man had entered – he didn't quite have the grizzled look of a warrior, but he wasn't a serf either. He wore a short sword and clothes made of linen and his beard and hair were clipped. Also, he wasn't covered in animal droppings and looked, for Llangollen, unusually smart.

'I fear, Lord King,' said the young man in the lazy, slightly bored voice of the well, or indeed **in**-bred, 'that Cadoc's gift of prophecy will not be improved by banging his head thus ...'

Ah, thought, Llew, a civilised person at last.

'My suggestion,' he continued, 'would be to cut it off completely.'

The druid managed to wrench his head away from the king's grasp. He stood to his full height to point his staff at the newcomer and hiss dangerously. Unfortunately, this meant he had nothing to lean on, which is why he fell over. Vortigern smiled a smile that is usually called wolfish, but usually by people who have never been that close to wolves.

'Ah, Lord Prince ...,' said Vortigern; then, with no small hint of lasciviousness, he asked 'and where is your lovely sister?'

'I am here, Father.'

A slight, pale and nervous-looking young woman came to the entrance of the hall. Dressed again in better garb than most of the serfs, she had the countenance of one who has not slept for a very long time.

'Will you not feast with me, my dear?' said the king. And now he was dribbling.

'She stays in my quarters ... with a chaperone and a guard,' said his son still lazily, but here there was a touch of danger in his voice. 'You will not come near her. Not while I live. And be warned, Father ... my men are more than you think and most are better with the throwing knife than Wyn was ...'

With that, the prince and princess turned and left the hall. Cadoc seemed to have suddenly found an inner strength, for he leapt onto the table and started babbling loudly and incoherently.

'What's he saying?' whispered Marcus to Llew.

'He's speaking in the Old Tongue,' Llew whispered back. 'I only know a few words of it ... er, he says ... "the Gods demand it ... it always was so ... copulate ... daughters ... sheep in the field ... dog in cold weather ... only when the tower is built ... I must have a virgin". Actually, that last one could be "piss". My lord, in case it hasn't occurred to you before, we have been assigned to one **seriously** deranged place.'

Marcus raised his eyebrows.

'So it would seem,' he muttered, 'yet it *is* promotion. An honour.'

Vortigern gestured to Griffith who, with a quick sweep, using the flat of his sword, had swept the poor druid off the table and sent him crashing to the floor, swearing in the Old Tongue.

'You were saying, Lord Marcus ...?'

Marcus was slightly taken aback.

'We could do this another time,' he said, 'if my lord felt the need ... after all, such an ... eventful feast.'

Vortigern waved a hand dismissively.

'Hardly an unusual occurrence round here. You'll learn soon enough.'

'Actually, my lord King, I am much afraid I will be denied that pleasure. As I was saying before we were interrupted, I have in fact been recalled to Rome. This ...'

… and here he gestured towards Llew.

'… this is Llewellyn ap Gwyddno ap Powys. He's to be the new emissary.'

… and it was at this point that the room started spinning, after which Llew could remember no more because he had fainted.

'You betrayed me!'
'No, I didn't …'
'You lied to me!!!'
Marcus thought for a moment.
'Well, yes, I think I probably did that …'

It was two days later. After the fiasco of the feast, Llew had woken up in his tent and decided that he didn't really want to speak to Marcus right now. He had also decided that he was in fact hungry and he had set about trying to find food. An investigation of the feasting hall had brought forth the revelation that only 'true warriors with a battle scar upon their cheek and the blood of the Scotti upon their hands' were allowed to pick at the cooling roasted ox carcass. That's what the warrior had said to him anyway, as well as drawing a rather cleverly jagged sword to emphasise the point. Llew had withdrawn and had also resisted the temptation to add that soldiers who tried talking like a bard reciting a great saga always looked a bit pathetic, in his humble opinion. The next thing to do was try one of the serfs from within the compound, but all they'd done was shrug at him and turned away. One, to be fair, had held a turnip out to him when he'd asked for food. However, it had turned out that the serf had meant for Llew to go and grow his own rather than eat the one he was being offered. Llew had gone back to his tent and tried to find ways to stop shivering. They had given him some sort of fur blanket for his bed, but it smelled of something unpleasant and Llew wasn't entirely sure whether the dead animal wasn't still in there somewhere. Finally, after a couple of days plotting how he was going to have Marcus killed in an extremely slow and painful way, the tent flap opened (letting in a really chilling draught), and there was the man himself.

'I can understand if you're angry with me …,' Marcus said soothingly.

' "**If?**" ' What do you mean "if"?'

'All right, let me rephrase. I can understand *how angry you are*,' he corrected himself.

'Actually, master, I don't think you can. Try not eating for two days and then you'll be able to understand how angry I am.'

'For Jove's sake, Llew, you're here at the behest of the most powerful empire on earth!' Marcus said wearily. 'You want food? You order one of the slaves to bring you some!'

'Tell **them** they're supposed to obey me, because so far it doesn't seem to have sunk in.'

The Roman rolled his eyes, sighed, then poked his head through the tent flap and ordered one of the Cymru guards to go and get some food for the ambassador, or Vortigern would hear of it. The guard was surly and plainly wasn't used to taking orders from anyone unable to beat him in hand-to-hand combat, but he went all the same.

Later, Llew was enjoying (well, consuming) a small plate of (cold) roast ox and a bowl of water, although his anger had hardly abated.

'Why didn't you tell me it was going to be my job all along?'

'Because you wouldn't have come and I couldn't have made you. You'd have run away if I'd tried. So I decided the easiest way was to trick you ...'

Marcus might have been cruel, but he was honest and he was also quite right.

'... Now you've come here, you're stuck; you'd never make it back home alone, so you may as well give it a try.'

Very sound logic, Llew thought. Then he thought 'bastard'.

'But why me? There must be hundreds of really experienced scribes, miles more suited to the job.'

Llew was right. There were. Loads of them. He could think of six colleagues at the governor's mansion in Aquae Sulis alone!

'You're right, my young friend, but the trouble is that – rather like me, they're going back to Rome.'

The empire, Marcus explained, was shrinking and there was nothing to be done about it. The last of the Romans were going home, the Cymru were being left to their own devices. And scribes like Llew, naturalised Britons, who knew the languages, were high born enough not to use the wrong spoon in front of a Gwentian princess (something they often took great offence too in Gwent), knew the land, could read and write **and** knew the way the Romans would want things done, so that wars didn't have to be fought too often ... well, they weren't ten a penny. Also, Llew was young – which meant he was slightly less likely to die in that pestilence-ridden land. Not immediately anyway.

'I tried to get you a decent post, Llew, I promise you. One at least a bit further south than this ... but they'd all gone. So, I was told to bring you here, before I returned home myself. And here you are – representing the empire. You've got to admit it is a promotion. Vortigern is the overlord of Ynys Prydein, after all.'

'And what in the name of all that's holy am I supposed to do here?'

Marcus shrugged.

'Making sure that old madman keeps the Saxons out is the main thing. No deals, no treaties, no ceding of land. If those Gothic bastards come here, that's it! You can forget the Romans **ever** coming back. No more baths, no warm buildings ...' – and, knowing Llew, he added for emphasis, '... no hypocaust.'

Llew's anger spurred him into attempting bravado.

'We can live without you lot! You're not taking the baths and the buildings with you, are you? We Cymru can make things work without you, you know!'

'Really?'

'No.'

It was sadly true and he knew it. Most people agreed that, since the first Romans had started returning homeward a few years previously, things in the country had started going slowly but steadily downhill ... houses had started falling apart without being rebuilt, institutions – like banks or tax-collecting services – had begun to disappear ... most importantly, from Llew's point of view, in Aquae Sulis the company whose business it was to maintain the hypocaust in the governor's palace had started reporting 'serious staff shortages'.

Llew shuddered. His worst nightmare was coming true.

That day, Marcus and the soldiers had left. Llew, his bravado pretty much worked through, had begged and pleaded with his master ...

'Please take me with you. I'll be no good here! I can't live in a place like this. I don't wear fur well. I can't grow turnips. I don't have the **strength** to turn over a table and go 'grooooaaaaaaha ha ha!!!', let alone heartily. I'll be killed here! Or I'll catch some fearful plague! Or freeze to death! Or all three! I'll do anything! I'll be your slave! Let me be your slave! Please? Here, I give you my freedom. Wrap me in chains and rip me from my beloved homeland. Force me to your Rome. I'll hate it, you know I will!!!'

... all to no avail. He'd watched the small company ride away into the hills and all he'd been able to do was call his farewells.

'You bastards!!! Come back you bastards and take me with you!!!! I demand you enslave me!!!! You baaaassstarddddssss!!!!!'

The people of the settlement watched him, bemused, before turning away and getting on with the daily grind. Llew stayed on his knees sobbing for some while. When he'd finally got a hold of himself, he got up, turned round, headed back to the settlement and asked the gatekeeper to let him in.

Chapter 3 – In the Court Of The Vortigern

Vortigern. How had such a man come to power? Llew tried hard to study the parchments Marcus had left behind explaining everything – the political history… the battles, alliances, oaths and, of course, breaking of them, that had led to Vortigern becoming overlord of the whole country (well, most of the country… I mean, no one in their right mind wanted to rule the northern wilderness of the Picts anyway).

It was, it seemed, possible to look at Vortigern's rise in a very simple way. Vortigern had started as a client king in Powys who'd bribed better, intimidated better, dissembled better and then, let's face it, murdered better than any other king around until he'd stopped being a small client king in Powys and become a full king of Gwynedd and, from there, the overlord of nearly the whole country – although not High King, as Marcus had said. None of the other kings would suffer to call him 'Majesty' and this was because they knew he needed them as much as they needed him – more now, since the Romans had gone. They needed each other to keep the lands of Ynys Prydein free from the outsiders.

Some hope, Llew observed to himself grimly.

Vortigern had four problems. One was small. One was big. One was getting bigger and had the potential of being huge. One was … well, more than a little strange. The small problem was in the west with raiders from Ireland, known as the Scotti, who plundered the coast. The scenario went something like this:

One day you'd have a nice little fishing and farming village, with people happily farming, fishing, paying taxes and enjoying the breeze. The next day, a sail would be seen on the horizon and the **next,** all you'd have was a smoking ruin and a lot of fishermen, farmers and their wives and children contemplating a new career in Irish slavery. Without protection, the farmers, fishermen, farmer's wives and fishwives and their progeny lacked the motivation to pay tribute or tax to their king. And as a result **their** king lacked motivation to pay tribute to Vortigern or provide soldiers for his armies.

Vortigern needed swords and men to protect the west coast.

Now, the **big** problem was in the North, coming from the land of the Picts. These wild, hairy and strangely decorated men that lived in those untamed lands had always been a difficulty for any ruler with a connecting border –

they were natural pillagers, figuring why make or grow stuff when you can always take it by force from someone else? So, what the Romans had done years before was build a great wall across the country garrisoned with a massive number of troops. And then, as a buffer zone, they'd fed up, paid off and generally made rich, the tribes that lived closest to the wall, so that they became slightly more pro-Roman and less pro-pillaging. This had managed to effectively seal off Pictland and for a while raids from the north had been virtually unknown. Then the Romans started evacuating, leaving a few slightly less wild northern tribes realising they were getting the brunt of the raids from their wilder, more northerly cousins and noticing that they sure weren't as rich as they used to be. So they'd reverted to type and started raiding again. This presented a similar problem to the west, but on a much larger and barbaric scale with people not so much taken as slaves as … well, in some cases, eaten.[13]

Vortigern needed swords and men to protect the northern borders.

The problem that was getting bigger and potentially huge was in the east. It had started with raids, but worse, unlike in the west, it had been followed with settlers. Saxons, or Sais, they called themselves. Strange, tall, fair-haired people, who worshipped foreign Gods with strange names. And instead of returning home with a few slaves and livestock after raiding and pillaging, they were staying and building halls and starting to work the land. And the rumour was that there were more to come from over the sea – a lot more.

'**Men**, what-ever-your-name-is! I need **men** to defend the coast of the whole country!' said Vortigern as he limped along, wheezing and sweating as he did so, while Llew tried to respectfully follow, splashing through the wet mud and dung (for it had surprisingly been raining again) without at the same time getting too close. You didn't get too close to old Vortigern, not if you could help it – you were never sure what you might catch.

'… But there aren't enough! There are never enough! So I must look to the Gods for an answer!'

And thereby lay the roots of Vortigern's fourth problem – the strange one. Always a religious man, he had decided that the answers lay, not on the earth, but in the heavens. That way, as is often said, madness lies …, which may explain why the king insisted on using a druid like Cadoc.

The king and his retinue were now approaching the tall structure that Llew had seen from the top of the hill on the day they had first arrived. It had progressed quite a lot since then, higher and stronger, criss-crossed oak beams nailed and roped together, pointing at the sky. It was really high. Llew hadn't seen anything built this high since Aquae Sulis. And they were still building upwards.

---

[13] Or so it was said.

'My dream tower!'

Llew had seen a dream tower before, back in his home village. Built and blessed by druids, they were usually about ten feet tall with a platform at the top. If a chieftain wanted to talk to the gods about the crops growing, a maiden about finding a husband, a wife about having a baby, then he or she would be given a few selected herbs and mushrooms by their druid and would climb up to the top. There they would lie down on the platform and spend the night waiting for the gods to come to them. In the morning, they'd awake, hopefully with an answer or two, because their dreams would have told them something. In Llew's village, just before a major festival such as Beltain[14] or Samhain,[15] the druid himself would climb his dream tower to talk to the gods about matters much more important that birth, or food. Quite often, the next morning he'd find himself prostrate on the ground ten feet below where he'd gone to sleep, to which he would say that the power of the Gods had lifted him up out of the tower and hurled him down to the earth. And everyone else would mutter that in reality he'd probably had a few too many herbs and mushrooms and during the night believed he could fly.

But this … this was taller than any dream tower Llew had seen. Vortigern must *really* want to get close to the gods.

Supervising the construction was old Cadoc, Vortigern's druid. He was hobbling around and shouting in the Old Tongue at the construction workers who were now straining to raise the tower even higher. Ropes and pulleys squeaked and creaked as the wood groaned. Men balanced precariously on the tower's upper storeys, hammering large iron nails into the timber, or tying pieces together with hempen rope. Vortigern limped forward to talk to him and the druid began ranting and raving in the direction of the king until the king had to hold him by the ear and keep twisting it to calm the old man down. When the druid's eyes started to water, Vortigern let go and Cadoc started babbling again, although apparently more reasonably.

'What's that halfwit saying now?'

Griffith, the bodyguard, had approached. Llew had managed to get the big man interested in a game of Nine Men's Morris[16] a few days back and wisely he'd made sure Griffith had won. He was quite a few coins down as a result, but afterwards Griffith made sure that Llew was tolerated so that he no longer had to go begging turnips from the settlement peasants. Llew was even allowed to eat in the king's hall – albeit in the corner away from the warriors. Griffith was the king's champion, he was hard as nails and he was wholly respected – mainly because if you didn't wholly respect him, bits of you did. Spread over a wide area. Griffith was also very good with a battle-axe.

---

[14] Summer Solstice.

[15] New Year.

[16] An ancient board game that you can still get. It's completely impossible to play.

Llew strained to hear and tried to translate a language he'd never been very sure of.

'Something about … "the daughter … tower … Samhain eve … must be finished by then … I am a little ant bee". Not sure about that last bit…'.

Griffith shook his head.

'With a bit of luck it'll fall down again! Always does! Then the old letch'll have to think of something else and that poor girl will be left in peace.'

Llew turned to Griffith, puzzled.

'What's going on, Griff?'

Griffith shrugged.

'He's building a dream tower to get closer to the gods.'

'So what's his daughter got to do with it? No one'll tell me.'

Griffith shook his head.

'Not for me to say.' He pointed to Cadoc, who was once again haranguing one of the men working on the construction.

'You speak his confounded tongue. Ask *him*!'

'I don't,' said Llew, 'not really. I only know the few words of the Old Tongue my grandmother taught me. To be honest I didn't think *anyone* only spoke it all of the time, not any more. I thought the Old People had all died out, before the Cymru came. Besides I'm … oh, ***crap***!!!'

But Griffith was already running. The only difference being that he, unlike the construction workers and now Llew, was running **towards** the rapidly toppling tower, which had suddenly begun to shudder and now was starting to collapse. Whereas everyone else was running away from it as several tons of timber threatened to fall on them.

Llew, still running, glanced back at the chaos behind him. As if in slow motion, he saw Griffith bodily pick up Vortigern, swing the old man onto his shoulders and then manage to lumber (pretty fast considering he was now straining under several hundred pounds of bloated king) as, with an enormous crash, oak tree and rock thundered down behind him, bouncing and cascading every which way, splintering and splitting and sending a wave of mud spraying out in every direction. Llew winced as the pair *just* dodged a large flying log and continued lumbering on, Griffith for all the world looking like some giant bear carting off a fat man for dinner.

Griffith reached Llew and the rest of the retinue, as they stood huddled together staring at the destruction. He and his master collapsed on the ground in a heap with almost the same speed as the former dream tower.

Silence.

Vortigern forced himself to his feet, breathless, helped by Griffith. He looked at the pile of rock and trees that had once been the tower.

'Cadoc!' he called, alarmed, and then more panicky, 'Cadoc!! Cadoc!!!'

There was a slight sound of some rocks being displaced and then a withered bony hand appeared from a small hole in the pile. Dusty, but otherwise unhurt, Cadoc appeared. He pulled himself up, steadied himself on his feet, raised his arms to the skies and yelled to the sky in the Old Tongue. Griffith looked to Llew for a translation – what was this? An invocation to the Gods or a curse?

' "I didn't ... touch ... anything ... don't ... blame ... me"?' Llew interpreted.

And here was Vortigern's strange problem. His druids told him that to find the answers to his other problems, to find how to get more men to fight for this sacred land, the Island Of The Mighty, he must talk to the gods. Yet every time the king got closer to Them, They knocked his tower down.

It was a sombre feast in the hall that night. The king said nothing. He just stared sullenly at his food and his warriors muttered miserably to one another in the firelight. Even Cadoc seemed content just to sit cross-legged in a corner and twitch to himself. Llew pulled his cloak tightly around him, observing that at least in the hall it was slightly warmer than the stall he'd been given with the animals.

'Almost warm. For the first time! Ha!' he muttered to himself bitterly, and noted it wouldn't be for long. It was nearly time for bed.

He took in the room. Something was different. The king at table. Warriors all sitting around on the floor eating. Then a noticable gap. Then more warriors on the floor. Then at the other end of the room at the other usually empty table ... ah, their highnesses the prince and princess. That was what was different. That explained the gap. The warriors were sitting closest to the faction they were most loyal to.

So there it was, the court of Vortigern spread out before him. And he could see that, although most of the soldiers were sitting at the king's end of the hall, there were enough on his offsprings' side to cause a hell of a fight should it come to a civil war.

And that's how it'll work in the kingdom with his feudal lords, he thought, with many loyal to the father, but just enough loyal to the son. Probably the same with all the other kingdoms as well. Same over the whole country. And the only reason no one starts a war is because they're waiting for that bloated old man to die. Then, if enough people *don't* want to be loyal to the son ... maybe another (ambitious) contender can be pushed forward.

And, he thought, of course the Saxons would benefit if there **were** war, because then they could come and take over while we were weak. So could the Picts. So could the Irish for that matter, although that was unlikely. He didn't know why he was thinking like this, but he thought it might be useful all the same.

Then he noticed that the king's daughter had seen him. She was staring at him. He reddened, looked down and got on with his food.

Llew trudged to his hovel that night, trying to fulfil the impossible task of hugging ill-fitting furs around him to keep out the freezing wind whilst at the same time holding up a torch so that he didn't slip over and land on his face into pig/goat/sheep dung. A peasant had warned him that it was not a good idea to bring fire into a place full of straw and designed to house animals. The danger didn't bother Llew. The straw (which he slept on) was always nice and damp. Mainly because the two goats and a sheep he shared the hovel with always did their best to make it so. Admittedly it was always a nice *warm* dampness at first, but it never stayed that way. Oh well, this accommodation situation was his own fault, he had to admit. He had started in the tent. This had proved an impossible state of affairs. It was Roman – designed for manoeuvres in southern Gaul – and very flimsy. The wind had rent a large hole in it on his first day. Vortigern had suggested he sleep in the hall with the soldiers, but Llew had declined. It was warm yes, but one warrior called Edwyn had started staring at him in a funny way, so he'd insisted that he be provided with his own quarters. A place where he could keep his scrolls and file his reports that would eventually be sent, or even taken by himself (oh please! Please!) to Rome.

So he'd been provided with the hovel; it was freezing, damp and all scrolls and/or reports were now kept securely filed inside the goats, who'd eaten them along with most of his clothes, which is why he was now dressing in what could perhaps be described as this season's 'Llangollen Warrior look'. The season was winter and the look was furs furs and more furs that you sort of tied on with something that Llew could only hope was string.

Llew knew why they were treating him like this. Yes, this was a barbarous place, yes the facilities were a bit … well, basic … but he was technically the emissary from Rome. And Romans got treated well, even by barbarians like Vortigern. They normally did anyway. Well, in the past they had. Right up until they had the usual 'hunting accident' for upsetting the king, or trying to nick the king's mistress, or whatever. But that was the point – the past. Rome had begun to matter less and less. The less soldiers Rome provided, the less the king wanted Roman advisors. And now the great empire of the Caesars had taken all its soldiers and the only advisor Rome was now providing was a Briton called Llew – not much more, as Vortigern had frequently pointed out, than a boy. And, frankly, Vortigern didn't care if Llew was there or not (neither did Rome for that matter). Llew was a courtesy. And, thought Llew grimly, if this was courtesy, he'd hate to find out what it was like to become a **dis**courtesy.

Llew arrived at the hovel, closing the gate behind him, kicked a goat and the sheep out of the way and lay down, trying to find a bit of the straw to lie on that didn't seep. This, he knew, could not go on. He could not stay in this place. If he didn't catch some horrible disease or fever from the cold, he'd be murdered by some mad warrior like Edwyn, murdered by some peasant for the extra turnip he got in wages or clobbered by one of Vortigern's regularly falling towers. And it was with this pleasant thought that Llew finally dropped off to sleep ...

He awoke suddenly. It was dark in the hovel because the torch had gone out, but moonlight streamed through gaps in the planks that made up the wall and he could just make out the sleeping forms of the goats and the sheep, oh and the princess sitting in the corner and ... whoa! The princess? Llew sat up suddenly and pulled the furs about him up to his neck – a pointless gesture and one which would be repeated in a thousand bedchambers in stories to come, but this was the Dark Ages, so it's quite possible Llew was one of the first.

'Princess!'

She was staring at him. In the moonlight, her face was still hard and worn, but lost the sleeplessness that it had in the daytime, so she had a kind of sickly beauty.

'You must help me,' she said.

It wasn't a plea, it wasn't an order; it was a statement of fact.

'I would greatly like to help you, Princess,' he said, with an amazing presence of mind for that time in the morning, 'but if your father or brother were to find you in here with me, it is quite likely they would bury their differences for just as long as it took to "send me out hunting", if you see what I mean –'

'It's from my father that I need helping!' she said urgently. 'They're going to start building again. Another dream tower! Cadoc has prophesied!'

Once again – the dream tower. The tower that everyone watched being built and falling down. A tower with a mysterious secret – something that no one would talk about.

'I don't understand,' he said. 'Why?'

'Prophecy is what he does! He's a druid.'

'No, the tower! Why do you care about it?'

'Has no one told you?'

Llew was beginning to find this frustrating.

'Has no one told me **what**?'

Now she was looking confused.

'I don't know. How could I possibly know that? Oh! I should never have come!'

She put her arm to her forehead in what would have been a clichéd dramatic way had it not, as been stated before, been around about 450 AD. It still, however, looked pathetic, but Llew, knowing his place, felt disinclined to tell her so. However, she seemed to read his thoughts, because she took her arm down and shrugged.

'I'm a princess,' she said. "We're supposed to be like this. It's part of the job. You know, in the same way that warriors are supposed to go –'

'Please. Just tell me what's going on …'

She came and knelt next to him, tucking her shift under her knees as she did so. Llew noticed with a sense of wonderment that, even in this place of mud and muck and dung, the princess seemed to have kept the shift perfectly white. She flicked the long dark hair out of her eyes.

'You know we're in trouble, yes? From the Picts and the Saxons and the Irish and all sorts. Well, there'll never be enough men and father needs divine inspiration and –'

'Yes, yes, I know all that. What's it got to do …?'

'According to Cadoc, that's not enough – the Gods demand more. So Cadoc has said on the night before Samhain I must go up into the dream tower with my father and …'

She trailed off and shifted uncomfortably.

It took a few seconds for Llew to understand. Then he wrinkled his nose and said, 'Ewww!'

'Vortigern's not my real father,' she said hurriedly, 'he just married my mother after he *murdered* him – my real father, that is – but still …'

She trailed off again and Llew resisted saying 'Ewww' for a second time.

There was a pause. Llew could feel that somehow the ball had landed squarely in his court. She'd come for his help … advice … he was a scribe, a counsellor and emissary of Rome, blah blah blah, after all. Maybe he ought to try and offer some words of wisdom.

'Don't worry. It'll probably fall down again. They say it always has till now,' said Mr Helpful.

'But it won't, you see! Cadoc says he's found a way to make it stay up. He says the gods demand a sacrifice! A human sacrifice! A child of the Old People! And Cadoc says he found one! A boy!'

The Old People. Llew felt himself shiver. He knew of them from tales and bits of language that only old druids like Cadoc spoke any more. It was said they inhabited the land before the Cymru came – thousands of years ago. They lived in the caves and the forests and they even built the great stone circles – temples to worship the sun … or so the stories said. And then the stories went that one night a dying god of theirs had streaked across the sky trailing a huge fiery tail, before crashing to earth far away out at sea. And then a great cloud had risen up, making the world dark. The Sun God went away. The crops wouldn't grow and the Old People had started to die. By the time the Cymru came in boats from lands far away, the Sun God had come back, but there were only a few of the Old People left. And seeing the Cymru with their iron swords and axes, they were afraid – because they couldn't stand iron – and they crept away to die in the mountains of Pictland and Gwynedd and Elmet. Llew had always been suspicious of the last part of the tale – he knew how these things went. Oh, he didn't doubt that the Old People, or Fair Folk as some called them, had seen the Cymru swords and axes and been afraid. It was just that the Bards had been less than specific about **how** close up. The Cymru had been raiders then just like the Saxons were now and he suspected that when the last of the Old People had gone to the mountains, they ran very fast rather than crept and that, yes, they couldn't stand iron, but neither can most people if the iron in question is being used to chop or stab at you. Either way…

'All the Old People are dead,' he said decisively. 'Everyone knows that.'

'Cadoc says not!' insisted the princess. 'He's descended from them! And he says he found this boy in the mountains near Eryri.[17] If the boy's blood and entrails are spilled on the tower's foundations, it will stay standing. That's what he says!'

'And you believe Cadoc?' Llew found it very hard that anyone would take the blindest bit of notice of a twitching druid who couldn't even point his staff dramatically without falling over.

'Yes! Yes! He has the gift of prophecy! Touched by the Gods, descended from the Old Ones, he Cadoc, who was given the staff of Dafydd Ap Gwyddion –'

'All right, all right, what about your brother? What's he say?'

'He says he's willing to stand up to my father, but he's badly outnumbered and if they go to war with each other, the alliance of kings falls and the Saxons will come. You've got to help!'

Now here was the rub. He'd 'got' to help, had he? He was sharing a hovel with a goat and two sheep and he was supposed to demand from the overlord of Ynys Prydein and his warband that the old man did not have sex with a young woman he plainly wanted to have sex with. Yes, that *was* a task he was born to, he thought dryly.

'What exactly do you expect me to do, your Highness?' he asked, trying hard and failing not to make the word 'highness' sound sarcastic. However, if she noticed, she didn't show it.

'Persuade my father not to sacrifice the boy. Or rescue him from the sacrifice. Or anything, but please, *please* help me. Save me from my fate!'

And once again she raised her arm dramatically to her forehead. And what should have followed was a speech along the lines of 'you cannot be serious, how on earth am I supposed to achieve that in a way which will not make my life any worse than it already is and believe me that's pretty bloody awful', but – and it may not have been deliberate – when she raised her arm *this* time, she made sure that her shift showed just a little bit more neckline than it had previously. Then she leaned forward earnestly and took his hand in hers.

'Please,' she added one more time for effect.[18]

He reddened – something quite difficult in the moonlight.

'I'll … erm … I'll see what I can do,' he said.

The next day, work started on the dream tower again.

---

[17] Mount Snowdon.

[18] In those days, also not a cliché.

Chapter 4 – Sacrifice

It wasn't long after, that a small band of warriors arrived on horseback from the mountains. Llew had seen these particular warriors around the camp before, but not lately. They were part of some sort of personal guard of Cadoc... odd looking men with strange tattoos that kept apart from the other warriors, always did Cadoc's bidding and, more importantly, understood him. As well as the horses there was an ox-drawn cart on which was placed a wooden cage. The arrival caused some excitement and people – serfs and soldiers alike – crowded round as the gates of the settlement were opened and the caravan was brought in.

Llew tried to peer over the heads of the crowd. At first he thought that there was some sort of animal inside the cage. It seemed to be all hair and fur. Then it hurled itself at the bars and hissed at the crowd outside, causing small children and at least one (later embarrassed) adult man to run away squealing, and Llew could see its ... *his* hands. It was human anyway ... Llew presumed it was a boy – it was really too mucky and hairy to tell. Probably about fourteen or fifteen. With bright, very bright blue eyes, shining like a pair of stars in that dark, dark face.

For a moment the creature's gaze connected with Llew's and the scribe shivered. It was like he heard a voice in his head saying, 'I know you'.

There was a screech from the back of the crowd and the cart stopped. The crowd parted as Cadoc came hobbling through. He rushed up to the cage and stared at the creature/boy, who started jabbering at Cadoc in the Old Tongue, a cascade of words and Llew could barely make out a few.

'A curse ... one that is to come ... you ... no true druid.'

Cadoc was evidently taken aback, because he turned round without a word to the boy and started to limp away. He yelled to one of the soldiers as he did so and these words Llew did understand.

'Prepare him.'

Llew understood what this meant as well. It meant 'prepare him for sacrifice'. Not 'prepare' as in, 'sit him down with a trained counsellor and say "something quite difficult is going to happen to you and I have to say it will hurt, but I want you to look at it this way – one minute, there'll be a flash of golden sickle, the next, you'll be feasting in the Otherworld with the gods, so try and see this challenge as an opportunity ... a learning experience if you will".' No, 'prepare' as in 'wash him, shave him completely, dress him in a white linen robe that everyone can see through and make sure he turns up to the altar stone on time'.

Llew had never seen a human sacrifice before. Unlike most of the smaller rural tribes, his clan had been Christian for a long time and the local monk said that Christianity forbade sacrifice of any kind ... yes, there was that one very bad winter where a small pigeon had been ... well, they'd needed the snows to melt or they'd all have died, after all. Gwyddno had allowed a druid to practise in the village, yes, but nothing too bloody. After all, Gwyddno had maintained, religious tolerance was the mark of a great chieftain, after which he'd always muttered something about not putting your eggs in one basket and the monk might be right about his One True God, but then so might the druid about his fifty or sixty. However, there were rumours about some remote clans in the hills who ... well, went in for the human skull school of house décor in a big way.

Llew knew only one thing. The idea filled him with horror. And here ... was this child ... maybe the last of his kind. He had to do something.

'What?!!!!' Vortigern screamed. 'You **dare**?! You **dare** to question me?!! The Vortigern! You **dare**!!!'

Cadoc jumped up onto the high table and jabbered at him with a thousand old world curses. He pointed his staff at Llew and, ruining the effect of everything he'd just done, toppled over to the floor.

'A miserable little worm like you! The maggot from the arse of Rome!!' Vortigern continued, his high voice reaching new and alarming pitches.

Llew cowered on his knees in front of them. He was thankful there were just him, the druid and Griffith in the hall with the king right now. If other warriors had been there, Vortigern might have felt he was losing face, what with Llew questioning his decision and everything. And Llew did not want Vortigern to lose face, because it would end with Llew *also* losing face. As well as his neck, scalp, jaw, ears and the back of his head. All in one go.

'With respect, Lord,' Llew stammered and heard Griffith groan just audibly from behind Vortigern. Apparently 'with respect' was not a good phrase, possibly because it nearly always *really* meant 'without respect'.[19] Nevertheless, Llew soldiered on.

'With respect, Lord Vortigern,' he said, 'human sacrifice is no longer practised by those who consider themselves ... you know ... civilised.'

Griffith, unseen by the king, had one hand over his eyes and was shaking his head in despair. Cadoc was now raising himself up from the floor and

---

[19] In the same way that people who say 'in my humble opinion' really mean 'in my very important opinion'.

leaning on his staff again. He was grinning wickedly at Llew, as if he was watching someone dig their own grave, which Llew almost certainly was.

'Are you saying,' and now Vortigern affected a wide-eyed look, 'that I'm not **civilised**?'

Llew quickly realised his mistake and hurriedly tried to back-pedal in a world without bicycles, metaphorical or otherwise.

'No, Lord, no. Of course not. I just … imparted the information by way of conversation … that's all. You? Not civilised? Ha! Ridiculous! I believe in Kernow you're actually **known** as Vortigern The Civilised. And not in an ironic way either. Anyway, thanks for the audience. Must be getting along … got lots of scrolls to … you know–'

He had used this speech as cover for getting to his feet and starting to move backwards towards the entrance of the hall, while still bowing madly. He could actually feel the wind from outside blowing against his back when heard the scrape of two spears being crossed behind him. The guards at the entrance were evidently on full alert.

'Nice reactions, boys,' he muttered, bitterly.

Vortigern paused and then, without looking at Griffith, said, 'Disembowel him.'

'Lord,' Griffith affirmed without hesitation and began to walk towards Llew, at the same time drawing his sword.

'Wait! Wait!!' Llew was panicking. 'If you kill me, what will the Romans say?'

'They won't know, they won't care!' Vortigern shrugged dismissively. 'If they ask, I'll say …' and here he grinned … '… hunting accident.'

Cadoc was cackling evilly. Griffith had already reached Llew and had him round the neck.

'I'll try not to make it hurt too much,' he muttered to Llew, 'but he said "disembowel". Now, if he'd said "*decapitate*", that'd be a whole lot …'

'But I wear the purple of Rome!' Llew shouted, but he could now feel the blade of Griffith's sword against his stomach, 'and … and if you kill me you won't get the **troops**!!!!'

'Hold!'

Griffith had been about to do it. He had been about to slice Llew open like so much sausage meat when Vortigern had held up his hand.

'What did you say, worm?'

The blade was still pressed against his belly.

'Three crack legions! From Gaul! To be deployed against the Saxons in the south. **If** I give the word …'

Vortigern looked at Cadoc, who shrugged.

'When?'

He indicated for Griffith to release Llew.

'Two years, Lord, when the campaign in Gaul is over.'

Vortigern looked thoughtful, weighing things up.

'That's a long time. Still, three legions is three legions. Why didn't you tell me about this before?'

Llew was thinking on his feet and was pleased to find that he was very good at it.

'Can't be guaranteed, Lord. There's a chance the campaign in Gaul could take longer, or less time. I just know that they have reserved three of the best legions for Britannia.'

He knew he was being really clever now, using the Roman name for Ynys Prydein – it made it sound so much more official.

'However,' he continued, 'the legions come on my recommendation. A Roman emissary must go to Rome and talk with the Emperor. I was originally sent here to assess the situation, you see. Well, now I think it can be said, I've assessed it – the situation is worse than we thought and you badly need those legions. Sooner rather than later. Certainly sooner than two years …'

Yes, oh yes! He was **so** good at this! He was surprised how good he was.

'… Mind you, were I to meet with a "hunting accident" … well, Rome won't be appointing another ambassador for a long time.'

Vortigern was thinking.

'And why should I believe you?'

Now *that* was a good question.

'Why should I lie?' said Llew.

'Because I'm about to have you killed.' Vortigern looked puzzled.

Oops. Someone might just have overreached himself.

'Good point, Your Majesty, *very* good point and indeed … I *had* letters given to me by Marcus detailing everything when I arrived. These would have provided the proof you want – the Romans are very keen on writing everything down, as you know – but if you remember you did insist I share my hovel with the goats …'

He trailed off. Either Vortigern was going to fall for this, or he wasn't. And the only thing that Llew really had to bank on was that, more than anything, Vortigern *wanted* it to be true. If the king could just hold the borders for a little longer, then the legions would come back and all would be well again. Vortigern's hope didn't stem from patriotism – from a need to restore pride, for the Island Of The Mighty to become exactly that again, however. Llew had learned that, above all, Vortigern was a vain man and it rankled that the other kings as well as the Romans refused to acknowledge him as High King. If the people thought that Vortigern had saved the country … well, maybe now they'd give him his due.

The old king turned to his druid and spoke to him in that strange guttural old-fashioned language. The druid shrugged and jabbered back. Llew could understand something about still having the boy and the tower. What, the druid appeared to be asking, did the king have to lose?

Vortigern thought again.

'When could you leave? For Rome, I mean,' he grumbled finally, obviously slightly annoyed he'd been able to avoid some unnecessary pain and bloodshed.

Llew couldn't believe his ears. He'd done it! He'd just bought his ticket out of this hell-hole. He could have an armed escort to the coast, he could be on a ship, he could be gone forever. He would disappear in Gaul or Italy. Or Greece. And Vortigern would sit and wait for the legions to come.

'Any time you like. If you think it would be helpful.'

Later, he was walking towards his hovel, with Griffith beside him.

'He's still going ahead with the sacrifice, you know.'

'Hm?' said Llew, absently. To be perfectly honest, he didn't care any more.

'Well, those legions can't be guaranteed for two years, can they? If at all. He needs men now. So he's going ahead with the sacrifice and the dream tower.'

Bugger! He'd forgotten about the girl. Big eyes, she'd got. Well, in the moonlight anyway. And she'd held his hand as well and ... no, he had to be firm about this. It wasn't *his* fault if the king wanted to sacrifice some feral kid from the mountains. I mean, he had tried, after all. And it wasn't his fault either that the old king had a ... thing for his stepdaughter. Or indeed that the king was being counselled by a lunatic druid that both abominations were a really good thing! Llew would be gone by morning. Griffith and two others were escorting him out of Langollen and down to the coast, where he was to get aboard a ship and away! Away, to wherever he wanted. Preferably somewhere they wore togas and such-like, because furs were never necessary. At first light, he was, as far as Langollen was concerned, history. Not even history. A footnote in history. In years to come, he'd be entered into the archives by some monk as the 'little bloke who was supposed to bring soldiers, but do you know, we never heard from him again?' If they ever learned to make archives. If the country still existed, because the Saxons would probably have overrun ... no, no, he must stop thinking like that! Or about the girl! Or about the wild boy! And yet ... all it would take would be for someone to sneak up to the cage at night time, force open the door and the kid would escape. That little savage could get under the holes in the stockade walls and be out in the hills, eating stoats or whatever it was he ate, within minutes. Then, if Cadoc was right ... the tower wouldn't stay up and the girl could wait for her stepfather to just ... well, die, which couldn't be too long, surely. The man was positively a walking crucible of horrible diseases. And it wouldn't matter that someone had let the child escape, because that someone'd be gone. He'd be on a horse somewhere between here and Aquae Sulis.

He had to admit, it was the logical thing to do.

Night time. Llew sneaked through the settlement, avoiding drunken guards and the serfs that were huddling around fires in the sullen unfriendly way they always did. He'd got good at sneaking about, finding that the best way to get anything you really wanted in Langollen was not to be noticed so you could steal it. There was a hut near the edge of the stockade. Cadoc's hut – where the druid slept and practised his art. And next to the hut was the wooden cage.

Llew glanced behind him. The new dream tower, now nearly completed, loomed in the moonlight.

Getting down on his hands and knees (never a pleasant thing to do in the stockade), Llew left the cover of the huts and crawled up to the wooden cage. The child sat inside, right in the centre, cross-legged, awake, staring with those blue eyes. Even in the dark of night they seemed to pierce Llew. That was scary. The boy, now completely shaved and wearing his white sacrificial tunic, looked less like an animal and more like some sort of ... spirit. He was thin, almost too thin, it seemed. And it seemed to Llew that he could hear voices, lots of them, not close up – almost as if they were off in another room – talking at him in a language he couldn't understand. Then he heard one voice in his head, clear as a bell ...

'I know you, Llewellyn Ap Gwyddno'

Llew's hands had just been about to slide the bolt back on the cage door and free the boy, but his hand jolted back.

'What?' he hissed, looking at the boy. 'Was that you?'

The boy's grin got even bigger.

'Of course it was me, you fool! Who did you think it was?'

Llew stared at the boy wide eyed. The voice in his head sounded like that of a man. An old man. There was definitely the air of long white beard about it.

'Who are you? How do you know my name?'

'My name is Merlin. And how I know yours is my business. Aren't you going to let me out?'

Llew thought. He had been, obviously, but now ... now he wasn't sure if it was a good idea. And then he thought how powerful this ... creature seemed. It could talk inside his head in the voice of an extremely powerful old man. Anyone who could do that, surely couldn't be held inside a simple wooden cage, could they?

'Cadoc has put iron bolts on the door,' came the voice as if in answer. *'He's not as stupid as he looks. I can't get past iron. My people never can.'*

So it was true – this was one of the Old Ones. And they really did fear iron. And not just because it nearly always came in the form of a sword or an axe.

'So open the door, Llewellyn Ap Gwyddno. Open the door and learn your destiny ...'

Llew didn't like this. That was druid talk. 'Learn your destiny' and it generally meant that the person in question was about to find out how he or she was going to die.

'*You want to save the girl, don't you?*'

He did. He wanted to save the girl. He wanted to release the kid, sneak back to his hovel; in the morning he'd be off with an armed guard while Cadoc gnashed, wailed and Vortigern got closer to being dead. A few weeks later, Llew would be a Greek or a Roman and no one would be any the wiser. Most importantly, the girl would be saved. His hand went back to the bolt and slid it across. He opened the cage door. The boy stood and ambled out. He walked into the middle of the space between the huts and stood still.

'Well, go on then,' Llew hissed, 'there's a gap under the stockade wall, get out of here ...'

The boy, Merlin, grinned once more – his teeth shining in the moonlight, his eyes glowing like two sapphires. And, at this this point, Llew thought to himself, 'Oh bugger', because he knew that what was about to happen didn't figure in a sneak-out-while-no-one's-looking type plan.

Merlin began to let out a fearful howl ... although 'howl' wasn't quite the right word. It was feral and high pitched yes, but it was one long note, never ending, no pause for breath, and it seemed to echo around the hills and mountains, bouncing off them back and forth, to and fro. It was as if Merlin was releasing some sort of screaming spirit made entirely of sound. Llew was waving his hands madly, making pathetic little shushing movements at the boy, which of course were having no effect at all, while all around he could hear 'what the bloody hell is that?' and variant phrases coming from the surrounding huts, along with the distinctive '*shhhinnggg*' noise that a sword makes when it's being pulled out of its scabbard for emergency use, only in plural. He realised that there was nothing for it but to run. To be caught here having let the boy go free had the potential to seriously jeopardise his chances of leaving the next morning. He turned, but it was too late, there were soldiers all around ... and Cadoc with *his* personal guard and then there was the girl and the prince and Edwyn and Griffith and finally, pushing his way through the gathering crowd, Vortigern himself.

And the howl stopped. Merlin stood, the people forming a clearing round him. Llew saw what he thought would be his only chance.

'Your Majesty! Look! I caught him trying to esca–'

He didn't finish. Edwyn had a sword pressed to his throat. The time for him to talk was ... well, not now.

Merlin spoke – aloud this time – in the booming old voice that didn't fit his boy shape.

'Know this, Vortigern! Your tower will not stand because the dragon that lives under this land has been awakened by another. Every time they fight, the ground shakes and your tower falls!'

Vortigern looked from the boy to Cadoc and back.

'You speak our tongue,' he said.

'I speak yours and a lot of others besides. I am Myrddin of the Old People.'

Vortigern shook his head.

'What must I do?'

'You want to meet your Gods? Do as you are doing – build your tower ... but remember this is about the **land**, Vortigern. The two dragons that fight below your tower, one is red – that is the dragon of the Cymru – one is white ... the dragon of outsiders. If you want the red dragon to win, first you must sacrifice an outsider! Not I! I am one of the Old People. Kill me and you strike at the heart of the red dragon. I must wait in this world for the one who is to come ...'

And Llew had wanted to say 'hang on, if the red dragon represents the Cymru, it can't represent the Old People can it, because to the Old People the Cymru **are** outsiders; besides, it's all bound to be symbolic anyway – there aren't really dragons underground ...' However, the sword that Edwyn was pressing against his neck made him unable to say anything other than 'ccccccchhhccchhhh'.

Vortigern turned his attention once again to Cadoc, who nodded that this indeed could be the case and jabbered back at Vortigern in the old tongue. Merlin's voice appeared in Llew's mind once again.

'He says the best example of an outsider we have here is the one who represents Rome, Llewellyn Ap Gwyddno.'

And the voice sounded more than a little amused.

And Llew noticed to his horror that Cadoc was pointing at *him*. Oh, he thought, that's my destiny is it? And he fainted.

'Course, it won't be me what does it, which is a shame really. ... I mean, not for me, obviously. ... I quite like you as it happens ... but, you know, more of a shame for you, 'cause it'll be that bastard Edwyn and he really likes his work, if you know what I mean – killing, that is – so it'll be quite slow. So, sorry about that ...'

Griffith had brought Llew some food, but his conversation wasn't very cheering to the scribe whose new (but very temporary) home was a (recently vacated) wooden cage and the roast ox he'd bought wasn't very tempting either. Roast ox could get a bit ... well, samey if you had it every day; and if that day was, in fact, the day when you were under sentence of death, it could be just plain unappetising. Especially if it was served cold. Which it was.

'You want to know how they're gonna do it? Some people find it helps if they know how it's gonna be done ... no? No, I don't blame you.' There was an awkward pause. 'So they shaved you then.'

Indeed they had. Or rather Cadoc had. And he hadn't done it with the delicate hand and sharp blade that Llew had hoped for. In fact, most of his hair, beard and … well, other hairs, had not been so much shaved as, well … pulled out. And this would have brought tears to his eyes, had not he already been weeping hysterically.

'… So they're gonna take you to the base of the tower, right, while the king's up in the dream chamber praying to the Gods, right?' Griffith burbled on. 'And they're gonna do it there. And then the princess'll climb up to him – apparently, it's very important she walks through the remains of your entrails on the way … and then she and him … well, they'll you-know-what. Horrible, I know. Not that you being disembowelled'll be that pleasant either. Looking good, by the way. The tower, I mean. And it hasn't fell down yet, obviously, so maybe that kid'll turn out to be right. Wherever he is. Oh, didn't I tell you? He buggered off at first light. Seems he got out by that hole under the stockade wall – which somebody's now gonna mend. Finally.'

He shifted uncomfortably. Griffith knew that to go on like this wasn't good for his image. He'd found early on that warriors who kept babbling about the price of fish or changes in the weather tended not to get verses dedicated to them when the bards composed their epic songs. But he just couldn't help himself, especially when he was uncomfortable. Like now, for instance.

'So, come on then … say something.'

Llew just looked at him. There was nothing *to* say. So this was it. He'd been *that* close to getting out of there and he'd let his conscience get in the way. Well, his conscience *and* his inability to not look at the neckline of a female shift when a bit of flesh was exposed. In his head he was cursing … cursing his father for taking him to Marcus, cursing that bastard Marcus for bringing him here, cursing that senile old lunatic Cadoc and the scabby, *gullible* old lunatic Vortigern for believing anything that he was told, cursing the girl for getting him to do anything she said, but most of all he was cursing as hard as he could that little sod Merlin for waking everybody up to do his show-off prophecy bit! He made himself the solemn vow that if he *ever* got out of this mess he was going to track that kid down and give him an arse kicking he'd never forget!

'Oh, and it's gonna happen when the moon's at its highest tonight. Thought you'd want to know.'

Night. An owl hooted. In his hall, Vortigern was being dressed in ceremonial robes and the two guards watching the door noticed he was not only grinning in anticipation of the evening ritual, he was also actually starting to salivate. Their eyes met and each knew instantly what the other was thinking.

'Yuk!'

In her hut, the princess Megan was also dressed in ceremonial robes. There were rather more guards stationed around her quarters. Vortigern had made sure there was no attempt at rescue.

And in his cage, in *his* ceremonial robe, sat Llew. It would be nice to say that by this point he'd become philosophical, almost calm and resigned to his fate. But he hadn't. Fear had driven him to keep spitting at the wooden slats that made up the cage bars in the forlorn hope that the damp would very (in fact, supernaturally) quickly rot the wood and he could make his escape. It was, he knew, pathetic and in vain, but it was all he could think of.

He saw legs outside the cage. Big chunky warrior trew-covered legs. Then he heard the bolt slide back and the cage door opened. The evil, leery face of Edwyn appeared in the doorway.

'Hello, boy,' he said, cheerfully, 'I'm gonna enjoy this.'

Much of what happened afterwards was difficult for Llew to remember. He hadn't gone nobly, he knew that. He'd been pulled out of the cage, with some considerable difficulty – which was quite an achievement seeing that those dragging him by his legs were Edwyn and three of the strongest warriors in the whole of Llangollen. And he would later recall that he'd been screaming really loudly, promising them all sorts if they didn't do this … everything from riches and honour in Rome (neither of which he could provide) to sexual favours (he'd been working to the strengths of his relationship with Edwyn). The escort, of course, had completely ignored him, preferring instead to lift him by the elbows so that his feet could pretend to run in thin air. It probably, he thought, would have looked quite comical, had not his bowels just turned to water, which was not helping the white ceremonial shift he was wearing keep clean.

They started to head downhill towards the great tower. And then … well, all that he remembered was that he fell face down on the ground and that the guards carrying him seemed to fall with him. Then they picked him up again in the same way … only this time they had helmets on, which they hadn't done before. And he could have sworn he saw some bodies on the ground. And one of them, the one on his left, had muttered, 'Will you **stop** whining like a girl?!'

'Griff?'

'Just shut up and thank your lucky stars I'm on the right side. If I hadn't been with the prince …'

'You're with … ooh, is this some sort of uprising?'

'Tell you what, why not shout it? Just see if we can't rouse a few loyalists and have the sacrifice go ahead as planned. How'd that be?'

'Shutting up now. I … I could probably walk on my own if you want.'

As they walked down the hill towards the tower, they could see the bloated figure of Vortigern struggling up the ladder to the dream chamber – a small walled room, like a bird hide – at the top. The bitter wind blew his ceremonial robe up and for one second the world was a particularly unpleasant place. At the bottom of the ladder Cadoc was hopping about on one leg and chanting druidic spells, while the girl stood by, surrounded by Cadoc's special soldiers. Then, a few paces back from them and surrounding the tower, was everyone else. At the front, all of the warriors of Vortigern's band, behind them the rest. The whole tribe. Well, all except one.

'Where's Prince Britu, then?' muttered Llew.

'I'm here, idiot,' said a familiar, lazy, but helmeted voice next to him.

'Oh, sire! How can I ever thank you?'

'I shouldn't bother. We're only using you as cover so we can get closer to my sister. And if my plan goes wrong we'll all be cut to pieces anyway.'

'Oh ... plan?'

'I'm rather hoping,' said the prince in his usual lazy way, 'that once I've got Megan away from Cadoc's men, the soldiers will follow me in an insurrection against my father. If, of course, they don't, we'll all die. Slowly and painfully, I imagine.'

Oh, great. Out of the frying pan into ... well, into another bloody frying pan.

They were now nearly at the tower; a single drum was beating a slow funereal-like beat and warriors parted to let the sacrificial victim and escort pass through. Llew was led once in a circle in front of the crowd assembled at the tower, then he was taken to the foot of the tower's ladder and made to kneel. Cadoc approached, spat a few times, hopped on his good leg, pointed his staff, muttered a couple of benedictions ... the usual druidy stuff ... then indicated it was time to decapitate Llew. Llew's chin was forced onto his chest and he heard the sound of a sword being drawn from its sheath.

'Now!!' the prince shouted.

Keeping his chin very firmly on his chest, Llew heard the *'shhhinggg'* of several more swords drawn and the sounds of running, grunting, steel clashing on steel, wooden shield on wooden shield, followed by the customary 'ughgh!' of warriors dying. Also, the drumming stopped and there was the unmistakable noise of it being used to hit someone. Then silence. Only then did Llew dare raise his head.

Cadoc was staring open-mouthed – his special guards all lay dead, the princess was now with the prince and Llew's escort stood, living, their swords drawn and bloody. The ceremonial drummer had had his instrument pushed over his head.

'Hear me, Llangollen!' the prince yelled at the assembled warriors, 'I do proclaim myself King Vortigern the second. The time has come for me to claim my birthright! Which of you is with me?'

Silence.

Uh, oh ...

Only to be broken by ...

'What the bloody hell is the hold up?' said a far-off high voice.

Everyone to a man looked to the top of the tower, where Vortigern the

Elder had pushed his head out from behind the curtain at the entrance to the dream chamber.

'Is she coming up here or what? I'm freezing! I've got no bloody clothes on!'

Llew shuddered, and not from the cold. He was pretty sure he saw the princess shuddering too.

The Prince, still hoping for a sudden surge in his favour, yelled up to the top of the tower.

'Yield to me, Father, and you shall come to no harm! I am king now!'

'Oh?' the old man looked out to the assembled warriors. 'What say you, men?'

It was Morfans who was first to answer, one of Vortigern's most loyal men. He drew his sword and raised it to the sky. This was followed in turn by other men still loyal to the king drawing their swords and doing the same; more followed and soon the sound of iron being drawn from scabbard had become like a great steel chorus to the night sky ...

Shhhinnggg!!! Shhhinnggg!!! Shhhinnggg!!! Shhhinnggg!!! Shhhinnggg!!! Shhhinnggg!!!

Llew had a horrible feeling that this didn't look good for the prince. Of course, the drawing of a sword *could* be interpreted as affirming the authority of the new young king. But what it actually *looked* like ... well, what it meant was that they were going to take it in turns to have a go at cutting bits of him off.

'I'm on the wrong side again, aren't I?' he said, turning to Griffith.

Griffith nodded slowly.

'Me too, old lad, me too. Oh well. See you in the Otherworld.'

And then the voice was heard again. All around them, echoing in the valley, bouncing off the mountains. Merlin's voice.

'Know me, Llangollen! Know me! I speak for Taranis, god of the lightning!'

Clouds seemed to be gathering very swiftly around the moon. In the distance they could hear the rumble of thunder.

'Know me! Vortigern! Know that you are cursed by the gods.'

Llew looked towards the mountains. High on the rock above the stockade he could see a small, boy-like figure in a white robe with a staff. The voice was now echoing round the valley, overlapping and colliding with itself.

The sky rumbled. Black clouds had all but covered the moon.

'You would be High King, but it shall not be. Only the one who is to come shall be High King. Know what Taranis thinks of your dream tower!!'

'What's he say –?' yelled Vortigern down to Cadoc.

And the lightning struck. The top of the tower burst into flames, illuminating the night sky, a great golden flower of fire. Cadoc screamed. Not for the first time, Llew found himself running away from the tower as it slowly, slowly started to collapse in on itself, sending bits of debris and flaming oak somersaulting in every direction, the others running with him. He turned to look back to see that one person had stayed. Cadoc. Cadoc, who was standing directly underneath. Looking upwards, frozen in terror as the flaming, bloated and extremely overweight body of Vortigern crashed through the floor of the chamber and plummeted headlong towards the druid, followed by the solid inferno that was the rest of the tower. Fear of tripping over made Llew face forwards so that he could keep running until he was out of harm's way. Behind him, the creak of burning timbers followed by a mighty crash told him the tower was no more.

And that was the last anyone saw or heard of Vortigern the Elder and his druid Cadoc.

Chapter 5 – Llew's Quest

'Actually,' the old warriors would say, 'that was what we had meant all along. When we drew our swords that night, it was in affirmation to the new king. We knew it was over for old Vortigern.'

Never mind that they generally said it in a muttered sort of way, looking into their half-empty mead horns and not meeting anybody's eye. And why? Well, perhaps *before* the tower had been struck by lightning, the broad feeling for those on the king's side had been 'there's probably more of us than there is of them, let them try something', while the feeling on the prince's side had been 'there's probably more of them than there is of us; I don't mind trying something, but I'm buggered if I'm going to be first'. Whereas, *after* the tower had caught fire, everyone said 'bloody hell, they've/we've got that Merlin kid to call down the lightning god on their/our side. ... I'm pledging loyalty to the prince right now!' Proving that experienced warriors become so because they know a thing or two about survival.

Such was the balance of power in Llangollen.

So the prince became Vortigern II, also known as Britu, overlord of Ynys Prydein. Ceremonies were held and so were feasts. And Llew, in recognition of his attempt to save the honour of the princess Megan, was given the choice of either his own warband or, now that the young King had moved into his father's place in the great hall, the chance to live in the princely quarters – a stout stone hut with its own fur bed and proper fireplace.

Guess which one he chose? And he spent the first night in his relatively warm(ish) quarters, writing down the story of Vortigern, the dream tower and the change in succession. He supposed he should send the scrolls to Rome, but he still hadn't quite got rid of the idea that he might take them there himself one day. It was a thought that was to stay with him.

Meantime, Spring was starting to show the first signs of appearing. Yes, it was still freezing and rainy and the north wind howled most nights, but the odd snowdrop had started to appear and there was much less sleet. And, thought Llew, in a place like Llangollen, you had to be grateful for small mercies. There was, of course, still the question of the three promised Roman legions ...

'Llewelyn. Those legions ... the ones you told my father about ...'

'Yes, Majesty?' Llew was careful not to make those two words sound like anything other than 'I refuse to commit myself until I know exactly what the follow-up question is'.

'I presume it was a complete lie you made up to stop him from killing you?'

Llew hesitated. For a second, he imagined himself in a toga on Capri, cavorting with half-dressed Numidian slave girls. Then he looked at the new king properly for the first time, sitting in his father's old throne. Vortigern Britu was young, he was honest and he seemed to be giving Llew the opportunity to be honest as well. Besides, he had remembered Llew's name (unlike his father) and it's always a big risk lying to someone who remembers your name – especially if they're more important than you are – because they may start talking about you in high places.

'Yes, Majesty,' he said. 'In mitigation, your father had just ordered Griffith to disembowel me.'

The King nodded sagely and acknowledged Griffith, who had taken up his old position of bodyguard. Only this time to the new king, obviously.

'Princess Megan is very grateful for what you did,' Vortigern Britu said and added quickly, 'and I am too, of course.'

The change in the princess had been almost tangible from the day after the dream tower had fallen for the last time. Colour had come back into her face, she'd smiled again, she'd lost the dead-woman-walking look and Llew could see that his previous instincts had been right on the money – she was gorgeous! She'd spoken to him several times since, even sat next to him at one feast or another, even squeezed his hand again. A couple of times! Llew had to admit to himself that he was getting a bit of a crush on her. He liked being around when she was around, had even volunteered to go hunting with her at one point – although that had come to a bit of a sticky end when Llew had been chased on his horse for ten miles by a really angry white hart, with big antlers and which apparently didn't know that it was supposed to be afraid of humans. Llew even convinced himself that maybe one day …, okay, admittedly there was a bit of a divide between their stations in life, but … well, he was the emissary of Rome after all! I mean, she'd have to marry *someone*! *She* remembered his name too. And she talked to him shyly and told him little secrets. She'd also dropped the 'woe is me' hand-to-forehead stuff which made conversing a hell of a lot easier. It'd all seemed to be working out beautifully. Then there'd been *that* evening …

'Nevertheless, it is a pity about those legions,' said the king in the half-bored way he had of talking.

The news was not good. A messenger had arrived at court a week previously. And the messenger had decided to follow the rules of narrative by falling off his horse with an arrow sticking out of his back. In a croaky voice, the messenger had managed to warn those assembled that a huge Pictish invasion had occurred in the north of Elmet.

Meanwhile, Scotti raids continued in the west, such that one king had refused tribute altogether until something was done. Ironically, the Saxons weren't causing much trouble at all from their stronghold in the east, although they had sent a few raiding parties into Gwyrangon.[20] Their chief, Hengist, seemed to be biding his time, although his brother Horsa was supposedly more aggressive. It was then that the messenger had expired, but not before the settlement's new druid, Owen, had noticed some marks on the poor man's skin and come to the conclusion that if the arrow hadn't killed him, plague almost certainly would have (which had the effect of clearing the crowd around the dead messenger very quickly). It meant that not only was war coming. Plague was coming too.

Llew saw the opportunity for, at the very least, a short holiday in the Mediterranean.

'I could go to Rome and plead our case, Sire? Just because I lied about those legions, doesn't mean they aren't a possibility.'

'Kind of you, but not necessary. I have sent Cuneglas to Consul Aetius in Rome, this very morning.'

Llew was stung. Hang on just a minute, he thought, someone from Llangollen's gone to nice, warm, sunny Rome and … it's not me!

'Sire! I … I must protest! I am … the Roman emissary! If anyone should have –'

'Yes, yes, it should have been you; but I was rather sure you wouldn't have come back …'

Llew couldn't help noticing Griffith standing behind the seated king, trying not to smirk.

'Besides,' the new Vortigern continued, 'I have other work for you. I understand you have a gift for languages, yes?'

'Yes, Majesty …'

Hey hey, maybe it's a trip abroad he wants me for after all! Hello sun, here I come.

'You speak Sais?'

'What? … I mean, I beg your pardon, Majesty?'

'You speak the language of the Saxons?'

'Oh yes, of course, Majesty.'

Ah. It's a bit of a long way, where the Saxons come from. Although not as far as Rome itself. Our side of the Roman Empire, isn't it? Next to Gaul? Not sure I like the sound of that. The cakes had better be bloody good.

'Excellent. Then you can go to the south-eastern sea with Edwyn and translate for him. See if we can persuade Hengist to come up north and fight a few Picts for us. You leave tomorrow … that will be all.'

---

[20] Kent.

Once again, Llew felt his world collapsing around him. Vortigern was looking at him in a way that was both surprised and bored at the same time. It was a look that said, 'goodness are you still here?'

'You're letting Edwyn negotiate with the Saxons?'

'I'm letting Edwyn lay down my conditions. There's a difference.'

'What conditions, if I may be so bold?'

'You may not. It is a matter between myself and the Saxon king, the details of which I am entrusting to Edwyn. You are merely there as translator. … I don't want you mucking about with the deal when you get there. I know what you scribes are like. Start a little debating society over every little point. Never use one word when ten will be more confusing. Edwyn's going because he'll keep it simple. He'll offer them some land and allow a few boats of their people to settle, that's all you need to know for the present …'

For a fleeting moment, Llew remembered Marcus's words before he said goodbye.

'*Make sure that old madman keeps the Saxons out! No deals, no treaties, no ceding of land. If those Gothic bastards come here, that's it! You can forget the Romans **ever** coming back. No more baths, no warm buildings, no hypercaust.*'

But he dismissed it from his mind, because he wanted to focus on making a last ditch attempt to save his own life.

'Majesty, I am a skilled scribe, Edwyn is a former warrior who has only one arm and who … well, is not exactly the brightest star in the sky, begging your pardon. He's not known for his diplomatic skills and the Saxons are not known for much other than burning, looting and killing. If we go into Saxon territory and Edwyn's allowed to do the negotiations … I mean, lay down the conditions … we'll both end up dead.'

The king shrugged.

'I admit it's a possibility. But as you say, he's a one-armed warrior and you're a scribe. Right now you're the two people I can most afford to lose. Now,' said the king and he looked like he really meant it, 'that really will be all. Thank you.'

It was raining again.

The fact that Griffith **hadn't** killed Edwyn on his way to the dream tower was something that really rankled with the warrior. Edwyn, that is. You see, it should have gone thus: his time had come, he was caught from behind and he'd died a noble death obeying the orders of his lord and master. His spirit had then crossed into Annw, the Otherworld, where, according to Edwyn's very personal view of the afterlife, there was much feasting and young men wearing very little but the oil they rubbed onto their firm and bulbous muscles.

Only it hadn't gone thus. Griffith had merely immobilised Edwyn by chopping off his arm. Edwyn, having fought in many a battle, was no stranger to pain, but the wave of agony that had hit as his limb went somersaulting over the rest of the escort, had caused him to faint. And when he had woken up, there was a new king on the throne, all his warrior friends looked a bit embarrassed and he learned that he'd lost his place at the front of the battle line.

To be fair, the new king had tried to appear sympathetic.

'It's been felt that in the current climate, a one-armed warrior is simply not efficient – the modern soldier cannot fight with shield alone, alas, although you should understand we appreciate all the work you've put in over your long career. Still, try not to look at it as being "dismissed". There are many opportunities for someone of your skills. For instance, with a disability like yours … have you considered a career in begging? I understand there are quite a few opportunities outside the third wall of the settlement.'

It had taken a lot of angry reminders about the noble lineage Edwyn had come from and how the king needed the support of that lineage – a tribe in the kingdom of Dyfed – to keep the Irish savages out of the country at all, before Vortigern Britu had sighed wearily and asked Edwyn to leave the matter with him. He'd try to find something for Edwyn to do.

In short, Edwyn was a very bitter man and the person he most held responsible for his troubles was currently attempting to ride a donkey through the rain next to his horse. Why hadn't the little runt just let himself be killed, eh? Why allow himself to be rescued?[21] And they were going to have to go all the way South together. Ha! No chance! Translator be blowed! He'd top Llew as soon as he got the opportunity and then hope that the Saxons spoke better Cymru than he spoke Sais. If they wanted to live here, they ought to learn, after all.

Llew for his part did not relish the partnership either. It was a long journey to the South-East. Many miles of swamp and woodland packed with wolves, bandits and fierce tribes who were not always respecters of Vortigern's authority. At least not until *after* they'd killed you and might then say 'oops. Sorry. Didn't realise. You should have said you were working for the king!' However, if it had been, say … Griffith at his side, he'd have been a lot happier. Indeed, if it had been Edwyn *before* the arm had come off, i.e psychotic but generally pretty well disposed towards the world, it'd have been a lot better than the current situation, in which Edwyn was psychotic and mumbling to himself all the time about being the 'god of death incarnate'.

And supposing they made it to the small enclave in the south that the Saxons were now calling their territory? What then? Would they find the chieftain Hengist smiling outside the gates of his own hall, sword firmly put away, big grin on his fair-bearded face, saying 'come in, come in, my friends.

---

[21] It's *just* possible Edwyn was rather looking for someone to blame.

Have a bowl of fine Saxon ale and let's talk. This is my brother Horsa, by the way, he's into flowers'? Llew somehow doubted it.

All this aside, however, Llew now had good reason to want to be away from Llangollen for a little while at the very least. He'd made a bit of a fool of himself if truth were known. It had started when Princess Megan had sneaked over to his quarters the morning before he was due to leave. She was looking extremely pretty – she'd even put a few spring flowers in her hair. And when she'd said they were to meet over by Cadoc's old hut as soon as it got dark and then left with yet another squeeze of his hand, he'd thought ... actually, he'd thought 'Yum Yum'. So that night, after dinner in the great hall and lots of meaningful glances across the table to each other, Llew got away from the meal as quickly as he could, back to his quarters, put on his best cloak (this was the one without the lice) and headed for the spot which had once been the place of his darkest hour, his heart beating like a blacksmith's hammer. Only very fast. He noticed the little wooden cage was still there – empty, of course. How things had changed, he reflected to himself. Then he was the lowest thing on God's earth and now he was about to be elevated to the level of kings.

Then she appeared. And she looked twice as beautiful as ever he'd seen her. And she took both his hands, this vision of loveliness (*both* he noted, *both*) and she said, 'I'm so happy you came ...'

He managed to somehow stammer out that he was pretty happy too. Then she said it.

'Guess what? I'm to be married to King Pelinore of Elmet! Isn't it brilliant?'

He was dumbstruck. He didn't know what to say. This didn't help matters, because she started babbling on about how Pelinore was supposed to be the handsomest man in the world and that it would help seal the alliance of kings in the North and she'd get to see a bit of the country outside of Gwynedd and probably have lots of babies and everything.

Of course, what she may as well have been doing was ripping out his heart, throwing it in a pile of animal dung and saying 'you won't be needing *this* any more'.

But it did, of course, give him a few seconds. Time to get over the shock, time to formulate what he was going to say next, so that at the very least he could walk away with a broken heart, but a little bit of dignity.

Ha! Some hope.

When she stopped he burst into tears, called her a stupid cow and wailed that she couldn't possibly leave him because he loved her, didn't she understand that? He was totally smitten and surely she must know it and surely she must deep down feel the same way, I mean *surely*!

And by the time he'd got this out he was producing a hell of a lot of snot.

Megan, of course, by now had decided that holding both of his hands wasn't really an option any more (which somehow made him feel worse). In fact, a *ten feet radius* wasn't really an option any more. She wasn't smiling. She wasn't happy. But she wasn't angry either. Worse, she was embarrassed. Embarrassed to have ever talked to this person, to have confided in him, to have believed him a friend. She backed away quickly and headed back to her chambers. After that happened, Llew went home and cried himself to sleep.

So it was lucky that he and Edwyn had to leave at first light as the royal household, or even the warrior classes, would not normally be up at that time. So he wouldn't have to speak to her and if she had told her brother about it … well, hopefully, by the time Llew came back … *if* he ever came back, it would all have blown over. She'd probably be gone and already married. Fine. Just fine. He never liked her anyway. Women! Who needed them?!

It was the 'if' concerning his return that he started to ponder on as he rode through the rain on the donkey that had been provided for him (Edwyn, of course, had his own warhorse, but Llew had to make do with any mount going spare in Llangollen – especially as, the stableman had pointed out, Llew probably wasn't going to make it back, not alive anyway). He was finally, he reflected, going South. Something he'd been trying to do now for around … good gods, five years! That long! Okay, he was heading a little further to the South-**East** than he'd really hoped for, but it was South nevertheless. And if he could find a way to change direction slightly, he might be able to get … well, maybe into Dumnonia[22] – where Saxons weren't heard of and neither were Irish raiders and which was miles away from the Picts and where the climate, as he remembered well from his salad days under Marcus, was a hell of a lot warmer. Maybe he could escape from Edwyn and get as far as Aquae Sulis. There he could lose himself in the big city … hire himself out to any merchant needing a scribe – Aquae Sulis was an important river port after all – maybe get on a boat to …

As Marcus had always said, no one stays anywhere for long.

A plan was starting to formulate. Llew was going home. Just as long as he didn't get as far as Saxon territory. And just as long as Edwyn didn't kill him first.

It was still raining.

They'd been on the road for several weeks now and, in spite of the fact it was mid-Spring, the weather had done nothing but pour down. Llew was unsurprisingly miserable, but it wasn't just the damp and cold. His feelings were compounded by the fact that he'd had little or no sleep since they started and the reason for this was … Edwyn. Several times Llew had woken up by the campfire to find Edwyn staring at him, smiling, while sharpening his sword. This was unnerving enough, but twice now he'd woken up to find Edwyn holding a knife to this throat. So, he had no choice but to try and stay

---

[22] Old kingdom – Devon/Somerset/Dorset.

awake at night and catnap whilst riding on the donkey during the day. Which meant he kept falling off. Edwyn, of course, being the powerful, if appendage-challenged warrior he was, could have killed Llew at any time, but he obviously relished the night-time terrors he was putting the scribe through. They never spoke. Any time Llew tried to talk to the warrior, Edwyn would just ignore him.

So Llew was having to live with silence during the day and fear at night. With no sleep. And after a few weeks, that's enough to drive anyone mad, or at the very least drive them to take a few risks. Llew decided that no matter what those risks were, he was going to make a run for it at the next opportunity. They had been in a forest for a few days now and Llew figured that he had the advantage of being nimbler on foot than Edwyn, who would have to run, finding it impossible to ride after him through the trees. That was the theory anyway. He knew that many Cymru warhorses were trained to push through thick woodland from very early in their lives. Llew was hoping against hope that Edwyn's horse, a fiery chestnut mare called Deathgiver,[23] had been bottom of her class.

They had made camp and Edwyn had taken his sling to hunt some game for the evening meal. Llew was at first hesitant to use this occasion to bolt because he was hungry and, for some reason, Edwyn had been letting Llew eat a portion of the food he caught. The condition, although unspoken, being that Llew organised the gutting, plucking and cooking of the animal and then took less than half. However, it seemed that Edwyn had gone further off than he usually did, because Llew could hear birds singing. And normally any birds singing when Edwyn was around stopped involuntarily after hearing the last two sounds they ever heard. These being the 'swish' of a sling-shot followed by a 'thok' of a stone hitting them.

Llew decided to take his chance and, grabbing anything he thought might be useful,[24] he made off into the woods, as fast as he could, leaving the campfire, donkey and everything else behind him. He noted that dusk was coming down fast. Soon it would be dark and he would be much harder to find. He pushed hard through branches and brambles ... everywhere in fact there wasn't a natural path ... in the hope that Edwyn and/or Deathgiver wouldn't be able to follow him. The branches cut his face and hands, but he pushed on, glad when they sprung back behind him to provide the same obstacle for any pursuer. On and on he pushed, harder and harder and ever more deeper into the undergrowth.

He must have been going for at least ... oh, four and a half minutes, when he heard Edwyn's roar of anger as the warrior arrived back at camp. Panic made him realise he had no choice but to take one of the natural paths along the forest floor and run like mad in the hope that Edwyn, slow and bulky,

---

[23] The Cymru didn't believe in cosy names for their mounts.
[24] Which was actually a small dagger and that's about it.

would try to follow him on foot. The sound of reigns jingling, horse's hooves and the words, 'Come, Deathgiver, let's teach that little turd a lesson he'll never forget' not too far away, dashed that hope pretty soon afterwards. He ran on as the hooves came faster and louder up behind him. This was it! This was finally it! He'd now given that madman a legitimate reason to kill him, by running away. Edwyn could easily go back to Llangollen and say 'the translator ran off and I didn't speak the language and I've only got one arm so I didn't go to see Hengist; sorry, but I'd like my pension now, thanks'.

The hooves were almost on him when he tripped, went flying through some bushes, out through the other side and fell about thirty feet down a steep slope, landing in the bracken and dead leaves at the bottom. Every bit of him hurt, even the inside of his nostrils, but he managed to refrain from groaning and listened, breathing deeply. Above him, he could hear Edwyn wheeling the horse round and round, looking for a way to follow him down the slope ... Llew realised that not only was the slope too steep for a horse to follow him, but that it went on either side of him indefinitely. Edwyn would either have to come down the hill on foot or ride on and find another way.

He didn't wait to find out. He leaped up out of the bracken and ran like the wind. Behind him in the distance he heard Edwyn's voice.

'I'll get you yet, you little turd! You owe me for one arm!'

A warhorse is the most valuable thing a warrior can own. Evidently, Edwyn wasn't about to leave his most treasured possession untended and alone in the middle of a forest, even if it had meant the chance of catching Llew.

Llew ran on, knowing that no matter how driven Edwyn might be, it was getting darker by the minute and soon he'd be impossible to follow. Hunger and fatigue didn't matter quite so much now. For the time being, he was free.

It's a bit of an old cliché about the forest at night being scary. For ages immeasurable, mothers and stepfathers, fathers and stepmothers (wicked or otherwise) have been warning children and stepchildren, whether red-cloaked or simply being abandoned for spilling milk, not to go into the woods at night. There are wolves and bandits and bears and witches living there. Ever wondered why a cliché is a cliché? Maybe because it's true.

This forest was, unhappily for Llew, no different. Any hope he may have had about perhaps it being a forest with a bit of imagination ... a forest that eschewed all that nasty wolfy/witchy/banditty stuff from tales of old[25] for a few bright, cosy little hamlets of forest people, friendly to strangers with plenty of warm shelter, food and drink for the weary traveller, perhaps with comely daughters who weren't – unlike certain princesses – so easily swayed into marriage with a handsome king ... any hope of this was quickly dispelled at the first wolf howl.

---

[25] Because they *were* old even then.

Wolves, it is well known, generally keep away from man. However, this man, albeit rather thin and stringy, was limping, bleeding, completely unable to see in the dark and the wolves were hungry after a lean few weeks. To them, Llew was an offer too good to be true. And slowly and carefully, because they knew that you couldn't be too careful when it came to man, they started to circle him as he stumbled along. And he was stumbling. Actually, he was *falling* more than he was stumbling, because that's the trouble with forests – they're always full of tree roots just made for you to trip over in the pitch black. Actually, it wasn't quite pitch black, to be honest. The eyes of the wolves shining in the darkness, getting closer and closer to him did give off a bit of light, although not enough to *see* anything by. And, to be fair, it wasn't much comfort.

Still, at least it had stopped raining.

He could feel rather than hear them growling to each other, signalling a tightening of the pack circle as he lurched onward. In the cool of the night he fancied he could even feel the warmth and smell of wolf breath. A wet, hungry dog smell. There was some sort of growling dispute going on between two of the wolves – maybe debating who was to be allowed first go at a kill.

And then, not too far in the distance, he saw a light. Firelight! A camp fire! Someone in the middle of the forest was … well, alive for a start. He broke into a run. He didn't care what was between him and that fire, he was going to get to it. The wolves started to speed up too. They knew that if he got close to that fire, they could kiss goodbye to their evening meal. Wolves do not like fires and they do not like the generally dangerous men who sit around them, often wearing wolf furs. They started to bark and growl at each other, each issuing instructions as to how the kill was to be made. Llew was going as fast as he could now, praying to any and every god he could think of – because even the most devout will look to any port in a storm – but most especially to the gods of the trees, because if he found favour with them, maybe he *wouldn't* trip over one of their roots. If he did, he was wolf meat.

Evidently, tree gods were involved in other matters that evening. Either that or they liked a bit of fun, because Llew *did* trip over a root and, after flying through the air, landed right next to the campfire.

The wolves swerved around just away from the camp, growling, barking and howling their disappointment before getting away as quickly as they could. Llew lifted his head up slowly to take a look at his new hosts. They'd none of them moved since he'd fallen into the clearing. They were mid-meal, eating some sort of stew from wooden bowls while a cauldron bubbled on the fire. They stared at him with thin, pinched faces, the bowls held in thin, pinched limbs. The ragged furs they wore could barely be called clothes. Every one of them wore a dagger in a belt of rags. They were all hairy and the only way you could tell the men from the women was that the beards were slightly thinner. These were forest bandits. Llew had heard about forest bandits. He began to wonder if he wouldn't have been better off with the wolves.

About half an hour later, having been stripped, hogtied and thoroughly beaten up, Llew was appreciating that, if nothing else, his instincts were never too wide of the mark. The bandits, meanwhile, were in the middle of an argument in their strange dialect – a sort of bastardised version of Cymru and something much more ancient.

'We noshin' all right! We's plenty big belly for now!'

This was from a young woman. She was pointing at Llew. The leader of the robbers turned on her, gnashing his teeth.

'You wrong. Oi's hunger good!'

'Thee just ate big time, feller!'

'Oi just ate squirrel stew, lady! Want with proper dinna dinna!'

It occurred to Llew that in some way he was connected to this argument. As far as he could understand, the meal they had just eaten had not satisfied the leader, who wanted the woman to cook something else. And somehow he, Llew, was invited. The leader was now wearing Llew's cloak and, in spite of the man's slight frame, it was still several sizes too small for him. Other items of Llew's clothing had been draped over other members of the crew. One was wearing Llew's trews on his head. It occurred to Llew that, in spite of the injuries they'd caused him, he ought to feel sorry for these people. They were scavengers, obviously rarely venturing out of the forest, living off what they could find or steal, which by the looks of them wasn't much. And now they were going to eat with him. One of the men in the corner raised a hand, wanting to make a suggestion. The leader indicated for him to speak.

'We can cook 'im and smoke 'im. That keep 'im chucklebutty for nigh on. Or we can keep 'im runnin' till we wants 'im.'

'Nah,' said the leader dismissively, 'we'd have ter fed 'im or he gets no meat on 'im. Anywise, oi wants 'im now, oi does. Oo's with oi?'

Most of the bandits raised their hands. What a wonderfully fair way of doing things these bandits have, thought Llew; they all have a say in what goes on! It's not just some leader ordering them about. Maybe we can learn from these people. A kind of natural way of doing things from the people of the forest – aaaaaaaaaghgghg!

The 'aaaghghgghg!' was, of course, thought *and* screamed. For the bandit leader had now drawn what looked like an extremely large and sharp-looking axe, walked over to Llew, raised the axe high, ready to bring it down with force and speed right on Llew's skull. Llew braced himself for the shock, but once again found himself pleasantly disappointed, as the bandit leader folded up and collapsed to the ground, his head neatly bouncing in the opposite direction of his body. Then, into the clearing came a whirling, mad, sword-wielding, one-armed killing machine. Edwyn. The bandits cried in panic and anger, each attempting to draw one of their rusty, blunt weapons and take on the attacker … the young man who had proposed smoking Llew was the first to fall and then two more were sent to their graves by the warrior, who was roaring in mad battle cry. The remaining bandits decided that discretion was the better part of valour and ran wailing into the dark of the forest night. It's quite possible that, from outside the circle of light, the wolves were watching, then turning to each other and – as much as wolves can – shrugging.

Edwyn stuck his sword point down in the earth and sighed with what seemed like relief.

'Gods, I feel so much better!'

Then he noticed Llew again, cowering, tied to a tree.

'Hmm,' he said, pulling his dagger from his belt and moving towards Llew. Llew was getting good at bracing himself for death … he'd lost count of how many times he'd had to do it this very evening, in fact. Edwyn leaned forwards and cut the ropes.

'Get your clothes on, will you? It's embarrassing.'

A short while later, Llew was dressed again, and together he and Edwyn were searching through the bandits' plunder. That is, if 'plunder' it could be called. It looked as if their biggest 'haul' had been mugging a turnip farmer – that or a bankrupt ironmonger. There were rusty bits of iron everywhere, which Llew was sorting through to see if there was anything good.

'… I think it was pent-up frustration. I mean, put yourself in my position – you're one of the top soldiers in the land, you've joined the elite squad of the overlord's personal warband and then some bastard's come up behind you and you've lost an arm! And then the new chief tells you, you're no good to him. I tell you, I needed to go crack a few skulls.'

Llew had uncovered what looked like a rusty short sword.

'… so you don't want to kill me any more?'

'Not for the time being. Got it out of me system, see? Course, I do still totally blame you for all … *this*.' He waved a hand in the direction his arm used to be. 'I mean, if you hadn't rescued that kid … whatshisname …'

Llew could see that the sword was well made, in spite of the rust. He wondered where the bandits had got it from. Then he heard a voice in his head.

'Keep it well, Llewellyn Ap Gwyddno.'

'Merlin?' he said aloud.

'That's the fella. Anyway, point being, I've relieved myself of the frustration I was feeling and I need you to translate for the Saxon.' He shrugged. 'After that, I probably will kill you. But,' he added quickly, 'without malice, obviously.'

Llew watched an owl alight from a branch nearby and fly off into the night. He wrapped the sword in some old sacking. It had been Merlin who saved him before, maybe it was Merlin who'd saved him this time. Perhaps he should do as he was told.

Chapter 6 – Hengist

The journey South continued, comparatively uneventfully … 'comparatively' being the important word here, as the trail of bird feathers, animal bones and bandit helmets that lay in the wake of Llew and Edwyn would attest to anyone who might have been following them.

But, as no one *was* following them, there was no attesting either.

And so it was that at last they came to the borders in the south-eastern lands where Cymru finished and Saxon territory began …

It was raining. It had done nothing but rain for the last four days and nights. Llew knew it must be high summer, because five days ago it had been sunny and – here was a strange feeling – warm. The birds had sung and the flowers were a riot of colour. They'd passed peasant folk singing as they tended their crops and livestock – all sorts of fol-de-ra-do-day-type songs in joyous uplift, because winter was behind them and summer had indeed a-comed in, hey-ho.

Next day it pissed down.

My lot in life, thought Llew, as he trudged along on foot through the quagmire that rather cheekily was calling itself a path. He was trudging, because the donkey was gone and *this* was because after about five days of wandering in the forest after the incident with the bandits, they had started to discover why it was that the bandits had looked so emaciated. Nature is not stupid. Oh, individually, your average nice, plump game bird is not going to attempt to build a better mousetrap, or solve a crossword puzzle … but *collectively* local wildlife gets to hear about strangers in the forest who are unusually good at firing well-aimed stones at other members of their fraternity and collectively they act accordingly by running away. Which is why, after a while, Llew and Edwyn began to find that the forest seemed incredibly empty of anything alive and/or worth eating. Ah, thinks the Nature Lover in all of us, so why didn't they live off nut and berry and mushroom?[26] Mother Nature is bountiful if you know where to look, or so 'tis said.[27] This is true, but the two

---

[26] You know you're in trouble when someone gets all lyrical and refuses to pronounce things in plural.

[27] For Nature Lover read the type of people who talk funny and sing songs with words like 'Hey Nonny Nonny' in them for a hobby.

important words here are 'if' and 'know'. Truth is … red's a nice bright colour and can look quite attractive if you're out picking berries and **don't know any better** … which is why Llew and Edwyn spent one day unable to travel because they'd both been squatting over holes in separate parts of the forest. And they'd also investigated the possibility of mushrooms. However, after *that* evening's meal, Edwyn had drawn his sword and whirled it around his head terrifyingly, convinced he was being attacked by thousands of giant snails called Evan Blod. Llew would have been scared, had he not passed out after the first bowl of mushroom stew. He woke up next morning high in the branches of an oak tree with no trews on. So, after a couple of days of this kind of thing, they decided in the interests of survival that roast donkey looked very tempting indeed, especially as the donkey was also using up precious food supplies.

And actually it was quite tasty.

But now Llew trudged through the mud, while Edwyn rode Deathgiver loaded with what provisions and equipment they had left. Neither of them spoke much. The incident with the bandits and starving together and the donkey had done little to bond them. Llew tentatively had tried to find out what the fundamentals were as regards the proposed deal with the Saxons, but Edwyn had not unkindly said that for now it was none of Llew's business and that if he asked again he'd get his knackers cut off. Llew would find out soon enough, he was told – when they got to deal with Hengist and Horsa personally.

Little was known about the Saxon chieftain and his brother, except that they were large, blond and were both quite capable of turning over tables and going 'grooooaaaaaaha ha ha ha!!!' in the international language common to all warriors of the time. Hengist was meant to be the brains of the outfit … but again this was apparently comparative and by all accounts merely meant he was less likely to chop his feet off while trying to cut his toenails.

The little caravan continued on through the driving rain. They were now coming into what Llew was assuming was Saxon territory – Lloegyr. The small enclave at the borders of the Cymru kingdom named Gwyrangon. They didn't, as was customary, call in to pay respects to its king, Bruenor. The king had fallen out with old Vortigern a long time ago and had now stopped paying tribute to the overlord altogether. The only clue as to how he featured in the new overlord's plans was Edwyn snorting 'Britu will make amends with Bruenor' and laughing in a not altogether pleasant way. Llew had not liked the sound of it. Years later, he had cause to reflect that perhaps if he and Edwyn *had* taken the trouble to simply introduce themselves to Bruenor, things might have turned out differently.

Llew took in the view. Basically, in the campaigns to take this land, Hengist and Horsa had followed what later might be referred to as a 'scorched earth' policy by the kind, or a 'massacre' policy by the fair minded. It was a charred and blackened wasteland. Llew was mystified.

'Why do this? Surely the Saxons could use the land as well,' he said.

He hadn't expected an answer, so he was surprised when Edwyn turned in the saddle and spoke to him.

'Say you're an invading Saxon chief. You got two problems. The first is getting the land, the second is *keeping* it, right? So you come off your boat, you send your armies and you get rid of the population and the soldiers and whatnot. But you got a problem, right? Your men can't be everywhere all of the time and sooner or later some farmer's gonna come back. At least as far as your borders. And he's gonna work the land again right next to the territory you just captured. And then there'll be a few soldiers to protect him, then a fort, then suddenly you got a raiding party right on your doorstep ...'

Llew was puzzled. 'So ...?'

'So you take what land you need. Then around it you burn *everything!* All the farms, all the villages, all the churches ... the grass the hedges ... *everything!* You take the crops, mind ... so that you can feed your people while they're settling – but you make the land around you much more unworkable. Make it so no one can live there. Then, any farmer who comes along and tries to resettle knows he's got to work that much harder to get things going again and might *still* get raided by your warbands. Basically,' he added, getting uncharacteristically poetic, 'Hengist has ring-fenced his territory with a little tract of Hell.'

'And presumably the next stage is to expand outside this border and then ring-fence that?'

'Catching on quick, Llew,' smiled Edwyn.

And, strangely, Llew felt that, at last, he and Edwyn were ... sort of becoming friends.

It wasn't to last long. Friendships don't in Hell.

They were now coming to a ridge spreading across the horizon. A large earthwork as it turned out ... maybe it was some sort of border mark ...

'Hengist's got people coming ashore all the time. He needs more land, or they'll starve. And there's enough spears down here to keep him from bursting that. ...' Edwyn nodded towards the earthwork. 'That's the official beginning of his territory ...'

As if on cue, about a hundred fully-armed Saxon warriors marched up from behind the earthwork onto its summit, becoming silhouetted against the sky.

'Well guarded, then,' muttered Llew grimly as he took in his first sight of Saxons. Everything he'd heard about their appearance was true. A race of blond giants, people had said. All blond beards and hair ... it was like looking at a line of human haystacks. Well-armed human haystacks, obviously. But the weapons were different ... shorter, thicker swords ... but not so many of them, because most of the warriors wore or carried axes. At either end of the line some warriors had huge wolf-like dogs straining at the leash and barking.

Edwyn pulled his horse up and stopped about a hundred yards from the earthwork while the border patrol watched in silence. He raised his one arm as a gesture of truce and waited for the Saxons to react ...

... Which they did by shooting him directly in the chest with an arrow. It hit him with a 'phok'. He looked down at it, said, 'Just my sodding luck', then, in front of a totally shocked Llew, slowly slid off Deathgiver and fell to the ground, dead. His loyal horse reacted with the mildest of snorts. Two of the Saxons now left the war-band and started strolling down towards Llew, who was looking from them to the late Edwyn, then to the middle distance, wondering what sort of chance he'd have if he broke into a run now. ... It was only this time that he remembered his original plan – to abandon Edwyn just before they reached the Saxon lands and head west. Fine time to remember.

'Sorry about that,' said one of the Saxons in the Sais tongue as he approached, 'your friend is obviously a warrior. He is supposed to raise *both* his arms if he is making the truce, I think?'

Llew could not help but be perplexed.

'He's only got one! *Had* one.'

The two Saxons looked down at the dead body.

'Ja?'

This confirmed to them that Llew spoke the truth. The other shrugged.

'Our mistake, then. But you know, up there' – he pointed to the earthwork where the rest of the war-band was looking down on them – 'it was quite difficult to see them. His arms, I mean. And in our culture one armed raised is like a ... you know, challenge to battle ...'

'Oh and he was riding a horse!' put in the other ...

'A horse?' said Llew.

'Ja, we don't use them ... and you Welsh[28] ride them in battle ... so as far as we were concerned he was going to attack; no doubt about it ... so you see, we had no choice ...'

'Ja, no choice,' the first joined in, in the same chatty monotone; 'so any suggestion that Edgar up there was aiming his bow at the man simply for target practice and accidentally fired would be completely, er ...' he searched for the word, 'incongruous ...'

The other nodded enthusiastically.

'Normally we would only use a bow for hunting game ... not for battle ... but, as I say, Edgar had good reason to think we were under attack and he tends to react quickly. He's a good man – you'd like him. So ... er, sorry about your bodyguard ... how may we help you? And may I add that any of

---

[28] The Saxon word for foreigner. It's true!

your people found wandering these lands without leave of Hengist gets put to death anyway ... so I hope you have good reason ... ja?'

Llew noticed that one of the men was already drawing his battle axe ...

'Otherwise you will have to go in the report as a spy or something, I don't know ...'

Llew thought quickly ... okay, they had assumed Edwyn was the bodyguard. He didn't have much choice.

'Er, I'm an emissary from Vortigern. I have come to speak with Lord Hengist.'

Hengist's hall was not so different from, say, the hall of Vortigern or even the hall of his father, except in the latter case perhaps in scale. Okay, the woodwork was slightly chunkier, the warriors a lot bigger and certainly blonder. Instead of mead they drank ale and instead of songs about ancient battles of gods like Bel and Lugh, they sang about gods called Wotan and Thor. All of them turned with interest to see this new arrival under guard.

Hengist sat at the end of the hall at the high table and, just like a Cymru king, he had a druid of sorts, or what in Saxon passed for one, sitting to one side of him, and a huge bodyguard behind him as he ate. Hengist was pretty big himself, again all fair beard and wild fair hair. The beard, Llew could see, just about disguised a number of heavy scars, presumably won in battle. Next to him was another man, less fair than Hengist, but other than this he was almost an exact copy – clear blue eyes, thin aqualine nose – of the Saxon chief. This, Llew assumed, must be Horsa. When Llew was brought into the hall, Hengist and Horsa were arguing ...

'No! No! I am not going to let you go and massacre that village!'

'Why not?' said the other petulantly.

'... because it is your answer to everything, that is why! ... There's a problem with crops? Horsa says let's go and burn a Welsh village ... the fishing boats are in disrepair? Horsa says let's go burn down a Welsh village ... I had loose stools this morning? Horsa says we should incinerate a Welsh village ... this is a new land, can we not at least try and do something a bit *different* for a change, ja?'

Horsa growled. 'It is well that our father is not around to hear such talk!'

'Our father is not around ,Horsa, because you killed him! You hit him over the head with the fire poker! Let us not discuss that again!'

'He insulted me! He called me *Shiksa!*'

'Ja, ja! I am not interested! I *am* interested in you staying within our borders until I decide otherwise! Are you getting this all down?'

This last comment was made to a reedy man Llew had not noticed before. He sat at a table separate from the chief, surrounded by scrolls of parchment and in his hand was a quill pen. A scribe! So the Saxons wrote things down ... that was a turn-up for the books! Llew had been a scribe once – he still was officially ... he'd been trained as a *Roman* scribe and it was an important job because the Romans wrote *everything* down. However, when he'd been 'promoted' up in Llangollen, the title had sort of ... been forgotten. The tradition of the Cymru was still oral and aural, and anyone who wrote things down was somehow ... mistrusted – even though nearly everyone forgot everything ... whereas these Saxons ... well, look at the man! There he was. His own table next to the Saxon chief!

'Ja, sire,' said the reedy man in answer to Hengist, 'although I'm not sure you want it immortalised that your brother committed patricide for the reason that he was likened to a small vole! Makes your family seem a little ... petty, you know?'

He could be honest with the chief too!

'Hmm. So what would you suggest?' asked the chief, thoughtfully.

'Well, how about I put down that the mighty Throthgar – your father, not the guy from Bremen ...,' and he started to write as he spoke, '... Throthgar poured scorn on the honour of Horsa until Horsa could bear it no longer ... and Horsa said "give mine honour back or give me your life". And Throthgar drew his axe ... blah blah ... then I write something about a mighty battle lasting for twelve days – you know, the usual stuff – and we end with Horsa parading Throthgar's head around to the clamour of all his warriors ... ja?'

'Ja,' said Hengist perfunctorily, 'I like it.'

'Did I really do that?' said Horsa, impressed. 'Hey, I'm pretty good! Ja?'

So the Saxons, far from being the bunch of barbarians everybody said they were, had a liking ... a *respect* for the written word, eh? Then, it seemed for the first time, Hengist noticed Llew. And the rest of the hall, noticing that Hengist had noticed Llew, quietened down.

'Who are you?' he said.

'I am Llewelyn ap Gwyddno, sire. I am an ... emissary from the Vortigern.'

'Emissary.' That word again. He'd been the Roman emissary – even though he'd never been to Rome, and now he was emissary from Llangollen even though he wasn't and the man who *was* had been 'accidentally' shot dead with an arrow. Llew looked at the man writing everything down and wished he were a scribe again.

'You? A man who would float away if the wind blew hard enough?' Hengist seemed doubtful. 'Is it not part of your tradition to send a mighty *warrior* to parley with a warlord such as myself?'

The men who had brought Llew from the border shuffled uneasily. It was probably lucky for them that Llew was good at thinking on his feet.

'Times have changed, mighty Hengist,' he said, the old magic kicking in again. 'There is a new overlord on the throne at Llangollen. Vortigern Britu – son of Vortigern – and he is much less likely to ... to ...'

'Fancy his immediate family?' said Hengist. 'Forgive me, I don't mean to be insulting … but you know … we hear stuff? One of my spies reported something about a tower falling down …' He turned to the scribe. 'Ja?'

'Ja,' the scribe nodded casually.

'See, the reason I ask is because we knew of Vortigern as a … you know … a barbarian? So, any time I get a messenger from him … I take the message, thank you very much, then I, you know … cut off his head. This is an honorable death for a warrior, no?'

Llew could feel the conversation getting away from his control, and now he knew he really needed to keep a rein on it.

'… But, you,' continued Hengist, 'you are no warrior. What are you? Tell me so I can decide your fate when you have given me the message.'

Llew smiled inwardly. Hengist had given him a way out.

'Sire, by trade I am a scribe.'

Hengist looked impressed. *His* scribe stopped writing and looked up from his parchments. He studied Llew quizzically.

Hengist smiled. 'So I can send you back to your overlord with a parchment and writing?'

Llew nodded, 'With our agreement written on it.'

'Agreement? We are going to reach agreement?'

'Oh yes, sire? That is why I was sent!'

It was at this point that Horsa decided to growl his viewpoint.

'Why should we trust you?' He turned to Hengist. 'Get the message from him then let me rip his innards out! It will be one less Welsh we should worry about!'

Hengist smiled wearily with an expression that said 'I'm sorry, I just have to deal with this' … then, without looking round, he drew up his fist and expertly punched his brother on the temple. Horsa's eyelids fluttered briefly, then he seemed to deflate and slid down to the floor, where he lay gurgling.

'You,' Hengist said to his druid, 'get him … whatever it is he takes to have less of a headache when he wakes up, ja?'

The little old man nodded philosophically and wandered off, leaving Horsa groaning on the floor. This was obviously something that happened regularly.

'You have to forgive my brother,' said Hengist. 'He does not understand this is a new country. He wants to do things the way we always have done, which is not going to work here. There are more of you than there are of us … we cannot beat you, but we are fierce and increasing in numbers … you cannot beat us. Therefore, it's like you say, we must come to an agreement, ja?'

Llew nodded dumbly. This was not the way he'd expected Hengist to be. Okay, maybe it was down to stereotyping, but one of the reasons he'd planned to escape before they got to Lloegyr was that he knew … everyone knew … Saxons were violent maniacs. Even more so than Cymru. And yes, Horsa seemed to confirm this as true; but here was at least one man who, in spite of his size and obvious strength, was a chief and didn't look like he needed to overturn a table to make a point.

Hengist stood up.

'Walk with me ...,' he said, beckoning to Llew.

Llew, blinking, followed him out, noticing that the big bodyguard stayed within spitting distance.

They walked through the settlement surrounding Hengist's hall. Llew hadn't really taken it in when he arrived. His mind had been on other things. Like not getting dismembered. For the first time he noticed that there was something odd about the buildings ... yes, they were typical Saxon design – which was not too different from Cymru design ... thatched roofs, rough stone walls, but in a strange way, they didn't look quite right ...

Hengist appeared to be reading Llew's mind, because he said, "This was a Roman settlement before we came along. Those Romans knew how to build, ja? The foundations were very good. Very strong. So we built our houses on top of their foundations ... look at this?'

He pointed to a square hole at the base of one of the buildings.

"For some reason they had a fireplace in the floor outside. Weird, ja?"

Llew felt a little tear of nostalgia form in his eye.

'It was for the hypocaust,' he whispered hoarsely.

'Uh?'

'Slaves would tend a fire ... here, see? And the heat would go under the ... under the ...' – Llew was desperately trying not to weep now – '... under the wooden floorboards. And make the house warm.'

Hengist nodded sagely.

'Hm. Clever idea. Clever damn Romans. Something the matter with you?'

'No, no,' said Llew, wiping his eyes, 'just ... remembering stuff.'

Hengist, however, was transfixed.

'Clever, ja? But stupid also. Not so much of them now. Bastard Visigoth coming west and taking everything. Crazy! That's why we come here, ja? ... but bastard Cymru won't give us no bastard land and with no bastard land we starve, which is why we come raiding damn Cymru! **Bastard**!'

Somehow, Hengist had managed to work himself into a state of anger. This wasn't a good sign and, seeing the bodyguard's hand was lingering close to the axe currently tucked into his belt, Llew knew there was at least one possibility of the way Hengist's anger could go.

'I mean, I try, you know? I got people to feed, ja? I got to stop Horsa riding off with a hundred men every few seconds and putting half the population to the sword and do I get thanks? No! I get some bard come in with miserable damn saga about warriors killing each other all the time. Tell me something, how come they never tell a bard "hey, write a funny saga", huh? Or better, a *short* one? Listen to me, Scribe, ja? Never be a leader! **Never** be a leader! **Never be a leader!!!**'

This last was shouted to the sky. The shout of an angry and confused man far from his homeland trying to stop his people from starving. Llew realised he was ... well, he was feeling sorry for him. For Hengist – the Ravager, as he was known. The people of the settlement, who were busy going about their daily business, hadn't even looked their way. Either they were used to Hengist's tantrums or they didn't want to get caught in the middle of one.

Hengist sighed, sat down on a rock and pulled out an evilly large-looking Saxon knife, causing Llew to gasp in fear. Hengist waved his fear away casually.

'Don't worry. It's made by one of my blacksmiths. Saxon knives ... no edge on them at all. We don't use them to cut our meat so much as tenderise it, ja?'

He picked up a stick from the ground and began an attempt at whittling. Which was pathetic because, as he had said, the knife was not sharp. He sighed.

'So what am I to do, Scribe?'

'Sire?'

'You come here as emissary. You come with a message. What's the message? What would you have me do?'

'Fight for us, sire.'

Hengist blinked. This was something he hadn't expected. Llew went on.

'My king would have you send men north. Help him keep the Picts at bay.'

'In exchange for ...?'

Ding! In his fascination watching the manic depressive episode of Hengist, Llew had forgotten to stay one jump ahead of the proceedings. He looked blank. His mouth was opening and closing, but nothing was coming out. He was lost for words.

'You see, this is what happens when you don't write things down, Scribe. You forget them. Now come on ... think ... what did your king want to offer me in exchange for my men?'

Llew could see that he had to say something ...

'Er ... it'll come to me in a minute ...'

He'd never been told. Britu had given the details to Edwyn who was, of course, dead ... so he was going to have to think what it was Britu would be offering. Luckily, he remembered something his king had said just before they left ...

'Edwyn's going because he'll keep it simple. He'll offer them some land and allow a few boats of their people to settle, that's all you need to know for the present ...'

... which was good, because Hengist was starting to seem impatient. You could tell because 'I am getting impatient, Scribe' was what he said. And the bodyguard had casually removed the battleaxe from his belt and was tossing it from one hand to the other.

'Land! Settlers!' Llew cried out.

Hengist didn't look surprised. He shrugged.

'How many settlers?'

'He'll offer them some land and allow a few boats of their people to settle ...'

'A few ...,' Llew stuttered vaguely.

Hengist didn't look too pleased at this and now the bodygard was making the axe do little somersaults in the air. Llew could understand the chieftain's impatience – after all, what was 'a few'?

'A few hundred!'

Hengist shook his head and Llew noticed the somersaults of the axe had become double somersaults.

'Thousands. I meant thousands!' and, realising this still wasn't working ... 'Three thousand.'

Whump! The axe embedded itself in the ground right by Llew's feet. The guard came over and picked it up, grinning at Llew. Hengist nodded thoughtfully.

'How much land? I cannot take so many in this place ...,' he said. 'Where will they go? The three thousand.'

Now Llew really had to do some thinking. Hengist was right. You couldn't expect them all to live on top of one another. So where would Britu have thought to put them? Three hundred thousand ... well, you'd need a small kingdom, wouldn't you? Then he remembered something Edwyn had said as they'd rode down together ...

'Britu will make amends with Bruenor.'

And then he'd laughed evilly. Llew now understood! Bruenor was about to get his come-uppance for not paying his taxes. Bruenor was about to become a king in exile. A king without a kingdom.

'Gwyrangon, my lord,' he said.

Hengist looked at him interestedly.

'The overlord is going to give me a whole kingdom? For the use of my army?'

'Well, with respect, Lord Hengist, you've taken a large chunk of the kingdom already. And it's not a very big one, either. Your people will be permitted to settle and you will rule the ... the rest.'

'And Bruenor? Vortigern can do this? He can take a whole kingdom away from one of his kings?'

I bloody well hope so, thought Llew; but aloud he said, 'he is the Overlord, sire. High king in all but name. He can do whatever he wants.'

Hengist was still for a moment. Then he stood briskly and said, 'Come, let us go and make it official, Scribe, ja? Let us write it down.'

And he strode towards the hall.

And so it was that evening Llew found a degree of contentment he hadn't felt for a long time. He sat outside a hut that had been provided for him – with a proper straw bed and he didn't have to share it with any animals either – looking up at the stars, remembering the fine meal he'd eaten next to the chieftain at the chieftain's table and the fine Saxon ale he had drunk and reflecting in the fact that for once he wasn't too cold either. He'd found he admired the Saxon Chief. Even liked him. Hengist was a reasonable man. A warrior yes, but reasonable. Someone you could do business with. Like all the Saxons, really. Llew couldn't help but think that maybe these foreigners had been given too much of a bad press by his own people. Sure, they were invaders ... but, well, wasn't everyone when you came down to it? The Romans were. So were the Cymru, actually. There were old stories about the first of his kind stepping off the boats to find the land populated by the Old People. He suspected that if you went back far enough, the Old People had come to the land from somewhere else. Not that there were any left to ask. Except for that Merlin. And if he were ever to run into *him* again the first question would not be 'what is the history of your people?' but the more brusque, 'how'd you like my boot up your arse, fairy man?' Anyway, the Saxons, he thought ... very admirable race; and Hengist, very admirable king. Marcus had really got things wrong when he'd said ... what was it?

'*Making sure that old madman keeps the Saxons out! No deals, no treaties, no ceding of land. If those Gothic bastards come here, that's it! You can forget the Romans **ever** coming back. No more baths, no warm buildings, no hypocaust.*'

Some people were just prejudiced.

At the feast, Llew had also admired the Saxon women, who were tall and fair ... if a little, well ... beefy in some places ... and then he'd felt guilty about Megan. And *then* he'd remembered that it had been an awful long time since he'd thought about her. He wondered if she was married to King Pelinore yet. Good *handsome* King Pelinore, he thought bitterly ... everybody said how handsome he was. And brave. And bold. Of course, what they also said, he *hadn't* had a chance to tell Megan on account of him ... you know ... weeping uncontrollably, which was that King Pelinore was supposed to be so stupid he couldn't find his own backside without a map and even then he'd be too stupid to read it properly. In fact, he'd probably read it upside down, he was said to be that stupid! You know that old tale about the man who was so stupid he'd thought the moon had fallen from the sky into the pond? Well, Pelinore was the model for that! Honestly. Megan didn't know there were like loads and loads of Pelinore jokes like ... like: why won't King Pelinore ride a horse? Because he can't! He's too stupid! Well, he probably made that one up, but there were loads of jokes, like about her big handsome so-called husband-to-be and he'd have told them all to her if he hadn't ... you know ... been having a sort of panic attack and a snot problem.

He realised that this probably wasn't a healthy way to be thinking.

Megan was probably married by now and living it up in Elmet. There was, he reflected, nothing to be done. What he did have to think about now was what his next move would be. Before the banquet, Llew had sat down with Hengist, the druid and Hengist's scribe, who's name was Alban, and they had written it all down. The agreement. In full. Exactly how many boatloads of people Hengist would be permitted to bring ashore and settle. Just exactly when he could start moving his people into Gwyrangon timed to coincide, of course, exactly when King Bruenor would abdicate and leave unmolested to live in exile in Powys under the protection of the Vortigern. This would mean that not only would Britu now have a Saxon army at his disposal to go and fight in the North, but also Bruenor's army, who'd no longer be required to defend its borders from the Saxons, so perhaps they could be deployed in the West to repel Irish raiders. Britu must have already thought of all of this, of course, but Llew was pretty sure his master would be doubly pleased for making sure it'd all come off! Especially after not having been let in on the plan in the first place! Also very specifically written down were the sizes of the Saxon army to be put at the Vortigern Britu's disposal. The number of men exactly.

There it all was, in black and white. Two copies – one in Sais, one in Cymru.

Llew noticed that, in terms of serving Hengist, Alban had a role similar to that of a druid back home ... in that he was, as well as noting everything down, the leader's main counsellor, while the Saxon *druid's* role was to generally bless everything the chief agreed to and occasionally go off and make a hot drink for them all. He didn't seem to mind either. Llew reflected that, in this at least, the Saxons were much more like the Romans than the Cymru. Marcus had been the main counsellor to the governor in Aquae Sulis before the Great Day they'd all been sent north and, like Alban, Marcus had written everything down too!

Surely, he thought, surely this had to be the way forward. Men of learning and letters being the men who advised the kings! Mind you, he mused, of the three tribes – Saxons, Roman and Cymru – which was the one that had the staying power? The Cymru had been lords of Ynys Prydein since beyond memory; whereas the Romans had come and now they were gone – albeit, he hoped, temporarily ... and now these Saxons were only just succeeding in getting a foothold. What that said about faith in the scribes of the world ... he didn't like to think.

So now it was written down. The agreement. And Hengist had signed it and Llew had signed it on behalf of Vortigern, which he wasn't too keen on, but something he didn't feel he had much choice about. Something he *did* feel he had a lot of choice about was what he would do once he was released from Saxon territory. He could go back to Llangollen ... or ... he could sort of turn left on the way up and go to the coast. Maybe get a ship abroad. Maybe go to Aquae Sulis and disappear there. He could arrange to have the parchment sent to Llangollen ... there was always a warrior who could be paid to do what you wanted and he'd get cash from somewhere. After all, Hengist had said he would be given Edwyn's armour, warrior rings and weapons as a matter of honour. Llew was pretty sure he'd get a damn good price for them. And the Saxons' mistrust of horses meant they didn't want Deathgiver either. So he could, if he wanted, ride out with all that stuff, sell it and pay someone to take the agreement to Vortigern Britu ... and then he'd have even done his job without ever having to return to the hateful place. It was tempting.

'May I join you?'

Llew started. It was Alban. He had come up to Llew's hut, a leather bag bulging with parchment scrolls under each arm.

'What are those?' asked Llew, indicating the bags.

'History,' said Alban, 'our history. Hengist wants it all written down for the generations to come. Everything that was to everything that is, ja? It is the way we do things.'

'What for?' asked Llew, genuinely interested.

Alban looked puzzled.

'Presumably so that those who follow us *don't* make the same balls-up we have. So that they will learn by our mistakes. ... Of course,' Alban added whistfully, 'that is, if the whole lot doesn't go up poof!'

'I'm sorry?'

'In fire, ja? We live in troubled times ... parchment burns and all our buildings are made of wood ... now, if we were ... what were they called ... the Greeks? Then we'd be able to do something about it. Although, I expect we'd still lose it in the end, just like they did.'

Llew shook his head uncomprehendingly.

'I met a man, once,' Alban went on, 'a learned man and he told me that the Romans copied everything ... or nearly everything from the Greeks. And the Greeks had these giant stone buildings ... and they filled the buildings with histories. Not just histories. Medicines ... science ... poems ... all written down. Libraries, ja? Then the Romans came and burned the parchment ... but my learned man said ... the buildings stayed standing ... and if the Romans had not been so stupid, the knowledge would still be there ...'

'But ... why did the Greeks let them?'

'Because the one thing the Greeks did not know is how to fight as well as the Romans, ja? And the Romans lost all the Greek knowledge, which is why they fade so now. Maybe you think?'

Llew didn't answer him. We know how to fight, he thought. We know because the Romans taught us. But we don't write things down. The Saxons do write things down and they know how to fight, but they don't know how to build things properly. They just build over what's already there ... but we *can* build, because the stuff we didn't always know … the Romans taught us that as well. We could know everything there is to know! And if one of our kings was to collect all the knowledge there was and put it into one place … a big stone building, a library that couldn't burn, protected by men like Griffith and, yes, even Edwyn … well, that'd be one hell of a king to contend with. He'd know everything! He'd know how to beat anyone! You could get people to steal the parchments from people like the Saxons, so you could *know* what they'd done in the past and you could stop them doing it. You could go to the tribes in the West and ask them how the Irish liked to start a battle or make a raid and you *write that down* and you could put it in the building. And next time the Irish or the Saxons invaded, the king could go and look up what they'd done before and he would know how to beat them. Old Vortigern shouldn't have been building a tower, he should have been building a library! With a big enough library, a Cymru king could be the most powerful in the world. Ynys Prydein really would be the Island Of The Mighty!

Oh well. It wasn't his problem.

Soon he would be gone.

'We're none of us here for long,' he thought to himself.

Chapter 7 – The Warrior

It was time to leave.

Of course it was time to leave. It was sleeting. Autumn that year had come with a 'flump'…, which was the sound of the leaves falling from the trees. Llew had lived for a good part of his life in the South and generally remembered it to be warmer than his homelands or indeed in the north.

Not this year, obviously.

He wondered if the Christians were wrong. That there was in fact not just the one God, but, as the druid's believed, many thousands and that he, Llew, was one of them. A Cold Weather God. And the clouds and the North wind and every single drop of rain or flake of snow wanted to love him and be with him.

He rode Deathgiver, Edwyn's old horse, who was as placid and easily biddable a mount as you could hope for (if a little higher than Llew was used to) while he was being escorted to the edge of Llogeyr by the same border patrol that had brought him to Hengist. However, as soon as the Saxons were away back over the earthwork border, Deathgiver turned into the snarling, battle-hardened monster she had been before, bucking and whinnying ferociously, throwing Llew to the ground and absolutely refusing to let him get back on again – which he couldn't have done anyway because Llew didn't have a handy ladder with him and small flying machines had yet to be invented. So Llew had to walk and Deathgiver followed him in that 'I just happen to be going in the same direction as you' sort of way. However, he was lucky, because Deathgiver was still carrying all the gear … the exception being a big leather bag of scrolls – some Saxon histories that Alban had given him as a gift, along with the agreement that Hengist had signed for his people and Llew had signed for the Vortigern. The binding agreement.

They headed North. Llew knew that if he was going to head for Aquae Sulis, he'd have to turn West at some point, but he wasn't sure whereabouts. He wanted, if possible, to avoid the great forest that he and Edwyn had passed through on the way down … not wishing to repeat the experience of the man-eating wolves or indeed the man-eating *men*, character building though they may have been. He liked travelling across open, flat grassland like this. You could see what was coming for miles. Not that much did come, of course. No one travelled to where he'd come from. People did not, as a rule, wake up on a breezy morning and say 'you know what we should do today, dear? We should hitch up oxen to the cart and take the kids on a jaunt to Lloegyr. I hear the views of the charred borderlands are quite spectacular and once you've passed through them you can see real-life Saxons living and working as they have done for thousands of years! They say once you're there, it's almost impossible to leave!'

He did, however, as he got further away from the Saxon lands, encounter a couple of small hamlets. Three or four huts built close to each other in an attempt at 'safety in numbers' – the vain hope that, should a horde of armed barbarians decide to swarm past, they'd be dissuaded from attacking, because there was more than one of you sharing a turnip patch. These were not places used to strangers and to say they were disinclined to be friendly would be an accurate if understated description. Rocks were often thrown at Llew and the horse and at one place there was even the threat of things long, iron-tipped and pointy. However, when this happened, Deathgiver wheeled round, charged and headbutted the hamlet's chief aggressor, after which the attack stopped.

It was during the second week, Llew started to see something in the distance. A settlement? No, it was too big. There were multiple plumes of smoke rising into the air, indicating people and houses, but there were so many of them! They spread right across the horizon. ... He could just about make out the shapes of buildings ... blackened, ramshackle. And, as he approached, the grassland gave way to farmland ... corn was being harvested ... livestock – large flocks of sheep and goats were being tended ... all by swarthy and friendlier folk. And now he could see the place he was approaching really was a city. He hadn't seen one for an awful long while. And this one was even bigger than Aquae Sulis.

To reach it you had to cross a great fortified, but ill-maintained, wooden bridge, evidently built long ago by Roman hands and, as he approached its giant open gates, he passed a tattered old wooden sign. The paint was peeling. It had been put up there a long time ago and somehow had managed to not rot or be knocked over or burned. He could just make out what the sign had once said in Latin ...

'Londinium welcomes careful drivers.'

The name was one he'd heard before. It was a name that promised expectation of much. A name you whispered as if magical.

Londinium! The greatest city of them all!

Londinium! The city of a thousand sights and sounds!

Londinium! The city that never sleeps!

Of course, what was never whispered quite so enthusiastically was that it smelled like a giant cesspool and that you were likely to get mugged, conned, or both, once you were within three feet of the main gate. And Llew was no exception to this rule. It was as if he was wearing a large placard that said

'There Is One Born Every Minute And It Was My Birthday Sixty Seconds Ago'.

He had barely got past the city walls when a big man in a leather jerkin carrying what looked like an antique Roman sword came up to him and said ... 'Nice horse.'

'Er, thanks ...'

'It's mine now. Any argument and I'll cut your legs off, okay –.... ouououourrghghghg!'

Deathgiver had decided she didn't like the look of this man. The mare turned and swiftly inserted a back hoof between the would-be horse thief's legs. The man collapsed on the floor. Llew and trusty steed started to make their way through the bustle ...

Another man, shorter, with a ferrety expression, approached them. He spoke to them in what Llew remembered was a Pictish accent.

'Excuse me, sir, you don't know me, but my wife is pregnant and waiting for me at Hadrian's wall. I've lost all my money, taken by despicable thieves ... if you could perhaps lend me some for a steed ... or even loan me yours for a couple of days I'd be most grateful. If you supply me with your address, I'd be sure to pay you back ...'

Llew was touched by the direct honesty of the man and he was just reaching for his purse to give the man a couple of gold coins, but Deathgiver had turned round and used that all-too-powerful back hoof to send the man flying into a passing ox cart.

'What did you do that for?' said Llew to the horse.

Deathgiver shook her head and buzzed as if she couldn't believe how stupid her new master was. Which she couldn't.

Londinium. Love it or hate it, you had to hate it. The place was just one big mass of noise and movement. Or rather the lack of movement. Ox carts, wagons, horses and even wheelbarrows were queuing up along the streets, failing to move forward at all despite the protestations of their drivers. People were just shouting all the time! Sometimes it was to sell things, but most of the time it seemed as if it was simply for something to do. On every other corner there was what could be described as an 'entertainer'. This ranged from a bard down on his luck ('forced to sell harp') singing epic songs about brave and fertile warriors, to a man with a painted white face and large trews juggling bladders (like many that were to follow him, he was *fantastically* unfunny), to another who was simply banging two wooden spoons together without rhythm or reason. This last held his hat ferociously out at Llew (apparently he'd just done his 'big finish') and when Llew passed without giving him any money he shouted 'Sod you then! Philistine!' at Llew's back. This man was lucky – Deathgiver decided to ignore him.

Every other building was a church. Every other person was a monk, or a priest of some sort. One plainly drunken monk with a big beard, who must have been the only cleric in the city *without* his own building, was rampaging round one of the town squares, screaming at people.

'Art thou a Peleganist, brother? No? Thou wilt burn in hell! Bastard!!!'

Llew dodged into a side street and found what he was looking for. An Inn. He'd been on the road for a long time. He needed a drink, a meal and somewhere to sleep for a while. He hitched up the horse on the rail outside and went in.

It was busy – but not too busy – and warm. A roaring fire billowed welcome at the far end of the room. He sat down at the end of one of three long tables and was pleased to find himself almost immediately approached by the friendly red-faced and well fed looking proprietor – a man who, when faced with certain narrative conventions about the 'look' of a genial landlord, had obviously thought 'why fight it?' and grown a nice big fuzzy pair of mutton-chop whiskers as well.

'What can I get you, sir? Come far?'

'Something to eat. Something to drink. And yes. From Lloegyr … listen, I might need some help … I need to sell some things before I can pay the bill. Armour … weapons … a horse …'

He trailed off. The Innkeeper was looking at him in a slightly puzzled fashion and he noticed that there'd been a subtle shift in the general chatter. A shift down from talking to not talking.

'Lloegyr, sir? And now we're selling our weapons, is it? Ah well, I suppose you wouldn't be the first.'

'I …' Llew measured up the rest of what he was going to say carefully, '… wouldn't?'

'Oh, no. I'm afraid there's rather a glut of warriors deserting from the border armies and trying to sell their gear here. Particularly from King Bruenor of Gwyrangon. Not the most popular of men, if you get my meaning. You won't get much of a price for it, I'm afraid – even for a magnificent animal like that …' He indicated Deathgiver, who was in view of the front doorway '… although I might know someone who'd be interested. I'll get you some food.'

The innkeeper hurried off.

This man thinks I'm a warrior. He can't do! I mean … look at me!

Some other members of Llew's table were starting to shuffle along the bench towards him. They had a look of nervous interest, as if someone famous was in the room.

On the other hand …

Llew realised that he'd been on the road for a while and the extra opportunity to exercise that Deathgiver had given him had probably helped him look that bit fitter. He'd got a bit of a beard coming now as well. And he was most definitely mucky. So maybe … maybe he could just pass for someone who lived by the sword. Perhaps he ought to clear this up right now…

'So what was it like down there?' said one – a pretty, young, dark haired woman, earnestly. 'You kill any Saxons?'

…. and perhaps he oughtn't. … This could be very good cover. He could be just another deserting soldier from the borderlands of Lloegyr, trying to make some money from his weapons. If he managed to make enough, he could pay someone else to take the agreement scroll up north and head away west as per his plan. No one would be any the wiser. He shrugged in what he thought was a warrior-like casual way at the lady's question and adopted a slightly deeper tembre of voice.

'It's pretty bad. Johnny Sais has turned the borders into a hellhole – no one can settle there again. Meanwhile, that bastard Horsa leads raiding parties out day and night. You'll be out on patrol one day. You'll see some smoke on the horizon. By the time you get there, Horsa's raized what used to be a nice little village to a smoking ruin – the men are dead, the women and children have been taken as slaves. Pah!' He spat for effect. Almost successfully, as it happened, so that he only had to wipe a little bit of dribble from his chin. His audience managed to look both appalled and entranced with terrified fascination. They were completely agog, with the exception of one old man who was sitting warning his hands by the fire, who just carried on staring at the flames and warming his hands.

By this time a large loaf of bread had been put down in front of him. He broke a hunk off in what he hoped was a suitably 'tough' way and bit into it…

'Yes,' continued the woman, 'but did you kill any of 'em? The Saxons, I mean.'

Llew shrugged again. His answer, however, was completely incomprehensible because he had a mouth completely full of bread. And after that it was completely incomprehensible because he was choking.

'I did what I had to do,' he said finally. 'And now I've seen enough killing to last me a lifetime, which is why I'm here.'

He affected the haunted look of the battle-weary veteran. He'd seen a few in his time. Soldiers at home or in the Roman garrisons of Aquae Sulis, or some of those up at Llangollen. Men who'd been in one too many a skirmish. As well as the haunted and weary look, he *could* have gone for the optional extra that some of the veterans had – the trembling fit and waking nightmares ' but he thought that might be over-egging the pudding.

'Funny. You don't look much like a soldier.'

This was the old man in the corner, rubbing his hands. He still hadn't taken his gaze away from the fire.

'No … well … I was quite sickly as a child …,' was all he could think of, adding, 'My father thought the army would make a man of me …'

Everyone else seemed to take this on trust. There were a few nods and mutters of 'it's true' and 'if only a few **more** father's were like that' and 'yeah, we might not have the situation we have now with the bloody Saxons at our doorstep'.

'... Except,' continued the old man, still without looking round, 'you're running away from it. From the fighting. And you look as if you'd fall over if a dog so much as tried to piss on you. So it hasn't worked, has it?'

Llew remembered something Marcus had taught him. Marcus had said that there's always one – when you've got an audience – someone who thinks they have a better story, someone who thinks they're funnier or cleverer than you are, someone who just basically wants to rain on your parade. They've worked out what they're going to say in advance and they're just waiting for an opportunity to say it ... waiting for their cue, so to speak. Usually, they've got a big stupid grin on their faces, because they're absolutely convinced *they're* going to wow everybody from the wrong side of the stage and they've usually got an unsmiling mousy girlfriend in tow who they're *sure* knows how deeply hilarious and clever they really are. And when they've said it ... the crappy little comment to ruin the punch line ... they sit down *really* pleased with themselves ... totally convinced that everyone in the audience thinks they're the best thing ever ... whereas, actually, everyone in the audience (usually *including* the mousy girlfriend) ... wishes they would either shut up and go away or better, just shut up and die.

And this, Llew realised, was just such a someone.

'You need to examine my weapons and armour to prove it?' said Llew, just a trifle more snottily than perhaps he intended.

'Me? No, no,' said the old man, 'not me. No ...'

'Good. Anyway –'

'Although ... you could have just stolen them ... the weapons and armour. And the horse probably ... if you weren't a soldier. *Like* you say you are.'

And, for the first time, the man had turned round to look at him. And, as expected, he was grinning as smugly as he could. Llew paused. The others were looking at him. Well, he'd started this now; he had to find a way of finishing it. How would a real warrior react? Luckily, he had one of Edwyn's daggers tucked into his belt. It wasn't terribly sharp, but it did have a very ornate handle. Okay, he thought, let's go for broke ...

He took the dagger out, casually holding it by the blade and pretended to be studying the carvings on the handle.

'Yeah. That's right,' he said, 'you know what I could've done? I could've been on the road, found a big Cymru warrior and just ... you know ... mugged him. Stolen his horse, his shield, his sword, his armour and his dagger. Just like that. On the other hand ...' Llew waited for a moment before he looked up directly into the old man's face, '... the stuff could just belong to me because I earned it. What do you think?'

And for an added bonus, he managed to affect the cold-eyed look he'd seen Griff, Edwyn and others give just before a fight. The look that said 'remember I gave you the chance to back off'.

The old man began to fidget in his seat. He looked really uncomfortable.

'All right. I'm only sayin'…'

He turned back to the fire. Bloody hell, it had worked! Llew put his dagger in his belt like an expert, trying not to show that actually it had been sharper than expected and that his hand was bleeding. He reflected realistically that he'd been lucky. He shouldn't try this too often. On the other hand, it was a damn useful tool with the right people.

By now the innkeeper had returned with a huge bowl of stew for Llew with a wooden spoon stuck in it. The young woman eyed it hungrily. Llew, still playing the casually cool warrior, offered her the bowl?

'Want some? There's plenty.'

The woman hungrily picked up the wooden spoon and gulped down a few mouthfuls of the stew, explaining as she did so that she and her party had only been able to afford a bed for the night. They had no money for food as well.

'Where have you come from?' said Llew, still affecting his deep warrior voice …

'The East. We had to leave in a hurry.'

'Fleeing the Saxons?'

She shook her head. 'Fleeing the plague.'

There was a pause.

'Can I have another spoon, please?' called Llew to the innkeeper. The innkeeper brought one over and told him that he'd just spoken to someone who would buy his gear.

'He wants you to come to the old boat wharves when the moon's highest in the sky. This side of the river. There's a jetty for a boat called *Gwyn Dun Mane*. He says come alone … you being a deserter … well, he don't want no trouble.'

Llew nodded sagely. This seemed logical.

Had Llew been a **real** warrior, of course, he might have thought … 'bring a load of valuable war gear and a very valuable horse down to the docks? At midnight? In this city? That's a bit suspect' … but he wasn't, so he didn't.

Wooden boards. He was walking along the wooden boardwalks that line the river, leading Deathgiver. He could hear the clunk clunk of the horse's hooves as they walked past lines of moored-up boats, all of them deserted. This river – the Thames – had once been the gateway to the Roman empire and, with it, everything the empire could promise: silks, goods, fabrics, precious metals, swords, axes, horses, cows … and people. Of course people. Because there was once a time when, if you were Roman, Britannia was quite the place to be. They'd called it the River Of Gold – with a fair wind, you could sail out of the heart of Londinium into the Eastern Channel and be on the shores of Gaul within three days and vice versa. And because of this the city had become huge … the biggest in the whole of Ynys Prydein … until the empire had started to fray slightly at the edges. And now, of course, the sea was full of Frankish pirates and trade was much more dangerous. So the boats now were mainly fishing boats ... because even Frankish pirates could catch their own fish. A few of the more adventurous traders still sent their wares across the sea to the Thames – for which they got paid a lot more ... a hell of a lot more – and this was one of the reasons why Londinium had become a place where you were either very rich or very poor.

Llew was looking for a boat called *Gwyn Dun Mane*, and it was not proving easy. He'd been wandering up and down the river for hours now, wondering if such a boat even existed, but the innkeeper had been very specific. Besides, the innkeeper had also added that, brave warrior or no brave warrior, Llew was not getting any more food and he certainly wasn't getting a bed until he'd got some real coins to pay for them.

'Can't use that armour of yours, can I, son? And I can't eat horse neither. ... Okay, actually I *can* eat horse and would too, but anyone can see that's a well trained battle mount and you should be able to get a half-decent amount for it, even in these troubled times. You'd have some left over ...'

This was the other reason for him continuing to scour the riverside. He needed as much cash as he could get. If he wanted to set himself up in Aquae Sulis or head to the continent ... he needed the cash ... and if he wanted to pay someone to go up to Llangollen for him, he needed *more* cash. It had occurred to him that he didn't have to bother with this. Vortigern Britu had sent him on a mission which he wasn't really supposed to succeed at, that the odds said was supposed to end in his death, so he didn't really feel he owed the overlord anything. On the other hand ... well, it was important. He might well have stopped a major war and saved the Northern kingdoms from the devastation of Pictish invasion. God knows if that idiot Cuneglas *had* persuaded Consul Aetius to lend some Roman soldiers ... well, with Hengist and the Saxons on side as well, they could all start celebrating. Maybe the alliance of kings would vote to call Vortigern High King – something his father had always wanted. Bruenor wouldn't, of course. Bruenor would be one pissed-off monarch ... former monarch ... but everyone else would be pleased. So, if for no other reason than that he wanted to be safe in the knowledge that one day at the Llangollen feasting hall they would for once be toasting his name (as opposed to not recognising it), he really wanted those pieces of parchment to be sent North.

The agreement, along with all his other parchments and that rusty sword of Merlin's, were currently still with the landlord at the inn. He'd decided against trying to flog the sword, because ... well, he didn't want to get laughed at.

So why not sell the stuff legitimately? This was Londinium after all! Why not just go to one of the thousands of market places it must already have[29] and

---

[29] Actually, it had two – it's important to remember that, although large by contemporary standards, London was only one square mile and also that Llew was prone to exaggeration.

sell the stuff there. Well, this on the face of it had seemed like a good idea, but apart from wanting to keep a low profile before he absconded into the west, he'd found out that the markets all belonged to those two well known business partners – Mr Rip and Mr Off. He had in fact investigated one and been told that neither his horse or his armour were worth anything, but would he like to pay them two coins to take the lot off his hands? Llew knew what the stuff was worth, because Edwyn had, before his unfortunate accidents with a very sharp-bladed sword and latterly a Saxon hunting bow, been one of the country's most famous warriors and he didn't buy crap equipment. So now he was searching the waterfront for his potential buyer ...

He'd come to a basin. It went a little bit away from the river. It was packed tightly with moored-up fishing boats – all empty – and, on the shore, hundreds of huts were built practically on top of each other all the way up a steep hill. Quite a few of them were inns with drinking noises and light spilling out of them. There was hardly anyone about ... a few stray dogs scrapping over ... something ... some bone or other ... gulls circled lazily by. He pulled Deathgiver's reins and walked further along the boardwalk. He hadn't got far when he came to a slightly smaller, tattier boat than the others. And then he saw the name. *Gwyn Dun Mane.* At last!

There was no one about. He looked up at the sky. He couldn't tell how high the moon was because the clouds were obscuring it.

'Hello?' he called gently, 'anyone about?'

The large piece of sailcloth which had been covering the boat moved aside and a familiar grinning face appeared from beneath it ...

'Well, well, well. If it isn't the Mysterious Warrior,' said the smug old man.

Llew's first words should have been either 'You?' or even 'what on earth are you doing here?' but he just couldn't help himself ...

'So how long've you been waiting to say that one?'

Evidently, the smug old man hadn't been expecting this either.

'What?' he said.

'Did you come up with it at the inn? You were sitting there thinking "I'll get to my boat before him and I'll hide under the sail and when he gets here he'll think no-one's here and I can come out with a really smart-arsed line".'

The old man's grin had changed from one of extreme amusement at his one witticism to a stubborn 'I'm-not-letting-this-grin-fade' grin.

'Well, at least I'm not pretending to be a soldier, Mr Big Fat Liar!'

'And that's what passes for a spontaneous comment, is it?'

Now the grin did fade.

'You just shut up, you! You'll get what's coming to you, you will!'

Llew was on what might be called a sarcastic roll.

'Gosh, I am cut to the quick. Stop this lashing from your flint-like wit!'

The old man was getting angry.

'I mean it!'

'Yeah, yeah. You going to buy this stuff or not?'

There was a pause while the old man thought … he was thinking of something clever to say.

'*Not*, actually,' he said finally, and there was more than a hint of triumph about it. What's more, the smug grin was returning, 'I'm *not* going to buy it because I don't need to.'

Behind Llew there was the familiar sound (*shhhhingg!!!*) of men drawing their swords. If I turn round, he thought, I'm not going to like it, so I won't. However, deep down, he knew he was putting off the inevitable.

'This is Bryn, Urien and Britta,' said the old man, his grin now firmly back in place, 'they're deserters. Real ones. And they help me with things like getting rid of little brown-stains like you. We'll be taking the horse now and everything that's loaded on it …'

Llew very slowly turned round. And sure enough there were three men whose size and demeanour said 'warrior' a lot more than Llew's did. They were grinning too – not smugly, but rather like they were going to get something they really enjoyed.

Llew started thinking on his feet again.

'I should warn you, lads – the horse is called Deathgiver. Steed to Edwyn of Llangollen and he doesn't just let anybody go near him …'

'Thanks for the warning,' said one of the men, then to the smug old man, 'I'll take him and stable him for market in the morning, shall I, boss?'

The smug old man nodded.

The man then climbed up onto Deathgiver's back, wheeled her round on the boardwalk and rode off into the night. Llew looked on, totally amazed. That horse is a bastard, he thought.

The smug old man's eyes were now almost dancing and twinkling.

'And now, just to show there's no hard feelings, Bryn and Urien here are gonna give you the kicking of your life …'

Llew nodded sagely.

'What if there had been hard feelings?'

'I'd have had them kill you.'

'Ah … actually, you know, for *you*, that was quite witty.'

'Off you go, boys.'

And they did.

Llew woke up in the shallows of the river where he'd been thrown after being thoroughly beaten up. Luckily, his head was on a reed bed, so he was saved from drowning. He tried to move, but realised this was going to be difficult because his legs didn't seem to want to work. Actually, nothing did. Every time he tried to even flex something, he felt a screaming spasm of pain. One arm, he thought, just one arm … dear God, I if can just move one arm … aghghghghgg! Not one arm then.

He knew he couldn't stay there. Apart from being freezing, there were leeches and water rats and all sorts of other riverside creatures for whom if you stayed still too long you became a floating buffet. Eventually, his body screaming that it was never going to allow him to do this again to it, he managed to force himself onto the bank.

Okay, now what?

That was difficult. They had robbed him of all his possessions, including the clothes that covered him. Luckily, the bag of parchments and the rusty sword were back at the inn … that was a point: he needed to get those back if he was going to do anything; but just physically *moving* was going to prove a problem … and where was he anyway? Not where they'd chucked him in, certainly … he'd been washed down river away from the harbour … outside the city limits, it looked like. Damn, that would mean he'd got miles just to get back to the inn to see if he could find it again!

'Brother, what ails you?'

He turned his head slowly to see a bearded and bedraggled figure in a monk's cowl, standing on the bank beside him.

'I've been robbed. I need help,' he managed.

'Lo, for thou hast fallen!' said the monk, who looked vaguely familiar, 'but even whence thou hast fallen as low as thou canst, I shall rise thee up!!!'

'No, please don't – … aghgh!'

The monk had tried to pick him up and it had hurt quite a lot.

'My brother, you are sick.'

'Not so much sick as, well … beaten up, actually.'

'I shall heal you with the cleansing waters of the river.'

'Er …'

'Art thou a Peleganist, my son?'

This seemed to come from nowhere, but it was here that Llew remembered the man. The drunken street preacher from when he first came into the city.

'What does that mean?'

'It is the true religion! It is the way of the true Christian church. Everything else is heresy!'

Llew, as has been said before, was a Christian. When he'd first been taken into Marcus's service, he'd been offered the chance to become a monk, like many of the other scribes, but had declined on the grounds that they used cold water for the baptismal font. However, Llew's religious belief really was not so much 'Praise the Lord!!' as 'Well, yes, I suppose so'. His upbringing had been multitheistic in that he distrusted druids as much as priests or monks and he wasn't going to start doing so now …

'Let me baptise thee i'th name of the true faith!!!'

'No, please don't! I'm serious, please don't – …. aghghgggh!!!'

So Llew found himself in the River Thames for the second time that day. It was pretty similar – the only real difference being that the first had not included having his head held under the water by a mad monk. It was only when Llew's life – a miserable, cold childhood, a relatively enjoyable apprenticeship in the warm, followed by freezing Llangollen, a damp journey around England and back to Londinium – had flashed before him that he actually felt himself being lifted bodily out of the water and propped up against a tree on the bank. This hurt quite a lot too.

'In the name of the Father and the Son and the Holy Ghost, I baptise thee... whateverthynameis ... welcome to the one true church ...'

'Thank you,' Llew tried to say as he coughed out a few lungfuls of Thames water.

'No, no, thank **thee**,' said the monk. 'By accepting baptism, thou hast upped my convert count. Verily thou hast upped it quite a lot.'

'How many converts have you had since you came to the city?'

'Including thee?'

'Yes.'

'Two.'

'And who was the other one?'

'Me.'

Llew winced.

It was later. The monk was busily trying to find dry sticks to put on a small fire he'd lit. And as Llew got warmer and less wet, his wounds began to smart just a bit less. The thieves had left him with nothing but a sack to wear, but luckily the monk carried a spare cowl around with him while it dried. It smelled very much of a monk who has been preaching on the open road for a little too long, but it was dry and right now that seemed about fine. He looked at his new friend who, apart from the obligatory cowl and shaven tonsure, seemed to be made entirely of matted beard and hair. His name, it turned out, was Brother Nascien. Originally from Ireland, he'd been sold to monks as a baby and had been brought up to be one. Only they weren't monks as Llew had known them.

'We follow the doctrine of Pelagius. We believe not in the concept of original sin!'

Llew, who was now munching a leg of chicken – slightly different tasting chicken – that Nascien had cooked and was starting to feel a whole lot better, wondered what in the name of all that's holy 'original' sin was.

'Oh, the apple. Eve. Garden of Eden. All that. See?'

Llew didn't really.

'It meaneth everyone can ... thou knowst.' Nascien gave him a significant sideways look, a look that has said the same thing down the ages and still does today. '... With women and not commit a sin. 'Tis great! Well t'would be so if we could get a few more to convert.'

Llew was surprised that more people didn't ... considering the lifting of *that* particular restriction.

'Ah, well, they're scared! Thou knowst what I mean? The mother church in Rome likes it not … they reckonest Christianity be the only thing holding the empire together … so when we cometh on the scene they start threatening our brethren – sometimes with excommunication, sometimes with hot tongs. … Thou seest, I used to travel around. I have been all over this land and thou couldst tell people they'd get free food and all the gold, right here, right now, if they would only convert and thou knowst what? They'd still say "no thanks, I prefer hunger, poverty and a how's-thy-fatherless life" if they don't think anyone else will. People are sheep, Llew, I'm telling thee. How's thy water rat, by the way?'

Llew now realised why his chicken didn't taste like chicken. He was just about to start feeling nauseous when his inner realist kicked and told him to stop being such a baby. He'd liked it a minute ago. Try being more like his father.

'Fine.'

'That's why I came to Londinium. Only thing Londoners are afraid of is other Londoners.' He sighed. 'But it works not, mainly because that is all they really care about too.'

Llew thought that he had to agree with them.

'Anyway,' Nascien went on, 'what we really could doeth with is a king. Now, if a king were to convert … well, then we'd really be talking. Once a king comes on-side, well, the flock start falling over themselves to join him.'

Llew shrugged.

'Well, you've got one more baptism under your belt anyway.'

The monk looked at him, proudly.

'Aye, 'tis true. Tomorrow I can set thee on thy way – a good Christian – and I can go mine.'

This was the first time Llew had been reminded about the concept of 'tomorrow' – that one day generally followed the next – for a while. It wasn't a few hours ago that he'd pretty much assumed that he'd just about run out of tomorrows. Now he was faced with a new one. He wasn't ungrateful – in fact, if truth were told, he was quite glad – but he was faced with the problem of what to do about it. He needed his things back. Maybe the landlord of the inn could help. He surely wouldn't like it that a thief was operating under his roof. Besides, the landlord had Llew's parchments – and with them Llew was beginning to see a way of making his plan proceed … even without money, horse and armour.

'Nascien … how would you like to have access to a king? Not any king, mind you, but the Vortigern Britu himself?'

The next day.

Llew had to admit the monk was useful to have around. Not only had this lowly preacher found him some clothes, dried his old ones (what was left of them), lit a fire and then managed to hunt down some supper and this morning's breakfast, he'd also managed to carve a half-decent walking staff for Llew to use in a matter of minutes. Now, together, they were walking (well, Nascien was walking, Llew was limping) towards the city gates.

'And these ... parchments ... the Vortigern will want these parchments?'

'Oh, you bet he'll want them, Nascien. These parchments may save him and the whole country from the most terrible and bloody war. And before you go to him, I'll write down a way for him to become the most invincible high king there's ever been.'

'So ... if it's such a good idea and it belongs to thee ... why are not thou coming to share in the glory?'

Llew had thought about this and he had to admit he was tempted. To come with the treaty that was going to make Ynys Prydein safe from both the Saxons and the Picts was one thing, but to also come with the key to Vortigern Britu's total glory in the eyes of the client kings and the lords and the soldiers and even the lowly populace was ... well, if only Megan hadn't got married, that's all! But that was the thing – she had, or would have by now ... and he felt in his heart of hearts that, in spite of everything that had happened since that dark day when he'd set out from Aquae Sulis, his best bet was still to disappear. Playing politics was not his strong point. Besides, Llangollen at this time of year would be bloody freezing![30] So this was the plan: somehow retrieve his parchments from the landlord of the inn ... how he didn't know – he had nothing to pay the man and, as a result of Llew being mugged, the publican had effectively already been robbed of one bowl of stew. Llew's only hope was to rely on the man's genial nature. That and perhaps his mortification on learning he had sent poor Llew into a thief's ambush.

Well, it was worth a try.

Once this was done, he would quickly write down his treatise on the use of libraries for the king and a letter of introduction for Nascien. Then Nascien could head north and Llew would head west, perhaps to become the country's greatest unsung hero. Nascien was ready and willing to take the risk of the journey, because the prize for him was the big one. The conversion of a king. Llew reflected that it didn't seem like too much of a risk either. Nascien was a big man; well, yes, but that wasn't what made him intimidating. He was also very wild and mad-looking, which *was*. Well, everywhere but the streets of Londinium.

Slowly they passed through the city gates, and made their way along the streets through the throng of people shouting at each other, the street entertainers, the itinerant priests (quite a few who seemed to know Nascien, which they indicated by hauling up their cowls and showing their bare

---

[30] More bloody freezing than Spring and Summer, less bloody freezing than the oncoming Winter.

buttocks at him) … the conmen (who avoided what they saw as two monks walking up the street together … possibly out of respect, but more likely because they knew monks never had any money) until they rounded the corner and came upon the inn which had been so welcoming to Llew.

The place wasn't as full as it had been the day before, although it was hard to tell as drapes had been hung over the windows and the fire wasn't lit. A group of men were huddled in the corner with their backs to Llew.

'Ah. What can I get you two …. monks?'

The landlord had only seen the cowls and had evidently not recognised Llew from the day before.

'Mead, brother, and plenty of it! I hath a great thirst.'

The landlord nodded at a table, indicating for them to take a seat, and was already taking a couple of drinking bowls over to the mead barrel.

'Er, hi. Remember me?' Llew coughed as he sat.

The landlord gave him a look as he used a ladle to pour out a couple of bowls for them.

'No. Can't say as I do, young sir …'

He came over and put the bowls on the table in front of him. Nascien grabbed his without a thought and drank it down. Then he grabbed Llew's and drank that down as well, while the innkeeper watched disinterestedly.

Llew attempted to plough on.

'I came in yesterday. I had some things to –'

'Two more in th' name of the one true God! This mead doth quench my slaking!'

'You'll pay for them two first, if you don't mind,' said the landlord. 'I'm not emptying my barrels of finest to help a hedge priest like you get rat-arsed for free …'

'No, but that's the point, you see. I was the … deserter who came yesterday. You have some parchments of mine!'

The innkeeper peered at him.

'Oh, yeah. I thought Doug said he'd killed you. No, he let you off with a beating, that's right. He's a soft old so-and-so when all's said and done, Doug is …'

Something about the way the conversation was going gave Llew an uneasy feeling.

'I would have mead!!' yelled Nascien.

'Er … who's Doug?' said Llew.

'I am,' said a voice from the corner.

Llew turned to where the group of men had been sitting and recognised the grinning figure of the old man and the not so easily amused figures of Bryn, Urien and Britta.

'Mead, I say!!!'

Llew started as usual to make all the connections he perhaps should have made say ... any time earlier. The landlord was in on the plot. The gang operated from the inn and picked on lone stray travellers who they knew would make good targets. Whether they'd known Llew was a real soldier or not didn't really make any difference; what they had spotted almost immediately was that he was an A1, first class, prize mug – which probably explained why the landlord had been so genial in the first place.

'Oh ... bugger,' he muttered under his breath.

'Mead, by God's Grace! **Mead**!!!!'

'Look, I don't want any trouble. I just want my bag. It's got my parchments in it ...'

The sounds of steel being drawn from leather scabbards told Llew that he wasn't going to get his wish and he was probably going to get a lot of what he *didn't* want and, alas, this included trouble. However, right as he turned out to be, there was one thing he hadn't banked on. Nascien had a problem and it concerned the phrase 'yeah, I get a bit like that after I've had a couple of drinks, sorry'.

Which Nascien had in fact just had.

Realising he wasn't being listened to, the monk rose up volcanically, turned over the table and threw himself at Llew's opponents, screaming 'Blasphemers!!!!!'

What then followed was, of course, a bar fight and Nascien was a bar fighter in the very traditional sense, in that he liked to smash bar furniture over his opponents' heads and throw them through the inn windows, etc, with one hand whilst at the same time taking a slurp of mead from a barrel or snatching a leg of roast ox which had been left to go cold on the spit with the other. The innkeeper's heavies (and this included the innkeeper) also fought traditionally, always getting up almost straight away after what seemed to be a severe, if not knock-out, blow. Llew found himself being cornered by Doug the old man, who was wielding an evil and thin-looking dagger. However, just as Doug raised the knife, he was hit by a traditional flying stool, hurled by one of his own men at Nascien, who had traditionally ducked and Doug was immediately knocked cold. From that moment on, Llew decided also to resume a traditional narrative bar-fighting role. He was going to be the guy who hid down behind the bar and not show his face until all had gone quiet, save the odd 'clink' of broken pots. It was here he found his bag, complete with all his parchments and the rusty sword.

It was just possible today was going to work out all right after all ...

'The watch! Someone call out the watch! That monk's killed old Doug Briarbuff and his men!'

... or not.

Llew realised that, apart from the shouting he'd just started hearing in the street outside, it had in fact gone extremely quiet in the inn. Carefully, he raised his head above the bar. Nascien definitely wasn't dead. He was sitting, drinking straight from an open barrel. As for the others: difficult to tell how they were, as they were the makeshift stool Nascien was currently sitting on. Outside, in the distance, more shouting and clattering could be heard. The watch was coming.

'Time we were gone,' he said. 'I don't know about you, but I'm a little tired of Londinium.'

'That is life,' said Nascien, grinning.

Something kept wanting to come through into Llew's mind, but he never could quite work out what that was.

Getting out of London would have been a whole lot easier if Nascien had not insisted on a choice of either draining or carrying the barrel he was currently drinking from. This meant that whatever happened he was going to get more drunk and/or more biblical before the night was out and Llew, knowing he needed Nascien for the next phase of his plan, decided that it was better if this should be later rather than sooner. So, reluctantly, he agreed to help carry the barrel to the city gates. Once they had done this, they would find somewhere to hide and then Nascien could go on drinking himself into a stupor. Had he time, he would have reflected that this was the way of holy men all over. The druids back home had the strange herbs and mushrooms that they took in large quantities – to the point where they didn't mind being naked in public on a freezing December day (although the people around them often took exception). The Roman Christian priests had their communion wine often drunk to a degree that Eucharist must have been said about once every thirteen seconds during a day. And this monk needed his mead. To be spiritual, Llew would have mused, you really needed spirits.

But he didn't because he was being chased by a Londinium mob and he was trying to lug a barrel that was also being held onto by one very drunk monk. So he was rather too occupied to be a smart arse at that moment. They were running through the narrow streets and a mob that was getting bigger all the time was rapidly pursuing them. Trouble was, they had no way to blend into the background – word had spread like wildfire that two monks had raided an inn and murdered the inhabitants and there they were – two men in habits carrying a barrel with 'Property Of The Fat Ox' written on it.

However, as the mob got bigger, so did the rumour mill, and that started work in the fugitives' favour. Because every now and then they'd lose their pursuers for an instant or two ... ducking into an available alley and only being spotted as they sneaked out the other side ... and when this happened, newcomers to the mob (and there'd always be a couple) would always ask, 'who we after again?' and, although longer-term mob members would reply, the story would always get changed a little ... such is the way of these things. ... And then, if they were joined by members of another, just as experienced, mob, well, the story would change a lot.

So a kind of giant game of what would later be called Chinese Whispers evolved and …

… 'We're after two monks who killed Doug Briarbuff and his men at the Fat Ox Inn' became …

… 'We're after Doug Briarbuff who killed his men and two monks at the Fat Ox Inn' …

became…

… 'We're after the Fat Ox that killed Doug Men at the Two Monks Inn near Briarbuff tent peg, chapel, horsewig …'

By the time various of the mobs had met, split up, come together with other mobs, split up with them, come together with another two and split up again, the main rumour that everyone was looking for two monks to lead them to freedom and glory and that everyone – Doug included – would get a Fat Ox at the end, such that when Llew and Nascien suddenly found themselves cornered by a huge and angry crowd, rather than being lynched, they were actually asked if they would take over. And so Llew found himself running round the streets at the head of a riotous mob who actually were going in no particular direction whatsoever. And, as is often the case with riots and lynch mobs, people get bored after a while and start peeling off, either home or to the market or to the pub (there was a rumour going round that there was a great place to have a drink called the Fat Ox), so that Llew and Nascien found themselves alone and heading for the city gates …

So it wasn't long before they were walking out across the grassy plain and Londinium was a series of smoke plumes in the distance behind them.

It was about here, Llew saw a cat at one of the milestones on the Roman Road. He turned, looked back at the city, thought, 'nah', turned away and kept on walking …

Chapter 8 – Council Of The Kings

Once again on the road. It was true what Marcus said, *'We are none of us here for long, boy'*. Certainly true for Llew, anyway. That was worth adding to the scrolls, he thought. As he and Nascien travelled, he had taken to writing down all sorts – anything he thought might be worth noting, anything he could think of, Llew would try and find a spare few square inches on one of his parchments and scribble it down. This was not without its problems – ink, parchment, quills – none of them were readily available. However, a bit of burnt wood could make the charcoal that would suffice for ink and quill – and in the forest-covered lands west of Londinium there was plenty of wood – a bit of salt, of course, stopped the letters from fading. As for parchment … Well, they'd had a bit of luck. They'd found a monastery and of course they were dressed as monks. The abbot had been most welcoming, although it had been difficult keeping Nascien quiet – these weren't Peleganists like he was, after all – and Llew had managed to borrow a few scrolls on the understanding that there'd be a nice mention of the establishment to Vortigern Britu. It was wonderful, new, clean parchment – freshly made in the monastery – and on it Llew wrote down everything he could think of – his thoughts, his feelings, his life, all the history he knew … everything that had happened to him … his ideas about how a king like Vortigern could make himself truly invincible against outside attack. Then he came upon some ideas about how a king should rule justly and fairly, so he wrote those down too.

They walked during the day and rested at night by firelight, where Llew, huddled against the cold, would write. The writing was beginning to make him feel … well, 'powerful' was the wrong word, but certainly not useless … certainly that he could do something few others could. So involved was he that he almost didn't notice the chilly autumn wind that blew around him. Almost. Miracles don't happen every day and this was Llew, after all.

Nascien spent the evenings of their journey finding different ways to get blind drunk, or at least the plant-based equivalent. So, if they couldn't find or were nowhere near an inn at which they could plead for some 'bread and mead for two men of the cloth' from a reluctant, usually grumpy, but ultimately God-fearing landlord, then after making camp, Nascien would scamper off into the woods and return with various mushrooms and weeds like the druids back home used. The mushrooms he ate, but he also had a strange apparatus made of clay – he called it a pipe – in which he would put the weeds, light them and then breathe in the smoke. Llew quite frankly thought Nascien was out of his mind, which, to be fair, after a few puffs on the 'pipe' he usually was.

And so it came that one day … one frost-covered, bright, late-autumn morning, they came to a place Llew recognised. The Roman Road. One way went north to Llangollen, the other south to Aquae Sulis.

'This is it, Nascien. This is where I'm afraid we part company.'

'Wilt thou not come with me, brother?' Nascien pleaded. 'Show thy overlord what thou hast done for him?'

Llew once again had to admit to himself he was tempted – they were going to be **so** pleased with him – but he had already had this discussion in his head (and on parchment) for several nights. He knew he must resolve now to stick to his plan to become the (or even 'a') footnote to a footnote in history. Maybe, if and when Vortigern did build that fabulous library … Llew could send more of his manuscripts to become part of it and that way … people could learn by reading them what he was and how he'd saved them. Meantime, however, it was time to get south, get a boat – to Gaul probably, then maybe on foot to Italy – find Marcus, get a job with him (because even Marcus would have to say he'd given the emissary thing a a fair go), relax, find a broom and sweep if anyone was coming.[31] In that order. He declined Nascien's offer – much as he appreciated it – opened his bag and gave Nascien the necessary scrolls for him to take to the Vortigern Britu. He felt strangely unwilling to part with them, but steeled himself, embraced Nascien goodbye and set off down the road. Nascien turned, shrugged sadly as a man not quite understanding, then turned and went on his way.

Llew felt strangely elated. A few more days' travel perhaps and he would be in Aquae Sulis – yes, the road held the same dangers as always, but the monk habit did seem to provide a lot more protection than his old clothes from the scavengers that haunted the wild lands outside any settlement's gates, so he was probably all right. At last, he was finally doing it! Getting away. He thought of that time … goodness, how many years ago, where he had stood at the gates of Llangollen watching Marcus and his escort leave. And how he'd screamed at them not to go without him. Screamed and begged and pleaded over the wind and the sleet. It had felt terrible at the time, but, well … it almost seemed funny now. What *was* he like, eh? Such a big fuss and all those big sinewy Llangollen warriors watching – what must they have thought of him? Dear, oh dear … what a big baby!

Then, just in the furthest edges of his hearing, he started to pick up something. Horses' hooves. Horse hooves galloping. Big, warrior-sized horse hooves galloping. Big warrior-sized horse hooves galloping in *his* direction. Oh, bugger …

---

[31] Old habits die hard.

He started to run. He didn't really know why ... after all, it was possible that the rider of the horse simply wanted to get a move on, had to be somewhere in a hurry, but on the other hand ... on the *other* hand, instinct was telling him that a large horse galloping his way was not a Good Thing. He knew he couldn't possibly outrun a man on a horse, but if he could just get enough distance between him and it, he might be able to find somewhere to hide. Unfortunately, they were in open country, mainly grasslands with a few rocks and there were no trees to speak of. Bloody typical – the one time he wanted to be in a forest. Still, at least the Roman road was flat, which made running easy –

'Aghgh!'

... apart from that bit, obviously.

Suddenly, the horse was very, very visible and gaining on him fast. Llew picked himself up ... was it worth running now? Nah, probably not. Was it worth crying like a baby? Definitely. Llew was just about to start wailing when the horse arrived. Its rider was a colossal warrior ... all leather armour, big sword and masked helmet. And if the rider was big, the horse seemed *vast*, wheeling around Llew and whinnying like a thing from the Otherworld – the mist it snorted in the cold weather looked like great puffs of smoke – more like a dragon than a horse. Finally it stopped, breathing deeply, grunting and occasionally tossing its Otherworld mane. The rider – like some sort of giant from old, old stories, reached up and took off his helmet – only, as if in a dream, it seemed to take him centuries to do so.

'What's the matter with you, boy? Look like you seen a ghost,' said a familiar, amiable voice.

Llew gawped.

'Griff?'

'Found a friend of yours up the road. He told me where you'd be. How you getting on, then?' ...

Later, Llew was using Griffith's knife to slash the chords that bound Nascien's wrists.

'What did you tie him up for?'

'Well, it's like this – I met him on the road, see? And he tries to baptise me and I said not today thanks and then he asks me if I got any mead and gets all huffy when I told him yes but he couldn't have any, so he tells me that he's on an errand for Vortigern and I thought hey that's interesting I've not heard anything, only before I can say it he's attacked me trying to get my mead skin, so I knock him down and I'm gonna kill him but then he mentions your name – screamed it out actually – that he's carrying a letter for you and that you were just down the road, so I thought tie him up, come and get you then come back here for him, see?'

'So why did you gag him?'

'Cos he was talking too much,' the old warrior grinned.

And he was. Old[32] now, that is. Old*er*, anyway. He'd got a lot greyer in the time Llew had been away. His face had become craggy and lined.

'Aghghgghghgghg! Blasphemer!!!'

The gag had just come off. Llew decided to do the introductions.

'Griffith, this is Nascien. Nascien, this is Griffith. Nascien is taking the treaty I've agreed with Hengist to the Vortigern Britu, while I go for ... a well-earned break ... there's no need to worry, it's all written down. And now, Nascien, you've got an escort to Llangollen; isn't that nice? Well,' he clapped his hands genially, 'now that's been cleared up I can be on my way. ... Nice to see you again, Griff.'

He was unsurprised to find that Griffith had wheeled his horse round again to block Llew's path.

'Sorry, lad. I was sent to find you. I gotta bring you back. Vortigern wants you at the council of the kings.'

The council of the kings. It would later become legend – a time when all the great Lords came together to talk of the future of the Island of the Mighty. From all over they would come – chieftains of the Demetae, the Belgae, the Silures, the Iceni and many more ... all the Cymru tribes and the kings of the great lands such as Elmet and Dumnonia and Gwent ... in short, everyone who was anyone. It happened once every three or four years and usually was an occasion for lots of back slapping, or back stabbing (the metaphorical and the literal), a couple of big speeches, some gift-giving – to Vortigern – and general quaffing of mead or ale until everyone fell over. In the great scheme of things it was not usually very productive ... the real business of government being done behind the scenes in the diplomatic language known as 'bribery'. However, this time it was different. It was Vortigern Britu's first one for a start and everyone was anxious to see how the young overlord would perform. Could he be as effective as his father; could he bully and intimidate where bullying and intimidation were needed? Could he rag and cajole the right people, whilst at the same time persuade and wheedle where the wheedling was wanted? It was also different because everyone knew that things had been pushed as far as they could regarding what might be called the 'invader situation' and someone was going to have to do something before the Island Of The Mighty[33] became the Island That Belongs To All Sorts Of Foreigners – Friends And Strangers Alike.[34] What was needed, everyone knew, was a king – a proper high king ... someone who could unite all as a nation, not someone who could just about keep the peace.

---

[32] Bearing in mind that the mortality rate such as it was made you an 'old man' at about thirty-five.

[33] Ynys Prydein.

[34] Ynys O Lawer Iawn O Wahanol Fathaw O Bobl Frindliau A Diethrynau (not quite as catchy).

'And that's the trouble, see? There's no one! I mean, most of 'em are stark, staring mad! I seen 'em! I seen 'em in battle, I seen what they can do with a bloody great sword in their hand. You want to put someone like that in charge? 'Cause I don't, no fear! I'll stick with Vortigern, thanks. I mean, take Bruenor ...'

Griff had been burbling on like this for several miles. It was a one-way conversation – neither Llew nor Nascien were expected to do anything other than go 'mmm' and nod every now and again at they trudged behind Griff's horse through the sleet. Yup, sleet. If there was anything Llew had always hated, it was sleet – too cold to be called rain, not quite picturesque enough to be called snow. Oh, he could tell they were returning to Llangollen, all right. However, Llew had just heard a name that made him look up.

'Bruenor? He's going to be there?'

' 'Course he is!' answered Griff, puzzled. 'He's a king, ain't he?'

Not for much longer, thought Llew.

'He's a hard bastard is Bruenor. Good in a battle. I seen him back years ago. That man seriously can kill. Which is why he's king in Gwyrangon. Killed his way to the top he did, but not fair. Likes to stab in the back, if you know what I mean. Got this funny sword – really slim blade. Dunno what it's made out of, but it can split feathers just by dropping 'em on it. No one likes him. Not his people, not his soldiers. Kind of bloke picks a fight with you for looking at him funny. Now, can you imagine a man like that becoming high king?'

'If I couldst but teach him the love of Jesus, yea!' interjected Nascien.

Llew realised that the news of Bruenor's immediate abdication would now probably be announced for the first time at the council when the treaty was presented. He made a mental note to try not to be in the same vicinity as the Kentish king when that happened ... actually, to try not to be in the same *country* might be preferable. Speaking of which ...

'Griff, how did you find me?'

'Mmm?'

'Well, you say Britu sent you to come and get me – how did you know where I'd be? ... I mean, it's a pretty big island when all's said and done.'

'Oh, I was told. In a dream. You remember that Merlin kid? He come to me in a dream and said you'd be on the Roman Road heading toward Aquae Sulis.'

Griffith said this matter-of-factly, as if being visited in your dreams by a member of the Old Ones was a daily (or to be more precise, nightly) occurrence. However, it caused Llew to stop trudging.

'What?'

Griff wheeled his horse round to face him.

'I know. Odd, innet? I mean, normally I have dreams about ... well, mainly about cheese actually and I've never really understood why, but anyway, there he was in my dream. He told me exactly where I had to go and I was to bring you safe to council of the kings.'

Nonplussed, Llew asked, 'He say anything else? Like why, for instance?'

Griff screwed up his face, trying to remember.

'Something about your destiny and the "one who is to come". ... I couldn't make head nor tale of it, to be honest. And then he disappeared, or rather he turned into this great, big, bucket of curds and whey and I knew I was back to dreaming about cheese again. Come on. We got to hurry ...'

Griff wheeled his horse back and continued on, followed by Nascien.

'Why?' Llew called after him.

'I been looking for you for a month now. That kid told me where, but never said when! Been going up and down this city road like a bloody weasel!![35] Council will have nearly finished by the time we get there ...'

He wheeled his horse back and trotted on, followed again by Nascien. Llew watched them for a bit. He had an odd feeling ... a confirmation that everything that had ever happened to him right from the moment of his birth had been out of his control. That someone else had always been pulling the strings. Was it a good thing that he was in some way 'meant' for something ... that he had a destiny? It all rather depended. If destiny involved sitting by a big fire while beautiful maidens served you really delicious food – great! He'd go for destiny every time. If, however, it involved being *roasted* over said fire ... well, he'd rather opt out thanks, no matter how many songs they were offering to make up about him afterwards. He set off again, determined to keep a watchful eye on this destiny thing.

That night, when they made camp, he learned a few more things, mainly about Megan. The princess had indeed gone off and married King Pelinore. Good, *handsome*, King Pelinore of Elmet – Fair of Face and Brave of Spirit (as the Bards sang) ... neither of which mattered any more because he was now Dead of Body. Gorlois – king of one of the northern tribes beyond Hadrian's Wall, had killed him in some sort of border raid and, rumour had it, decided to take Megan as a wife. 'A' wife as in 'one of many' – Gorlois was a pagan and kind of liked marrying anyone he generally took a shine to. And apparently having his sister in Gorlois' family was no help whatsoever. Gorlois collected wives like cats collected mice. This worried Llew. Yes, he was relieved to be spared the embarrassment of seeing Megan again and yet. ... Well, he didn't like to think of her as ... well, something to be played with before being either killed and eaten or killed and discarded.

A few days later, in driving rain, they found themselves on the hill path leading towards Llangollen. Nothing much had changed, except that yet another wooden stockade wall had been added to surround the others. Obviously, Llew observed, some of the beggars had moved up in the world.

---

[35] Which went 'pop', presumably.

They rode down towards the gates, which opened slowly, pulled as usual by some burly bearskin-wrapped guards. Once again the smell of dung and turnips hit him like a shoe hammer – even in the pouring rain – once again he saw the small, hungry and ragged non-warriors being dwarfed and fairly often hit by the large bearded warriors; once again he found he was knee-deep in what for the sake of argument might be called mud. Ah, he thought, Home Sweet Home.

'Changed a bit since you were last here, hasn't it?' said the ever-grinning Griffith as they trudged up towards Vortigern's hall.

'Er … in what way? I mean, apart from the new stockade wall – impressive though that is.'

'No!' said the warrior with a look of someone talking to a lunatic, 'haven't you *noticed*?'

He pointed to a large iron cauldron situated in the clearing in front of the hall's entrance. Llew was nonplussed.

'Our first public bath!' he said slowly, as if talking to an idiot child, 'civ-il-is-at-ion, see?'

'Ah,' said Llew dryly. 'Civilisation. How far we've come. And they said the wheel would be the Last Great Leap.'

Griffith, to whom sarcasm had always been an alien concept, looked proud and gestured for them to follow him. Llew looked around for Nascien who, although once a humble hedge priest, had seen enough of the Big City for a satirical comment about their bumpkin so-called masters in Llangollen to have at least some effect (a smirk? A smug, knowing grin?), but it was only then that he noticed Nascien didn't seem to be there any more. It was too late, however, for him to go searching. Griffith was heading for Vortigern's hall.

'Llewelyn? That you?'

Llew turned around to see another familiar figure approaching. Like Griffith, this one was looking much older than when last seen.

'Dad?'

It was Gwyddno, all right. It'd been a long, *long* time, but it was Gwyddno. They looked each other up and down, unsure of what to do. Shaking hands seemed a little formal, but embracing … well, it wasn't the kind of thing Gwyddno and Llew had *ever* done. So the old 'looking-each-other-up-and-down-in-a-slightly-embarrassed-fashion' greeting it was.

'What're you doing here, Dad?'

'Here for the council, of course.' Gwyddno looked a little bit offended. 'I am still a chief, after all.' He indicated the hall. 'Just nipped out for a breather – bit smoky in there.'

'Course. Yeah. How's the clan doing?'

'Well, to be honest,' said Gwyddno, looking sheepish, 'there's not so much of it these days. We sort of merged with the Silures and they're very big, obviously … anyway, I kept my rank … I mean, it's honorary really – I haven't got any soldiers, or responsibilities any more. But I have got a hall ... well, it's more of a "hut" really, but I call it a hall. And I do get to come up here at conference time. Which is nice. To get out and about like.'

There was an awkward pause.

'So,' said Gwyddno, 'what's been happening with you, then?'

Llew took a deep breath.

'Well, I've been a scribe – for Marcus, as you know; remember him? – and *then* I was the Roman advisor to the last Vortigern – got sort of mixed up in the military coup that ousted him – and *lately* I've organised the treaty with the Saxons for *this* Vortigern – Vortigern Britu. Had to travel all the way to Lloegyr for that ... spoke to Hengist, then saw a bit of Londinium, you know. I'm writing an awful lot, of course ...'

'Oh. Very good,' said Gwyddno with all the enthusiasm of a distant unmarried uncle looking at a painting by his three-year-old niece while deep down knowing that it's really a bit crap.

There was another awkward pause, father and son each not really knowing where to look or what to say. When, at that moment, Griffith called Llew into the hall, Llew was actually relieved.

'I'll say hello to your Mam for you when I get back,' Gwyddno called after Llew as he headed towards the hall entrance, making Llew cringe with guilt. Luckily, he didn't have too much time to think about it.

There were shouts coming from inside. Not good shouts either.

'By Samhain and Lugh you shall pay for that insult with your beard, snaggle tooth!'

'Then come here and take payment from me, whoreson, whose mother lay with the beasts of the field!!!'

The guards at the entrance parted their spears, allowing Griffith and Llew to enter. The hall was pretty much as Llew had remembered: dark, smoky, full of warriors, a large ox spit roasting on a fire. There was, however, one new development. At the centre of the room was a *huge* round table. Around this sat all the kings, lords and chieftains; behind them stood their champions. Evidently this was another of Vortigern Britu's nods towards civilisation, Llew reflected, guessing (rightly, is it happened) that if you got all your kings and chieftains sitting at a big enough table together there was less of a chance of one of them leaping at the other with a sword in his hand, if only because there was a bit of space and a lot of oak between them. This was evidently the case now – two kings, or chieftains (it was hard to tell one from the other), red-faced and furious, were snarling at one other from opposite sides of the newly established piece of furniture. On the other side of the table sat Vortigern Britu, looking languorous and bored as usual (but again a little older), while the two men came up with the most foul and disgusting insults Llew had ever heard – poisonous, obscene, often physically impossible. Llew, who had been in the company of Roman, Cymru *and* Saxon warriors, who had spent time at the edges of the Langollen stockade and heard some of the peasant classes fighting over turnips and who knew insults in several different languages (including that of the Old Ones), was actually shocked. Finally, the overlord raised his hand in his usual lazy way and a guard shouted for silence.

'I have come to a decision,' said Vortigern Britu. 'Morfans …'

And here he pointed to one angry king.

'… is in the wrong. Cows last longer, but pigs **are** tastier!'

There was a mutter that went round the room. The king Morfans sat down, shaking his head and giving the other king the look a stag would give after licking a stinging nettle it'd just peed on. The other king, on the other hand, gave the impression of being about to burst with joy.

Vortigern Britu gazed across the room and waved his hand for silence again. He had spotted Llew.

'Well, well, well. Llewelyn. You've come back.'

Llew bowed deeply.

'Yes, Lord.'

'And where is Edwyn?'

'Um. Dead, Lord.'

'Dead? How?'

'Believe it or not, there was a sort of … hunting accident.' Too late he realised what this in the court of Llangollen had once been a euphemism for: 'No! No! You see, this Saxon was trying out his bow and –'

Too late indeed. Llew was already interrupted by a tumult of shouting.

'Revenge!'

'Edwyn is slain!'

'Slain by the Saxons!'

'Let us make **war**!'

This was followed by a roar of loud approval as almost every king and chieftain shouted for war to be declared on the Saxons. Vortigern Britu just sighed and sat back in his chair, giving Llew a look which said 'you see what I have to deal with? *Every day*?'

Finally, they quietened down.

'Idiots! We're *already* at war with them!' said Vortigern Britu; then he added as an afterthought, 'Although they have been rather quiet of late … staying within their boundaries even. Right, Bruenor?'

'Very quiet, Lord.'

Llew looked over and saw the Kentish king for the first time. He looked different to the others. He wasn't very big for a start, but he was sinewy. He had an angular, almost comical face, except that his eyes were ice blue and hard. He was clothed in black leather armour with studs in it. His beard had been clipped short, so that it hardly existed, and his hair was cropped close to the skull. He was the kind of man who, in another time, might have been the type you avoided spilling the pint of in a crowded pub. As a child in this other time, he might have been the kind of kid your teacher didn't trust with the scissors. He was *dangerous*.

And he was looking right at Llew.

'No raids on the borders of Gwyrangon for months now,' he added.

Llew unfixed his gaze from Bruenor and looked back towards Vortigern Britu.

'That is because they are waiting for the ratification of the treaty I have agreed with them, I expect!' he said proudly. He knew when to show his aces.

There was a mutter went right round the table.

'You? You agreed a treaty with Hengist?' said Vortigern, plainly surprised. 'But you couldn't have known what terms I would have accepted.'

'I … managed to glean enough information from Edwyn before he … met with his unfortunate end … and I used my common sense …'

Vortigern Britu was beginning to look impressed.

'So they will fight for us?' he asked, as the chattering around him got louder.

'Yes, Lord,' said Llew, starting to enjoy himself – he was the Big Man on Campus again.

'In exchange for?'

'Land and settlers, Lord. As you commanded. They are sailing towards Ynys Prydein as we speak.'

The chattering was not only loud, but pleased. Llew had, after all, offered them hope. Britu was smiling. Llew was really enjoying the moment, especially now as Gwyddno had wandered back into the hall and even *he* was looking impressed.

'I think the question is …,' came a loud voice over all this, causing them all to be quiet.

Everyone looked at Bruenor.

'I think the question is: How many settlers? How much land? And … who does it belong to at this moment?'

Vortigern Britu looked annoyed – as if someone was trying to rain on his parade.

'Enough to pacify them. A trifle,' he said irritably. 'My instructions to Edwyn were for no more than a hundred settlers and no more than three acres of land. Right, Llewelyn?'

Llew swallowed. Once more he was feeling, or he was getting the *beginning* of the feeling, that something was about to do something on him from a very great height. And that the creature in question was almost certainly a flying whale and its family. All of whom had just eaten a big bowl of laxatives.

'Llewelyn?'

He tried to stall for time. Holding up his knapsack, he said, 'I have written the details down here – the Saxons believe that written treaties are a matter of honour.'

'Then read it to us ...'

'Well, sure, I *could*, but it's very wordy and I've just arrived after a long journey and I notice you now have that public bath – which I think is a great leap forward ...'

'Llewelyn!'

Llew decided to come clean, but try and put an optimistic spin on it.

'Truth is I may have kind of gone over a bit ... in terms of the ... people ... the ... the, er, numbers.'

'By how many?'

'A few, Lord.'

'How many?!!!'

'Several hundred, Lord.'

'Several hundred settlers?!!!'

'Boatloads, Lord.'

'What!!!???' This last was shrieked and was followed by a tumolt of protest and oaths. Once more Bruenor's voice cut through.

'And how much of *my* land did you say you would give them? I assume it was my land you were "negotiating" away?'

Once again silence that you could slice through. At the periphery of his vision, Llew could just see Gwyddno with his hand over his eyes and shaking his head.

'Erm ... just your kingdom, Lord.'

Now no one said anything; everyone ... all the kings of Ynys Prydein were just too stunned at this monumental balls-up. Finally, Britu spoke ...

'So, you're saying that I am honour bound to take this man's kingdom from him,' he nodded towards Bruenor, 'or we will be at war with what ... three thousand Saxons?'

'Something like that, Lord,' said Llew, looking at his feet.

'... who are already sailing here to live?'

Llew swallowed. He was really sweating, in spite of the cold.

'Er, was that *not* what you wanted ...?'

Ah, 'home sweet home' .... that's what he'd said to himself as he arrived at Llangollen, and who'd have thought it after all these years? That he'd be back in the same wooden cage he'd once spent the night in waiting to be sacrificed to the gods? You had to hand it to the local craftsmen. When they built something, they sure built it to last. And who'd have thought, *who'd have thought* there'd be the *double* irony of being locked in the same cage, *once again waiting for his own execution*?!!! Oh, life was funny!

After going on like this to himself, Llew started to realise why he didn't have many friends – he was a smart arse. And few people liked smart arses.

Actually, *he* didn't like smart arses. That was probably why he was always in trouble. He wasn't a very good friend to himself.

'... So, anyway, that's how it's gonna be. Bruenor's demanding he be given the job of executing you personally – which is fair enough, I suppose. ... I mean, you did give away his kingdom without so much a by-your-leave. Can't blame him for being a bit piqued, really ...'

Griff was being his usual taciturn self while he brought Llew a bowl of slop masquerading as food.

'Griff, it wasn't my fault! What else was I going to do?'

'I dunno,' said Griff thoughtfully, 'but if it had been me – well, soon as I got the job of accompanying Edwyn, I'd have sneaked off to the coast and got a boat as far away as I could.'

'Thanks. Look, Edwyn said Britu was going to 'settle things with Bruenor' – what was I supposed to deduce from that?'

Griff scratched his head.

'With hindsight, probably that Britu was gonna let Bruenor off the taxes he owed in exchange for a couple of acres of land.'

'But Edwyn used to say it with an evil glint in his eye!'

'Edwyn said *everything* with an evil glint in his eye!' countered Griff, adding philosophically, 'He was in many ways a ... difficult and bitter man. Anyway,' he went on. '... you got one night and then Bruenor's gonna do you first thing. He says he can't wait around any longer than that. He's gonna try and attack the Saxons while Hengist is off his guard.'

'Well, he might do a bit of damage to Hengist's current forces, but he's not going to be much use against the three thousand extra –'

He stopped himself, not wanting to remind himself of the utter mess he'd made of things.

'That's what they're arguing about now. Bruenor's demanding Vortigern send a load of extra soldiers down south to help him out, like. Vortigern's saying he can't afford the men ...'

Something occurred to Llew.

'What about Cuneglas?' he asked as he passed his now empty bowl back through the bars of the cage to Griff. Griffith just looked at him uncomprehendingly.

'You remember? The guy Vortigern sent to Consul Aetius in Rome just before I left ...'

Griffith thought for a moment.

'Cuneglas. ... Oh, yeah. Cuneglas! I remember him – little bloke who was supposed to bring soldiers from Rome. Do you know, we never heard from him again.'

Llew ground his teeth.

'Anyway, sorry about all this. Still – fresh straw in cage every day. Not all bad, eh?'

Oh good, a few *more* touches of civilisation.

'Not that you'll know the benefit of it. ... They let you keep your scrolls. That's something.'

Llew looked at his bulging sack.

'What good could they possibly do me now?'

Griff shrugged.

'Least you got something to read tonight. Take your mind off things. See you in the morning.'

And Llew was alone and facing death once again. Actually, he was getting used to it. It didn't make him any less afraid, of course, but it *did* make it so that the utter terror was something more akin to a natural way of being. He looked at his bag of scrolls in the corner. This wasn't how it should be! Everything he'd done ... all his skills he'd acquired he'd tried to use to create lasting peace. Instead, it looked as if he had set the ball rolling for the biggest war Ynys Prydein had ever known. One that would engulf the whole country.

It would go like this. To pre-empt the Saxon settlers and the loss of his kingdom, Bruenor and whoever joined him (which was beginning to look like quite a few kings) would attack the Saxons now. If the Saxons *won*, Hengist would show no mercy – not after he'd signed a treaty in good faith and been betrayed. If the Saxons *lost* and they were pushed back into the sea, Bruenor would find himself the head of an army of kingdoms at least equal to that of Vortigern's ... which would almost certainly cause a civil war.

And whose fault was it? Whose fault was this utter, *utter* catastrophe?

A couple of years back he'd rather hoped that he was going to be nothing more than a footnote on the pages of history. Now it looked as if he'd have whole chapters ... no, *books* dedicated to him and the title of each would be 'Llewelyn Ap Gwyddno – History's Number One Nob-head'.

Not that it'd make a blind bit of difference to him, because he was going to be dead by first light. However, it galled him to know that all his efforts had come to this – total and complete failure – and this was how he'd be remembered ... if at the end there were any of his own people left alive to remember him.

He pulled his bag over to him, snatched out a scroll of parchment and a bit of charcoal. Well, he had all night. He was going to get his side down on parchment ... with a bit of luck, there'd be someone around literate enough to read it one day.

The next morning, Llew found himself in an uncomfortably familiar situation. That of being dragged out of a wooden cage by two burly guards and taken to a spot at the bottom end of the settlement where there had once stood a tall tower and now stood a little Christian chapel (looking pretty unused – but again more civilisation ... Britu really was what, for those times, would have been called a radical). The whole of Langollen had come out it seemed to watch him being publicly and painfully murdered. On the way down, they passed his father, who shrugged sadly at him in 'I-don't-know-what-you-expect-me-to-do-about-it-this-is-your-mess-you-clear-it-up' kind of way (which is not bad for one shrug). All the kings and chieftains had come out as well, it seemed, as their retinue.

Llew realised that he was to be today's diversion. Well, he supposed, loads of kings and chieftains hanging around with nothing to do all the while ... you've got to keep them entertained *somehow.*

On a clear patch of grass just before the little chapel was Bruenor. He was using a whetstone to sharpen a long, but thin-bladed sword which looked to Llew like it was pretty sharp enough already, thank you.

Someone was missing ...

Where was Britu? Surely Vortigern would turn out to see this. Llew knew the overlord was not as sadistic as his father, but he was pretty sure that Britu would want to see him chopped into very small bits, if only so he could dance on them! Llew had, after all, ruined any chance of peace and almost certainly ensured that Britu would not remain in charge for very much longer. Or that, if he did, it would only be after a doubtless bloody attempt at insurrection and a war with the Saxons. Wonder where he is, Llew thought, and he mused at how calm he was being. It must be, he mused, because every time he'd ended up in one of these situations, some miracle had happened and he'd always been saved. Except that, in those times, he'd always been really scared and he wasn't now, which probably meant that he *wouldn't* be this time. Saved, that is. That was how it was supposed to go, wasn't it? In all the old stories. The fool who's always terrified of death, faces it so many times until he isn't and he gets complacent, which is when he actually gets killed. Ho, ho, ho, how ironic. Which means, if I *think* I'm going to get rescued, he thought, then I almost certainly *won't* be!!!

Suddenly, Llew was terrified again.

Which was actually a relief.

The warriors were starting to bang out a rhythm on their shields with their swords. Louder and louder, faster and faster. Llew was forced to his knees. Bruenor had started practising with his sword – very fast swishes in arcs of a figure eight[36] so that it whistled as it cut through the air.

Oh well, thought Llew (not for the first time), this is definitely it. Then ...

'Praise the Lord!!!!'

'In the name of God, I command thee to *stop*!!!!'

And everything did stop. The soldiers stopped the shield banging and Bruenor stopped with the arcs of eight. Everyone looked on and started to mutter in astonishment.

---

[36] Not that they used the figure '8' in those days. They were still doing Roman numerals, but 'VIII' is not something that looks very impressive when you make it in the air with a sword.

Two figures had emerged from the little chapel. The command to stop had come from one of them. It was Nascien. The first cry had come from a rather more surprising source.

'Lord Vortigern?'

It was indeed, but not as anyone had seen him before. He was wide eyed and smiling, standing, shoulders back and head high. He looked … joyous. There was no other word for it. Definitely joyous. And he was wearing a monk's cowl.

'Good grief, Nascien, just how many of those have you *got*?' Llew couldn't help himself from exclaiming (which just goes to show the surprising things that occur to you when you seem to have just narrowly averted a painful death).

'Praise the lord!!!!' said Vortigern again.

'What are you talking about?' said Bruenor.

'He sayeth that thou must worship the one true God!' said Nascien haughtily.

Bruenor looked puzzled and annoyed at having to delay his morning murder.

'We all do!' he said testily. 'All good Christians here; right, people?'

There was a general murmur of ascent from the assembled throng.

'There! So can I get on now?'

'Noooooo!!!!!'

Vortigern threw his arms around Llew – a deeply unexpected occurrence. Especially to Llew.

'You shall not touch a hair on his head, my brother! That is not the Pelegianist way!'

'Pel– what?' said Bruenor.

It began to dawn on Llew what had happened. Nascien must have converted Vortigern Britu! Somehow he'd got to him in the night and … well, it sort of made sense when you thought about it. A man like Britu, trying to keep control, trying to keep the Saxons from destroying your country, trying to keep the Picts or the Irish from destroying your country, trying to keep your chieftains and your kings from going to war every five minutes so they don't destroy each other. And you manage, *just* manage to hold it together. It could so easily fall apart, but it doesn't. Then everything gets blown to bits by a scribe who you ignored because you assumed he was harmless and, if you hadn't, he might have been.

The day that happens to a man like Vortigern Britu, Llew mused, he's going to start asking, 'what's the point of it all?' And then up pops this evangelical monk and, like all good preachers, he's got the answers for that long dark night of the soul. Come the morning, the overlord's got a big grin and –

'Praise the Lord!!!'

'I wish you wouldn't keep saying that!' said Bruenor, now more than a little annoyed. Llew wished it too, mainly because Britu's mouth was just adjacent to Llew's ear and the overlord wasn't being shy about shouting.

'Pelegianism is the true Christian way!' said Nascien, 'it teaches brotherly love. Now the king has embraced the true faith, no one shall be harmed.'

'No one!' cried Britu, still hugging Llew (and this was becoming slightly embarrassing). 'We will all love each other. There will be no more bloodshed! Praise the Lord!!!!'

Ruddy Nora, he's got it bad, thought Llew. Nascien must be really good at this! The other chiefs and kings were all giving each other slightly uneasy looks. Looks which said, 'this is going to cause problems, isn't it?'

Bruenor wasn't having any of this.

'What about my bloody kingdom?' he yelled, pointing his sword at Llew and making Llew glad to be a bit more intimate with the new monk-king than he had been previously.

'Your kingdom is merely an earthly possession,' answered Britu piously.

'No, it's not, it's *my* earthly possession and I don't want to give it to those bloody Saxons!'

'Neither shall you, my brother!' said Vortigern.

'Praise be!' said Nascien.

'For we *shall* defeat the Saxons. But with *love*!' said Vortigern.

And inwardly everyone, Llew included, said, 'oh, crap'!

War followed. Of course war followed. The Saxons brought their ships and settlers and when the armies of Bruenor and others met them at the borders of Gwyrangon, apparently not as a welcoming committee, they fought and fought hard, taking the kingdom and renaming it Kent. Instead of a few square miles of scorched earth, they now had a kingdom. Just as importantly, Bruenor **didn't** any more – and he wanted one. He didn't have much of an army now either and so he lived in exile in Gwent, plotting and persuading other kings to overthrow Vortigern Britu. Which they then did.

Other kings joined in on various sides; there were lots of battles in which most people were killed, lots of towns and villages were put to the flame and sword, as were their inhabitants. The Irish raiders saw this as an ideal opportunity to start raiding again in the West – the kingdoms of Lleyn and most of Gwynedd – as did the Picts in the North.

Everything the Vortigerns had tried to prevent had happened twelve-fold. It was at this point that the Romans finally heard the plea of the Britons for help and so they sent as many men as they could spare.

One.

His name was Ambrosius. And, to be fair, he was a general and a brilliant tactician. His story is to come.

As for Vortigern, no one is sure quite what happened to him. Some said that he had died a broken man after Kent fell to the Saxons and Bruenor persuaded others to march against him. Some said he was taken as a slave by Irish raiders. Some said he had become a wandering monk – preaching the Pelegianist doctrine to anyone who would listen. Those people said he had started singing in public as well. Some said he had become a hermit with the strange monk who converted him.

All that was known was that he had gone. And with him went the dream of a united Cymru people, ruling and prospering in their homeland, Ynys Prydein, island of the mighty. The Cymru were under assault from the north, west, south and east. And from each other.

It was the beginning of the dark times.

END OF PART ONE

PART TWO

Chapter Nine – The Votadini

A wild and windswept hillside, covered in bracken, heather and dotted with wattle and daub huts. Early morning. Megan moved the fur curtain that covered her hut's doorway aside and began the walk down to the bottom of the hill where the stream lay, carrying her big wooden bucket, shivering slightly. It wasn't, she reflected, how she'd envisaged the life of a princess (queen, actually … well, technically) should be. Okay, she was no fool – she'd known how it was for Royalty in Llangollen and how it differed greatly from the stories by the bards …. no cushions and sweetmeats while she was waited on hand on foot, not in *that* place. But she had thought once she was grown up and married there might be a bit less fetching and carrying. Those bards! Always singing of summer and sweet wine and in her head she knew that it must have been true for at least one princess *somewhere*, otherwise where would the idea for the song have come from?

With Pelinore it had at least seemed a possibility. He was as handsome as everyone said. Swarthy, muscular, hair black as jet, obviously a great warrior … although it had to be said not the brightest jewel in the dagger hilt when it came to brains; but then he did have a very trusty counsellor in the form of a plump Christian Bishop called Derfel, who was the best corrupt official money could buy. He was open for bribes and kickbacks of all sorts – like most senior priests – but never too much at the expense of Pelinore and/or the kingdom. He just took enough to keep himself in robes, attentive nuns and pudding.

Megan had been taken to Pelinore's huge hall in the fortress of Din Guayrdi[37] in Elmet.[38] And there'd been a wonderful ceremony in the castle chapel, with servants and feasting and the odd nice gown to wear. And she'd thought this, *this* is how it's supposed to go. This is what being a princess is supposed to be like.

It hadn't lasted long.

---

[37] Modern-day Bamburgh Castle, Northumberland.
[38] Modern-day North Eastern England.

Her husband had been called to arms not more than a month after their wedding. A horde of Pictish raiders were coming South, burning everything in their path. Pelinore had raised his levy, called his men to his side and off he'd ridden. That was the last time she ever saw him. Well, the last time she saw *all* of him. She did come across his head again, but that was after. After she'd woken up one morning to find all the servants in panic, trying to throw things into chests and load up the ox carts very quickly. No one seemed to be able to tell her what was going on, and then she'd run into Derfel. Quite literally, in fact, for they were both coming around the same corner in opposite directions and they collided, causing him to drop the small chest he was carrying and spreading the jewels which looked remarkably similar to the ones given to her as wedding presents all over the place. She helped him pick them up hurriedly and put them back into the chest.

'Derfel, what's going on? Where's everyone going?'

'Has no one told you? All is lost, my lady, our army is overrun. The Votadini are coming – we must leave.'

'But my husband –'

'Is dead, my lady; they're all dead. The Votadini are coming!' he said again for emphasis.

'But what about –?'

'Dead.'

'But the army –'

'Dead.'

'But –'

'Your majesty, which bit of the word 'dead' do you not **understand**?'

His voice was becoming panicky, which was pretty unusual for Derfel.

She was overcome by two sensations. One was fear. The Votadini were the most feared tribe of the north. They were said to live on three mountains. On two of them, Gorlois, scourge of the lowlands, was king, on the third his nephew Uther (known as Dragon's Head) ruled as a client prince. Those three mountains were known as the Mountains of Blood.

The other was shock. She had just been told her husband was dead, although she hadn't really had a chance to get to know him yet. And if she was perfectly honest, that what she *had* known of him she'd not really liked – he was terrifically dense. However, her narrative instinct told her that there was, in situations like this, a way in which a princess was expected to behave. She hurled herself to the ground, sobbing violently and crying to the Gods in torments of her grief.

'Highness. There isn't time for this! The barbarians are but a few minutes away! We must get to the carts,' Derfel said urgently. 'Seriously, will you just … put a bun in it for a few seconds!'

Megan had stopped sobbing. 'Put a bun in it' was not a phrase of comfort a grieving princess should hear from a consoling priest, even if he was a bishop.

Okay, if he wasn't going to play story-ball with her, she would do likewise. She stopped crying and sat up.

'I'm not going anywhere.'

Derfel went white.

'*What*?'

'I am queen of this land now! I will stand at the gates of the settlement and face Gorlois – *alone* if needs be.' She said it just a little too over-dramatically for it to be effective – and she knew it.

The Bishop was now shaking his head in disbelief and making nervous glances out of the window.

'If I set an example, the people will stay and fight! I can be a Boudicca for this country! All I require is my most faithful servants and you, Derfel, you who has sworn fealty to me, you will also stand by me as we await the onslaught.'

Derfel was sure he had a better understanding of human nature than her.

'Bugger that!'

Which is why she ended up defiantly stood at the gates of Din Guayrdi very much alone – the rest of the clan making a long line of refugees, heading south, a couple of miles away.

The gates had opened, the Pictish army had come in, she'd been thrown on the back of a horse and it was around about this time she saw her late husband's head being fixed to a spike to be displayed on the castle walls.

And that had been that. She'd been taken to Gorlois – very similar to most warrior chiefs,[39] but with more tattoos ... in fact, he seemed to be more tattoo than actual skin, and they weren't nice, tasteful, swirly Celtic patterns either. They all seemed to be of strange mythical animals either fighting or copulating or both. The Pictish chieftain had announced that she was his wife now. Some terrified, poor old pagan priest had been forced to mumble a few words over some (she thought) pretty tacky bronze rings and hey presto! She was married again without so much as a by-your-leave. And this was infuriating at first – she'd have liked at least the *pretence* of some say in the matter – but then she started thinking. Yes, she was married again.

Married to a *king* again.

Not as nice as the last king she had to admit – Gorlois was pock-marked scarred, had very few teeth and was, as has been said, an ode to the tattooist's art – but a king nevertheless ...

Having pillaged as far south as he wanted to, Gorlois had decided to turn back home. Megan was put on an ox-cart which rode beside him. He rarely spoke to her. And when he did, he kept calling her Ygrain. She thought this must be a Pictish word meaning 'Queen' or something and she'd thought, fair

---

[39] Large, hairy, the ability to overturn a table laden with food and drink and go 'grooooaaaaaaha ha ha ha!!!' heartily.

enough; it was only later when she asked the slave who drove her cart that she found out the truth.

'Och, all his wives are called Ygrain ...'

'He's been married before?'

'Aye and still is. See yon king's never really got round Christianity and he's no' so fond of the old gods neither, so he sorta ... mixed them up. He's figured that if you give your wives all the same name ... well, yeh've only been married the once. Which gives him the blessing of the new church and all the fun of the auld one, ye ken? Besides, it's easier for him to remember.'

Megan could feel the positive aspects of her situation become less and less.

'Are you telling me his other wives are still *alive*?'

'Oh aye. About half of them. The ones that dinna displease him. The ones that do ... well, there is this big cliff near his hall, see? Lot o' the wives get flyin' lessons.'

'So who's queen of the Votadini?'

'Why, none of them! He dinna trust women! Actually, he dinna trust anyone, but especially he dinna trust women. You're all just wee princesses tae him.'

Megan had sighed. So, with the Votadini she'd be no one special except that by her very accident of her birth she'd be living in fear, until Britu came to rescue her. In many ways it would be just like being in Langollen all over again. Only much, much further away ... And *would* Britu come to rescue her? She hadn't heard from him since he'd come to visit just before the Votadini raid. He'd had some monk with him and, to be honest, he really wasn't his normal self, babbling something about 'a simple, more Godly life' before leaving on some sort of pilgrimage ... she hadn't really been paying attention – she was thinking about her new queenly duties at the time – which, in retrospect, might have been a mistake. There'd been some talk about 'trouble at the council'. She'd missed that too.

She was now down by the river. Someone had to bring the water up for cooking and, being the least senior 'princess' in the 'royal household', this was her job. She didn't get on with the other Ygrains, who made her do all the chores – they'd seen her for what she was as soon as she arrived ... just another rival as far as they were concerned ... and some of them weren't so 'wee' either. They were big, sinewy women with red hair and as many tattoos as the men. Usually they were seen carrying two babies apiece. She wondered if this was to be her fate. Build up the muscles by sending her to carry huge buckets of water for a couple of miles every day, then a couple of visits to the local tattoo man and then Gorlois would come calling. Hey presto! A couple of babies to carry around.

On the face of it, this last part didn't seem very likely. Gorlois himself had forgotten about Megan almost as soon as she'd been dumped off her cart at the wives' hut. Unlike most of his tribe, Gorlois didn't speak much Cymru anyway, so there wouldn't have been anything to talk about. It was not long after she arrived that she began to think that maybe her 'defiant stand' hadn't been that good an idea. Gorlois hadn't intended to occupy her country, merely to plunder it, and now she was … well, part of the plunder. If she'd run off with Derfel and the rest of the populace out into the hills or wherever they'd hidden, she could have come back to Din Guayrdi as soon as the Votadini had vacated and then she really would have been queen, because the king – Pelinore – was dead. She could have ruled! It wasn't unheard of, after all. Boudicca had been one of the most powerful warrior queens ever. Actually, she'd been the only warrior queen ever as far as Megan knew, but that wasn't the point. The point was Megan could have been Queen of the Elmetians.

Actually, she still *was* queen of Elmet technically. She wasn't dead after all and Pelinore had no legitimate heirs. It was one of the reasons he'd wanted to marry her in the first place. So, in theory, she was in charge, albeit slightly in the wrong place at the wrong time. She'd then resolved to escape and head back to her rightful kingdom and claim it as her own before some upstart chieftain vassal of her late husband's got the same idea. All she had to do was find her moment. Wait and watch, watch and wait. One day, they'd all be looking the other way and she could make a quick run for it. … Okay, grab a horse and make a quick ride for it … all right, a *long* ride for it. The main point was that she had to find a moment where no one was watching her. Except …

… Except that not long after she'd arrived, she'd found she got a sort of … fan.

'Hello, Princess Ygrain,' said a slightly smug-sounding voice as she started filling up her bucket. She looked up. There he was again. Prince Uther, the king's nephew on his oh so brilliant white pony. He ruled one of the mountains in the country of the Votadini. She had decided she really didn't like him from the moment she laid eyes on him. He was too full of himself by half, too fond of the sound of his own voice … really thought he was something special. It didn't help him having that ridiculous title – all that 'Dragon Head' business! I mean, per-lease! It wasn't as if he was even particularly good looking. But he obviously thought he was. And for some reason he'd taken a shine to her. Which would have been all right if he just stayed on his own mountain, but he had taken it upon himself to ride every morning over to the borders of Gorlois' territory, which was marked by the river she drew water from (which was the one time in the day she was alone). Every morning. There he'd be, smiling arrogantly, showing off his legs (all the men of the Votadini wore kilts) and big chest and slightly cheeky moustache and beard. She really, **really** couldn't stand him.

And now it wasn't just mornings – wherever she'd be during the day, there he'd be too. Smiling, watching her. And quite frankly it wasn't making her chances of escape any easier.

'I said hello, Princess Ygrain,' said Uther.

She looked up at him and smiled in an unamused and unfriendly way.

'My name's not Ygrain,' she said, lifting the bucket and struggling up the hill.

'No. Yes. You told me. Sorry. Megan,' he blurted out, apparently nervous about something, still smiling that wretched smug idiot smile. He wheeled his horse round and started to follow her up the hill. 'Princess Megan,' he added.

'Queen Megan in my own country as it happens. So you can call me Your Majesty.'

She didn't look very queen-like, she knew, struggling up a muddy hillside with a wooden bucket spilling water all over the place.

'Can I give you a hand with that?' he offered.

'No, thank you, I can manage,' she said abruptly, as she did every morning.

There was an embarrassed pause.

'Well ... I'll bid you good day then, Your Majesty.'

She couldn't *hear* anything of a mocking tone in those last two words, but she was sure it must be there – she knew what he was like. She turned to watch him wheel his horse away and ride off. Actually, he looked more than a little cross. Obviously he hadn't been able to wind her up like he'd wanted to.

That'd teach him.

The fearsome reputation of the Votadini was perhaps not quite as warranted as they liked to believe. True, as a people they were (and were known as) great fighters. They'd had to be. These were the people that had caused so much trouble for the Romans, but had then made peace with them and part of the deal was that they kept other Pictish tribes well away from the borders of the Roman Empire in exchange for bribes of cattle and sheep to see them through the hard winters. This didn't make them terribly popular with those other tribes of the north, so the Votadini'd had to fight *them*, of course; but, generally, they lived a simple life and enjoyed the bribes while they lasted – trying not to pick fights if they could help it.

As for the 'Mountains Of Blood' – they had been so named because of the reddish lichen that covered the rocks on the land there. It was the Roman storytellers who'd started making up stuff about the battles, intrigues and murder that had been the making of the clan Votadini. The stories had spread and the Votadini didn't do anything to discourage them. They found that when people were scared of you, they gave you things that you barely had to ask for. So, living in the Mountains Of Blood had perpetuated the Votadini myth.[40]

---

[40] In fact, it had been suggested recently that maybe they should change the name to the 'Ruby Mountains' – it sounded nicer and might even attract some rich

However, once the Romans left, the bribes dried up, while the winters still remained harsh. With the extra food coming in, the Votadini had basically become a lot bigger, even having to spread from one mountain to two, then three – Gorlois had decided that the kingdom was too big to manage on his own, so he'd put Uther his nephew in charge of the third. Not because he didn't trust his three grown-up sons and myriad nephews, but because once he'd appointed one, the other two would unite to kill the new vassal and this would go on until he'd have no relatives left – favouritism being frowned on in Votadini culture.

There still remained the problem of what to do regarding the food situation, ie there not being enough of it for the harsh winters now the Romans had gone. So the Votadini went back to being what they'd always deep down been – marauding thieves. They'd go south, rob a few places, burn them out, defeat their armies so they wouldn't be pursued, then they'd return north. They didn't mean any harm – they were just hungry. And on that point, yes, they'd heard the rumours. Of *course* they didn't eat people! Well, hardly ever. And that hadn't happened for years, not since those Christians had come up from Holy Island preaching the Good Word. And *they'd* been a bit stringy.

Still, a fearsome reputation was a fearsome reputation – one you didn't drop lightly. It kept folk away.

Gorlois himself was a pretty fearsome character. He was from a long line of the clan's warrior caste, which was effectively how you got to be chief. You kept hitting the other guy over the head until he a) gave in or b) died – in either case you were the winner and the more you did this, the more people were either a) your servants with sore heads or b) dead. He had a dreadful temper – again useful in battle – but in spite of this he was not like other leaders of the time, say Vortigern I, a man of intrigues. He said what he thought, thought what he said and wasn't shy about saying it. Or hitting it.

He did, however, have one golden rule.

You Do Not Take Anything That Belongs To Me.

He didn't care what you did to other people. He didn't care who you were. He just wanted what was his and anyone who tried to take that from him ... well, they'd better have a good place to run to, that's all. This made, say, family marriages quite difficult with 'try not to look upon this as losing a daughter, but gaining a son' definitely being the motto of the Big Day. Gorlois liked his possessions ... sheep, cattle, slaves, wives (and he didn't care about the order) ... he collected them all and once he collected them they stayed collected.

This presented a problem for Prince Uther.

Uther was most honoured among the Votadini. He'd been made the

---

merchants to the area; but this idea had been generally frowned upon and the person who suggested it called a 'big Jessie'.

prince in charge of a third of the clan – one of the three mountains, in fact. And for good reason. Uther, as son of Gorlois' late brother Kustenhin, had one advantage over Gorlois' sons. He was quite bright. Actually, he was particularly intelligent and he was also, like his father and uncle, a great warrior, earning several times over the title of Dragon Head. And thus being most honoured, it meant that, ultimately, he'd have to marry one of Gorlois' daughters (probably Morag – who right now still had three of her teeth left, which was why she was known as Morag 'The Fair') and relinquish his part of the kingdom when Gorlois died, so that his sons could fight over it. And inevitably, he'd have to choose a son to fight for and if he, Uther, was lucky, that son would win, who he'd then have to work for, which would mean fighting someone else's battles until the day he died – probably at the hands of one of the sons who hadn't won the civil war, but who had survived it.

To Uther, this didn't seem like much of a future. His mountain principality was a job without prospects.

And then, on top of all this, Gorlois had gone off on one of his raiding parties and come back with *the most beautiful woman* Uther had ever seen. And Gorlois, the selfish bastard, had married her! Another one! Another wife! How many did the old fat-arse need?! And this one was lippy, which meant that if she wasn't careful it'd be flying lessons time and he really didn't want that, because to him … well, she was special. It wasn't just because she was beautiful, or that she was feisty (the Gods knew that women who speak their minds were fairly common place among the Votadini, to say the least), but … well, she just *was*! However, she was married to Gorlois and therefore he had to leave well alone.

And yet somehow he couldn't.

So he'd taken to exercising his horse in the place where she was sent to fetch the water. You know, just 'happening to be there'. And then trying to start up a conversation. He was, after all, probably the second most important man on the three mountains; you'd think that would warrant a kind word or even a smile, but no! Nothing! Just plain … well, rudeness was the only word for it. He was Uther Dragon Head, one of the most feared warriors in all Pictland! He'd cut men's heads off and thrown them on ant hills for just looking at him in a funny way, and yet here was this woman and she just didn't seem to care!!!

It was, he knew, going to drive him mad.

Megan got her first chance to escape at the beginning of winter.

Firstly, she'd never known cold like it. She'd known some pretty cold winters in Llangollen, but nothing, *nothing* like this. It felt as if she was walking through a cloud of ice. It was a cold that actually *stung*. And snow. Yes, again, there was lots of snow in Llangollen, but not like this. Not huge drifts of the stuff that people could get lost in and never be seen again. And it was one such person – a small child, in fact – that had wandered off and no one had seen for a while which gave Megan her chance, because anyone who could ride a horse was out looking for the child, and that included Uther.[41]

It didn't occur to her at first. She was down at the river trying to break the six inches of solid ice with what was proving to be a deeply ineffective twig when something occurred to her.

'Good gods! I'm all alone!'

It was true. The other Ygrains were all huddled together in the wives' hut; the other women were going about their daily chores. All the men were up on the high moorland looking for the lost child.

This was it.

She had no food and only the clothing she was standing in, but this might be her only chance. She threw the twig down onto the ice, which had the effect she'd been after for most of that morning and the ice broke. This was good because she was able to make a hole in the ice and sink the bucket so that there was no evidence of her ever having physically been there – apart from the hole in the ice ... which would soon freeze over. Then she broke into a run.

She was following the river downhill. She knew this was the way to go because she's remembered it from the day they'd brought her to the Mountains of Blood. In fact, she'd taken it upon herself to remember everything, deliberately, in as minute detail as she possibly could – every landmark ... rock, woodland, scrubland, hill and tree ... this determined she was to find her way back home. Plus, she was a Cymru girl, fashioned from the earth she stood on – in times past her people had worshipped the rocks and trees ... the very bones of the land. Those bones would guide her. She'd find her way back to Din Guayrdi all right.

Within about an hour she was utterly, utterly lost.

She was in a wood, she knew that; but she'd lost the river, couldn't see the sun and hadn't a clue which direction she was heading in. She was pretty sure she *wasn't* going in circles, but she was quite worried she was going in a series of spirals that eventually would end up in the same place she'd started from. A nice, swirly Celtic pattern. Very nice ... very artistic ... but absolutely no bloody good at all.

Meantime, her absence had been noted almost as soon as the search for the lost child had been realised for the wild goose chase that it actually was. One of the Ygrains – the eldest, known as Big Ygrain[42] – suddenly realised that there was 'nae watter to boil yon stoat in' (that day's lunch). A party was pretty soon by the river, including all the Ygrains, a few warriors and farmers, Gorlois himself and Uther.

The first thing that was noticed was the bucket, which, being made of

---

[41] In actual fact, the child in question was found several hours later sitting on Gorlois' lap by the fire while he told it stories – and when he was discovered and everybody scowled at him, he said, 'What? **What?**'

[42] Imaginative nicknames for women not being a Votadini strong point.

wood, had floated up to the top, where it could clearly be seen under the newly formed ice that had once been the hole in the ice it had been forced through. One of the farmers, a relatively intelligent member of the tribe, volunteered this explanation.

'Och, she went tae get some watter. She made a wee hole in the ice, filled the wee bucket, but the watter made it too heavy, see? So she fell through and got washed awa' by the current.'

He didn't have an explanation as to why the bucket had stayed where it was.

Well, I did say 'relatively intelligent'.

One of the women (a younger Ygrain, known as 'Young Ygrain') stepped forward and spoke to Gorlois.

'What will ye do, oh majesty, noo yon pretty young wifie is gone?'

She was sucking up and all the other Ygrains knew it.

Gorlois shrugged.

'I've got plenty o' others,' he said, and lumbered off. And after a while everyone shrugged also and went away.

Except for Uther, who remained staring fixedly at the bucket. He had seen the flaw in the farmer's theory. He'd also seen the footprints in the snow heading along the river bank. He spurred his horse on and started to follow.

A couple of hours later, Uther was lost too. Following the footprints hadn't been that easy on horseback, so he had tried walking and leading the horse behind him. This had worked for a while … it was weird – the trail seemed to show that although the fugitive wasn't actually going around in a circle, she was doing a series of spirals which would eventually bring her to pretty much the same place. Why, he mused? Some Cymru/Celtic thing? They did have all those lovely swirly patterns on their pots and stuff – he'd seen lots of them, usually before he smashed them with his war hammer. He liked the Cymru. They were very … civilised. Not like the Romans – all those bloody baths and writing things down and straight lines – but civilised nevertheless … their bards sang good songs, they didn't eat stoat … they didn't eat each *other*.

Uther had realised his mind was wandering, which wasn't getting him any closer to finding Megan. It occurred he hadn't a clue where he was. And it was at about this point disaster struck. A combination of heavy snow and fallen branches had disguised the fact that Uther wasn't actually walking on a proper path: he was walking on what was effectively a drop of about thirty feet. Which he fell as soon as the branches broke.

When he woke up he found he was at the bottom of the drop and his horse was at the top … or he guessed so; he could hear it buzzing contentedly to itself. And then it stopped and whinnied, alarmingly. Uther had not heard it do that since he was last in battle. Then he'd heard it gallop off. He'd struggled to his feet, miraculously found nothing was broken and then found a way to struggle to the top of the cliff (for cliff it was). The horse was gone. Something had caused it to bolt. He could see its hoof prints going off in the opposite direction to Megan's footprints. He had a choice: go after the horse or go after the girl.

Uther knew this: in an inhospitable forest in midwinter, with night not so far away and snow all around, your horse could mean the difference between life and death. Uther sighed. He knew it was no choice, really.

He set off, following Megan's footprints.

Brolger was a bear. He should have been hibernating, but his family had all been killed by the man creatures for their skins and he was afraid to. So a combination of fear, cold and fatigue did not put him in the best of moods.

He was actually the original Bear With A Sore Head.

He had been hungry. Hungry for most of the winter.

Luckily, for today at least, he wasn't hungry any more.

Uther had not been going for half an hour when he saw it ... the blood. A lot of blood. And not much else ... well, not that was recognizable. And what ever it was that had been killed by ... by what ever it was that had killed it ... was of a fair size. Certainly this was not the blood belonging to, say, a chicken ... or even a sheep. This was ... bigger ... and whatever it was had been dragged off by something really, *really* big. Uther had that sinking feeling in his stomach ... the kind where you know something truly dreadful has happened and you're just waiting for the pleasant surprise that actually it hasn't only that surprise never quite seems to come.

He started to follow the trail of blood and found to his dismay that it led to a cave from which the very definite sound of a bear eating (nay, *guzzling*) something large ... maybe human-sized ... was in fact emanating.

Now, Uther had a reputation in battle. A fury would come on him, a raging fire that only his enemy's blood would quench. His eyes wide with pure anger, spitting the worst curses and insults you could imagine, he would hurl himself into the fray, a whirling mass of sharpened steel. It was where his fearsome nickname 'Dragon Head' had come from and it was a reputation he had earned well. It would therefore have been a bit shocking to any of his fellow clansmen had they been watching him now, because he fell to his knees and burst into tears.

'Oh no, no, no, no, no, no!' he moaned to himself, sobbing, 'no, no, please no ...'

This continued for a while and probably would have continued a while longer if a voice hadn't said, 'Don't you think this is all a bit full on? It was only a horse ...'

'I'm not crying for the bloody horse!' an exasperated Uther tried to say through the sobs, his eyes streaming with tears. 'I'm crying for the princess! Gods have a little pity, will you? I just lost the love of my life –'

And then he stopped. And he realised to whom the voice belonged and he tried to swallow the last sentence, which was impossible because he'd already said it and so it sort of sounded like he added the word 'broohjghingff' at the end. He wiped his eyes with the back of his hand (and, it has to be said, his nose too) and looked up into the rather puzzled but still definitely lovely face of Megan. The pleasant surprise had come, but it had taken its own sweet time.

'The bear got it. I saw it. Dragged it into the cave. Obviously very hungry,' she said, before a penny suddenly dropped. 'Sorry, love of your what?'

But Uther was unable to answer this question because all his attention was now very focused on the mouth of the cave, where the slurping biting chewing sound of bear-eating-horse had now stopped and been replaced with the growling getting-louder sound of angry brown bear approaching.

He turned to her and had time to say just one thing …

'Run!'

… before the bear came bounding out, roaring.

Brolger didn't like the man creatures. They'd killed his family and then had the temerity to wear bits of them while they were out hunting for *him*. However, he didn't as a rule chase after them, because he feared them. Even when he'd seen there were two of them in his forest – and yes he'd seen them long before they knew about him – he did not jump on them and immediately bite their heads off (something a bear with a sore head often does, metaphorically and in this case physically speaking) even though he was Hungrier Than He'd Ever Been.[43] Instead, he'd let them get lost and he'd got their horse and eaten that instead. But then, he'd heard their voices outside his cave.

And he'd decided this was Not On,[44] because this was *his* cave in *his* forest and they were strange, dangerous creatures who he'd seen wearing bits of his family. Then, I think it's fair to say, the red mist set in and suddenly the two man creatures were running like mad across a snow-covered forest away from a ton of highly motivated, pointy-toothed bear.

Uther and Megan hurtled headlong over the brow of a steep embankment and tumbled down as the bear followed them, roaring. They hit the lower ground – a clearing – rolling, both knowing it was hopeless, because there was no way they could outrun a bear … the best one could hope for was to outrun the other and neither of them were thinking like that at present. Tripping over each other, they struggled to get up, but Uther caught his leg in

---

[43] For a bear? Pretty hungry.

[44] This way of thinking, ie in Title Case, may point to Brolger being an ancestor of Winnie The Pooh.

a hole (probably a badger sett ... but again, working this out was the last thing on his mind at the time) and fell flat on his face again. Seeing him struggle, Megan ran back to help him up.

'Don't wait for me, you daft bat! Get out of here!'

Possibly not the most heroic thing a man has said to the love of his life, but the sentiment was noble enough.

And then Brolger entered the clearing. There was nothing they could do. He was lumbering up to them and he was going to eat one if not both of them. He stood on his hind legs, stretching up to his full height,[45] and roared triumphantly.

And then stopped. In the distance he could hear something coming. It was animal definitely, and it was also roaring.

'Oh, great!' groaned Uther. 'Another bloody bear!'

The thing was getting closer and closer, the bushes parted; but then, instead of a large furry creature with a huge head and pointy teeth, into the clearing stepped a figure ... a human figure. A man, tall, with long, long wild black hair and a beard that seemed to go down to his knees – oh, and roaring like a bear. How old he was they couldn't tell, but Uther reflected that the stranger didn't seem to be of any clan that he knew, appearing to be some sort of creature of the forest – a wild man. He was wearing rabbit skins and carrying a tall staff, which he pointed at Brolger. The man then uttered a series of grunts and growls. The bear, still on his hind legs, roared back furiously. It appeared, though neither Uther nor Megan could believe it, that the two creatures, man and bear, were having some sort of ... conversation. It was also becoming apparent, by the mad and furious roars of the bear, that the conversation wasn't going very well.

But then the man pointed his staff at Uther and Megan, each in turn, and uttered another ear-blistering roar. The bear, for his part, *stopped* roaring. It then got down on all fours and left them. They heard it lumbering up the slope, through the snow and presumably back to its cave.

The stranger turned to look at them. For the first time, Megan could see his face full on. Not that there was much to see – it was all hair and beard, but the eyes ... they were very bright and as blue as ... well, it was like looking at two, small blue flames. And she knew she'd seen those eyes before.

'I know you!' she said in wonder, struggling to get up. 'You're him, aren't you?'

He looked at her and grinned, slowly.

'Who would 'him' be?'

The voice didn't seem to come from his mouth, but rather inside her head. It wasn't the voice of this (albeit hairy) young man either, for now they could see that he was younger than them. It was a voice older than time itself.

'The boy ... the one they were going to sacrifice. You're Merlin!'

---

[45] About eight feet.

Without answering, Merlin strode to the still prostrate Uther.

'You owe a life-debt to the bear, Uther Pen Dragon. One day you will honour that creature.'

Uther shook his head, not understanding.

'When the time comes ... you will know ...'

Merlin pointed his staff in the direction of the setting sun and began to move towards the edge of the clearing.

'That is your way back.' Then he pointed his staff at Megan. 'Protect her, Uther, there will come a time when the land is glad of it ...'

'Look, wait a minute!' said Uther, struggling up. 'Who are you? How do you know my name?'

But all that was left of Merlin were the leaves that scattered as the wind blew. Uther looked at Megan.

'You going to tell me about him? Or am I supposed to guess?'

Megan shrugged.

'I suppose I'd better tell you on the way,' she said.

So they limped back towards the Mountains Of Blood.

At first, it was awkward. Certain words hung over them, something that neither one of them had expected to hear or say. The words were 'love' 'of' 'my' and 'life'.

Walking in silence gave Megan a chance to reflect. What was it about men? They seemed to divide into one of two categories. The first regarded her as ... well, a thing. Something you owned and used as you basically wanted to ... whether that was a trophy (Pelinore and Gorlois), a bargaining chip (her brother) or a seriously twisted way of sucking up to the gods (her stepfather). The other type looked at you all moony-eyed and, yes, did what you wanted them to most of the time (except when you wanted them to go away, obviously), but had this extremely annoying way of getting all emotional – by which she meant crying enough to produce a lot of snot – about you. This third type were, she had to admit, more like the men in the stories the bards sang about. Into this category fell Uther, but also that weird little guy who used to work for her stepfather and brother ... what was his name again? Now *there* was an embarrassing incident, she remembered with a shudder. Gods, what was his problem? And they'd been getting on so well! At least this one (by which she meant Uther, who was trudging along beside her) had a ... well, he was a bit more her type, that's all. What's more, for better or for worse it did look like he was the only friend she had right now.

So she said brightly, 'Thanks for rescuing me, by the way.'

He shrugged and muttered, 'I didn't rescue you, did I?'

'Well, thanks for trying.'

And he felt a little better. And a little less embarrassed. So much so that he shot back a little conversation her way – something about how they'd be travelling back without a horse, which would be hard going, but he knew the land pretty well once they got out of the forest. And to this she offered a little conversation back to him.

And pretty soon the conversation was flowing back and forth between them pretty well indeed. Uther learned something of Megan and, more importantly, Megan learned something of Uther. She learned that underneath the fearsome exterior there was actually quite a kind man, whose lot in life wasn't dissimilar to hers. He would never be king – not properly – just like she would never properly be queen.

'Yes, but there's a difference,' said Uther. 'I've never wanted to be king. Well, not here anyway. I wouldn't mind being in charge of some place where you didn't have to go out and fight someone every fifteen seconds.'

'But what would you do if you didn't fight?' she said. 'You're a warrior, aren't you?'

'It's not pleasant, lass, dealing in Death every day. The one advantage I had of being made a prince was that I got other people to do it for me. And believe me, that dis'nae count as much compensation,' he said grimly; then he added, 'Beats me why you want it so much. The Queen bit.'

'Power. I quite liked the power, but not just that. I wanted to be remembered.'

Uther glanced over at her, baffled, and seeing his bewilderment she tried to explain.

'You've got bards, you've heard the stories …'

He shook his head.

'What stories?'

'The stories about women.'

Now he was really puzzled.

'Stories? About women?'

'That's my point. There aren't any …'

'Well, I don't know about that …'

'Oh, there are a few stories with women *in* them, but usually they're fair maidens and for some reason they're all so fair and none fairer – so I don't know how *that* works … I mean, one of them must have been fairer than the others – and they're usually princesses and they usually get captured and have to be rescued. Either that or they're goddesses who get impregnated, so that another bloody hero can be born!'

Uther didn't know what to say to this, so he didn't say anything.

'What I'm saying is … I'd like to be remembered by the bards as a woman … who *did* something! You know … like Boudicca!'

'You want your family murdered so you can become a warrior?' Uther wasn't following this at all.

'No! I meant I wanted to be a … a queen who … people remembered for something other than being rescued or being pregnant with someone famous!'

She paused. 'Well, I *did*. Now I don't know what I want at all any more. I mean, basically now I think I could do with a quiet life …'

It was true. She didn't know what had changed her, or why. Maybe it had been the experience with the bear, or Merlin turning up; maybe it had just been something she'd realised as she trudged through the snow with Uther. She just knew that running away to try and be queen in Elmet didn't matter any more – for her, it seemed, life wasn't going to be like the tales the bards sang of and … well, fair enough.

Uther grunted.

'Huh! A quiet life! I could do with some of that myself!'

And they trudged on.

Chapter 10 – Uther And Ygrain

And so Winter turned to Spring which turned to Summer. The Votadini hunted, gathered food, got married, had children, hunted, had more food, had hunts, gathered children. Occasionally, they fought the odd skirmish with other Pictish tribes … occasionally, Gorlois would announce that they were off to raid some poor Cymru kingdom on the other side of the wall; but generally life went on as it always had done for them. Nothing changed for the Votadini. Oh, they heard tales from the South … of wars and invasions and councils and more wars. They heard that the One God was now worshipped by much of the country beyond the wall – certainly by the Cymru anyway – although these strange creatures called the Saxons were spreading ever westward and northward and who knew **what** they worshipped? They'd heard tales, of course. A travelling bard had visited them and he had said that the Saxons' Chief God had only one eye. They'd laughed at that. Laughed and laughed. Only one eye? What kind of God was that? Couldn't he afford two? Oh how they laughed. Proving, thought the bard as he left with a bagful of old Roman gold coin, that these Picts were seriously starved for entertainment and boy, was he right to come north instead of scrabbling for a living down in Londinium or what? They also heard news from the Kingdom of Orkney, where King Lot still ruled – he who sacrificed all strangers from the mainland to the local sea god – and they wondered perhaps if they should have warned the travelling bard about this when he'd announced his intention to visit there.

And Megan and Uther fell in love.

It was not an immediate thing – not for Megan anyway. And, actually, Uther tried to distance himself a little once they'd returned to Mountains Of Blood, because he felt embarrassed and also because, when all was said and done, Megan was the wife of his king and the king tended to get possessive about what or who belonged to him.

Their arrival back home had not been eventful. Most of the women had said, 'Oh she's alive, is she?' and reflected that at least they still had someone to fetch the water first thing. Most of the men had said, 'Aye well, this proves young Mac Airn isnae as relatively intelligent as we thought.' Gorlois simply said 'Who?' when he was told that his new wife had been miraculously rescued. Then he asked for a description and was still none the wiser.

And so life went on.

And every day (or nearly every day), Uther would exercise his (new) horse by riding the edge of his lands, taking care that he was at the river in the morning where Megan was fetching the water. They'd exchange a few words and then Uther would ride on, usually smiling, because although Megan would never actually gush with joy, she would make the effort to be a whole lot more pleasant to him than she had been in the past. And this made him happy.

Megan for her part, meanwhile, also found herself being pleased to see him – which made her water-fetching duties seem a tad less onerous – and (here was something new) disappointed when, as happened on occasion, Uther didn't show up. This was bound to happen, of course. After all, Uther was a prince and he had a whole mountain to run – taxes to collect, crops and livestock to inspect, petitions to hear, justice to dispense – so there were often occasions when he didn't have the time to take his horse on a trot round the kingdom to where one of Gorlois' wives (or rather 'wife', because officially Gorlois only had one) happened to be drawing water for that day's breakfast of boiled rodent. When this happened, Megan found it put her out of sorts for the rest of the day and the other women would notice, muttering things to each other like 'whit wee beastie crawled up *her* jacksie and died?'

Then came the Rising of the Selgovae.

The Selgovae were a neighbouring tribe of the Votadini and, as things went, the two communities had always got on passably well. Yes, there was the odd border dispute and on occasion a few heads would end up on a few spears, but by and large it'd been a case of trading furs for corn and vice versa and then ignoring each other for years.

Until, that is, they'd got a new Chief called Urien. And Urien had decided that he rather liked to know what the view would be like from the top of the highest of the three Mountains Of Blood, so he then got some druid or bard to come up with some cock and bull story about how those mountains had always originally belonged to the Selgovae, but then the evil Votadini had cheated in a game of dice or something and they'd stolen the mountains from them. It was, he declared to his tribe, a matter of blood and honour. And his tribe, who were easily led at the best of times, yelled approval before running to pick up their trusty swords and spears.

The first the Votadini knew about all this was the plumes of smoke on the horizon. And knowing that, expanding city though it was, there was no way Londinium could have spread *this* far North, they assumed correctly that someone was raiding their borders. Horns were sounded and soon every able man was donning armour and sharpening some sort of pointy weapon. Then, as the army made ready to mobilise, the first of the refugees came into the settlements – farmers burned out of their homes, their wives looking ashen, their children crying, told the captains that, as they'd suspected, the Selgovae were on the march. They had come in their hundreds and they didn't look as if they were going to stop.

Megan watched all this, knowing that among the men now donning armour, getting weapons and saddling up, one must be Uther. As a chief, he'd be expected in the front line – he'd be leading the first charge, or in the middle of a shield wall. And then she saw him riding past with four or five other horsemen as escort, barking orders to the foot soldiers, telling them to get a move on because Urien wouldn't wait for them, even if they were prepared to wait for *him*. And then he was gone.

The waiting nearly drove her out of her mind. For days, all she could do was pace up and down the hut. It didn't seem to bother the other women. They sat and sewed, weaved or ground corn and after a while they got annoyed with her pacing. They sent her out to fetch more water. While she was at the river, she saw an ox cart arrive filled with some of the wounded and dying. She ran over to find, to her relief, that none of them was Uther. However, news from the battle wasn't good. It was rumoured that both Uther and Gorlois were dead – this was from one of the wounded soldiers. She must have looked horrified because the ox driver said, 'Now don't worry your pretty wee head about that, lassie, there's always rumours like that in times of warrin'. Most likely your husband bides fine.'

Husband? She blinked. Of course! The driver must have thought she was worried about Gorlois! Well, of course she was! He was her husband after all! Then she paused. Who was she kidding? She didn't give a stuff about Gorlois! The man had hardly spoken more than three words to her since she'd met him. And two of *them* were to say 'I do' at the wedding ceremony!

So she waited. And she waited some more.

Then, the soldiers started coming back. First, in ones and twos, joyfully saying that yes it was over and yes the Votadini had won and then in tens and twenties and then more! A whole crowd marched! They were cheering, singing and yelling, all massed around a horse on which sat the hero of the hour …

Gorlois.

He was bloodstained, one arm was hanging limp at his side, but he was looking pleased with himself. In his good arm, he held a spear and on the spear was a head. The head, she later learned, of Urien.

Then the arrivals of soldiers began to trail off. Tens and twenties arrived. Then ones and twos. Still no sign of Uther. No one seemed to know what had happened to him. One soldier pointed to a large plume of smoke in the sky.

'We burned all the bodies,' he said. 'Maybe that's his bale fire!'

And this time it was *her* who got that feeling in the pit of her stomach. The kind that Uther had told her about – when he'd seen the blood of his horse on the snow.

She didn't like the feeling, she didn't like it one bit.

She stayed by the river now, hoping against hope, waiting for him to come back.

Which he did. Of course he did! There'd be no story if he didn't!

As the sun began to set on the mountains, a figure came limping towards the settlement. He too was bloodstreaked, and his leather armour had been sliced open in several places, but there he was, nevertheless.

'Sorry I'm late,' he said. 'Lost my bloody horse, didn't I?. Middle of the bloody battle and I fall off my horse and I'm shouting "anyone who gives me a horse they can have my whole bloody kingdom"; but was anybody listening? Were they f–'

But he couldn't say any more because she'd thrown her arms around him and was kissing him. And it was lucky no one was watching them really because she was actually married to someone else. The king. And this was about to become a problem.

Two things decided to go wrong at around about the same time. The first was that Gorlois decided that Uther had gone unmarried for long enough. People were starting to talk, suggesting maybe that Uther was one of them fella's who ... 'didnae like women'. This was no sin as far as the Votadini were concerned, although the local Christian priest – a Monk called Andrew – had voiced his doubts, but there was the question of progeny. Uther was to all intents and purposes royalty. And without a marriage bed there would be no wee princes or princesses to continue his line. Uther had protested that he would find a wife in his own good time and there had been a falling out between the two men, causing the beginnings of a rift that only seemed to get worse with time.

The second thing that went wrong was the death of Gorlois' wife Ygrain. Big Ygrain. The main Ygrain-of-the-moment, that is. There was always one. The one Gorlois kept hanging about, cooking for him, cleaning for him, the one Gorlois would take to his bed. Usually, they'd last for about a year, then he'd get bored, accuse them of infidelity and two guards would take the unfortunate woman to a cliff top and have her hurled off. Then he'd choose a new Ygrain to do the same job – and somehow ... in his weird and twisted logic, having a wife with the same name meant that Gorlois hadn't killed his other wife and so hadn't broken the one God's law. Andrew had once attempted to explain the difference to his lord between committing murder and not committing murder ('just because you give them the *same name* lord, doesn't mean they become *the same person*'), but the argument had fallen on stony ground (rather like all the Ygrains) and the monk decided not push it, because he'd seen that cliff and it was very high in a non-gender-discriminating type of way. Now the thing was, this latest Ygrain didn't go in this untimely fashion, although Gorlois was beginning to tire of her, so she probably would have, given a little time. However, the fact was that Big Ygrain met her maker in an entirely different way. She was killed by a bear.

A bear wouldn't usually kill a human, not unless the human annoyed it and not many humans are either a) that stupid or b) get so bored they think to themselves 'what the hell am I going to do with myself today? The only thing I can think of is to go and annoy the big brown bear over the way'. However, in exceptional circumstances – say, when a small war between two bands of humans has scared all the prey from the bear's feeding territory and/or the bear has been scared by human activity away from its normal eating habits – a hungry bear might try and hunt down the odd bi-ped, as long as they didn't smell too nasty.

Well, as it happened, Brolger's feeding territory was slap bang in the middle of the forest located between the Selgovae lands and the Mountains of Blood. When the Selgovae had risen, they'd smashed through the woodlands, eating and burning everything in their path. Brolger had hidden in his cave with his eyes shut and, when they'd gone, he looked out to find there was nothing left to eat. Literally nothing. They'd taken all the berries, they'd taken all the nuts. They'd taken all the good roots. They'd taken all the fish. They'd taken all the small mammals and they'd taken all the large mammals. They *hadn't* taken all the birds, but Brolger didn't care about birds because, Being An Animal Unable To Fly, he couldn't eat them.

So that was that – the man creatures had crossed his path yet again. And just like last time, he found he was down on the deal.

Then, later, he smelled something … something like … well, he knew that the man creatures used to burn meat and that when you ate this, it almost tasted nice. He'd had found this out when frightening a few of them off from around a campfire once. And this scent was not dissimilar. So he followed the scent, which took him for miles and miles, out of his forest – further than he had ever been before – and he found himself in a green valley. There in the middle of the valley was a big pile of dead man creatures on fire – hundreds of them. There were some live humans too – they were pulling dead man creatures from all around the area and throwing them onto the fire. There were also crows. They were feeding.

Brolger decided it was unfair that the crows should have all the good scoff.

Then one of the live man creatures saw Brolger approaching, so he screamed and started to run away, which caused the other man creatures (the live ones) to see Brolger and also to scream and run away again, leaving the bear all alone (bar a few carrion crows) in what was – if he so chose to modify his eating habits – a great big larder.

Brolger decided to evolve.

Brolger learned to eat man's flesh. First cooked … then not so cooked … then he started hunting live ones.

Not long after that, rumours started circulating in the settlements and farmsteads on the Mountains of Blood about a monster that had been seen on the battlefield first and later wandering in the woodlands around the mountains.

' 'Tis said it has the body of a bear!'

'Aye, and also the head ... of a bear!'

'Aye, but it has the *roar* of ... well, of a bear, but 'tis a monster all the same!'

As is always the way in times like these, people started barring their doors at night and leaving little offerings of food for it, which the next morning would always be gone (of course, people then said the monster had accepted the offering – which was ridiculous really as any number of night creatures could have taken it, but most people don't let things like facts get in the way of a good story).

Then a child went missing. Never found.

Then a hunter from one of the settlements. Never found.

Then a farmhand along with one of his cows. Two weeks later they found his bones (but, curiously, never the cow's).

Now Gorlois' found he was being petitioned. Farmers, soldiers, lords and vassals all wanting to know what was he doing about the Bear Monster problem. Gorlois shrugged. What was he expected to do? Who'd died and left *him* in charge? Didn't people realise he had bigger problems at the moment? Had they *any* idea what it was like to live with a wife you were really bored by?

No one knew why Big Ygrain went into the woods that day. The bards later would sing a song of a fair wispy maiden going to pick bluebells, dancing in the trees as she did so. Then they sung of her coming upon a great monster, who was really a bear (or was it the other way round?). After that, for some reason, in the songs, monster and wispy maiden always had some sort of conversation in the vein of 'oh, will you come back to my cave, oh wispy bluebell-gathering maiden? For I have comfits and sweeties to give you'; 'oh, thank you for your offer, kind sir, but I must gather my bluebells' – which seemed to go on for *hours*, culminating with the bear monster losing his temper and eating her anyway. However, it's doubtful the real incident went like that.[46] At the end of the song, the last fourteen verses would tell of how Gorlois took the news when the remains of his wife were found, which was not in a good, or indeed shy, way. And in this instance at least, the bards sang true, because Gorlois was bloody furious! Ygrain was *his*! He'd planned to have her thrown off a cliff! How dare that bear/monster/whatever it was supersede him!

He demanded that every available military man be called to arms. They were going on a monster hunt.

For once, Uther didn't mind donning his armour. Unlike most of the other men, he was pretty sure that, whatever was out there, it couldn't be as

---

[46] Apart from anything else, Big Ygrain was built like a barn and wouldn't have had much truck with picking bluebells because you couldn't eat them.

dangerous to a hundred fully armed men as, say … a hundred fully armed *other* men could be. He also knew that most likely what ever it was (and if, as rumoured, it had the head and body of a bear, then it probably wasn't a giant Land Octopus) would be scared off by the sound of all of them tramping through the undergowth and run like mad – with a bit of luck into what remained of the Selgovae and then *they'd* have the Monster Problem. He also didn't mind because he was in love and the person he was in love with was in fact in love with him, which, as far as he was concerned, was all that mattered in the world.

Megan and Uther had kept their meetings since the battle discreet for various reasons – the main one being that if Gorlois ever found out, he'd kill them – but as it was they'd had precious little chance to see one another. Uther's princely duties rarely allowed him down to Megan's settlement and even when they did they were lucky to get even the shortest conversation. It was a question of the odd glance, whisper and/or smile. Not usually all at once. However, the secrecy seemed to make it even more exciting for both of them. Uther had talked to Andrew in private.

'Look, priest, how can he be legally married to more than one woman in the eyes of your God?'

Andrew had nervously – for he was a nervous man – held his hands up in exasperation.

'Quite frankly, my Lord Prince, the eyes of my God must be popping out on stalks at the effrontery of the King! But do you want to tell him, because I sure as hell don't?'

Uther had to admit Andrew had a point. He just wanted to find a way of marrying Megan. There had to be one, he mused, as he climbed on his horse … there surely had to be a way of persuading Gorlois that he could part with one of his wives when he had another twenty – at least least six of which were likely to be Gorlois' new Ygrain-of-the-moment before Megan was. That was assuming Big Ygrain … well, that those bones were hers. She might still be alive. You never could tell from a skull, could you?

And he rode off into the woods with the rest of the men on the beginning of the great monster hunt.

It was by sheer luck that one of the men best at tracking had managed to get ahead of the mob. He picked up Brolger's trail pretty quickly and it wasn't long before he was able to send word back that the monster wasn't far in front. Uther managed to divide his men into groups, instructing them to attempt surrounding the creature with the intention of driving into a particular clearing he knew of.

Again the bards later had their own version of the story. About how this mighty bear was cunning enough to realise that some groups of men were more isolated then others, how it'd pounced on them and brave warriors had fought the bear, which was as ferocious as … well, a bear. The truth of it was, that some of the men only had to hear a rustle in the bushes behind them and Fight Or Flight instinct kicked in – the latter very much winning over. Others, however, had better luck and soon the bear was on the run. Once it was on the run, some of the men decided that cruelty was the better part of valour and soon they were shooting their arrows and throwing their spears, not to kill, but merely for the sport of it.

When Uther rode into the clearing, all he could see at first was a great crowd of cheering and crowing men with spears, arrows and such-like being fired or hurled into the centre. He roared at them to stop what they were doing and they parted as he rode through them to see what had happened. There, in the centre of the crowd, was the bleeding, sweating version of the bear that had once been Brolger. A child had been taken, some others had been taken and the chief's wife had been taken. The warriors had decided to be cruel. Brolger tried to raise itself and then fell to the ground, making a deep groaning sound, the sound of a creature for which it hurts to simply breathe. One of the men raised his bow to shoot an arrow – an arrow that would just add to its pain. The man was still grinning at the thought of this when he was knocked to the ground by Uther's spear butt, the prince wielding this whilst spurring his horse into the centre of the fray. The warriors all looked at one another and started muttering grumpily, but the message had got home. The chief didn't want the bear to be taunted any more. Uther urged his horse forward and trotted up to the bear. Their eyes met and Uther was sure he could see them pleading to him to do something, to end the misery. And in his head a voice came back to him.

'You owe a life-debt to the bear, Uther Pen Dragon. One day you will honour that creature.'

Uther nodded at the creature slowly and then hurled his spear hard. Brolger gave a brief spasm of pain and then died. The warriors all cheered because they felt it was what was required of them. Uther sat slumped on his horse, thinking to himself about this creature that had managed to terrify the life out of whole tribes of his people. A creature who made all its enemies fear it totally. And a voice came into his head reminding him of the word for 'bear' in the Old Language.

Arth.

Somehow it didn't feel quite ... right.

There was a great feast in Gorlois' hall that night. Roast venison. The plan had been for bear meat, but the carcass had mysteriously disappeared not long after it had been skinned – someone said they'd seen a holy man ... one of the woodland hermits, the ones who were supposed to live off nuts and berries, but everyone knew they never did ... in the area which, as far as everyone was concerned, explained the disappearance.

Gorlois was given the pelt of the creature, as a gift, which he announced was a great honour both for him and the clan, before throwing it on the big pile of animal pelts (some of which were the remains of Brolger's family) that had accumulated over the years in one corner.

Gorlois also demanded that all the Ygrains be brought into the feasting hall so he could find one to be his new wife –

'Ahem,' Andrew coughed.

… find one that was *already* his wife, Gorlois continued expertly. And afterwards there would be a great feast and much quaffing of big horns of mead, after which Gorlois and his new wife –

'Ahem.'

… *same* wife would retire to the bedchamber for nookie.[47]

So it was done. Not half an hour later, Gorlois' other wives (who were also one and the same wife, you understand) were lined up in front of him. Trying to hide at the back of the group was the wife who, after Big Ygrain, was considered most likely to be the Chosen One. Her real name was Dioneta and it was she who was next in line to the rather precarious Queen's throne, simply because a) she'd been around for the longest and b) she'd been passed over a couple of times. It never occurred to anyone that actually this might have been down to a deliberate strategy of hers. Dioneta, just like Megan, had been abducted on a Votadini foraging raid a number of years ago and, once she'd realised what the usual fate was for one of the King's wives (who were, of course, one and the same wife, you understand) – that is, you got thrown off a cliff once he got bored – she made it her mission in life not to be the one he fancied. This was quite an achievement considering that, even though she was getting on in years, not only was she dazzlingly beautiful with fiery red hair and deep *deep* blue eyes … eyes that bards and poets would kill to describe (which is why I'm not going to bother) … she was also a good foot taller than any of the other women in the Mountains Of Blood. Right now, she was trying to dig a little hole with her feet – just to see if she could get a few inches off the top.

It wasn't working.

It was pretty obvious, Uther observed as he stood with other clan notables watching Gorlois walk up and down inspecting the group, that the king had eyes for only one woman and that was the tall one at the back, currently trying to bend her knees and screw up her face so as to pretend not to be very tall, or good looking. And failing miserably. This was a big relief to the Prince, since it meant Megan wasn't even vaguely in with a chance.

Having inspected the group of women thoroughly, Gorlois turned round and opened his mouth to announce his choice …

'I'm sorry, but this is really demeaning.'

Everyone gaped. Not only did King Gorlois never use words like this, but

---

[47] Gorlois had never quite got the hang of kingly speeches.

also he didn't have a sweet girly voice with a Cymru accent. What was going on?

'It was me! I said it!' said Megan.

Everyone realised their mistake. One of the women had spoken. The little one on the end. Wasn't she the one who'd gone missing that time? A muttering broke out ... generally things about women speaking at solemn ceremonies such as this and them wanting to be priests next and over my dead body, etc, etc.

Uther's eyes were popping out of his head. He was willing her to shut up shut up shut up shut up, because he knew the way Gorlois' mind worked and was generally for women to know their place, be it at their husband's side or off a cliff top. But Megan was on a roll.

'We're ... people! We're not cattle, you know! How would you like to be treated like this, eh? We do everything for you men! We cook, we clean, have your babies, we ... draw water! Isn't all that enough without us being wheeled out and inspected like a herd of prize pigs or something?'

Outwardly, Uther was being as still as a statue and his face was an expression of curious amusement. Inwardly he was slapping his own face with his hands and screaming 'aaaaaaaaghghghg!!!!'

Gorlois himself looked appalled. His eyes were bulging like they'd never bulged before (and most people there had seen those eyes *bulge*). No one in the room had any doubt what was going to happen next. He was going to blow his top and demand that Megan be taken to the cliff. To be fair to be Megan, she obviously realised the folly of this outburst because, noticing the stoney faces staring at her in absolute shock, she said, 'Just an opinion, obviously.'

Then something odd happened. Gorlois' expression changed to one of extreme amusement; then he threw back his head, laughed loudly and announced that he liked a woman with spirit. He had, he said, made his choice and he held out his hand to Megan who, just as gobsmacked as everybody else, took it. There was a quiet 'yessss!!!' from the back of the group of women as Dioneta tried to privately celebrate another reprieve that she then turned into an unconvincing cough.

Then Gorlois announced that the feasting should commence.

As feasts went, it was not spectacular. There were no fireworks. There was no entertainment of any kind – no bards or jugglers. There wasn't even very much food. What there was a lot of was drink and the Votadini, or rather the Votadini *men,* drank it.

It wasn't long before the night sky was filled with the traditional Votadini sounds of men throwing up, singing bawdy songs and getting into fights.

Gorlois himself managed to do all three before retiring to his bedchamber, where poor Megan waited, fully clothed and dreading what was about to happen. It would be nice, she had thought to herself, just once for the person who wanted to have sex with her to be a person she wanted to have sex *with*. There'd been Vortigern … (eeewwwww!!) … lucky escape there … there'd been whatshisface – the scribe (well, she assumed he'd planned on having sex after he'd stopped reciting poetry and running round in slow motion) … she had to admit she'd quite liked Pelinore … but, well, he'd lasted all of a month, and now she was waiting for a half-drunken thug who she really couldn't stand when in fact the person she *did* want to be with was – … oh well, this was obviously going to be her lot in life. At least it wasn't *King* Lot, she joked to herself, because then she'd get sacrificed into the bargain as well –

This train of thought was interrupted by the aforesaid half-drunken thug lurching into the chamber in a way that didn't suggest half-drunken thug at all. It suggested a very thoroughly *full*-drunken thug who was now clumsily trying to take off all his clothes. And all would have gone badly for Megan had not another figure entered the room and hit the king over the head with Megan's bucket, causing him to keel forward and collapse on the floor.

'Damn useful this,' Uther said, holding up the bucket.

Megan was staring at the recumbent Gorlois.

'Have you killed him?' she asked, worried.

Uther snorted.

'I'd have tae cut his hede *off* tae kill *him*, and even then it'd be touch and go,' he said.

He held his hand out to her.

'Coming?'

And she took it and followed him out.

Next morning, a deeply happy Megan sneaked back into her bedchamber and slipped in beside the snoring form of her husband Gorlois, still lying on the floor. When he woke up half an hour later, he announced that he had an appalling hangover which would only be made better by lots more drink, at which he got up and went in search of a cure, although Andrew did later manage to persuade him to put some clothes on.

Megan was, over the coming months, through a series of cunning wiles and lucky coincidences, able to avoid any sort of major contact with Gorlois. The main one being that Uther managed to make sure the king got good and drunk every night and was always on hand with the bucket at bed time. Not long after, Uther was left to mind the kingdom while Gorlois went off with his army, pillaging.

Which left Uther on his own with Megan for weeks on end.

And a change came over Megan. She started feeling very hungry all the time and being forgetful. Then she began getting sick in the morning. And the women started smiling, giving each other meaningful looks and nudging each other, muttering something about another 'wee Gorlois' being on the way.

And Megan thought, 'I wonder what on earth they're talking about.'

Then one day, it was with horror that she realised. That was the same day that she saw a figure hobbling towards the settlements. He was covered with dried blood and his clothes – such as they were ... an old monk's cowl and trews ... were torn to shreds. He was carrying a bag stuffed to overflowing with what looked like parchment.

She thought he must be a holy man ... the cowl indicated as much – one of those mad hermits from the hills. But for some reason he looked incredibly familiar.

Chapter 11 – The Further Adventures of Llew (Part I)

He went through quite a few adventures after the council of the kings.

The first was, of course, his escape from death at the hands of Bruenor. It had all been very well Vortigern Britu – 'loved up' as he was – ordering that no man harm a hair on Llew's head. That would keep him safe for the next couple of hours, but he knew damn well that, as soon as he was out of the overlord's sight, Bruenor and his men were going to come looking. So, as soon as he got the chance, he escaped, sneaking out from under the hole in the outer wall (yes, it was still there) with his bag of scrolls and that old rusty sword Merlin had told him to look after. Although why he was bothering, he couldn't think! What had that weird kid ever done for him?

Actually, he wouldn't be a kid any more. But the point was the same.

He knew where he was going to head for. The plan now seemed even more urgent. He was sure the new, improved Vortigern-Who-Jesus-Wants-For-A-Sunbeam wasn't going to last for long. The alliance was going to collapse, which meant that Hengist wasn't going to get Gwyrangon – not without a fight – and the various interested parties from outside the Island Of The Mighty would cry havoc and let loose their dogs of war.[48] Llew had no direct experience of war as such, but he was pretty sure it wasn't something you should hang round for if you could avoid it. Maybe he was mistaken – after all, it's arguable that seven million warriors all insisting on getting together for the very *purpose* of mass slaughter can't all be wrong – but Llew was determined *not* to find out either way.

So he was heading for the Aquae Sulis road again.

I suppose it's sort of my fault, he thought to himself as he trudged along through the famous Powysian drizzle. And he'd sort of got a point. The wars that were about to happen were to be directly caused by the breaking of a contract he'd negotiated and agreed to on behalf of the Britons. *However*, they'd probably have happened anyway and if he'd been given the proper information (thank you, Majesty!) in the first place maybe he wouldn't have negotiated such a daft contract. Not that he'd had a lot of choice about *that* at the time either. I mean, if that Saxon bodyguard hadn't been mucking about

---

[48] It's Shakespeare, who wouldn't be born for another thousand years. Yes, I know – teach me to use a quotation as a metaphor.

with that axe, maybe *maybe* he'd have been able to do some proper negotiating. And he wouldn't have even had *that* job if Edwyn had managed to keep alive for five minutes. Plus ... *plus*, if they'd sent him to Rome like he'd been asked to (thank you again, Majesty) instead of that little twit Cuneglas ... well, maybe he wouldn't have been around to muck things up in the first place.

It is perhaps a credit to Llew's character that he was feeling so guilty about everything, which is why he was able to continue with this monologue of self-justification for about three days while he travelled. In the end, he decided to write it all down – which made him feel a whole lot better. He didn't know why ...

It wasn't long before he realised he was being pursued. Hoof beats in the distance, just on the edge of his hearing; only, unlike the time when Griff had found him, he was travelling through woodland now and there was somewhere to hide.

So he hid. Or rather, he climbed a tree.

Three horsemen rode past – warriors and a scout ... a tracker. They were all Gwyrangon men – Llew recognised them from the council. They hadn't gone ten yards beyond him when the tracker pulled his horse to a halt and dismounted. The two soldiers, who were just behind, also stopped their mounts.

'What's wrong?' said one of the soldiers. 'You said he came this way ...'

'Yes,' said the tracker, 'but I can't see his trail any more ...'

Oh bugger, thought Llew. He began to sweat.

The tracker carefully moved away from the path and began to follow, almost to the footstep, exactly where Llew had gone. Llew looked down, praying that neither the tracker nor the soldiers would look upwards, because this was autumn and the absence of leaves meant that it was a bad time to climb a tree if it was for the purpose of hiding.

The tracker was now directly under Llew's tree.

'What are you doing?' said the other warrior impatiently, 'every moment we stay here, the further he gets away. And I want those gold pieces!'

Oh good. A price was on his head. That was all he needed. On the other hand, maybe they weren't after him – maybe it was someone else.

'And Buenor wants that Scribe!' said the tracker. 'And he'll get him if you let me do my job ...'

Maybe it was another scribe ... oh, who was he kidding?

And yet, still they didn't look up. Why? The scout was pacing round Llew's tree now.

'I'm sure he came this way ...,' he said.

'No one's stupid enough to go into that forest. Not alone,' came the reply, '... it's filled with wolves and half-starved bandits ...'

Bloody hell! Not here again!

'… come on!'

The warrior plainly had no more time for the tracker (proving that they weren't very bright) and the tracker reluctantly made his way back to his horse without looking up (proving he wasn't very bright either). Once the tracker had mounted up, the three rode off at top speed. Llew climbed down from his tree. He knew after a while they'd realise the trail really had gone cold, but that gave him a couple of hours to cover his tracks and disappear.

He hoped all his pursuers would be as dim.

He spent many days on the run, keeping to the road until he heard the sound of hooves behind him, then he'd always be able to find somewhere to hide. Luck was on his side it seemed – for once. Every now and again he'd come to a hamlet and again the monk's cowl would come in handy for a bite to eat, shelter and occasionally somewhere to conceal himself. This latter was a revelation to Llew. Poor people with nothing to gain, but one hell of a lot to lose by lying to a troop of burly soldiers, would, without question, stand outside their hovel and put on what Llew began to call The Bumpkin Act.

The Bumpkin Act was where a farmer who, only fifteen minutes previously to the horses pulling up, had been intelligently discussing the forecasts for this year's harvest or the state of the wars, would mess up his hair, put on a goofy expression and lean against the doorway in a way that was both nonchalant and sullen. The leading soldier, usually a captain or a warrant officer, would for some reason decide that the farmer must be deaf and shout[49] at him, 'have you seen a scribe come this way?'

The farmer would go 'Arrrr?', which could, of course, mean anything.

So the warrant officer would repeat himself even more loudly, at which the farmer would sort of half laugh half snicker as if the soldier was an idiot talking nonsense. Then the soldier would repeat himself yet a further time and at another dozen decibels.

This was the cue for the farmer's wife. Previous to the soldiers' arrival, she was attractive and intelligent – now she'd come out, half falling out of her clothes and complaining loudly that she should never have married him (the farmer) and should have married her *other* brother instead. Another cue. This time for the farmer's previously well behaved, well scrubbed and quiet children to appear, covered in filth and fighting over a mutton bone.

And it worked every time. The soldiers would look at each other as if to say 'this is what they get up to in the country, is it?' and the leader would bark, 'let's get out of here!' At which the soldiers would ride off into the distance.

The scrolls also came in handy if any farmer asked for more identification

---

[49] Not that this is a good way to communicate with deaf people either.

as any fool could put on a cowl and pretend to be a monk. Llew would show his writing to them. It was well known that only monks and scribes could write, so it was believed that Llew must be the genuine article.

Life on the run, however, does have its disadvantages – the main one being that it quite often means you don't get to choose the direction you get to run in. Every now and then Llew might see a patrol on the road up ahead of him, who might or might not be after him, but, just in case, he'd have to nip over a hedge and, rather than wait for the patrol to go past, he'd head off across the field, knowing that for now at least he'd changed from west to east. Thus it was that Llew ended up travelling all over the place rather than getting to his beloved Aquae Sulis. And what's more, his travels took quite a long time. Long enough, he hoped, for some of the fuss to die down and maybe have Bruenor come round to thinking he was wasting time and soldiers hunting Llew. However, after several months, he did find himself in a place he recognised. It was a hill, a big one, and he remembered a conversation about the Romans trying to build a road there …

'… One of the druids has pronounced Badon Hill sacred. Anyone who lays a stone down there gets an arrow up his arse, begging your pardon, sir.'

Badon Hill.

Badon Hill!!!??

He was just a couple of miles from Aquae Sulis! He was nearly home! And they had finally finished that road then. He could tell they had because, as he approached it, he could see the road itself was full of people. More than full, it was packed – worse than Llew had ever seen, even in Londinium – men, women, children, their aunts, their uncles, their grandparents, whole families, not so much walking slowly as marching wearily … and their belongings packed onto carts pulled by whatever animal they could get to pull it … and if they didn't have a cart, they carried everything. Llew noted that every cart was overloaded, that every person was carrying more than they really physically should be able to. This was a people on the move who'd decided to take everything with them. It could only mean one thing. They were refugees. And refugees were nearly always moving away from one of four things – war, plague or famine.

'What are you running from?' he asked one.

'There's plague in the east. Oh, and the Saxons are coming. Oh, and everyone's starving since the Saxons took all the food.'

Oh well, three out of three wasn't bad.

And they were all heading into Aquae Sulis. This tide of humanity was currently engulfing the city of his dreams. There had better, he thought, be a space in a warm house for him.

Of course, if he'd said this aloud, the resounding phrase from any who heard him would of course have been 'You'll be lucky'. When thousands of refugees converge on a city, it's not just a question of 'first come first served'

– and Llew wasn't even close to being the first among the refugees to arrive there. Nor is it normally a question of 'each according to his needs' – in times of public strife there are a few who make sure the weakest, the ill and the children are looked after first, but they are usually exactly that – the few. In this town, the motto of the day was 'Aquae Sulis Is Open For Business'. All the prices of the shops and inns immediately went up threefold and for those who couldn't afford them there was … well, nothing. You paid up or you slept in the street and you didn't eat.

This was why Llew spent his first night back in Aquae Sulis on a nice comfy stretch of pavement about a hundred yards down the road from the governor's palace where he used to live. He had, of course, gone straight there in the vain hope (and yes, even he knew it was a vain hope, but he didn't have any money) that Marcus and the governor's retinue might still be there. Or, at the very least, someone who might remember them and therefore might give a bed for the night.

Some hope.

The old place was full of Cymru soldiers … some sort of military headquarters, and he'd been told to go and sling his hook. Or words to that effect anyway. He didn't argue – messengers might have been sent out by now. He didn't want to draw attention to himself where soldiers were concerned.

So this was his punishment, was it? The wars he'd caused were starting and he was being made to sleep rough in the city that had once held him in high esteem.[50] Fair enough, he thought, as he tried to find a comfortable position on the cobble stones; he hadn't planned to be around for long … what was it Marcus had said? Oh, something or other, but anyway, come first light he was off down the docks to get a boat out of Aquae Sulis to anywhere other than Ynys Prydein because, even if he starved there, at least he'd die hungry but warm.

Just then a drunk came past and tried to wee on him.

Next morning.

Aquae Sulis had a thriving river dockland area. Boats would sail up the Avon with goods from all over the continent. Llew knew that all he had to do was look and he was sure to find one that would take him to the country of his choice. During his time as an apprentice, Llew had paid several visits to the docks for Marcus – usually to ensure that goods the governor had bought made their way to the palace without getting portions of them pocketed by unscrupulous dockhands on the way. This had always been unlikely, which was why Marcus felt able to send his thin boy-apprentice as a security guard. In those days, the place was watched by Roman or Roman-trained soldiers and, in that time of prosperity, most people who worked there were very well off and therefore petty corruption was minimal.

---

[50] It's *just* possible that he was prone to kidding himself.

It was very, very different now. Most of the wonderful portside Llew remembered was gone. Buildings had fallen or been pulled down. There were no soldiers keeping order. There was, however, a number of inns that Llew didn't recognise. These were mainly full of drunken and/or brawling sailors, dockers and prostitutes. The drunken brawls spilled out onto the streets, which were also crowded with *more* sailors and dockers wanting to get drunk and more prostitutes wanting them to do so and thus being able to part them with their hard-earned gold. And there were also refugees, lots and lots of refugees, all trying desperately to get a boat out of Aquae Sulis. It occurred to Llew that, if there were refugees this far west, then the Saxons must not be far behind, which made his need to escape even more pressing. It was bad enough being hunted down by the kings of Ynys Prydein for giving the Saxons a kingdom, but to be hunted down by Hengist as well, for not providing it … well, that could make things difficult.

As it turned out, Llew was wrong. The Saxons were marching, yes, but they were still a long way off. However, the migration of people in the east had started a domino effect amongst the Cymru – a sort of mass hysteria … 'these people from the east say the Saxons are coming, therefore I better go too before they come here'. Llew could see that he was going to have to use all his powers of persuasion to get himself on any, if not the right ship. Asking around, Llew found himself pointed towards an old, rickety wooden hut on the quayside in which there was an even older and more rickety drunk who called himself the harbourmaster. He told Llew the name of a ship currently moored up that was setting sale for Italy the next day. Llew pushed his way through the crowds towards the part of the quay he'd been told the ship was. He had a problem – similar to the one that he'd had at the governor's residence. The Saxons were coming and everyone was trying to get out of the country; therefore, a berth on a ship could be sold to the highest bidder. And, as far as bidding went, Llew could bid with the best of them as long as he didn't go above a certain price. That price was no gold coins at all. As long as no one upped that, he was fine. What he hoped to do was to talk to the captain and persuade him that what every modern ship needed was a scribe. There must be, he thought, a chance. After all, surely every seafaring man would love to have his voyages and heroic deeds graphically described on scrolls of parchment for posterity. Surely! Actually, thought Llew, no he wouldn't, and he realised his only real hope was becoming a stowaway. With a bit of luck he could stay hidden on board a ship for long enough, so that if he was discovered they'd be too far away to turn back. It wasn't a brilliant plan, but it was the best he could think of as he made his way to the gangplank of the large vessel and tried to attract the attention of the bulky and bald moustachioed man guarding it.

'Er … hi … hello. I want to speak to the Captain …'

'What for?'

'I want to talk to him, that's all.'

'What for?'

'I think that's my business.'

'What for?'

Llew looked at the man quizzically. He was obviously a seafarer – eye-patch, weathered windblown face, squint from looking at the sun too often – and, judging by his clothes and the fact that his job was guarding the gangplank, a fairly lowly one at that. However, the fact remained that, lowly or not, he was currently blocking the way and Llew didn't have any money to bribe the man. Therefore, it was time …

'Look, do you always talk like this to the Ship Inspector?'

… for Llew to think on his feet again.

'What?'

'I'm this port's official Ship Inspector and you, Sunshine, are currently obstructing me.'

He thought 'Sunshine' was a nice touch.

'What the hell's a Ship Inspector when he's at home?'

Not nice enough, apparently. He obviously needed a bit more petty officialdom about him to convince the man if this was going to work. He thought of all the petty officials he'd ever come across – and having worked in several government organisations, he'd come across a few … store masters and stable masters and kitchen masters … well, pretty much anything with the word 'master' attached to it, which was ironic really, because how could you be a 'master' if you were also 'petty'? – and tried to think of the one thing they had in common. Then he remembered.

Sarcasm. Ask a store master if he's got any, for example, boots in stock and he'll say 'yeah, it rained boots yesterday' because, if nothing else, stuck in the stores all day, he's got very little to entertain him.

'What's a Ship Inspector? Well, I wonder? Could it be someone who *inspects the ships* to make sure they're seaworthy or is it someone who dances with no clothes on for a living? You tell me.'

The gangplank guard looked uncomfortable.

'I've never heard of a Ship Inspector, that's all!'

'Haven't you? Haven't you indeed? Let me tell you, Sunshine' (again with the 'Sunshine') '… let me tell you that I wouldn't be surprised if it wasn't the only thing you hadn't heard of. In fact, I wouldn't be surprised if there was a great big list of things you hadn't heard of, but let me also add …', and he was quick here because the guard looked as if he might get aggressive, 'that if you don't let me see your Captain, I will be forced to tell my boss that I have been unable to inspect this ship and therefore it may not be seaworthy and *therefore* will not be allowed to sail with the tide this evening. Now, what's your name?'

He knew this wouldn't fail. 'What's your name?' is a far, far more frightening phrase than, say, 'do you know who I am?' or even 'you're under arrest'[51] if used in just the right way, because it shows just the right amount of promise. It says, 'you are beneath me, so you tell me your name and then I can go away and find someone, someone who's also beneath me, but above *you*, someone who will do bad things to you' and it leaves the rest to the imagination.

The man snapped to attention.

'Bryn, sir, able seaman.'

He stepped aside smartly and Llew officiously walk passed him.

'And where's the Captain, *Bryn*?'

'In his cabin on the stern.'

Good, thought Llew, then I'm going to the bow. Actually, I'm going to go below the deck, *then* I'm going to the bow. And then I'm going to get amongst the stores and I'm going to cover myself with some sheeting or something and I'm going to get some sleep. By the time I wake up, this thing should be in the Severn estuary, then we'll be a couple of days at sea and *then* I don't care what anybody says, I'm a Roman.

That was the plan anyway.

Sure enough, he managed to sneak past various crew members and get into the ship's hold, which was, as he had guessed, full of all sorts of goods – barrels, sacks, wooden chests – ready for shipping back to the continent. At the far end were piles of fabric ... blankets, he thought, weaved by the women of Elmet, taken by cart to Aquae Sulis, then to be sailed up the Avon, down the Severn sea and into the ocean ... and then wherever ... Italy in this case. With modern transport, he mused, the world had become a very small place indeed. He lay down, covered himself with blankets and waited, the gentle rocking of the ship sending him very slowly off to sleep ...

All too easy, he might have said afterwards. All too easy.

When he woke up, the ship was heaving to and fro and he could hear the shouting of ship's officers and the singing of sailors as they went about the business of managing a ship in choppy waters. He didn't know how long he'd been asleep, but he realised he must have done it! They must now be at sea! All he had to do was lie where he was and soon enough it would be 'Rome, here we come'.

Then something at the edge of his perception started annoying him. Something in the general swim of things was not quite right – like the beginnings of a sort of mental cold sore. He tried to think what it was. Ah, that was it! When he'd seen or even been on ships before, ship's officers usually shouted at each other things like 'Haul the main sail, Mr Bosun!' Or 'steady as she goes, Mr Fo'castle!'; they did not shout 'well, where is he then,

---

[51] Although obviously not as frightening as 'I'm going to stab you' or 'ready aim fire'.

you stupid little git?' And sailors sang sea shanties about Neptune and Davy Jones' locker. They didn't just go 'ow! oww! owww!'; and there was usually more than one of them.

'All right, search the hold. When you find him, throw him over the side.'

'Aye aye, sir.'

Llew had this horrible feeling they might just … might *just* be talking about him. And if they were far out at sea … well, being thrown over the side might not be a terribly good thing. He peeped out from under his blanket. There was a bang as the hatch above him was thrown open and a pair of stout sea boots attached to stout sea legs and an able body descended the ladder into the hold. It was followed by several bodies of similar stout and ableness, one of which belonged to the enraged and now battered face of Bryn.

The sailors spread out and started poking among the goods in the hold. What they were poking with was short but extremely pointy swords and they weren't poking gently either. And Bryn was now getting closer to Llew's end of the boat. Well figured, Llew, he'll have to be a bit gentler when he comes to the fabric. He won't want to tear it, will he? It's valuable after all …

Rrrrrrrrrrrrrrrip!

On the other hand, thought Llew, he's not exactly the brightest star in the mariners' sky. He decided to take his chances with the briny blue, just as Bryn narrowly missed slicing off his ear. As soon as Bryn had withdrawn the dagger from the folds of fabric covering the scribe, Llew leapt up with his hands raised.

'All right, I surrender! But I demand to speak to the Captain!'

Llew was hauled up on deck, but not before he'd been given a damn good kicking by Bryn and his fellow crew members. Llew tried bravely to fend off the blows by keeping the scroll sack clutched firmly to his head. It was only when he'd been able to stand up that he discovered the second disappointment of the day.

They were still in the river, barely a mile away from Aqua Sulis. He could see the town in the distance. He must have been asleep for all of … three minutes … just enough time for the ship to push off, he supposed. The captain, no less rough-looking than the seamen currently manhandling him, but wearing slightly better-tailored clothes, was staring at him coldly as Llew launched into what he knew was going to be the most imaginative defence of his life.

'Yes, sir, I am but a humble stowaway. However, by trade I am a scribe. See? Here are all my adventures on parchment. Here I am immortalised in print. And for you too, the same could be true. With my pens and parchment I could tell your story. I could immortalise a great sea captain such as yourself. I could tell of your adventures for the great and the good to read. Soon all the world will have read the story of the great captain …?'

He looked hopefully at the captain, indicating that he should tell Llew his name.

'Fflib,' said the captain, his look daring Llew to make something of it ...

'Oookay ...,' said Llew, carefully, 'the exciting and fantastic adventures of Captain Fflib! I like it! It's catchy!'

The captain sighed, shaking his head.

'Throw this tosser off my ship. Over the side. Now.'

Llew was led protesting over to the side of the boat. He was hurled head-first, still clutching his bag. He closed his eyes and waited to feel the cold water envelope him. He wondered how far they were from shore and how deep the water was. He could be in for a long swim.

Clunk!

'Ow!'

Surely water wasn't meant to sound or indeed feel this hard and, well ... wooden. He opened his eyes and looked around him. He was on the deck of a ship. *Another* ship. He could see the one he'd just been on sailing off up river, away into the distance. They must have thrown him over the side onto a passing ship.

A passing ship that was going back to Aquae Sulis. Ye Gods, would he never get off this confounded island?[52] He realised he was being watched by several curious sailors. Well-dressed sailors.

'Er, hello?' said Llew.

One of the sailors came up and spoke to him.

'Looks like you were saved a soaking ...,' said the sailor, grinning.

And all Llew could do was gawp, because the sailor was speaking a language he hadn't heard for a good long while.

Latin.

'Come on,' said the sailor, 'we better take you to see the general.'

'They call me Aurelius Ambrosius,' said the Roman, 'and you are ...?'

Llew had been forced to his knees. However, as the floor of the luxurious cabin was carpeted and he'd been given a cushion to kneel on, this wasn't too bad. The Roman in front of him, currently striding around and eating bunches of grapes in one go, was really, **really** handsome. He was tall, crew-cut blond and square jawed, with dark brown eyes. He wore his Roman uniform well and had one of those gravelly, but well-bred voices that people usually associate with the words 'action' and 'man'. Llew swallowed.

'My name is Llewelyn Ap Gwyddno,' said Llew, swallowing. He was in awe of this man, before he'd even met him. Ambrosius *had* something ... charisma, maybe ... what ever it was, he had it in spades.

'I am a scribe ...,' he added.

'And you speak Latin well,' said Ambrosius seriously.

To his great surprise, Llew found he was blushing with pleasure.

---

[52] No.

'Llewelyn ap Gwyddno …,' repeated Ambrosius to himself softly, 'why does that name ring a bell?'

He appeared to think for a moment and then he barked, 'got it'!

He strode over to Llew and picked him bodily up by the shoulders.

'You're Marcus's protégé. The one he left up with that old madman Vortigern! Well, well! Still alive, eh? And of all the ships on the Avon you have to land on mine. That has to be a sign! You, my young friend, are manna from heaven.'

Llew was staring at him, wide-eyed.

'You know Marcus?'

'Course I know Marcus!' Ambrosius bellowed in reply. 'Chief advisor to Consul Aetius! Got that funny little assistant. From round here somewhere, actually. Cuneglas, is it?'

Yes, thought Llew bitterly, it would be Cuneglas.

'Marcus speaks of you often!' said Ambrosius.

He dropped Llew, who fell to the floor as gracefully as he could, and strode over to a chair which he sat down on.

'He ever talked about sending for me?' ventured Llew hopefully. 'In Rome?' he added, even more so.

'No.' Ambrosius shook his head.

'Oh. Only I'd quite like to go to Rome and if … you were going back that way … maybe you could give me a lift?'

'Oh, I'd love to,' said Marcus, 'but I'm here for the duration. The emperor has sent me to lead your armies and I'll only go back to Rome when the Saxons are defeated or I'm dead. But,' he added, 'I could really do with a good scribe and translator. How would you like the job?'

Llew could tell that, for the time being at least, it would be churlish to say no.

It will come as no surprise to learn that Ambrosius was a roll-your-sleeves-up-and-get-things-done kind of person. The Roman boat had barely moored up at the harbour before Ambrosius was out on the quayside ordering people about, telling them to unload, fetch, carry, find him accommodation, get him an audience with one of the local Cymru chiefs and so on. And the weird thing was that no one seemed to mind. Even the most surly dockhand could be brought to attention, saluting when Ambrosius barked an order, and sent away glowing with pleasure. People really liked doing things for him, Llew noticed. *He* liked doing things for him – which was pretty damn unusual for Llew.

The first thing Ambrosius did was take over the governor's palace. It was full of warriors anyway – all belonging to some absent Cymru chieftain. Ambrosius addressed their captains in the building's main hall with a rousing, stirring speech (translated by Llew) at which they all cheered heartily and, as a result, within hours of arriving, Ambrosius had a small standing army awaiting his command.

It was extremely strange for Llew to be back in the palace after so long. It was, of course, filled with so many pleasant memories ... over here was where he'd pretended to sweep ... over there was where he'd curled up all lovely and warm. However, they weren't comforting, these memories – this was a place that was his home no longer – and they came back to him as melancholy ghosts might, beseeching him impotently to recreate a time that once was and never would be again. Besides, the hypocaust had long since fallen into disrepair and the place was ... actually, it was a bit too draughty for Llew's liking.

Llew barely had time to formulate a plan of what to do next. Ambrosius had kept Llew by his side from the moment they had stepped ashore. He'd already negotiated Llew's pay and conditions, which were, Llew felt, very fair indeed.

Okay, thought Llew, I can't get abroad without any money and this guy is offering gold for me to help him. I may as well stick around for a while ... just until I'm a bit richer ... then I can pay my way out this place. He mused that there was still the Bruenor problem, but Llew had the feeling that he was about to be less of a priority for the Kentish king. Besides, Llew now seemed to have the protection of Ambrosius.

Of course, there was the war. It'd be good to be away before that really kicked off.

One of the first things Ambrosius had done once he'd amassed a few troops was to assess the situation militarily. What he found out was that the Saxons had risen up and started pushing hard against Bruenor's forces in Gwyrangon. These forces – badly led and under-equipped – were easily defeated and Bruenor had fled alone into the kingdom of Gwent. The Saxons had now gathered at the River Medway, which meant they threatened Londonium and they looked like taking it too. As soon as they heard Hengist was coming, most of the populace of that fair city had headed west, which was why the roads were so crowded now.

'What I need, boy,' said Ambrosius, pacing agitatedly in the palace's main hall, 'is just enough men to hold them back. If I can spearhead an attack into the centre of Hengist's army and hit him hard enough ...'

And he punched his left palm with his right fist for emphasis.

'... then he won't dare come any further west. Not this year anyway. And then maybe ... just maybe we can get the kings of the Godforsaken island together *just* long enough to push 'em back into the sea altogether!'

It was, however, going to prove to be a problem. Most of the kings had decided that, as they were almost certainly going to lose their lands to the Saxons anyway, they might as well start fights with each other. It was a strange logic, but it was *their* logic. The most fashionable civil war going on at present was the one between King Ynyr of Gwent and former King Bruenor, in which Ynyr was trying to get back his throne after leaving it with

Bruenor for five minutes. He'd left it, taking his army to rise against Vortigern Britu's army in Llangollen – something Bruenor had persuaded him to do in the first place. Ynyr wasn't the only king persuaded to do this. Everyone seemed to want a piece of this action. To get in on the ground floor, so to speak. And what none of the British kings seemed to have noticed was that there was a large Saxon army creeping up behind them.

Ambrosius spent his first few weeks in Aquae Sulis sending out messages to as many kings as he could think of, imploring them to send men, as many or as few as they could spare, to Aquae Sulis and thence to the Saxon border, where it was known that Hengist and Horsa were amassing their armies at a place called Egelesprep. One push and they would almost certainly take Londinium, which would mean they controlled the rivers Medway and Thames, plus the trade routes that went with them. However, most of the kings either didn't hear or pretended not to hear Ambrosius's pleas, and no reply came.

Llew, meanwhile, got used to sleeping with a roof over his head again and having breakfast regularly. He would, he reflected, be quite happy to stay in Ambrosius' headquarters for as long as it took. He was amassing quite a pile of gold for himself as well.

This was why it was a bit of a blow to wake up one morning to find that breakfast was going to take the form of a packed one on horseback. Llew was heading back inland with Ambrosius and such forces as he'd managed to gather so far.

'But ... what about the other kings? Shouldn't we wait for them?' he tried to say breathlessly as they rode at speed through the western plains.

'There is no time!' shouted Ambrosius, plainly enjoying being in the saddle after weeks cooped up in the palace, 'If the other kings would join us, so be it! If not, we die defending Ynys Prydein!'

Llew swore quietly under his breath.

Chapter 12 – Egelesprep

It was a small town on the River Medway. 'Was' being the most important word here, because now it had acquired that 'burning ruin' feel to it and, if any of the populace were still alive, it was quite likely they were contemplating a career in servitude (without pay) to their new Germanic masters. At the river, the Saxon army had stopped. More than an army, in fact – this was a horde, which meant it carried with it women, children, slaves, farmers, artisans, craftsmen, bards, druids, scribes, cooks, prostitutes, accountants, general-hangers-on[53] ... every level of Saxon society.[54] This was a currently mobile civilisation looking for somewhere to set down and form.

Llew looked down from the hilltop at the hundreds of Saxon campfires, spread out over the valley in the winter half-light. He imagined the warmth of those fires and almost wished he was down there because, lying on the damp grass verge as he was now, made him sure he was going to catch some sort of pneumonia. He could be sitting by one of his own army's campfires right now, but Ambrosius had sent him to do a little reconnaissance and he wasn't about to disobey the Old Man's orders.

'Old Man's orders'? Yes, he was thinking like that. Like a loyal ... well, not soldier, but underling, certainly. It felt strange, not just because Llew had never really felt loyalty to anyone but himself, but also because Ambrosius was, for a general at least, quite young. And yet that was how everyone in the Cymru army referred to him (when he wasn't present). 'Can you go up to the main tent? The Old Man wants a word?' someone might say, or 'what's the Old Man planning now?', or 'you try that one in front of the Old Man – see how far it gets you'. It was a sort of grudging term of respect, a nickname picked out for a person who didn't have nicknames by people who didn't use them. It was ... a soldier's term of affection. And they did hold him in their highest esteem, the warriors (as did Llew). Ambrosius did everything right. Even when it was *wrong* it was right. His clumsy attempts, for instance, to speak to the men in their own language rather than his native Latin could, if

---

[53] No particular order here.

[54] If there'd been such things as Advertising Salesmen, they'd have been around too, but one of the very few advantages of living in the period known as the Dark Ages is that, as far as we know, there wasn't.

attempted by some other leader, have seemed condescending. Not the way Ambrosius did it. He made it seem as if he was trying to *understand* the way they thought, even if he did send waves of saliva over anyone he was having a conversation with in his attempts to master the throated, phlegm-dominated Celtic dialect. Or his insistence on marching like the foot soldiers rather than riding like the chieftains, even though everyone kept having to stop so he could catch up. Then there was his ability to know when to encourage, when to cajole, when to bully. And his ability to be a friend when necessary.

That, Llew realised, was it! Ambrosius was a friend to every single man in that army.

Unless he had to execute them for desertion, or spying. Obviously.

And there had been instances of these on the journey from Aquae Sulis. A man had been caught riding away from the marching army at speed and when his animal had been searched there'd been several sacks containing Saxon gold. The man had vehemently protested his innocence, coming up with a story about inheriting the money from his grandfather who'd had some Saxon in him from his mother's side … it was a story he stuck to even under torture. And then Ambrosius had come and spoken quietly to him. The man had burst into tears and had confessed – to his eternal shame – that yes, he was in the pay of Hengist and his job had been to inform the Saxon king of Cymru troop movements as they approached the Saxon border. Ambrosius had given the man a kindly smile and a comforting pat on the shoulder. The man had sniffed and smiled, obviously feeling better, and never intending to do such a terrible thing again, which turned out to be exactly the case, because it was at this point that Ambrosius grabbed an axe and cut his head off. Personally mind, personally. No delegating to some poor so-and-so who might have been the traitor's mate. Oh no, the Old Man did his own dirty work.

And, as a result, everyone respected him. He'd done what had to be done – tough job though it was – and moved on.

Consequently, the army that had headed southeast was a fiercely loyal one. An army ready to follow its leader into death. Good thing really, because the size of the Saxon army made death pretty much a certainty. Yes, word of Ambrosius's gallant march to save Londinium had spread throughout the Island of the Mighty and several kings with (perhaps more importantly) their armies had joined the march on the way, but there were nowhere near enough men. Not as far as Llew could see right now anyway. The valley below him was completely filled with armed men. Armed Saxon warriors as far as the eye could see.[55] This, he thought, does not bode well.

Llew made his way back to the Cymru encampment, which was in a valley

---

[55] 'And who *was* the genius who invited them all here, I wonder?' said a smart-arsed little voice inside his head.

a few miles off. The first thing he did was go to Ambrosius's tent, partly because he wanted to report to his commander, but also because he knew there'd be food and a fire there. Ambrosius's guards recognised him and let him past without a comment, and he strode in, almost cockily. It was a strange feeling to be amongst such men and not feel ... well, that you were in immediate danger of having something lopped off. It was like when he had pretended to be a warrior back in Londinium. Llew realised he'd developed a sort of 'tough guy' swagger.

He quite liked it.

However, the swagger was about to be his undoing because, had he not been using it, he might have tiptoed into the tent, seen who was there with Ambrosius and tiptoed straight out again. Unfortunately, tough guys don't tiptoe. There was someone familiar conversing with Ambrosius at his table. Llew could only see the stranger from the back, but he should have recognised the black leather armour and the hair shaved close to the skull. He should have recognised the voice too.

'... I have no longer a kingdom of my own and my army is all but wiped off the face of the earth. Yet I would serve you, my Lord Ambrosius.'

'That's very noble of you, my Lord Bruenor.'

Oh ... crap.

By this point, though, Llew was in mid-swagger right into the centre of the tent. He was about to turn round and go straight out again when he was seen by Ambrosius.

'Ah, Llewellyn, come in, come in. No, don't dither in the half-light, man, come to the table! I'd like you to meet Lord Bruenor, who I believe is the former king of ...?'

'Gwyrangon,' said Bruenor darkly, 'as Llewellyn ap Gwyddno knows well.'

Ambrosius looked surprised.

'Oh?' he said, 'Have you two already met?'

Bruenor wheeled round, knocking the table over as he drew his thin-bladed sword and made to run the scribe through, the point aimed directly at Llew's heart. Luckily, the guards were on the ball and had made a 'V' shape with their weapons protecting Llew so that Bruenor's sword slid on them upwards slicing rather too close to Llew's nose. In the same instant, Ambrosius, in his usual dashing fashion, somersaulted over to them head first, drawing a dagger as he did so, landing on his feet and placing the dagger exactly at Bruenor's throat. Llew would have been impressed if he weren't currently concentrating on the need to go to the toilet.

'Now, what the blazes is going on, Gods damn it?!'

Ambrosius' turn of phrase, if a little melodramatic, was succinct. So Bruenor told him. The whole story. And, as all history is, it was a slightly biased account. In it, Llew was described as … well, many things, the most flattering of which was 'an odious treacherous reptile' who'd let a brave warrior die (Edwyn) and then who'd sold Bruenor's land to the Saxons out of pure malevolence. *Then* he'd had the temerity to come up to the Council of the Kings and boast about it! What was more, he'd brought some sort of weird priest with him – definitely not allied to the Church of Rome this one – who'd turned the Vortigern Britu 'a bit funny'. And as a result of *that*, the overlord wouldn't fight properly any more!

And look at what had happened! These Saxon traitors, far from volunteering the promised army to fight the Picts in the North or the Irish in the West, had risen up and started marching against the Cymru! And what was more (here Bruenor pointed at Llew), it was all *his* fault!

Ambrosius took this and nodded sagely.

'Well,' he said to Llew gruffly, 'is this true, boy?'

Llew found himself torn between his two selves. His older, more cynical, but-very-good-at-thinking-on-his-feet self was desperately trying to come up with a way of contorting the story so that yes, he'd be in trouble **but** his punishment would be that he was banished to the first ship heading for Rome. His newer, improved, dewey-eyed-recruit-looking-for-a-father-figure-in-his-commanding-officer self, on the other, had wanted to tell the truth even if, in fact, he ended up in front of an executioner because he knew this sort of upright behaviour would gain Ambrosius's approval.

In fact, it was the latter, the New Llew, which took over.

'Yes, My Lord,' he said stoically, 'yes, it was insane … a moment of madness, but you see, I had a dream.' His voice started to rise. 'I had a dream where there was no war or hatred. I had a dream where little Saxon children could walk hand in hand with little Cymru children down any street in any city or settlement in the whole of this island! Our island! Ynys Prydein – Island of the Mighty! A dream of peace! And the only way, the **only** way to make that dream come true was to **give** something. Give a little of **us**. And then maybe they would trust us! Yes! Yes we could have just attacked them for what they'd done to us in the past, but if you have an eye for an eye and a tooth for a tooth, then soon the whole world is blind and toothless!!!'

He realised he was shouting now, like Nascien when preaching on a street corner. Everyone in the tent was looking at him, astounded. He could see that New Llew was someone he was going to have to keep a tightish rein on.

'Mmm,' said Ambrosius.

Then the Roman turned to his two bodyguards.

'Swords down, lads.'

The two men sheathed their swords and stood back to attention. Bruenor stood there with his thin-bladed pig-sticking thing naked and ready for use.

'Bruenor, this man is my scribe and my translator.' Ambrosius' tone was brisk and business-like. 'He has certainly made some grievous mistakes as far as you are concerned and you are entitled to kill him. If I were in your shoes, I would probably do just that. I offer him no protection …'

Oh … crap, thought Llew.

'… except this. If you do kill him, you will earn my undying enmity …'

Bruenor looked at Ambrosius, nodded very slightly, then sheathed his sword. Ambrosius nodded back.

'You shall be next to me in the battle line, Bruenor Of – … *formerly* of Gwyrangon'; then he barked to his guards, 'find the former king some quarters. Now!'

Ambrosius turned to look at Llew, who felt more than a little sheepish.

'Not a good move, old lad, not a good move,' said Ambrosius. 'Now, let's have that report of yours, shall we? How many Saxons would you say there are in Egelesprep?'

Over the coming days, Llew came to feel less sheepish and more … well, *resentful*. He found that, once he'd given his report, he'd been perfunctorily dismissed and only been called on for translation duties (not so often either, because these days Ambrosius, although not skilled at languages, was especially keen) and the odd occasion when Llew might be required to write things down. Again, this was rare, and Llew resented it bitterly. Especially as the General's new Pal Of Choice was now Bruenor, who seemed to be accompanying Ambrosius wherever he went.

Llew, of course, wasted no time in adding to the travelling parchment store that had come with them in one of the wagons (several sacks-worth now) by writing these events down in the form of a diary. It has to be said, some of it got quite vindictive. He particularly resented Bruenor – why was that over-shaved … upstart always allowed in Ambrosius's company? It wasn't as if he'd done anything brave. He'd been made king and then he'd run away from the Saxons as fast as possible. Llew had faced them down. Llew had walked right into the centre of Hengist's camp once and yet, because Bruenor wandered about with black leather armour and a cool haircut and a fancy sword – which, let's face it, was a girl's sword anyway – Ambrosius had practically made him Second In Command!

Every scroll was stuffed in the new and additional sacks that he'd had made.

By the time the Cymru army had amassed properly, ready to start the final march towards Egelesprep, the bitterness had become a nicely simmering cauldron of bile. A kind of madness had overtaken him. Perhaps it was the effect of all the testosterone and male camaraderie around him. Tales of great warriors being told around campfires at night making him wish he was one, or had been one, surviving through strength and skill rather than just dumb luck. It was all very well being lucky like he was, but what about respect? A man had to have respect, or he was ... well, he was nothing. Those men around him respected each other and they respected the Old Man and the Old Man respected the warriors, but what about Llew? Where did he stand? All right, he wasn't a warrior – he'd never trained as one, anyway – but he did have a sword ... rusty as it was ... and he didn't see why the man he was now referring to as 'that big fake' should be in the battle line next to Ambrosius! He resolved to do something about it. He'd got gold. There was a man on an ox cart travelling with them that sold military supplies – weapons, armour, helmets and whatnot.

He was going to get himself kitted out.

Next day.

Yet *another* New Llew was seen wandering round the camp. This Llew was wearing black leather armour and a sword (the old rusty one that Merlin had made him keep) and had a wooden shield slung over his back.

Llew The Warrior. It sounded good, although he was, in truth, having a great deal of trouble standing up. Leather surely wasn't meant to be this heavy! It couldn't have been this heavy when it was on the *cow*. However, he was getting a few admiring looks from the other warriors. He thought they were admiring looks anyway. Certainly they were smiling. And anyway, what was he *supposed* to spend his money on? He didn't drink – not very much – he had no family ... there was no wife on the horizon ... he'd tried talking to some of the women who followed the army around (and some of *them* had indicated they'd happily take his money), but none of them seemed very keen on the whole marriage front. Besides, he was a bit young for all that. He was at the prime of his life! Time to roister![56] Time to sew some wild oats![57] Time to ... spend huge sums of money on a load of war gear that didn't fit and was too heavy to move in properly.

There was a girl, actually. Well, sort of. Her name was Ceridwen and she was a bit different from the other camp followers. For a start, she didn't laugh at him. They'd had some quite interesting conversations together about ... actually, about the fascination of writing things down, mainly. In one of these conversations she'd said she was very keen to learn to read and he'd said he'd teach her one day, but then she'd had to go because some soldier was calling her and had her money, apparently. Was it 'her' money she'd said or just *some* money?

She was quite pretty in a way.

'Llew? Is that you?'

With some effort, Llew managed to turn round. His new steel helmet slipped over his eyes and he had to push it back to see the speaker.

---

[56] Whatever that is.
[57] See above.

'Oh,' he said awkwardly, 'hello, Dad.'

Gwyddno was now very grey. Grey of moustache and beard, that is, because there wasn't very much hair on the top of his head to be able to tell either way. Like Llew, he was dressed for battle, but his gear looked used, which, of course, in its time, it had been.

'I thought it was you. What you dressed up like that for?' said Gwyddno, apparently puzzled.

I'm fine thanks, thought Llew tersely, but he decided not to say it. Last time he'd seen his father was ... well, when there'd been that bit of awkwardness over at Llangollen and he was – thinking about it – probably rather lucky his father was speaking to him.

'Well, I'm ... going to take my place in the battle line, of course.'

'Oh. Nice,' said Gwyddno with his usual air of I-don't-really-know-what-to-say-to-that.

There was an awkward pause.

'What brings you here?' Llew asked finally, giving up the idea that Gwyddno might actually be the one to lead the conversation.

'The battle, of course!' said Gwyddno, sounding vaguely offended. 'Got to keep the clan's end up. To save Prydein, like. From the Saxons,' he added, as if talking to an idiot.

Llew could have mentioned that the clan didn't really exist any more – there was time too, because they were on another lengthy and awkward pause – but he didn't.

'How's ... Mam?'

'Fine.'

'Evan, Daffyd and Culhwch?'

'Fine.'

'Gwen and Sian?'

'Fine.'

'That's good then.'

Indeed it was. Considering the mortality rate at the time, having your whole family survive into adulthood was a bloody *miracle*! Llew could have said so. But somehow it became yet another comment that didn't seem worth adding.

'Right ... well ... I'd better be getting on then,' said Gwyddno after another awkward pause. 'I'm in a tent on the edge of the encampment if you fancy popping over for a chinwag some time.'

'Popping over for a chinwag'? – that's a laugh, thought Llew; his chin would not be so much wagging as staying stock still: 'popping over for a chin*still*'[58] more like! Then something else occurred to him as his father turned and started to walk away.

---

[58] There is, of course, no such word.

'If we both survive, of course!'

Gwyddno turned back, looking puzzled.

'How d'you mean?'

'Well, the battle? It's supposed to be this afternoon, isn't it?'

Gwyddno nodded, unperturbed, as if he hadn't thought of that, turned again and started walking away.

'Point,' he said.

Ceridwen lived in an ox-drawn wagon that she shared with three other women who were also known as 'camp followers', which was a gentle euphemism for 'Working Girls', which was a not-so-gentle euphemism for 'prostitutes'. She was from Ireland originally, but had been taken as a slave by British raiders[59] when she was a child. From then on it had been downhill really, culminating in her current profession (which, basically, meant a lot of travelling because you had to go where the work was and the trouble with wars is that they're never always in the one place). Thus it was very strange that, in spite of all, she retained the sunniest of dispositions and a rapier-like wit. If rapiers had been around then and they weren't, obviously.

'Hello, Llew,' she said brightly. 'Ooh, you look *nice!*'

She was admiring his new 'look'.

'Thanks,' he said simply and trying not to go red.

Llew had never tried to engage Ceridwen *professionally*, so to speak. He had far too much respect for her and he was also too embarrassed to ask how much. So what had happened was that they had become sort of friends. This was much better than the 'I-Can't-Live-Without-You' poetry writing way he'd sort of felt about Megan, which still made him cringe when ever he thought about it.

'What's it for?' she said.

'What?'

'Did you borrow it? The armour, I mean.'

'No, it's for going into battle,' he said, looking puzzled.

Of course it was for going into battle! Why else would anyone spend his hard-earned cash on this stuff?

'You're not serious!' she said, and then the look he gave her made her realise that he was, so she made her voice sound a little kinder. 'Llew … Llew … lovey … I mean … you can't! You'll get killed!'

Llew attempted to look rugged.

'If it be so, then let it be so. For I will have fallen at my captain's side!'

'Why are you talking so funny?' she asked, perplexed; then she said, 'Wait a minute! Your "captain"? You don't mean Ambrosius?'

She was the only one in the whole camp who didn't refer to him as The Old Man. However, Llew did mean Ambrosius, and he said so. She shook her head worriedly.

---

[59] Oh yes. People forget that it happened the other way round. The Dark Ages wasn't all Good Guys Bad Guys you know!

'This is because he likes Bruenor better than you, isn't it?'

He'd told her all his innermost thoughts – something some men are prone to do with prostitutes, but usually *after* they've had sex with them.

'No. *No. **No!*** Pause. 'Oh, all right ... a bit. But why shouldn't I want a bit of respect? I've been through lots, I have! Just 'cause I don't have a thin sword and a nice haircut ... just because of my humble origins ... the Old Man thinks I'm nothing.'

'And because you let the Saxons in,' she added.

'Oh, yeah. You had to bring *that* up,' he said, miffed. 'Everybody always has to bring *that* up.'

She took both of his hands and sat him down on the step of the ox cart.

'Llew,' she said, looking directly into his eyes, earnestly – something he rather liked, especially when her face was as close to his as it was now. 'Llew, you've never seen a battle. I have. And I've also seen men like Ambrosius before. They're always very good at saying things like "well done that man" to people who don't get a lot of well dones in their lives. They're also very good at shouting things like "charge!!" or "attack!!" And after they have, you can bet your last chicken[60] that they're going to be one of the few at the end of the whole business looking sombre and saying "what a tragedy" and "how sickening is this business called war" and "when will it all end?", but you know what? They'll be back for the next battle and they'll have a whole load of *new* young men to say "well done that man" to! You get my meaning?'

This was, thinking about it, a highly articulate outburst.

'What's all this got to do with me?' said Llew, puzzled and not that day being too smart on the uptake.

Ceridwen sighed, and let go of his hands.

'One of the reasons I liked you more than the rest of the rabble round here is that you're a survivor, but if you're just going to go off and get killed like they are ... well, I guess I'd better find myself another project.'

Llew was too insulted to take in what Ceridwen was actually saying to him. The words that should have permeated were 'I liked you more than the rest of the rabble'; instead, the male ego being what it is, the words that *did* permeate were 'go off and get killed like they are'.

'Yeah, well, maybe I'm *not* going to get killed! Ever thought of that? I might see you afterwards!'

And in as unhuffy a manner as he could possibly manage ' which was, in fact, *tremendously* huffy ' he turned and walked off, or tried to walk off without falling over in his new outfit.

---

[60] Ceridwen liked to be paid in livestock. Gold had to be transported and could be stolen. Whereas, with a sheep or a pig, if the army was on the move, *it* could walk and if it got fed up with walking, you could eat it. And if someone tried to steal it, there was always the chance it would bite.

He was going to see the Old Man to find out where his place was to be in the battle line.

'Your place?'
'Yes, sire.'
'In the battle line?'
'Yes, sire.'
'Your place in the battle line?'
'Yes, sire.'
'Let me get this straight, you want me to tell you where you will be standing in the battle line?'
'*Yes*, sire!'

This was not going how Llew had hoped. He knew it had probably been too much to expect 'come to my arms, good Scribe, for if every man is as brave as you we will indeed win the day! You shall be by my side and if we fall together t'will have been mine honour to have served thus with you!!' On the other hand, it might have been nice to get 'well, do you think you could squeeze into the mass of foot soldiers on the left flank?' But no, all he was getting from Ambrosius, currently poring over battle plans in his tent, was very, very, blank looks.

'Old lad, are you under the impression you're going to … *fight*?'

Llew was now becoming aware that one of the guards in the tent appeared to be developing a smirk that was threatening to evolve into a snigger.

'Why not?' he said, trying not to go red for the second time that day.

'Because, my young friend, you are not a warrior,' said Ambrosius as kindly as he could, 'and no amount of new armour is going to change that!'

Llew found he was trying to blink back tears of humiliation.

'I thought we were badly outnumbered! I thought you could use every man you could get!'

'Llewellyn, have you ever fought in a battle in your life?' asked Ambrosius patiently.

'No, but I've run away from a few!' stated Llew, and immediately regretted it.

'Well, then …'

Ambrosius turned away and signalled to one of his servants for help donning his own armour, which lay on the floor. There wasn't much of it – silver roman breastplate, silver helmet, red plume, a short sword.

'People on a battlefield who don't know what they're doing are going to be more hindrance than help. So I'm sorry, Llew, you can stay on the hill and watch the show from there. There is no place for you in the battle line.'

To be fair, Ambrosius was being fantastically kind to Llew. In about an hour's time he was to be leading thousands of Cymru warriors into the biggest fight on these shores in living memory. His forces were badly outnumbered and many of them appeared to be elderly men, who hadn't fought since the days when animal skins and wooden clubs had been at the cutting edge of technology. Only this morning a load of grey, balding old veterans had arrived from some obscure Silurian clan and although, yes, you had to admit they might be quite good (you don't get to *be* a veteran without surviving a bit of action) it was just as likely he'd be shouting at them 'go left! ... no, **left** ... no, **LEFT ... <u>LEFT!!!</u>** ... before the Saxons take that hill ... **I said before the Saxons take** – ... oh, never mind!' Therefore, to try and be kind to the puny Scribe who'd decided he was suddenly going to be a Mark Antony or a Bran The Blessed[61] when really he should have been shouting 'get the bloody hell out of my tent! I haven't got time for this!' However, this last thing he didn't have to say because, as he turned round from having his breastplate buckled on, he realised that Llew had gone anyway.

Llew was now storming through the encampment, furious! How dare he! How dare that jumped-up nobody ... *Roman* try and stop him from being brave! Llew had spent all his life running away and the one time he'd decided to face the thing full on the man he most admired in all the world, even if he was a jumped-up nobody Roman, was trying to prevent him! Well, he'd see about that. In fact, he'd make *them* see about it! They couldn't stop him turning up at the battle, could they? It wasn't like it was a ticket-only affair. It wasn't going to be fenced-off with large men guarding the gate in ill-fitting jerkins saying 'sorry, mate, you ain't getting in to this battle! Not with that armour on. And that sword? It's casual! How old are you, anyway?'

All he had to do was go and join the throng of the other troops as they marched towards the battlefield and then, if he so desired, he could squeeze his way through to the front, right next to Ambrosius' horse. With his oversized helmet on, they probably wouldn't recognise him anyway. Then they'd see who was warrior material or not. He went back to his tent to write this all down. If he didn't survive, they'd all know why.

The site of the battlefield agreed on by both sides through intermediaries was a valley just on the Cymru side of the river. From dawn onwards, the soldiers had started arriving, taking up position. Llew's first view of the battlefield was as he, with many of his countrymen, came to the top of the hill that only a few days ago he'd been using as a vantage point to spy on the Saxon troops. Now, as he came to the summit of the hill, he saw both armies amassing.

He gasped. He had no choice. The sight was totally overwhelming. He'd never seen so many people in all his life! It was like looking at two huge, shapeless creatures, grey-brown and scaly, with a sea of green turf between

---

[61] A legendary Cymru warrior king.

them. And the noise … men chanting war songs, pipes playing, drums banging, horses screaming, the scraping of steel, dogs barking, officers shouting incomprehensible orders at one another. A pure cacophony without any apparent logic to it; yet, if you concentrated hard and long enough, there was a sort of pounding, a rhythm, driving the armies forward in a strange, hypnotic harmony, that was almost … stirring. Perhaps this was what made men brave in battle.

As Llew got down the hill, he and the other men moving with him added themselves to the throng of the British side, pushing and shoving, becoming a part of one of the two rippling monsters. Others, many others, fell in behind him, making the monster ever larger. Llew, however, had noticed from the top of the hill that the rippling monster on the Saxon's side was dwarfing the British one. Two dragons, he thought, remembering the boy Merlin's prophesy all those years ago.

He realised that he'd completely underestimated the number of men there would be. He was sure there hadn't been this many at the camp. He couldn't even see where Ambrosius *was*, let alone get to him. There were a few horses and riders just off on the edge of his vision, but they could have been anyone. One of them was carrying a cloth banner on a wooden pole, but the standard just looked like a red and blue blob to Llew. He was having trouble seeing anything other than the backs of the men immediately in front of him. They were taller than him for a start, plus his helmet kept slipping down in front of his eyes. Then there was the problem of staying upright – the fact that the crowd was continually pushing back and forward as crowds are wont to do, coupled with the fact that Llew was wearing armour too heavy and too big for him, with the additional problem that, after a couple of hundred thousand soldiers swarm over damp grassland, it becomes a deep quagmire, meant Llew was basically concentrating on keeping his balance.

He wanted to shout 'keep still, for goodness sake! With all these pointed weapons around, all you need is one slip up and you'll have someone's eye out' … but he felt it would not go down well with the other warriors assembled close by him and no one else would be able to hear anyway.

Still, amongst the crush of men, it was at least quite warm – that was something.

Far away to his left, he could see some ox-drawn wagons assembling on the top of the hill. He assumed that Ceridwen would be on one of them, there to watch the day's 'entertainment', along with all the camp followers and non-combatants. They really needed a scribe up there too, obviously, he thought to himself. Because a scribe could look down and have a brilliant view of the battle, after which he could write it all down and, for years to come, people would know exactly what happened and it wouldn't get changed by some exaggerating bard or some old soldier who'd had one two many bowls of ale and who wanted to make himself into more of a hero.

Two phrases of his own came echoing (well, sort of[62]) back to him in his mind.

'They really need a scribe up there too ...'

… and ….

'... someone who wants to make himself into more of a hero ...'

And this was the point where he realised. What the bloody hell was **he** doing **down here on the battlefield**?! He was a scribe, not a soldier! He was standing in the middle of a load of very doomed people, he was wearing stupid clothes and he was going to get killed! He had to get out. He had to turn round and get out of the crush of men before he got cut or something really nasty. However, when he tried to, he found he couldn't move. He was completely penned in by the mass of armour-clad bodies on all sides. He tried to turn his head, but could see practically nothing from inside his helmet. All he could see was that behind him there seemed to be as many bodies pressed up together as there were in front. He was trapped. Completely trapped. His left arm was pushed against his body by the press of soldiers on his shield and his other arm was pinned to his side. If he was going to survive, he knew that was one thing he was going to have to unpin, pretty quickly.

'Erm, excuse me,' he said in the tone of someone who wants to make themselves heard, but does not want people to think he's shouting. 'Er, is there any chance we could all spread out a bit, only I'm rather unable to get at my sword.'

No one heard him. Or at least no one answered him.

The drums and pipes far over to his right seemed to be getting louder, building to a climax. Were they Saxon or Cymru? He couldn't tell. Never mind that, he said to himself …

'No, really,' he said, his voice a little louder now, 'all it needs is for someone to move a thumb's length away and I can get my hand on my sword –'

Again, no answer. Again, the drums and pipes were increasing in volume. Why were they just ignoring him? Then, as the crowd surged forward, briefly he caught a glimpse of one man's face. His eyes were wide, as if the eyelids didn't exist; his expression was taut, as if it had been frozen or chiselled that way. The man was plainly terrified. Was everyone like this? Quite probably.

'No, really,' he shouted, 'I know you've all got your minds on other things, but –'

The drums, the pipes, the yelling, the chanting; in fact, everything suddenly stopped. In the silence that followed, he heard himself shout in his most effeminate, panicked and high-pitched voice …

'… I'm going to be no bloody use to anyone if I can't get my sword out!'

---

[62] In actual fact, your own voice talking to you as if it's in a big cave only ever happens in films. Just try listening to the voice in your head now. Is it echoing? No, I thought not.

The words seemed to waft across the silent armies, echoing far across the battlefield. Llew thought there was some sort of irony in him wishing that the ground would open and swallow him when it was now so muddy, it was quite likely – within the course of the day – that it would.

And then, as one, apparently on some signal from the front that Llew never saw, the Cymru roared and charged forward. Llew was swept along with them, trying desperately to keep upright and even more desperately trying to retrieve the rusty sword from his belt as a little, although not much, space had opened up between him and the other men.

And, of course, it was stuck.

Then, not so far in the distance, through gaps in the jostling crowd, he could see men falling forward and backward, keeling over. Sprays of blood flew through the air, as did bits of people … limbs, slices of head … they were flying too fast for Llew to tell what they actually were. Some of the men in front tried to stop and back up, some tried to turn and run, others tried to stand and fight: it was chaos. And all the while Llew found himself being pushed inexorably towards the bloody mayhem in from of him. And just over the tops of the Cymru warriors' heads he could see other blond heads, higher heads, on taller people's shoulders. The heads of Saxon warriors. Llew had seen men like them before obviously and had thought them pretty fearsome-looking then, but they had seemed … somehow civilised. These beings were machines of dread and slaughter, whirling their axes and swords, which, in spite of what Hengist had said to him before, looked pretty damn sharp from where Llew was standing. Or not standing exactly. He was being propelled right towards them. One of them had had his helmet knocked off. He was bleeding from a gash in his forehead, but was still fighting as if nothing had happened – hewing down Llew's countrymen as if they were stalks of corn and he some sort of blond grim reaper. Llew recognised him almost immediately.

'Horsa!'

Llew had not meant to shout the name out. It had been a reflex action on seeing someone he recognised in an extraordinary situation, which afterwards made him glad he hadn't cheerily added, 'fancy seeing you here!' However, it had the effect of making Horsa change direction and start cleaving towards Llew. This was not good. Two men directly in front of Llew went down, Llew tripped over their falling and now headless bodies and found himself face-first in a sludgy pile of bodies and mud. Rolling over quickly, because he knew his life depended on it, and wiping the mud and blood from his helmet's visor, Llew's next view was of Horsa bearing down with his war axe. It sliced just past Llew's left ear and buried itself in the saturated earth. Llew decided he was going to play his only card before Horsa pulled the axe out of the mud and took a shot at what was likely to be a fairly open goal.

'Hi, Horsa! Remember me?' he shouted in perfect Sais as brightly as he could. 'I'm that Cymru scribe your brother liked …'

The axe head was already plummeting down towards Llew's rather less hardy one when it stopped mid air – a miracle of strength and control on the part of Horsa. If air had friction,[63] there would have been a screeching sound. Horsa looked at him, puzzled, and Llew looked back, the pair of them almost frozen in time there while the carnage went on all around them. Llew seized his chance before the moment had gone and rolled out of the way, trying to upright himself at the same time. By now the Cymru soldiers seemed to have rallied a little and were starting to push some of the Saxons back. Llew was fumbling frantically at his sword. Why would the bloody thing not come out? It was like it was willing the right person to unsheath it and Llew was not that person. It was only a bit of rust-covered iron, but it was all Llew had got. Any moment now that big Saxon madman was going to awake from his trance and come after Llew. He needed to defend himself. But something had distracted Horsa – he was no longer interested in Llew. He had turned and looked to his left and then started off in the opposite direction, pushing and slashing through the throng of fighting men. Llew saw what had distracted the Saxon warlord. Horses. Horses and riders. They were some way off, but they were causing the Saxon troops to scatter in all directions. At the point the sword decided to unleash itself from the scabbard – and, yes, it *did* seem to have decided for itself too. The momentum of it doing so seemed to drag Llew along with it, making him whirl round in an arc, just as a Saxon warrior came at him, bringing his sword to parry Llew's. He was a big man. Big as Horsa and just as powerful looking. Llew braced himself for the rusty sword to connect with the Saxon's and break or shatter, probably causing his shoulder to be dislocated at the same time, but the Saxon went flying, tumbling over backwards, crashing into other Saxons, who went flying too. That was lucky, thought Llew, amazed. He didn't have long to think. Another Saxon was bearing down on him. His war axe was aimed right at Llew's skull. Instinctively, Llew put his sword over his head to protect himself, remembering too late that this was what the shield was for. The axe made direct contact with Llew's sword and shattered, pieces of it flying out in all directions. The warrior screamed. Somehow his hand was no longer there. There was a stump and a lot of blood spurting out of it, but no hand. Llew looked around for somewhere to run to. In the distance he could see the Cymru cavalry making short work of some Saxon warriors and decided that was a good place to be. There was a little more space now. Either people had spread out to fight properly or more of them were dead, so that the battlefield could now be described as a bit roomier than it had been before. Llew pushed his way towards the horses. He didn't seem to be having much trouble getting there for some reason. It was weird. Just like before, every time a Saxon warrior would get close to him, Llew would attempt to defend himself with

---

[63] Actually it does, but not very much.

his rusty sword, it would make contact with the Saxon's weapon and the warrior would literally go flying, somersaulting backwards into his comrades. Llew noticed the Saxons were starting to give him a wide birth now. This sword, he thought, would be great in the hands of someone who could use it. This surprised him. He was thinking calmly; in all this mayhem he, Llew, otherwise known as Mr Panic, was thinking calmly!

There was a mass cry behind him – what sounded like several thousand Cymru shouting 'chaaaaarggeee!!!'. It turned out that Llew's hearing was right on target once again as he was swept forward by yet another surging wave of bodies. He was now getting closer to where the cavalry were and Llew realised that this must mean there was some sort of weakness in the Saxon line. There was a chance, if the Cymru army pushed hard enough to break through. This would cut the Saxons in two. And two small armies were not as strong as one big one. A Saxon of ample dimensions was suddenly right in Llew's face and screaming at him. Llew raised his rusty old sword and attempted to stab at the Saxon. He failed miserably and just brushed the side of his enemy's armour. Luckily, this seemed to do the trick and the Saxon warrior collapsed with a deep cut in his side. Still surging along, Llew now found he was amongst the horses and there above him, his horse rearing, was the one person on the battlefield Llew probably should have avoided.

Bruenor.

The Kentish king lifted his own sword and swung it down, directly at Llew's head. Llew dived under Bruenor's horse for protection. Maybe Bruenor had mistaken him for a Saxon.

'I'll get you, you little scribe bastard! Get out from under there!'

Or maybe not. Llew was now crawling on all fours, trying to keep under Bruenor's moving horse. He knew there was going to be a problem if enough space opened up for Bruenor to gallop. Then there was a familiar roar and Llew saw Bruenor come tumbling off his horse, with a Saxon warrior attached to his midriff. It was Horsa again. The pair landed on some passing fighting soldiers, who collapsed under the momentum and weight of two flying kings, and then Horsa was sitting on Bruenor's chest, with his axe raised.

Llew was never quite sure why he did what he did next. Perhaps he felt he owed Bruenor for the loss of a kingdom. Perhaps, deep down, he was actually a chip off his father's block. Or perhaps, and Llew always felt deep down this might been the case, perhaps the sword made the decision. Either way, he stepped out from under the horse, wielded the rusty weapon in a fearsome arc and cut Horsa's head off. The head went flying off into the battle somewhere and the body slumped forward onto the man it had not a second before been about to kill.

'Get this bloody thing off me!'

Llew sheathed his sword and struggled to remove Horsa's remains off Bruenor. Around him, he could hear the Saxons shouting to one another over the fighting.

'Horsa is slain!'
'Horsa has fallen!'
'What?'
'I said Horsa is slain!'
'No! Really?'
'That's what I heard!'
'It can't be! I just saw him this morning!'
'I'm just telling you what I heard …'

And so on. However, the Saxons in the immediate area that had seen what had happened had decided to withdraw. Which meant that more and more Cymru were pouring into the space and surging forward. The Saxon line had been broken.

One of the soldiers that Bruenor and Horsa had landed on was now getting to his feet (the other one was dead).

'King Bruenor has slain Horsa!' he shouted, before lumbering forward to join the battle that was now moving away towards the Saxon army.

'Er …'

'Yes, I killed him, you understand me?' Llew realised that Bruenor's face was right up against his.

'But …'

'Uh, uh. No buts. I killed him! Me! King Bruenor. Former king Bruneor! You saved my life and there's a battle on. So right now I don't have time to kill you, but you will tell everyone you know that I killed Horsa. Do you understand?'

'Er … sure …'

'Good.'

Bruenor strode over to his horse, remounted and headed off into the fray. Llew realised that he was alone amongst a sea of dead bodies. Crows were already landing to try out the pickings. The battle had moved forward without him. He had a choice. He could follow Bruenor into battle, which was continuing not a hundred yards off from him, or he could get on that hill with Ceridwen and the others and start writing things down. He weighed this up. Well, he'd experienced a bit of combat first hand … no one could say he was a coward. Besides, the Old Man had expressly forbade him to be there, so his withdrawing couldn't be seen as desertion. On the other hand –

A stone from a Saxon slingshot hit him on the side of the helmet very hard. He waited a couple of seconds, then folded up onto the mud for a nice long bout of unconsciousness.

'You know, I expressly told you there was no place for you in the battle line!'

He was sitting on a chair in Ambrosius' tent. The Old Man was standing and staring at him.

'I'm sorry, Lord.'

Both were covered in grime and dried blood. Both had bits of armour hanging off them. Ambrosius was looking exhausted but happy. He had good reason. The Cymru had won.

Llew had woken up on the battlefield, with a crow trying to peck at him while one of his comrades in arms tried to pinch his boots.

'What are you doing?' he had shouted, angrily.

'Ruddy Nora, this one's alive!' his comrade had replied, and run off.

'Corr!!' the crow had said, and done a similar thing, only upwards.

He had then limped back to the camp, where he had found a big celebration in progress. And the hero of the hour was the man they were now calling 'Good King Bruenor' and 'Brave King Bruenor' and even 'King Bruenor The Greatest Fighter In The World For It Was He Who Slew The Mighty Horsa'. Which meant it didn't take Llew much time to work things out. It seemed that the slaying of Horsa had been a turning point. Because Horsa had fallen, many Saxons fled. Their line, already weakened, had become even weaker and the Britons had managed, against the odds, to divide them. Seeing the problem, Hengist had tried to get the Saxons to retreat so that they could regroup as one force, but the Britons kept harrying them as they did so, with the result that half of them tried to turn and fight and were slain. The other half were spread all over Saxon territory. It was all Hengist could do to amass enough of his armies so that he could defend the territory he had gained so far.

The Saxon force had been stopped. For now. They would not be marching on Londinium. Not this year anyway. That very day, they were decamping and moving their forces, back over to the other side of the Medway. It was almost as if they had never been there in the first place. Although, the great quagmire that had once been a great grass plain, the sea of decomposing bodies and the smoking ruins of the town that had once been Egelesprep attested to the fact that they had.

'You know, here's an interesting thing,' said Ambrosius, 'I've been listening to some reports …'

Typical. Only the Old Man would want to study reports *after* he'd won a battle.

'Funny thing is … they say that Horsa pulled Bruenor down from his mount and was about to kill him when some foot soldier decapitated him with a very, very rusty sword.'

Llew looked at him dumbly.

'I've also had people tell me about a scrawny boy in ill-fitting armour, knocking out half the Saxon line with some antique. You know anything about this?'

'Well, I –'

'I'd like to see your sword, Old Lad. If I may.'

Llew drew the sword out of the scabbard. Again it took a lot of effort as if, once again, it didn't want to be drawn. Ambrosius took the sword from Llew and swung it a few times.

'There's something about this.'

He swung it again.

'It's … a piece of junk. Where on earth did you get it?'

'Some bandits in the forest, Lord. Years ago.'

Ambrosius looked thoughtful.

'Well, it's absolutely useless,' he said very seriously, 'do not under any circumstances let anyone else get their hands on it.'

Llew nodded. There seemed to be little else to do.

Chapter 13 – Return To Llangollen (again)

'The question is,' said Ambrosius, 'where to go next?'

He was performing his usual debriefing ritual of pacing up and down his tent while he thought aloud. It was Llew's job to write these thoughts down as Ambrosius spoke them, so that the general could review them later at his leisure. Llew looked at the page he'd just started.

'Hmm ... hmm ... what's for dinner today? Do we know? Asparagus? Oh ... by the way, did Madoc come for the thing ... you know, the thing ... the thing!!! ... come on, Llew, you know what I mean ... oh, he did ... hmm ... what did we say was for dinner? Asparagus ... oh ... now why have I got you here again? ... Oh yes ... the question is where to go next?'

As historical documents went, this one probably *wasn't* going to rank up there with Pliny The Younger's[64] description of the last moments of Pompeii. Mind you, Llew's own interpretation of history wasn't a great deal to (appositely) write home about. He'd tried to put his version of the great battle down on parchment and all he'd got was a paragraph about it being really crowded, lots of people getting killed and then being hit on the head. He realised that history was generally not written by those in the midst of it. History was generally written by those in the comfort of a wagon on a nearby hill. He also realised that he was having terrible trouble concentrating and the reason for this was that winter was now in full tilt and he was living in a tent. So, when Ambrosius asked, partly rhetorically, where to go next, Llew was very tempted to shout 'Aquae Sulis! Let's get that hypocaust fired up again!'; but he didn't, because he knew his master didn't like being interrupted when thinking aloud.

'What did we say was for dinner again?'

Llew sighed.

'Asparagus, master.'

'Oh.'

---

[64] A famous historian.

Ambrosius sounded a bit disappointed.

'So,' he said, whistling through his teeth, 'where to go next. Where, where, where … where-ity – where-ington.'

Llew reflected inwardly that this could be one of his master's long sessions.

'Could go to Pictland!' Ambrosius suddenly snapped, causing Llew to start. 'Could go there! Kick the arses of those damn savages north of the wall, make 'em stay in their own country … haven't really got enough men though…'

This was true. Although the Cymru appeared to have won Egelesprep, the main side effect of such a battle was that a huge number of their men had been killed.[65] And wherever Ambrosius decided to go next, he was going to have to leave a large force behind to secure the Saxon borders. Llew noticed that Ambrosius now accepted that the Saxons were a fact of life. There was no pushing them back into the sea. They were here to stay. It's also perhaps worth mentioning that, as far as the Saxons were concerned, *they* had won the battle[66] – the kingdom formerly known as Gwyrangon was now definitely theirs to keep and Hengist had even renamed the place Kent. Plus, the British forces were now so depleted they wouldn't be able to mount another attack.

So that much of Marcus' prediction had come true. Once they'd got a foothold, they weren't leaving, ever. Llew could only hope Marcus was wrong about the hypocaust.

'Of course, I would have enough men if a few more kings would come onside! I mean, where are the Iceni? Where are the Coritani? Tell me that, eh.'

It was true that many kings had not joined Ambrosius to fight Hengist. This was not due to lack of valour or national pride on their part (or *probably* not), but more to do with the fact that Ambrosius had been, before the battle, something of an unknown quantity. Any nutter could sail up-river to Aquae Sulis, say they were a Roman general and that it was time to attack the Saxons; but, as the old saying goes, 'a pig that says it's a dog is still a pig'[67] and many of the kings were not willing to risk sacrificing men and, more importantly (in their eyes), themselves so easily. *Now*, of course, things were different. Ambrosius had, for the time being at least, kept the Saxons in check. No one doubted that they would be back – more boats would start arriving soon enough … in the Spring probably, and there

---

[65] A lot of the Saxons had been killed too, but that was beside the point – there'd been more of them in the first place.

[66] It's certainly what they put in their written chronicles of the period, stating, with some justification it later turned out, that the retreat had been a 'strategic withdrawal' and that the aim had been to try and get the Cymru forces to spread themselves too thinly.

[67] Although the saying 'a nutter who pretends to be a Roman general is still a nutter' might have been more appropriate.

would be the inevitable spreading of a people demanding land, but for now they would keep relatively quiet.

'If we could get a few more of those buggers on-side, old lad, we might have enough men to send north. Bring the Picts into line before the Saxons start causing trouble again. So ...,' said Marcus thoughtfully, 'that's the next job. A bit of a tour ... bit of flesh pressing, bit of flattery, bit of negotiating, know what I mean?'

Llew hadn't a clue.

'It's very simple. We need to unite the tribes again. Vortigern did that, but *his* problem was that he had too many things happening at one time to contend with ... the Saxons ... the Picts, the Irish ... the plague. And when the alliance fell apart, the kings became very insular. Well, now we've got an opportunity! Job one – the Saxons – well that's done for the moment. So let's move on to job two – the Picts. But we need men, and the kings who aren't part of the alliance *have* men. So what I've got to do is travel to where those kings are and persuade them it's in their interest to join us. See?'

Ambrosius was becoming very animated now – he always did when he was on a roll.

'But,' said Llew, venturing a question, 'for that to work don't *they* need an overlord. Like Vortigern?'

Ambrosius stopped pacing.

'I don't see why,' he said, wrinkling his nose at what apparently was a distasteful suggestion. 'After all, who'd *want* the job?'

They all would, thought Llew; that was the trouble. You had to have a leader of kings because otherwise all the kings would fight over who was the leader; but Ambrosius just didn't see the world like that. It was amazing really – he was a veteran of goodness knows how many battles, he'd seen slaughter and atrocity on a scale no one could have dreamed, and yet he still had this unshakable faith in the good in everybody. In fact, he was the ideal candidate for overlord, or even High King, because of this. Especially when coupled with his leadership abilities. And yet, and *yet*, Ambrosius would no more have thought of himself for the job than he had a mind to fly in the air.

What a guy!

'Now, the thing is ...' Ambrosius was back to pacing again, 'the thing *is*, who to take and who to leave! Who can I trust to guard the border here and not cock it up and who can I trust to take with me into other kings' territories and not start a civil war?'

In neither case, it seemed, was the answer 'Bruenor'. If he was left with soldiers to guard the Kent border, he'd almost certainly try and take his old kingdom back. He would fail, there would be a massacre and valuable men would be lost. Maybe the Saxons would rise up again, taking more land as they did so, and the Cymru would be back to square one. On the other hand, if Bruenor went with Ambrosius to another kingdom, he'd most likely try to take *that* for himself. He'd pick a fight with someone – probably the king – and, before you knew it, they'd all be fighting a war with each other. It'd happened in Gwent, after all. Poor king Ynyr was *still* trying to pick up the pieces of *that* little adventure. He'd got back his throne all right (which was why Bruenor had come skulking over to Egelesprep), but he'd lost a great deal of territory and not a small number of his subjects in the unrest Bruenor had stirred up.

'On the other hand, Bruenor has been an honourable man. He fought bravely with us.'

Only because he thought you'd get his kingdom back for him after he'd single-handedly managed to lose his whole army, thought Llew to himself, but he knew it wouldn't be much use to say so. Ambrosius wanted to see the good in people.

What a guy!

'What Bruenor needs is a kingdom for himself.'

And had Llew lived fifteen hundred years later, he would have said, 'well, *duh*', and then he would have felt bad about it because Ambrosius didn't think like that. He wasn't cynical like Llew.

What a guy!

'What's happening with Gwynedd these days? How fares Llangollen?'

Llew sat bolt upright. Well well well – here was a turn-up for the books. Vortigern's old seat. Rumour was that once the overlord had abandoned the great stockade, the whole country had fallen apart. Various tribes had gone to war with one another and Irish pirates had been using the ensuing chaos as a good cover for raiding further and further inland. The place was a war zone. If it was possible for Llangollen in the kingdom of Gwynedd to be any more inhospitable than it had been, it was exactly that now. What was his master planning? Bruenor wanted a kingdom. Gwynedd had no king. Bruenor needed to be kept out of the way; Llangollen was right in the top left-hand corner of nowhere.[68] This could be good. What a guy!

'I think I'm going to install Bruenor as king there.'

Yes, oh yes! At last, some justice! That smug, vain, belligerent, chippy bastard, the one who told big porky pies about who he had and hadn't slain in battle, the one with the girly sword was going to be sent north to that country of snow and mad people and he was going to be stuck there!

'… and I'd like you, old lad, to go with him as his chamberlain. What did we say was for dinner again?'

What a … *what*?

---

[68] Please note: this is Llew's opinion, not mine. I love North Wales, particularly Lleyn and Gwynedd, visit regularly and would advise you to do the same. Anyone from the area now taking offence, please don't.

That night, Llew was shoving his things into a sack and making ready for a swift departure. His crush, if that is what it had been, on his great leader had all but dissolved, disappeared, exploded, or whatever it is crushes do when you find that the object of your affection really doesn't give a flying monkeys whether you live or die. Oh yes, that little flame will keep flickering as long as you think there's a chance, just a *chance* that the 'crushee' cares. 'Oh,' you say, 'he's rude and he doesn't take any notice of me and once he even nearly didn't stop his car when I was crossing the street, but *deep down* I know he cares.' Then, when you realise that *deep down* he really, really doesn't; *deep down* he is actively anti-caring, and not in a shy way. That's when you stop caring too, hopefully.[69] And Llew had realised that Ambrosius loved everybody as long as they were useful to him. Llew had been useful as a scribe and a translator. Now he was going to be useful to Ambrosius as a counsellor to King Ratface Warmonger Bully Boy No Hero. Or that's what Ambrosius *thought*, because actually Llew wasn't. He was going to sneak off with all his gear and his scrolls and his money. He was going back to Aquae Sulis. He was going to *pay* for a passage to the continent and then he was going to Rome to find Marcus. And no one was going to know about it. Ruddy Llangollen! *Ruddy* Llangollen! Never mind all the roads leading to Rome, all the roads lead to ruddy Llangollen! They did for him, anyway! Well, not this time. Forget that! He was going to buy a cart – and he needed one for all his bags of scrolls – and he was out of there. Gone! Once in Rome, he would sell his scrolls to the library … they must have got round to building one by now … and then that would be it. With his skills and his gift for languages, he'd have no problem.

But there was one thing he was certain of. He was not, *not* going to Llangollen.

His tent flap opened.

'Hello, son.'

Llew looked up.

'Oh, hi, Dad.'

Once again, the awkward pause. Llew reflected that if awkward pauses could be exchanged for coins, he and his father would do very well in business.

'Yes,' said his father, 'I did survive the battle. Thanks for asking.'

Oh, and guilt. Boy, if only you could sell that.

'So did I actually,' replied Llew. 'Thanks.'

Pause.

'I … heard you saw that Horsa fella get killed.'

'Yes, I did.'

Pause.

---

[69] Some people don't, which is a shame.

'Was it good?'

Was it good? What a bizarre question, thought Llew. How could watching a man having his head removed from his shoulders then collapse, decapitated, onto his foe, while blood and mud sprayed out like an over-colourful fountain, be described as 'good'? Or 'bad' for that matter? How could it be described as anything?

'It was all right,' he said.

Llew realised that he and his father were having that promised 'chinwag'.

Pause.

'So, it's Llangollen tomorrow for you then?'

That was interesting. The news had spread fast.

'Bruenor's being made king of Gwynedd,' said Llew, by way of an explanation.

Llew got back to packing – not intending to tell his father what he was really packing for.

'That's what Ambrosius told me,' said Gwyddno. 'So, quite an honour for the pair of us, isn't it? You know, you being Bruenor's scribe and that.'

'Scribe'. That was it. Llew decided that, once and for all, he was going to make his father for once *be impressed with something he'd done!!!*

'I'm not going to be his bloody scribe!' he shouted. 'I'm going to be his chamberlain! You know what that means? It means his chief advisor! At my age! Think about that! I've *been* a scribe, yes, but I've also been an emissary and translator to all sorts of powerful people. I've fought in one of the greatest battles of the age, I felled – … *saw* a feared Saxon chieftain felled, and now I'm going to be the chamberlain to the king – … Sorry, "the pair of us"? Honour for the pair of us?'

Gwyddno sniffed.

'They've not told you then?'

'Told me what?'

'I've been asked to be part of your escort. I'm to see you to Gwynedd before I go home to Dyfed. It's 'cause I'm an old and distinguished warrior, see? Which I think you will agree …,' and here Gwyddno puffed himself up a little, '… is quite an honour! See you at first light.'

And with that, Gwyddno swept out. Llew couldn't believe it! Not only was his father being deliberately unimpressed with everything Llew had done, Gwyddno was actually inferring that he had done something *more impressive*! Right, enough was enough! Llew'd had it! He was getting out right now and he didn't care what anybody thought …

He stopped. He sighed. He realised he wasn't going anywhere. If he didn't turn up to ride with Bruenor the next morning, who would be the dishonoured one? Gwyddno. And the old man would probably be banished and ride home alone and die of a broken heart. Or whatever the hell you did when you were once a proud warrior chieftain and got dishonoured by a wayward and cowardly son, fol-de-ray-doh-day, damn those bards. And whose fault would that be?

Which would be why Ambrosius had appointed such an elderly warrior as escort for the new king, because Ambrosius wasn't as unworldly as Llew had thought.

What a bastard!

The next day, Llew found himself as part of a reasonable-sized retinue heading north. It had not been easy getting hold of an ox cart to transport his stuff, as most people who had them lived in them and weren't willing to give them up, no matter what the financial incentive. However, Llew had managed to persuade Ceridwen that, for a small consideration, it might be worth her heading north with him – he would hire her wagon and she could be his driver. He also had to pay her two fellow wagon dwellers to move out; so, by the time they left Egelesprep, he was a whole lot poorer than he had been.

He needed to have a conversation about wages with Bruenor. And soon. It was not a conversation he was looking forward to. He'd had his first official meeting with his new liege lord as chamberlain and it had not gone well. Bruenor basically told him that Ambrosius had insisted Llew be given his current position and the only reason he wasn't killing Llew right now was … well, Llew knew why, and now they were quits. And if Llew ever told *anyone* what had really happened that day … well, Llangollen was a long way from where Ambrosius was going, even if he was Llew's sworn protector. All this was Llew's fault, that much was certain. Llew had pointed out at least Bruenor had got a kingdom again, even if it wasn't quite as nice and sunny as his one in the south-east had been. Bruenor didn't seem mollified.

'You forget, scribe, I've been there. I know what Gwynedd is like and I know what Llangollen is like. It's cold. It rains every day. It's full of mad people. I used to have a pleasant, bright kingdom by the sea. Then you came along. Now I've an impassable, snow-covered mountain range and mad people! So, your best bet will be to keep mum and out of my way. Oh, and if while we're there, some foreign invaders come up to you and say "please can we have this country", see if you can do me the honour of saying "no", okay?'

Good start.

However, things had got better once they'd started their journey. Being on a cart meant that he was going at a slower pace than Bruenor and his men (who included Gwyddno), so they were miles in the distance. Meanwhile, Llew was sitting next to Ceridwen and she was huddling against him for warmth. It was the first time *ever* he was glad it was winter.

'So, what was it like then? The battle.'

Llew shrugged.

'I didn't really see much of it … just tried to stop myself from falling over.'

'There's these really weird rumours going round.'

'What rumours?'

'That Bruenor didn't kill Horsa. That some kid with a rusty old sword did. And in so doing, the kid saved Bruenor as well.'

She looked significantly at the rusty old sword that Llew had placed in the wagon behind them.

'Yes, well, rumours like that can get people killed,' said Llew quietly as he watched Bruenor trotting his horse in the distance, 'so would you mind not repeating it. Them. The rumours, I mean.'

'There's another one – they say the kid scared off half the Saxon army with that sword of his. That was how we broke their line.'

Llew snorted.

'That's just ridiculous!'

She moved just slightly away from him.

'Don't you like being a hero or something?'

Llew realised he was blowing it again.

'No, no, I like it! I do! Really! I just thought … you know, before the battle… you, well … you seemed to think I was doing something stupid.'

She moved back to her original position.

'You were. But I still think it was pretty terrific. What you did. Or didn't do, of course.'

In spite of the bitter wind, Llew was beginning to feel quite warm.

'Listen, where did you get that thing?' she said, indicating the rusty sword.

'Bandits. In the great forest. I got rescued, they left it behind. Why?'

Wow, *that* seemed an awful long time ago! What was it, a year? Two years? Seemed longer.

'And why did you keep it?'

Llew paused. This was more difficult to explain. To say to Ceridwen that he'd heard a voice in his head, the voice of some feral child who he'd once stopped Vortigern from sacrificing … well, he didn't think it would up his heroic status in her eyes. It might, however, up his 'a-bit-mental' status, and he really didn't want to do that, not while she was snuggling up this close.

'Dunno. Just did.'

'Only I used to go out with this bard. And he told me there were stories about the thirteen treasures of Ynys Prydein. You ever heard of them?'

Llew had, of course. More of the old stories his grandmother had regaled him with when he was sticking close to the fire while others were out hunting – as *he* should have been. Each treasure was supposed to have extraordinary magical properties – made by the gods, his grandmother had said. She also said that they'd all been lost and would never be found again. The thirteen treasures were … let's see, he thought … there was the horn of Bran, and the cauldron of Diwrnach the giant … and after that it got a bit hazy… there was a ring of someone's and a coat … and a chariot … a wooden dish belonging to somebody and a halter which was weird – how could a halter be magic … a knife, a mantel, a hamper, a whetstone … a Nine Men's Morris board of all things and … a sword. Caliburn, the sword of Rhydderch.

'You're saying I've got a magical sword here?'

Rhydderch had been a legendary king. His sword was said to be able to defeat any other in battle. Mind you, it had to be said it wasn't the only one. The old legends had indestructible magic swords practically falling from the trees, every one of them thrown out of a lake, or somehow stuck in a rock, never actually made by a blacksmith unless, of course, it was the Blacksmith Of The Gods. And, of course, said magical sword would then go and defeat everyone on the battlefield. How come, Llew thought, no two magical swords in any of the old legends had ever, well … crossed?

'I dunno. I mean, don't get me wrong. You did a pretty incredible thing out there – or rather,' she said carefully, 'that kid whoever he was did … but face it, Llew, you could hardly stand in that armour, let alone wield a sword as well. And another thing …'

'Go on …,' he said warily.

'Well, maybe the reason Bruenor's accepted all this and *hasn't* had you killed … well, he's seen what you – that kid – can do with that thing.'

Llew took this in. So … she didn't really think he was *that* much of a hero. He had done it all because he had the sword of Rhydderch. His pride should be wounded but, funnily enough, it wasn't. Perhaps it was because she'd managed to orchestrate her position so that his arm was now round her waist and hers was round his.

It was, he decided, the wrong time to start their second row.

Curling up in the wagon at night time with Ceridwen was about the only good thing about going to Gwynedd. The rest of it was horrible. The journey took weeks in some of the worst weather Llew had ever known. Ice-cold rain poured down in sheets, non-stop. It was impossible to keep anything dry. The track, such as it was, became a quagmire and Llew and Ceridwen spent many unhappy wet hours trying to drive the oxen forward while Bruenor and the rest of the retinue got fed up with waiting for them. In the end, Bruenor shouted at Llew that he was going on with the rest of the company and he'd see them at Llangollen – if he made it that far. And, quite frankly, Bruenor didn't care all that much if he didn't. Llew once again considered the opportunity of heading for the coast and getting away; but, of course, his father was still riding with Bruenor, so it wasn't an idea he toyed with for long. Gwyddno himself had been his usual chatty self for the journey so far, pointedly ignoring Llew if they were ever within the same six-feet square area. So now that his father had ridden on with the others, Llew almost felt relieved. At least he wouldn't have to try to *make* conversation. Why, he reflected, was Gwyddno like this? When Llew was younger, Gwyddno had been grumpy and bad tempered with Llew most of the time, but at least he hadn't been *embarrassed* by his son. And in those days Gwyddno'd had more cause to be embarrassed. He had been the chief, after all! And he'd had several fine, fighting, hunting Cymru sons. Then there'd been Llew ... sickly, weedy, always cold, always complaining, whining ... my word, it must have caused some smirks among the other chiefs of the other clans ... 'all right, Gwyddno? How's the boy? The sickly one. Sickly? Yes, so I hear', smirk smirk.

Whereas *now*, when Llew had actually achieved something – finally – it was all Gwyddno could do to even look at Llew, so discomfited was he at his son's presence. Must have been all that business with the treaty and Bruenor's kingdom. It was quite embarrassing, now Llew thought about it; but, well, it was done now and it couldn't be undone and surely ... surely now the Saxons had been pushed back a little and Bruenor had got another kingdom ... well, surely amends had been made. Oh, he didn't doubt he was the butt of various people's jokes by some campfire, somewhere, but still ...

'What on earth are you brooding about,' said Ceridwen, as she laid a fur down in the back of the wagon.

'Nothing much,' he said.

'Come to bed then,' she said.

So he did.

Within the next few days the little wagon crossed from the green and rolling land known as Powys into the rocky, snowy country known as Gwynedd. They could tell when they had crossed the border. The country somehow looked ... ill, which it hadn't done before. It reminded Llew of the burned-out areas surrounding the Saxon lands that he'd seen when travelling with Edwyn. A wasteland is what it had become. Every now and again the little wagon came upon a village or hamlet and found it shut. Strangers were told to go round the village walls. No shelter would be given, not food either. Llew even tried the 'do you know who I am' line occasionally, but the gatekeeper would always reply that he didn't care. Some bloke claiming to be the new king had come past not so long ago and he'd been given the same treatment.

Ceridwen was appalled.

'We're travellers! You give succour to travellers,' she had yelled at one particularly recalcitrant gatekeeper, 'it's the rule of the open road!!'

'Used to be it was!' said the gatekeeper through the very closed gate, 'then one day, not far from here, some fine young bandit pretends to be a traveller and as soon as the gate's open he and his men burn a village to the ground. Now the rule is 'we don't like strangers in these parts'.

Bandits were also very much in evidence. Every so often they'd look up from the road and see three or four men riding on the ridge above them, watching them. Llew was starting to get nervous. Why hadn't they been robbed yet? He looked at his sword behind him. It had better be bloody magic, because those bandits had to be coming soon.

And yet they didn't. On the last day, when they were just a couple of miles away from Llangollen, they came across a spike sticking out of the ground. Not terribly interesting in itself, except that it had a head stuck on it. Llew pulled the cart to a halt.

'Wonder who he was.'

'Bandit,' said Ceridwen, 'look at that earring. Denotes where he stands in the gang.'

'And where does he stand?'

'He doesn't. He hasn't got any feet.'

Ceridwen's little witticisms had a habit of popping out at fantastically inappropriate times. Llew gave her a withering look.

'He's the leader,' she explained, 'that's Blue John stone ... think I'll have it.'

She got down from the cart and took out a knife.

'You're going to steal the earring from a dead bandit leader?'

She turned back.

'Why not?'

'Well,' said Llew, 'if you're right and he is a leader, whoever did this to him did so as a warning to other bandits – that we were to be left alone. If that's the case, it might be a sort of nice gesture if we left our new "friend" the earring.'

Ceridwen sniffed and put her knife away.

'Point,' she said. 'Wonder who it was.'

Llew had an idea, but he didn't say anything. He was back in that weird kid's country and that meant weird things might start happening.

Next day, they came to Llangollen.

Llangollen's brief sojourn into the world of civilisation had not lasted long. The large iron cauldron that passed for a public bath was still there, but it was rusty and full of holes. Britu's round table had apparently been chopped up for firewood. The chapel was still there mind you, and it was obviously used a lot. There was even a crowd outside, waiting for a blessing. Llew was disappointed to find that the monk currently in residence there was not his old friend Nascien. It was, in fact, a pious and extremely thin young man called Thomas.

'Ah, the Peleganist? Yes, he was here for a while, but then there was a papal bull pronouncing Peleganism as heresy – hardly surprising ... all that brotherly love nonsense – and he ran away before some soldiers came to have him stoned to death. Pity,' he added, looking most disappointed.

Thomas was showing Llew to his quarters: a sturdy thatched hut that had once belonged to the Princess Megan.

'They say he's still running around out there,' said Thomas, in a conspiratorial tone, nodding towards the hills, 'naked as the day he was born. Nothing but a big long beard to keep him company.'

Not if I know Nascien, thought Llew. He'll have found a cowl from somewhere. And he doesn't *need* company. All he has to do is find some of those mushrooms and he can converse with all the creatures from inside his head.

'Ooh, nice fur bed. Is it ours?'

Ceridwen had followed them in.

'Er ... yes, dear,' said Llew.

'Oh, I didn't know that the new chamberlain was *married*,' said Thomas with a faint air of distaste.

'Oh, we're not –' Ceridwen started to say, but Llew got in their first.

'Why on earth would you?' he said quickly and as sternly as he dared.

Thomas looked taken aback.

'I like to know everything that's going on,' he said coolly. 'I have told his majesty King Bruenor that I intend to be his eyes and ears on the ground.'

Oh good, thought Llew, not only do we have a zealot here, we've an *ambitious* zealot. And he seems to be after my job which my employer doesn't want me to have anyway. Cosmic.

'Why didn't you let me tell him we're not married?' said Ceridwen when Thomas had gone.

'Because a Christian priest with an appetite for stoning people is not the kind of guy I want with the knowledge that we've committed a mortal sin, okay?' he said, a little bit more irritably than he meant.

'Okay,' she said in a don't-get-shirty-with-me tone of voice, 'but he'll find out soon enough once I get back to work.'

'Work?' said Llew, puzzled; then he realised what she meant. 'Oh. Oh, you're not, are you?'

'We've got to do *something* for money!' she said, 'you're not earning anything, are you?'

'All right, all right. I'll go to Bruenor tomorrow. Try and sort out this wages business.'

'So what are we going to do about eating tonight?'

'Ah,' he said, 'you are about to find out the Llangollen speciality of cold, old roast ox and raw turnip. It's an acquired taste, but one you *have* to acquire, because that's all there is.'

She wrinkled her nose.

'How do you know?' she asked.

'I've been here before. It's all there *ever* is.'

Later that day, Llew sought out Griffith. He found the old warrior practising with his sword outside the smithy.

'All right, boy?'

'Griff!' he said, genuinely pleased to see his old friend, 'how are you?'
He looked him up and down.

'There's something different about you. Something's changed.'

'Probably the fact that I've only got one arm and I used to have two,' he said solemnly. It was true. Llew realised he should have noticed Griffith was practising his swordplay with his *right* hand and he'd always been left handed. Actually, he should have noticed that Griffith's left arm was gone, but he hadn't and now the *faux pas* had been made, so there it was – nothing to be done.

'What happened?'

'Oh, had a bit of trouble with some raiders. We heard some of them had come ashore near Ynys Mon,[70] right? It's nice down there – you'd like it. Anyway, we thought well, we could lose a load of the fishing community if we don't do something. So me and a few of the lads got together and rode down there, thinking, you know, it'd be about ten or twenty, only there was about a hundred of the buggers. And we had to fight our way out. And we lost oooh … Evan and Dylan – remember him? … and Owen and Bors and that little fella who used an axe, what was his name now? And, of course, I got my arm cut off – just like old Edwyn, see? Ironic, I know – bloody hell, I tell you, it hurt like buggery! Did I make a fuss about that at the time? Oh, you bet I did. There's a couple of them Irish sods might be alive now if one of 'em hadn't cut off my arm. I was that angry, I can tell you! I can see why Edwyn was such a moody so and so. Still, I'm all right now, mind, but I have a bit of a problem holding a shield. Oh, and scratching my arse if I'm carrying something. I hear you're married.'

Llew shook his head in wonder. Griffith was a walking miracle![71] You couldn't keep him down! They walked down through the stockade together.

'Sort of. You'll have to meet her. Griff, who's been in charge here? After Britu.'

'In charge? No one! Place is bloody chaos! It's all gangs and tribes and goodness knows what. Oh, and that flaming monk pronouncing judgement wherever he goes. Got his eyes on the big prize, that one. Bruenor hadn't hardly got in the gate when Thomas introduces himself and promptly disappears up the king's arse, pardon my language. And whose brilliant idea was it to put Bruenor in charge anyway?'

Llew remembered that Griffith had once fought alongside Bruenor. He'd also a fair amount of experience of Bruenor from the various councils the king had attended. He explained about Ambrosius and how he'd wanted to keep Bruenor out of the way.

'Pretty clever, huh?'

'I don't know, boy. Seems to me you don't give a treacherous headcase a

---

[70] Anglesey.

[71] A walking *talking* miracle.

knife then turn your back on him. I mean, all Bruenor's got to do is organise the place and suddenly he's got a standing army, hasn't he? One of the biggest around. That's why Vortigern got to be overlord. One of the reasons, anyway.'

'He'd need some pretty decent advisors, Bruenor.'

'He's got you, hasn't he?' said Griffith, 'And it seems to me, boy, that you just being here means you're smarter than you look, doesn't it?'

'Thanks.'

Ha, I wish, thought Llew. If I'd any brains at all I'd have been able to organise my way off this god-forsaken island. However, I can't actually get away from the same place! And now I've got a cartload of possessions ... parchments and stuff. I even appear to have acquired a wife along the way without getting married! How did that happen?

It did occur to him that Griffith had a point, though. Bruenor was now in a position to either become terribly dangerous or fall apart. If he had a half competent chamberlain, then it might just be the former. And much as Llew had ill feeling towards Ambrosius, he did actually think the Roman had got the right idea about uniting the kingdom. If Bruenor made a success of Gwynedd, all that could be threatened.

Unless he got rubbish counsel from his chamberlain.

Of course, that was a dangerous game. In the world of politics, rubbish counsellors tended to meet with hunting accidents.

Llew realised he was going to have to treat the situation carefully.

As it happened, Llew's half-formed plan to give bad advice to the new king became unnecessary. In fact, he found it didn't matter *what* advice he gave Bruenor, because whatever he said – good, bad or indifferent – Thomas always recommended his majesty do exactly the opposite, which was the line that Bruenor would follow. Thus it was that Llew gave the absolute best guidance he could possibly think of and was therefore able to let Bruenor systematically destroy his own kingdom without feeling too guilty about it.

Before this, though, there had been the question of money. Bruenor turned out to be one of those kings who thinks that the best way to 'create wealth' is to keep all the gold for yourself and not give any away, ever. It was therefore quite hard for Llew to persuade him that *he* needed such a thing as a wage.

'What do you want paying for?' Bruenor had said grumpily. 'If you need food, you just have to demand it from one of the servants or those peasanty people. If they won't give it to you, just get one of the soldiers to kill them. You'll soon find yourself knee-deep in turnips if you've got a soldier to back you up. Same goes with clothes. Get someone to go out and skin a couple of cows for you!'

'Sire,' said Llew, as patiently as he could, 'I would like to be able to save, so that one day I may buy myself some land and I can settle.'

'What, here? In this god-forsaken place?'

Llew really wanted to reply that where he chose to settle was his own damn business, but he knew it would not be politic so early in the financial negotiations. However, Thomas, who had already taken to standing directly behind the king's chair, had started whispering in his master's ear.

'Thomas says,' said Bruenor, with a glint in his eye, 'you already owe me one kingdom. When you've worked enough to pay that off, only *then* should I start to pay you.'

He smiled the smile of someone who thinks they've said something really clever. Thomas beamed behind him.

'With respect, sire, Thomas is an arse-licking toad.'

He knew it was a gamble, but he figured that the king was already surrounded by 'yes' men. Being the one 'no' man in the place might just get him a smidgeon of respect. He certainly wasn't going to get it being obsequious to Bruenor. The king disliked him enough as it was.

Thomas himself had tried to keep the smug smile, but it had gone seriously glassy and his face had gone very, very red.

'That's true,' Bruenor nodded thoughtfully.

'Sire!' Thomas protested.

'Oh, shut up, Thomas,' snapped the king. 'You know you couldn't get any further up my back passage without some forceps and a jar of grease. As for you ...,' and here he turned back to Llew, '... as for you, how much do you want?'

'Three gold pieces a week.'

Bruenor coughed in amazement.

'I do have a wife to support,' Llew protested, and the fare abroad is going to be double if we both go, he thought to himself.

'*You're* married?' said the king, astounded.

'Yes,' said Llew.

'What, *really?*' said the king disbelievingly.

'Yes!'

'Personally, sire,' interjected Thomas, 'I would like to know which man of the cloth performed the ceremony, because the lady in question looks to me like no more than a common –'

Sssshhiiinnng!

There was the sound of a sword being unsheathed at the back of the hall. Everyone turned. Griff was sitting at a table, not even looking in their direction, apparently oblivious to them, but weighing up the balance of his sword, nevertheless.

'Terrible thing, calling ladies nasty names,' he said, to no one in particular. 'Especially the wives of my friends.'

Thomas looked to the king for some support, but the king ignored him and spoke to Llew.

'Two pieces. Per fortnight,' he said.

With that he got up and swept out. And that was the first and last time he ever did anything Llew suggested.

King Mor of Elmet looked solemnly at his visitor. He hadn't been king long – he was a distant cousin of the late King Pelinore and his main strengths were that he knew when to stay, when to go and when to come back. He'd come back at the right moment after the Votadini raid and now he was king, advised by the ever-faithful, ever-richer and consequently ever-plumper bishop Derfel. The bishop's job was easy enough, however; for, although Mor was a young man, he was not given to flights of fancy. In fact, there were some in court who opined he was 'a bit serious for his age', which he thought was easy for them to say when they did not have his job. Despite all the trappings – fur jewels, admiring women – being king was not the most fun career in the world, and it had not been made any easier now that the old alliance had almost totally collapsed. The deposition of Vortigern had happened while Pelinore was still on the throne. By the time Mor took over, things had gone from bad to worse. Still, by thinking and working hard (yes, being 'a bit serious' to all those courtiers who thought his job was to simply go out hunting, drinking and roistering with fat people), also by listening to the good bishop, he'd managed to keep things ticking over – just – by what might be called an isolationist policy: put simply, 'we don't mess with anybody and they won't mess with us'. Admittedly, the barbarians in the north under that madman Gorlois had been no respecter of this, *but* everyone else – west and south – had. So he was successful at least, but the business of being king still puzzled him.

Right now he was sitting opposite a man who was probably the most powerful in all Ynys Prydein, but this damn fellow would insist on kneeling before him. This puzzled him too.

'I do wish you'd stand up, Ambrosius.'

'I am no king, sire.'

'Hmm.'

He had to admit he rather liked Ambrosius all the same. He had this deep desire to call him 'the Old Man', and he didn't know why. And he wanted to put on armour and follow him into battle, or go off on adventures. Luckily, despite his youth, Mor had the wisdom to be very wary of these feelings.

'So … you would have me join this new alliance of yours?'

'Yes, sire. And we can do to the Picts what I have done to the Saxons at Egelesprep. It was a great victory.'

'Yes, about that,' said King Mor. 'My bishop has some rather distressing news.'

'Oh?'

Bishop Derfel stepped forward.

'Yes, it seems that many boats – many, *many* boats – have been putting ashore in the new kingdom of Kent. They're not *actually* Saxons, apparently ... they're kinsmen of them – calling themselves Angles. But Hengist has allowed them to land and they have marched through his kingdom and are now settling all along the coast, next door, just to the north of it. They apparently intend establishing a new kingdom there under their King Aelle. We believe it won't be long before they start spreading inland and further north. Meantime, Hengist himself is marching back towards the River Medway.'

Ambrosius blinked. This should not have been happening. Well, not until after the winter anyway. This was not part of the Plan.

'So, I think what we'd like to ask is this ...,' said the bishop, 'you fight the Saxons, they seriously deplete your forces, they establish their own kingdom, they allow hundreds and thousands more settlers to invade and start to colonise the kingdoms next door and then, finally, they start marching back towards the place you fought them in the first place. How, Lord Ambrosius, can you call the battle of Egelesprep a "victory"?'

Ambrosius gave an embarrassed cough. Firstly to give himself more time and secondly because he was genuinely embarrassed, although it was, in fairness, he thought, a mistake anyone could have made. There'd been all those dead bodies at the end and one of their most important chieftains had been decapitated. Plus the Saxons appeared to have run away, didn't they? I mean, who would have thought they'd just ... come back? This was tricky. The bishop was right, of course; how could he now call Egelesprep a victory? However, Ambrosius' father had been a senator in Rome and Ambrosius knew that what he needed right now was a politician's answer. He licked his lips.

'I think what I meant was ... it was a victory in a very *real* sense.'

Chapter 14 – Besieged

'Canmol dy wlad a thrig ynddi'
'Praise your country and live in it'
                    Welsh Proverb

The winter passed without much incident. Everyone in Llangollen simply went about the normal business of not dying from the cold. Or the plague – which made a brief but unpleasant little foray into Gwynedd throughout the month of January, such that by the end of the month there was just about less of everything.

'And with half the tax-paying population wiped out, how am I going to pay the army?' shouted Bruenor, always a great sympathiser for his subjects. '… What's *left* of it anyway. How am I supposed to feed people when half the farmers are dead?'

It was a good question and one that Llew had thought long and hard about.

'My suggestion would be, sire, that you invest. You have gold reserves – use them. Help the families of farmers who have been worst hit. The sooner they get back on their feet, the sooner everyone else gets fed. As far as the levies are concerned, again I'd use some of the reserves – the more soldiers are paid, the less of them will desert – as,' he added through clenched teeth, 'they're currently doing.'

It was good advice. It was the *right* advice. He knew both Marcus and Ambrosius would have been impressed. Actually, even Gwyddno might have been impressed, had he been there. He also knew that there was no way in hell Bruenor was going to take it.

'And when you have spent all my gold for me, *scribe*, what will you do then?'

Bruenor always called Llew 'scribe' – it made him an object … a *thing*, and a lowly one at that.

As for spending all the king's gold … well, to put it mildly, this was extremely unlikely, because to spend that much would take a lifetime, assuming there was lots to buy in the shops.[72] Bruenor had (as usual, against Llew's advice) spent the whole winter taxing the living daylights out of

---

[72] Which, in a starving, plague-ridden Dark Ages feudal state, there generally wasn't.

everybody in the kingdom with the exception (of course) of himself. He'd then had a special building erected within the fortress, which he was now calling the treasury – mainly because it held all the treasure. It was guarded by a troop of Gwynedd's best warriors – all of whom would have been put to better use being out in the countryside attempting to protect the populace from bandits and Scotti (Irish) raiders – and there it stayed. It did not go back into the economy – into paying farmers and soldiers and craftsmen to try and get the country back on its feet – because Bruenor was evidently the type of ruler who believed that what being king meant was being *rich* when everyone else is *poor*. Llew wondered if this is what had happened in Kent – Gwyrangon, that was. Had Bruenor basically run the place into the ground for a pile of gold? Is that why the Saxons had been able to establish a colony there so easily? Because Bruenor's soldiers were too few and too inept to be able to defend the place properly. Or, more likely, because the Saxons had bribed his majesty with gold to be allowed to stay. And then, finally, when he'd needed to fight for his kingdom, he'd found he'd barely any soldiers left.

It might explain a lot.

Llew tried not to wince. He'd been kneeling for about an hour now – for the whole length of the audience, in fact – and he couldn't feel his knees any more. He wasn't made any more comfortable by the fact that he was wearing his rusty sword, as he always did when he met with his liege … just in case. A little reminder to the king of who killed whom at Egelesprep. It was no surprise, of course, that Bruenor was also the kind of king who insisted that everyone kneel before him – although even old Vortigern had never insisted on that – and had had his chair in the hall placed on a table, so that he towered above everyone kneeling in his presence, even when he was sitting.

He was shaping up into quite a nice little tin-pot dictator.

At the foot of this table-cum-throne sat, as ever, the thin figure of Thomas, simpering as usual. Thomas was now, next to the king, probably the most important figure in the court at Llangollen. Not just because he had the king's ear, but because, being the only Christian priest in the settlement, he had power over people's souls. And when the end of the world is nigh, people often start looking to the care of their souls. Every morning now, crowds of the newly faithful spread out in front of the little chapel as Thomas said mass outside (and there were so many of them, it was a *mass* mass) … all freezing in their faith; but, as Thomas pointed out, there were too many of them to fit inside. Interestingly enough, he was rather cagey about letting *anyone* inside, even if they were alone, for fear, he said, of damage to the holy relics he kept there – the bones of saints and such-like. And when the skeletal monk wasn't preaching, he seemed to be everywhere else, everywhere you looked, dissembling, putting his nose into the business of others, or, more often than not, whispering into the king's ear.

'If I might make a suggestion, sire –' said Thomas.

'Will I have to spend any gold?' said the king immediately.

'No, Majesty,' said Thomas, slightly taken aback.

'Then that's what we'll do.' There was a slight pause. 'What is it? This suggestion.'

'It is simply this, Majesty. People have been through a traumatic winter – plague, raids and so on – all throwing money at them will do is make them think that every time things get a little rough, the king will bail them out. The result will be them becoming lazy, or rather laz*ier* than they already are. My suggestion would be to raise taxes: it will make the strong pull themselves up by their boot straps and weed out the weak.'

There was, Llew reflected, only one type of person who called others lazy. It was the type who already has regular meals, a warm bed and, more importantly, the time to do so.

'Hmmm.' The king looked thoughtful. 'What about the army?'

'Every soldier is sworn to serve you in the name of God. Tell them they will be paid in due time and that any who desert in the interim will be condemned to hell.'

As opposed to the 'heaven' that is Gwynedd right now, thought Llew dryly. Something else was bothering him about Thomas's advice ... it wasn't just bad ... it was *ridiculously* bad! Almost deliberately so. Surely no one who wasn't an utter idiot would even *dream* of following it.

Meantime, Bruenor was nodding.

'You see?' he said to Llew accusingly. 'You see, scribe? Here is a man who *understands* government. I don't even know why I keep you on. I mean what, answer me this, what is the point of you, eh? **Eh**?'

Bruenor's voice had been getting rather high and whiny of late. He was also starting to lose his hair ... and there were a number of rashes and boils on his skin now. All this plus his ability turn everything he said into a rant against Llew was making him strangely reminiscent of someone.

'If your Majesty wishes,' said Llew, and not for the first time since getting his 'plumb job' at Llangollen, 'I will reluctantly resign and take banishment as my punishment.'

He knew it wasn't going to work, but it was worth a try. Yes, please banish me, he thought. *Please* banish me and I'll take Ceridwen as far away as I can. Griff too, if he'll come.

Griffith had, of late, become a permanent fixture of the Llew/Ceridwen household. He'd moved into the hut next door, and Ceridwen had taken to fussing, cleaning around him and feeding him like she was the daughter he'd never had, while he sat by their hearth fire, telling old stories. And in a funny way Llew had become more and more fond of the old warrior who he'd always *liked*, but ... well, these days Griffith seemed a bit more vulnerable. It was partially because he'd lost an arm, but also because, for a soldier, Griff was getting on and now it was starting to show – not that he'd ever admit it.

Somehow the thought of leaving Llangollen without him (and Llew's number one priority *was* still to leave Llangollen – this time for good) didn't seem quite right. He had realised that now he had another addition to his family. Damn! How did that happen?

Meantime, Llew's *real* father had gone back to Siluria just after the winter solstice. It had been the usual, slightly embarrassed parting, with the one exception. As he'd climbed on his horse, just before the stockade gates had been opened, Gwyddno had said, 'Well, take care now. It's not a bad little number you've got for yourself here is it? Well done.'

Llew had been so dumbstruck by this he'd hardly been able say his goodbyes as his father and fellow elderly Silurian warriors had rode off into the mountains. Gwyddno was actually impressed by something Llew had done!

'You think I'd let you resign? And leave?'

The high voice of the king invaded these musings. Llew snapped back to reality and bad knees.

'Oh, I don't think so, boyo!' The king was doing that incredulous unamused laugh of his. 'You leave this god-forsaken country when I leave this god-forsaken country; but in the meantime, don't think I haven't got my eye on you! I know what you're thinking! I know what you're up to!'

A tin-pot dictator and a paranoid one at that. Things *were* looking up.

'Now get out of my sight.'

Llew stood and bowed; he kept bowing and walked backwards until he was out of the hall, and it was probably a mark of his new-found status that no soldier stuck his foot out and tripped him up as he did so. However, the comfort Llew took from this was minimal. Big deal, no one's tripping me up for a laugh now. How the mighty have risen.

He returned home to find Griff putting his feet up by the fire (as usual) and Ceridwen cooking a pot of stew over it.

'Hello,' said Ceridwen, kissing his cheek, 'how was work?'

'Don't ask. What's new with you, Griff?'

Griff grunted a greeting and stared into the flames.

'Things outside are not looking good, boy.'

By 'outside', Griff meant outside the walls of the Llangollen fortress. It was Griff's job to take small patrols out and make sure all was well with the populace, which of course it never was. That, to be fair, is always the way with populaces generally. Go up to any farmer and ask how things are going, he or she will nearly always say 'ooh, terrible'[73] … ask your average working person how life is, they'll nearly always make a reply of the 'oh, overworked and underpaid, I don't know why I bother really' sort … but you really have to start worrying if they give you these answers through a small, horizontal

---

[73] Try it. It always works.

slot in their door which they've cut recently so they don't have to open it to strangers. And right now the countryside was full of doors with newly-cut slots.

The place was rife with rumour – always a bad sign. Spring had come, making the crossing from Ireland all the easier. The Scotti were all over the place, it was said, hiding in forests and mountains, just waiting for the moment to completely lay waste to the country. Paganism was on the move again – and not the nice tree-worshipping paganism of old. No, the type of paganism where hundreds of people had their heads chopped off at one time to pacify the gods. The Old Ones, the Fair Folk, were coming down from the mountains, coming to claim their own …the land that was taken from them. So you had to put iron outside at night – horseshoes and such-like. Powys was going to invade. Gwent was going to invade. Ambrosius was dead. There would never be an alliance again. The second coming had happened at a small coastal village called Pwllheli, but it had happened at the same time as a Scotti raid and the reborn Christ had been taken as a slave. There was a dragon on Mount Eyri. It only ate fish. You had to put fish on your doorstep at night as well or it would burn your house down.

Right now the countryside was also full of houses with fish and horseshoes outside their doors (as well as the newly-cut slots).

What it all boiled down to was that people were afraid.

'… And they don't think the king is going protect them,' Griff went on, lowering his voice and peering through the gloom to make sure no one was listening at the doorway. 'Truth is, neither do I.'

It wasn't the wilder rumours that worried Griff – dragons, Fair Folk and such-like – but the sighting of Scotti in the area was unnerving. There were plenty of places in the remote and mountainous areas for large numbers of them to hide out. If enough of them got sufficiently far inland, Llangollen itself would be threatened and, if the hill fortress fell, effectively the whole country fell to the Scotti. Of course, people might not have seen Scotti raiders at all. Cymru soldiers had been deserting in their hundreds once Bruenor had stopped paying them, and had started living as large groups of bandits. Not that there was much to tell between the two – when your village is being put to flame and sword, it makes little difference what language is being spoken by those with the weapons and the torches. Although, pleading for mercy is easier if the language is *yours*, obviously.

One whisper was particularly worrying. A feared Irish chieftain by the name of Matholwch had come ashore with a lot of men. Rumours varied on how many, but everyone seemed to agree that the force was closer to the size of an army than a raiding party. Villages had been attacked near Llangollen, food and grain taken and no one could tell if this was the man himself, or whether it was just a normal Scotti raiding party doing the usual, or bandits/deserters doing the same.

Smoking ruins tend to look alike.

Llew went to the fur curtain that was covering the doorway, peaked through, saw no one was there and then came back to the fireplace. It says something about the nature of Gwynedd under Bruenor that two members in a household of three would check the doorway to make sure no one was listening in.

'I think,' he said quietly, 'it's really time we got out of this country.'

It wasn't the first time he'd suggested it, so they didn't look surprised. There was no 'are you mad, where would we go?' or 'we'd never make it – Bruenor would hunt us down like dogs, I tell you, dogs!'

Griff carried on staring into the fire; Ceridwen carried on staring into the pot.

'Well?'

Griffith shifted uncomfortably.

'You know I can't! I mean, it's not just that I've lived in Gwynedd man and boy all my life or that I'm too old to change my ways – although I am, obviously – but you know, my job … see, really I'm sworn to protect people here, aren't I, see? I mean, that's what being a warrior *means*, really, isn't it? That was the whole point of turning on old Vortigern; far as I can tell it was, anyway. Man was a tyrant. And yes, maybe Bruenor's a tyrant too, but he's all we've got left between us and all them Scotti – Matholwch's a bad bastard, you know, famed for it – and all them bandits, see? So I can't, I'm sorry.'

Llew sighed. Griffith had said all this before. Obviously, he had felt the need to say it again, although why he had to do so *in full, word for word* would have been a mystery if Llew hadn't known what Griff was like.

Ceridwen didn't need to say anything. Llew knew full well she wouldn't go without Griff any more than had the situation been reversed, she would have left without Llew.

Llew sighed, frustrated.

'He's going to raise the taxes again. That idiot Thomas has persuaded him to raise taxes *again*! Can't you see what's happening? He's running the country into the ground! And I think he's doing it deliberately! I'm pretty sure it's what he did to his last kingdom. And when it's over he's going to be first at the border, hanging a sign up saying "will the last Cymru to leave Gwynedd please extinguish the torches".'

The other two stayed silent. He knew it was futile to harangue them like this – their minds were made up. Now, the Old Llew would have gone 'oh well, tough luck, I'm out of here, see you in the Otherworld', but New Improved Llew was, it seemed, not like that. So he was stuck. Actually, he was really stuck, because, unlike Griff or even, when it was relatively peaceful, Ceridwen, Llew couldn't venture outside the fortress. Actually, he had problems wandering freely outside his *hut*. This was because, being the king's chamberlain, everyone assumed the policy of continually rising punitive taxes and the general disintegration of the country was down to his advice. It was hard for him to get a hundred yards without someone throwing something at him – whether it be turnip or rock. He was about as popular, as the saying went, as plague.

'Look, if Thomas doesn't advise Bruenor to have me executed for treason, which, by the way, His good old majesty already suspects me of, then one of those poor so and so's out there trying to eke a living from a country that currently only produces mud is going to do for me with a well-placed, well-aimed rock or turnip.'

'Dinner's nearly ready,' said Ceridwen.

And that was that. End of discussion.

'Someone stick another log in the fire,' he said. 'I'm freezing.'

However, Llew's worries about personal safety soon were to become, if not irrelevant, certainly slightly less of a priority over the next few weeks after certain events took place.

It began when refugees started showing up at the gates of Llangollen's outermost wall, demanding to be let in. And when they were told to shove off by the gate captain (in so many words), they started throwing things at him, so he ordered a couple of soldiers go out on horseback to 'bonk a few heads', as they later put it; but as soon as the gates were opened, the refugees rushed at the horsemen and the rest of the gate guards and pretty soon everyone, including all the beggars and outcasts who regularly camped outside the fortress walls, were *inside* and the captain was left standing on the ramparts impotently shouting that he demand everyone leave right now or there really was going to be serious trouble.[74]

It was Llew who was first informed of this situation by the commander of the guard and he knew that one group of refugees coming this way generally meant that there was more to follow. He told them that those inside would now have to stay inside. It wasn't long (and he had known it wouldn't be) before he was summoned to the King's hall.

'Why have you let them close the front gate?' Bruenor demanded.

'It's my belief more refugees will be on their way, Majesty. And whatever is following them will be close behind.'

'Yes, but you've let those that attacked my guards stay *in*, you fool!'

'I understood from the guard commander that if we'd tried to evict them, there'd have been a riot, Majesty. I thought it better to cut our losses and secure the gate.'

'Oh, you thought, did you? *You* thought? You **thought**? Well, let me tell you, boyo, I don't pay you to think!'

Actually, you do, Llew wanted to say, but not enough, not nearly enough.

---

[74] And he was right. When the king found out what had happened, the poor captain lost his job and his head, in that order. This was bad news for everybody because it meant one less able-bodied soldier in the place.

He didn't, however, because he wanted to spare Griff the awkwardness of escorting him to his own execution in Llangollen for a *third* time.

'Now I've got the whole place full of refugees and they're going to demand to be fed, aren't they? *Aren't* they? Coming here, demanding asylum ... who do they think I am? Who do they think they are?'

'I have had an opportunity to interview one or two of them, Majesty – the refugees ...,' interjected Thomas. 'Some of them are quite ... pious.'

Oh, I'll bet they are, thought Llew, knowing that most people from the Gwynedd countryside were still pagan in belief; they've been travelling for days without food or drink and you come along offering bread and wine (not, on the way, mentioning that it's one sip, one crumb and *then* you have to spend two hours praying). Oh, I'll bet they just fell *over* getting into the chapel with religious zeal. Or rather to its doors, because nobody was ever allowed in.

'... and it appears they are running from a dragon. Who eats fish.'

Both Llew and Bruenor blinked and looked at each other before turning to look at Thomas, who did at least have the decency to blush.

'I merely am reporting what they said, sire,' he added, shamefacedly.

'Why?' Bruenor asked irritably, 'why do you think there is any reason *on this earth* I should want to know that?'

'Because it proves the rumour mill that *is* the countryside after a bout of plague has been ... well, working rather too hard. Some people have panicked, that is all. If you don't feed them, sire, they will get bored and hungry. In a few days, they will see that this fish-eating monster has not materialised and they will go home. Or, at the very least, away, which is what we want.'

Llew knew full well that people don't simply abandon their homes just because of wild rumour and he doubted Thomas's sources – the starving will say anything for a bit of wine and bread, no matter how small the portion. However, he decided to hold his piece. Griff would be down amongst the refugees by now and he'd find out what was really going on. But Llew couldn't help but wonder once again what Thomas was up to. Why was he propagating this rumour? He had known the monk long enough to be sure there was an ulterior motive, but here it was hard to see what it was. How could advocating that an influx of refugees into Llangollen was simply a bad case of peasant mass hysteria, when it plainly wasn't, possibly make Thomas look good in front of the king? Again, Thomas was assessing the situation and giving advice that was not just obviously wrong, but plain stupid.

As it happened, they were both dismissed at the same time and found themselves walking from the king's hall together. This had happened before and usually Thomas had put his hands together, pretending to be doing some sort of silent praying as he walked along, making him look, Llew guessed, more pious to those around him and giving him a way to avoid conversing with Llew.

However, Thomas wasn't praying this time. In fact, it was he who broke the silence.

'Rumour has it,' said the monk, 'you are planning to leave.'

Llew managed to keep walking even though his insides had just frozen. How did Thomas know? He'd only talked about this with Griff and Ceridwen and they wouldn't have said anything ... not (taking into account Griff's tendency for verbal diarrhoea) about this, anyway ... so how had Thomas found out?

'You need a thicker door, my brother,' Thomas explained.

Llew was torn once again between Old Llew and New Improved Llew. Old Llew wanted to throw himself at the monk's feet and plead for him not to tell Bruenor, promising gold, furs and sexual favours. The Improved Llew wanted to be sure just how much this obnoxious little man knew before he did so.

The result was silence.

'I wouldn't blame you if you did run,' said Thomas, cryptically; 'but if I were you, I'd go now. Before it's too late. I'd go tonight.'

Before Llew could think of anything to say, Thomas had skipped off down the hill, heading towards his chapel. Llew watched him go.

'There's an army on the move is what it is,' Griffith told him, 'them Scotti, right? But not just them. All the deserters from Bruenor's army, they've joined 'em and they're all marching here. Thousands of 'em there are. Apparently, that chief of theirs – Matholwch – he's been in the country for months preparing. Making little truces with all them ex-soldiers, burning villages for supplies. His plan is to take the country. See, he's a pagan, right? Only the pagans in Ireland are having a hard time of it from the Christians, yeah? So they're coming here, aren't they? Gonna start with Gwynedd, move to Lleyn, then take over Ynys Mon.[75] Be a little pagan Irish paradise here ... you know ... with the sacrificing and so on ... oh, and they'll be here by tomorrow ...'

Llew paced around the hut agitatedly.

'Then we've got to go! Get out of Gwynedd tonight!'

Still staring at the fire, Griffith weighed this up.

'Don't you think we ought to tell the king?'

'What for?' said Llew incredulously.

Griffith had plainly never quite got to grips with this 'fleeing' lark.

'About the Irish,' he said, reading Llew's thoughts. 'So he can warn everyone else, at least.'

Llew sighed. Sometimes he got tired of having to lecture people like Griffith on the realities of life.

'Look, if we go and tell Bruenor, what's he going to say? "Oh, we're

---

[75] Anglesey, N.Wales; lit. 'Mother Isle'.

doomed! No soldiers. Advancing Irish army. Logical thing to do is abandon Llangollen and run." Is that what he's going to say?' Llew was aware of his voice becoming a little hysterical.

'It's what you said he'd do the other day,' pointed out Ceridwen as she threaded a wooden needle, 'you said he was running the country into the ground just so he can abandon it. Well, isn't this his chance? He can bugger off east without loss of face and with plenty of gold.'

Llew stopped. Actually, that was a good point. Faced with overwhelming odds, the king was just as likely to empty his treasury onto a few ox carts and run like the wind. In fact, Bruenor had just enough men to escort himself and the gold out of the country. If everyone else abandoned Llangollen, then the Scotti could just march in and stage a bloodless coup. Point being that if Bruenor ran, then everyone else could run *as long as the king was given enough time to run in the first place*. Then everyone else could make their escape too. But if it were left too late, Bruenor would have no choice but to make a last stand and let the fortress be besieged.

It also occurred to Llew that, having been personally responsible for the Saxon takeover of the south-east of the country, he was now about to be responsible for the Irish taking over the north-west. Maybe *this* was why his father was never proud of him. However … needs must …

'If I go to Bruenor and tell him to abandon the place, he'll do the exact opposite of what I say,' he said, thinking aloud, '*but* if I can persuade Thomas to tell him …'

Within minutes, Llew was scurrying down towards the little chapel at the place where a giant dream tower had once stood.

'Thomas!'

He burst open the doors and hurried in. It was empty. Everything was as normal, or he guessed so, seeing as it was the first time he'd ever been in there … the wooden crucifix stood on the little wooden altar … rough embroidered pictures of the saints and the Madonna, made by the women of Llangollen, had been hung all around … but something wasn't right. He had shut the door behind him tight, the windows were shuttered up and yet there was still a draught. Llew had a knack of knowing when there was a draught – it was a gift – and there was one in this chapel, just a slight one. He walked slowly towards the altar and noticed it wasn't quite square with the rest of the room. He pushed it slightly. It moved. He pushed it again, harder; it slid away from Llew and there in front of him was a hole in the ground, with a ladder going downwards. It occurred to him that were someone, a monk for instance, say … a spy for the other side … this was a great way of sneaking in and out of the stockade would be via a tunnel that went under the wooden walls. It'd also be a great way for the enemy to attack from inside without a prolonged siege.

He knew he'd better get to work and fast.

He found the king, alone (except for his usual twelve bodyguards, of course – Bruenor was nothing if not careful) in his hall and sitting on his throne.

'So what is happening with this … tunnel now?'

'Griffith has some people filling it in. They've found the entrance as well. It was hidden in some bushes, just outside the outer wall. It must have taken him ages to dig it, but it means he's been able to sneak in and out at will without anyone noticing. No wonder he'd never allow anybody in that chapel.'

'Yes, this would also explain the long periods alone at prayer.'

Yes, it would. It had never occurred to anyone that maybe it was unusual for a holy person to disappear into a room without a toilet for weeks at a time. Still, that's hindsight for you.

Bruenor looked grim. He had good reason to. If he didn't look grim, there was a good chance he was going to look like a prize fool.

'So … what would you suggest I do, *scribe*?'

Still making it sound like an insult then, in spite of Llew just discovering an enemy spy.

Llew reflected that there was a chance, *just* a chance, that this might be the last time he would be kneeling before his king. He took a deep breath.

'There's an army on the move, sire. An army made up of Scotti raiders and deserters from our own side. We don't know how big it is, but the chances are they've got more soldiers than we have here. More refugees are coming by the hour, all wanting to get in at the gates. It seems to me we … that is, you … have a choice. Stay here and stand your ground, or my advice would be to take your men into the hills before we are beseiged. Mount a campaign from there. Harry them like they are harrying us until they too retreat.'

Llew knew that in actual fact what he was suggesting to Bruenor was this:

'Bugger off with your gold and what's left of your men, leave these peasants and this god-awful place. You may have lost another kingdom, but you never wanted to come here anyway and you'll still have the loot.'

And he was sure it was an offer that the king would not refuse.

'And where would you go, scribe?'

'Wherever you order me to, sire,' said Llew, perhaps just a *little* too enthusiastically. 'With you into the mountains, or stay here to … organise the refugees.'

And then, as soon as no one's looking, he thought, me and the family are off into the not-quite-as-wild blue yonder.

The king, seated on his throne, sat back and pondered silently.

'Hmm,' he said finally, 'so I should abandon this place?'

Nearly there …

'… which is, of course, exactly what you *want* me to do?'

Uh oh …

'You forget I know you, scribe! I know that you're plotting against me –'

'I think you'll find it's Thomas who –'

'You want the Scotti to come here! And then you'll hand them my kingdom, just like you did the last one!'

Oh ... crap! I forgot not to be a 'yes' man!

'And the only reason I haven't killed you so far is because I know that the best advice I can act on is precisely the opposite of everything you say.'

Oh crap, crap, crapity, crap!

'We will stay here! We will survive and when they have thrown everything they can at us, they will have no choice but to parley or leave. We will allow the refugees into the fortress. Let every one of them stand on its walls ready to defend it! And you shall help Griffith to organise them. You have seen battle. Now you will see a siege.'

Oh crap, crap, crapity, crap, crap, crapity, crap, crap crap!

'After all, to lose one kingdom could be said to be unfortunate,' Bruenor said in a moment of futuristic literary aptness, 'to lose two would look like carelessness.[76] Do you not think so, *scribe*?'

'Yes, Majesty.'

Later that evening, Llew found himself walking along the outer ramparts of the fortress with Griffith, trying to make sure they'd got enough men manning the walls for the night. They had. Just. They'd had to choose a large contingent from the refugees to help and they'd organised things so that there could be two shifts – day and night – one half of each watch would be professional soldiers, the other ... emaciated, starving, scared farmers, whose 'armour' was their thickest smocks and who had responded to the call to 'bring your own weapons' with wooden sticks – and the only chance of these being any use at all was if they made a marauding enemy die laughing.

Down in the grounds of the stockade was what might be called 'the reserves'. The reinforcements. Or, to be more accurate, the old people, pregnant women and children – a force to really strike fear into the heart of your average Scotti raider. Some of the refugees, a few, had their own bows and arrows that had been used mainly for catching game birds or small mammals. Now they would be put to a different use.

Llew had put his armour on. He realised now he looked (and had *always* looked) ridiculous, but if it stopped a spear from skewering him when it was chucked then, quite honestly, he didn't care.

'So, how do you think they'll come?' he said nervously. 'Will it be in one big rush? You know, like in a battle? Will they ask us to surrender first? Or what? Come on, Griffith – you know this sort of thing – what are they going to do?'

Griffith shrugged. Uncharacteristically silent, he shook his head slowly.

'Oh, great. Great help. You're commanding these forces, Griff. You're in *charge*!'

---

[76] Bruenor had a literary gift well ahead of his time.

Griffith nodded, admitting it was true.

'Not used to being in command, me,' he said finally, looking out across the hills and woodland illuminated by the moonlight. It was blisteringly clear. Get high up enough and you could probably even see the moon reflecting on the sea, which was miles away.

'Well,' hissed Llew at him, 'I don't want to have to remind you that we could have been out of here weeks ago, but oh no – big noble Griff had to honour his oath to protect the people, which meant that we had to stay here too.'

'Hmm, she's a nice lady, your wife, isn't she? I've got quite fond of her in my own way.'

'The point being,' said Llew, barely hiding his exasperation, 'that as we are here on your behest, it might be good if you thought about how we're going to survive this by working out how the enemy will attack!!!'

'Look, don't get all shirty with me! All the fighting I done, someone else has been telling me what to do! Not my fault if I'm the only captain left.'

'That's my point! You're a captain! You must have given a few orders in your time!'

'Not so'd you'd notice.'

Muttering a few inaudible swear words under his breath, Llew turned away and looked outside towards the lands surrounding the hill fortress. Something caught his eye.

'Is it me,' he said, puzzled, 'or has that woodland got quite a lot closer than it used to be?'

Griffith looked out to where Llew was pointing.

'Bugger me!' he said in wonder. 'It's moving.'

He wasn't wrong. The trees, bushes and whatever were very slowly but surely edging across the open fields towards the settlement.

'Good Gods!' said Griff, 'they've camouflaged themselves!'

'No,' said Llew flatly, 'do you really think so?'

'That's bloody clever, that is. Someone should use that!'

'Someone *is* using it, Griff!'

'No, I meant in a story or something. It's like a whole forest on the move. You could think it was magic or something. 'Specially if it was prophesied like … it'd make a great tale for one of the bards!'

There was a pause. Then …

'Shouldn't one of us sound the alarm?' said Llew as conversationally as he dared.

'Oh, yeah …'

Griffith raised his battle horn to his lips and blew hard. There was a very brief pause and then the whole place became a hive of activity ' soldiers running up stone steps … refugees and such-like following them and trying not to trip up. Shields were held rim to rim on the edge of the battlements;

between each, where the shields met and touched, a bow was drawn or a spear was poised for throwing and in rather too many places a wooden stick was pointed.

At exactly the same moment the horn sounded, as if it had been a signal for them too, the enemy dropped their foliage-based disguises and surged forward, screaming war cries of both Scotti and Cymru.

'Wait for it, wait for it!' shouted Griff, marching up and down the ramparts and thankfully, at the last moment, getting the inspiration of command, 'don't fire till I say so. Don't want to waste no arrows or spears, do we? Or sticks,' he added quietly.

Llew, peeking out between two shields from behind one of the archers (a soldier), watched with a terrible fascination as the enemy charged towards them. They had painted their faces in all sorts of weird and horrible patterns. Llew knew that by day the paint would be blue – a dye the Scotti used called woad – but in the moonlight it looked black and the enemy looked like an army of demons from hell charging up on them.

This was, of course, the point. The idea was to scare.

'Fire!' Griffith screamed over the noise.

Arrows, spears, rocks and sticks rained down, causing a mass of screams of pain and anger. Nearly everyone found a target, because they were aimed at a huddling mass of people. There was a swishing sound in the air as a few were returned – they in their turn managed to hit home once or twice … the odd refugee hadn't managed to dodge behind a shield in time. Most of the enemy fell away and now Llew could see that some of them had been carrying something other than weaponry.

Ladders. Rough wooden ones, obviously recently hewn from the same forest that had been the disguise for the attack. They were going to try and mount the fortress walls. Luckily for Llangollen, that first wave of spears and arrows seemed to have wiped out most of the ladder carriers, but one or two had made it to the edge of the ramparts. Enemy warriors were now scampering up them one after the other. Men on the ramparts were heaving against them to push them over, toppling the painted men to the ground.

'Something's not right …,' Griff shouted, '… this isn't a proper attack. There's hardly any men here …'

Could've fooled me, thought Llew.

'It's a distraction, that's why!' he shouted back. 'I hope you filled that tunnel up well.'

'Actually, I didn't,' said Griffith.

Llew looked at him, horrified …

… Inside the tunnel, a band of Scotti raiders were making their way through and reflecting on how easy this was all proving. All they had to do was come up through the trap door in the chapel's altar as instructed and they would be right inside the fortress. Every Cymru soldier would be on the fortress walls with the exception of the king's bodyguard, who, if their information was correct, would be sitting on a pile of gold. All the little band had to do was kill the king, sneak off and start opening the gates and the masses of Scotti warriors and Cymru deserters would rush in. It would all be over bar the shouting.

Oh, and the slaughtering and the pillaging. And slave taking, obviously.

The first of them had now come upon the ladder in the dark. To get to it, he had to kick away a large piece of wood that was propped up against one of the tunnel supports.

'Oengus,' said the man behind, whimsically to his leader, 'now would I be imagining things, or is there something creaking in here?' …

Meanwhile, Llew didn't have time to question Griffith about this because, with a crash, the top of a ladder had landed on the rampart right opposite him, knocking over the soldiers whose shields had been providing him with protection and now a painted and screaming face had appeared at the top of it. Llew did not remember drawing his rusty sword from its scabbard, only that it had appeared in his hand and he'd raised it above his head to protect himself. Somehow, the sword had connected with the ladder and, with an ear-splitting explosion, the ladder shattered into splinters, causing a whole load of Scotti warriors to tumble, crying, to the ground.

Then a horn sounded outside, far off towards the trees. The enemy, those alive anyway, turned and began to run back towards where they had come from.

'That's the first attack then,' said Griffith, over the cheering of the inhabitants of Llangollen.

Once the tunnel had collapsed, Matholwch had pulled all his men back to make sure he didn't lose any more unnecessarily. He'd hoped that this would be a quick victory. That had been the point of using the tunnel. Now it looked as if it was going to be a typical siege. He and his men would occupy the surrounding lands of Llangollen. They had access to all the timber and all the local food producers and just about anything they needed. Llangollen had only as much stuff as they had when they last closed the gates. It would take a while, but all he had to do was sit and watch them starve until they surrendered. By that time, of course, everyone in there would be so hungry they'd willingly be slaves for his people as long as slavery provided one square meal a day.

Either that or they'd have eaten each other. He'd heard the Picts did that.

Griffith had taken advantage of the enemy withdrawal. He had sent men out to retrieve any arrows, spears, sticks or indeed rocks that had been hurled and were still hurlable. Nothing could afford to be wasted. He also had the corpses piled together and set on fire.

'I suppose that's a message to the enemy,' said Llew grimly and perhaps a trifle too dramatically, 'the bigger the fire, the more men it shows we've taken.'

'No,' said Griffith, puzzled; 'it keeps away the plague. Lots of disease around when corpses are left to rot and that lot are right by a settlement, in case you hadn't noticed. You're a bit weird sometimes, you know that?'

Llew had to admit Griff wasn't the first to point this out.

'Daft thing is,' mused Griff half to himself, looking first to the fire and then toward the horizon where the Scotti had started erecting the first of several encampments, 'we could have beaten this lot hands down if that idiot Bruenor hadn't kept all the gold for himself. Could have paid for a proper army. Proper army could wipe the floor with 'em. They're only a bunch of pirates when all's said and done.'

Llew followed Griff's gaze into the middle distance. They looked like an *awful lot* of pirates to him.

So the people went about the grizzly business that goes on after any armed confict – salvaging or looting anything of use and burning everything else and Llew found himself reflecting that every time one of these things happened, a little bit of humanity, a little bit of civilisation was chipped away from those involved – whether it was because they became more used to the sight of burning corpses or because one or two might not see the harm in using a knife to 'liberate' a warrior ring from its former owner. He resolved to put this down on parchment as soon as he got a moment. Although he got precious few of those these days, he found that the sacks of writings were now starting to accumulate, practically filling up Ceridwen's old wagon. Almost, he mused bitterly, enough for a library. Ha! Whatever happened to that idea? It was not one he felt the inclination to share with his current lord and master. The idea of a reptile like Bruenor being in charge of all the information to make him the most powerful king in Ynys Prydein didn't bear thinking about. It'd be like setting a wolf in a packed sheep field and successfully teaching it to use a bow and arrow. In retrospect, it was an idea he perhaps *could* have discussed with Ambrosius. Then again, Ambrosius was the bastard who'd sent him here, so why should *he* get any favours?

Meantime, the next day, two Scotti warriors approached the settlement under a flag of truce. They said their king would parley, which was diplomatic language for 'negotiate a fairly unconditional surrender'. The meeting was to take place in the middle of the open ground between Llangollen and the Scotti camp. It was agreed that three from each side would be allowed to attend – one king, one advisor and one warrior to act as bodyguard and king's champion – and, although Bruenor practically choked on the notion, he had little other choice but to have Llew come along. Now that Thomas had gone, the king had virtually no one he could trust – well, no one who could walk and think at the same time, which discounted most of his personal guards. Indeed, the champion Bruenor had chosen to accompany them was a warrior called Gwyr, who could perhaps be described as the living embodiment of this in that asking him his age gave him problems because he only had ten fingers.

As they rode up to the agreed meeting place – a small pool surrounded by trees – Llew could see the delegation from the enemy approaching. There was a big bearded man almost entirely clothed, it seemed, in weapons, a man well disposed to throwing over a table and crying 'groooooohahahah', and Llew assumed rightly that this must be the king's champion. He was surprised to see riding almost immediately behind him none other than Thomas. Well, well, well, thought Llew, not only was Thomas a spy, he must be pretty high up in Matholwch's court to be brought here as advisor. And this meant that the older, long-bearded man with a ... dead seagull tied to his head, must be the Irish chieftain himself. Oh good – they were going to be negotiating with a nutter.

The three horses stopped a little way off from them. Then the Irish champion rode his horse forward a few paces. Gwyr did the same thing.

Tradition held it on occasions such as these that the first action should be an exchange of insults between the two sides. What the purpose was, no one really knew, but tradition was tradition and you didn't go changing it just because you hadn't a clue what it was for. Over the years, the practice had evolved so that the exchanges were meant to be as cutting, witty and satirical as was humanly possible. However, as it was the job of the king's champion to do the insulting, Llew had been working very hard that morning at coaching Gwyr so that the insults went a bit beyond the 'you're-a-big-fat-pig-who-smells-like-a pig-an'-looks-like-a-pig-an'-that' kind. It had not been easy, but Llew had done his best to get Gwyr to learn, parrot fashion, a witty phrase about the clumsiness of the Scotti, the cowardice of their warriors and the general easy virtue of their women.

The Scotti warrior went first.

'It is said that the Cymru fights like a woman! It is said that he runs and cries like a baby without milk every time he fights a battle! It is said that even now the Cymru hide crying like children in their halls soiling their own armour in fear!'

And he spat proudly. Not bad. The Irish were obviously good at this. However, Llew was confident that, if Gwyr remembered what he had been repeating to himself over and over all morning, they would at least be able to say that Cymru had stood their ground with honour. However, Gwyr's forehead was a virtual sea of wrinkles as he tried to remember his lines, which was not a good sign.

Finally, he gave up.

'Yeah, well, you're a big fat pig who smells like a pig an' looks like a pig an' that,' he finally managed.

Llew sighed and clapped his hand to his forehead.

'Oh, splendid,' muttered Bruenor, in a tight-lipped monotone; 'such a shame there are no bards here for truly they would have writ *that* into song.' And then, because he wasn't as good at sarcasm as he thought, he added, 'I don't think.'

He spurred his horse forward so that he was now level with Gwyr – the opening ceremony of the parleying now completed – and Llew followed. Meantime, Thomas and the other rider had pulled their horses level with their champion. It was Thomas who spoke first.

'Greetings, Bruenor, King Of Gwynedd.'

He had an Irish accent, which made sense, but it was strange to hear all the same. The poncey posh one he'd used when pretending to be a monk would have been a disguise and, now that Llew thought about it, wasn't terribly convincing, actually. He sheepishly thought that if there was a God of Hindsight it must be a very smug one.

'I do not parley spies and traitors,' said Bruenor, proudly, 'I will speak with your king and no other.'

'Then you will speak with me,' said Thomas, 'for I am Matholwch, chieftain of Scotti. This …,' and here he indicated the man with the seagull on his head, 'is my druid, Parsan.'

Now here was a surprise to everyone.

'What?' Llew could not help himself blurting out, 'you're a king and you do your own spying?'

'Well now, scribe,' said the man, smiling, 'you and I both know that if you're not big and violent and you want to survive in this world, you have to learn a trade. Yours is writing things down. Mine is learning people's secrets. And I'm good too, you have to admit.'

There was an uncomfortable silence. It was quite true, but to admit it would have seemed like giving ground and they hadn't even started negotiating yet. However, Thomas, or Matholwch, as he was actually called, didn't seem to mind. A silence was something he could fill.

'And, being a monk … well, that just made things easier. I could go anywhere, find out anything, nobody suspected. And people came and confessed things to me. For instance, Bruenor, I happen to know that, for the past six months, your quartermaster has been selling off sacks of flour to people outside the settlement on the quiet. Which means that, in a few weeks time, you're going to completely run out of bread … all sorts like that. Only mistake I made was trying to let on to your man here …,' and he indicated Llew, 'that he ought to get out while the going was good. If I hadn't, the tunnel would've worked and –'

'And we wouldn't be here parleying,' interrupting Bruenor, rightly assuming that if this chieftain/spy were allowed to do all the talking they could be there all day. 'What do you want?'

'Oh, it's very simple,' said Matholwch, looking at first his champion then his druid. 'I want here. Gwynedd. I mean, in reality, I've already got it … I just don't have …'

He pointed towards the hill fortress.

'Now, if you give me that. Open your gates, let my men in … then only you Bruenor and you scribe will die. If the king and his chamberlain are killed, then it will show your people they belong to me. I promise you it'll be quick. If you don't, we will sit it out here and eventually *everyone* will die, because they'll starve to death and the ones that don't, we'll kill. What do you think?'

'I have to say,' said Bruenor carefully, 'it's not an agreement I'm amazingly keen on ...'

'Yes, but in the circumstances you don't really have a lot of choice, do you? I will outlast you and I will kill you one way or another, so what's it to be?'

Bruenor sat there thinking. Llew knew what he was doing – he was trying to work out a way to save his skin and some of his gold. Bruenor would be damn sure by now he'd have to leave the kingdom – the lack of food in the fortress now effectively quashing Bruenor's plan to outlast the besiegers – but there was a chance he could negotiate his freedom and the price would only be most (but hopefully not all) of his gold and probably the enslavement of everyone inside Llangollen. Llew was pretty sure the Irish chieftain was thinking along the same lines. After all, what would he profit from the death of a defeated king and a scribe? It was plainly a subterfuge to get Bruenor to make a compromise – say ... the execution of Llew, but not Bruenor? Which Matholwch would accept and offer to throw in some gold to sweeten the deal. That way, both men would have pretty much what they wanted without having to go through a prolonged siege.

Llew wouldn't, of course.

'Supposing,' said Bruenor, 'I were to offer you a compromise?'

This was it. Llew decided to take the plunge.

'May I speak with you, Majesty?'

Bruenor looked surprised and annoyed to be interrupted.

'What?'

'I would speak with you, my liege. In private.'

Bruenor gave Llew a black look, but the scribe had already trotted his horse away so that they were out of hearing of the others and Bruenor, although uncomfortable, had no choice but to follow.

'Yes, this is all *very* good, isn't it?' hissed the king through clenched teeth, as he approached Llew, 'not only have I got the pig line as my searing opening gambit, I've got you *ordering* me – the king – away from negotiations. More for the bards to sing about when I've gone, eh?'

Llew took a deep breath and then, with all the venom he could muster, he began to hiss back.

'Now listen to me and listen to me good, you little *turd*! You are not selling me and everyone else in that fortress down the river into death or slavery just so that you can ride out of here with a few bags of measly coins!'

Bruenor was open-mouthed in astonishment. Llew carried on regardless.

'You cannot trust him!' he hissed, pointing at the former 'monk'; 'he will not let you go with or without the money, whatever he says. He will kill you as soon as you open those gates and he will take the gold and kill or enslave everybody else! You were stupid enough to trust him before and what did he turn out to be? Not only an enemy spy, but an enemy *king*!! Now, *I* know you're mean and greedy and full of your own self-importance, but that doesn't mean everybody else has to! Everyone else *thinks* you're king and a king loves his country and lives in it – he doesn't try and make it so crap he can just abandon it. Or at least,' Llew added, 'he doesn't do so *twice*! Not while I'm his scribe, anyway. So, if you're going to be king, just try behaving like one!'

Bruenor did at least have the grace to look sheepish.

'And while we're on the subject of me, I am not going to be executed by that Irishman to save your worthless arse, so let me make this clear right now …,' and he lowered his voice right down, 'you make a deal with Thomas, or Matholwch or whatever he's called, one where I am to be executed and I will make sure … *personally* make sure that all those rumours – and, oh yes, there are lots of them – about who actually killed Horsa – are confirmed as the truth to the whole of Ynys Prydein. You want to know how? Because *I've written it down!* Lots of times! So you'll have to find my parchments and burn them … all of them … but you know the funny thing about writing is, you can leave it anywhere, with anyone and – no matter how secret you tell them to keep it – they always give it to someone to read. *Do you understand?*'

Bruenor understood all right – his face seemed to have developed quite a severe tick.

'Good,' said Llew, 'we'll go back to it then. Let me handle this.'

He wheeled his horse back to the negotiations and Bruenor followed dumbly.

'I have his majesty's reply to your proposal,' said Llew.

'Go on,' said Matholwch, still smiling charmingly.

When Llew had finished telling him, the chieftain had stopped smiling and had started wondering whether such a thing was physically possible. He looked at Bruenor for confirmation and Bruenor nodded sullenly.

The two parties then turned and went their separate ways.

At least, thought Llew, they had managed to get some decent insults in.

Later on, Llew found himself being thoroughly beaten up. He was in the king's hall where he had been dragged by two members of Bruenor's personal guard. The king had then ordered the guards to set about Llew in as comprehensive and meticulous a way as they possibly could. The equivalent today would be a battering with several tyre irons followed by a good rub down with sandpaper. And while they did this, Bruenor paced to and fro, agitatedly berating the scribe for what he had done.

'Never mind the way you spoke to me – and, believe me, no one, **no one** speaks to me like that! Just what are we supposed to do now? Just what do you think we are going to do? Sit here and starve? He has us surrounded! He has access to every grain store in the land! We have a few months of rations and then we have nothing! Apart from gold, which of course I love, but **I CANNOT EAT!!!**'

Llew received a painful kick and watched a tooth spin away across the floor. He was, he gratefully began to feel, starting at last to lose consciousness. He also had another reason to be grateful – that he wasn't the bloody, limp mass in the corner that had once been Llangollen's quartermaster. The guards had really gone to town on *that* guy. Oh good, Llew realised, he was starting to lose all feeling …

The doors of the hall burst open and there, framed by them, was a one-armed figure clutching a sword in his right hand. Griff may have been old and slightly subtracted from, but he was still large and scary.

'All right, that's enough!' he cried.

The two guards did at least have the sense to stop kicking Llew. Bruenor sighed.

'What do **you** want?' he said irritably.

'I should have thought that was obvious,' said Griff, puzzled. 'I want you to stop beating up miladdo there!'

Bruenor shook his head frustratedly.

'I have had enough of this!' he said, his voice rising. 'I am still the bloody king of this awful country, but suddenly everybody thinks it's all right to give me orders! **I have had enough of this!!!**'

He looked at Griffith, still standing there with his sword drawn.

'Just … kill him!' He waved his hands distractedly at the other guards in the hall. 'I don't have time to muck about any more … just kill him.'

The guards drew their swords, but hesitantly and cautiously began to approach. Griffith may only have had one arm, but he was a feared veteran of many of the bloodiest campaigns in the land. He had a fearsome reputation in battle and no one wanted to be the first to take him on. However, he was outnumbered eleven to one. If a couple of them took a chance, his odds would not be good.

'Ambrosius …!' Llew tried to croak as loudly as he could through a swollen lip, 'Ambrosius! Ambrosius!'

Luckily Bruenor was close enough to be able to hear him.

'Hold!'

The guards stopped advancing on Griffith.

'All right,' said Bruenor testily, 'exactly what has he got to do with this?'

Llew attempted to find the strength to speak.

'He has … an army … in the north. He … owes you, majesty … for Egelesprep … for Horsa …'

Bruenor blinked and looked thoughtful. Finally, he nodded.

'Hm. A point, I suppose. Of course, someone will have to go and get him.'

Chapter 15 – Llew's Dillemma

'You can't go! You can hardly go to the *toilet* on your own, let alone drive all the bloody way to Pictland!'

Ceridwen was shouting again and it wasn't pleasant, because Llew had a multitude of aches all over his body, *not* including his head, that (contrary to medical opinion) were made worse by loud noises. Actually, his head was aching too, quite a lot. The last time he'd been beaten up, it was by thugs who wanted to rob him. This time, it was by experts who believed it an important part of the way they earned their living and, comparatively, the first lot were rank amateurs. There's nothing like being beaten up by craftsmen if you want to learn how it's done.

Griffith had carried him back to the hut and Ceridwen had bathed him, bandaged him and generally said soothing things like, 'Oh stop making such a *fuss!*' when, during the course of these ministrations, he'd gone 'Ow! Ow! Oweee! Ow! Ruddy Nora, that hurts!'

And then a message had come from Bruenor. Llew was to make ready to travel North to the land of the Picts as soon as possible. Or tomorrow. Whichever was the sooner.

'I'll be all right,' he'd muttered. 'I'll be on a cart.'

He was lying on the bed, just letting all the bruises and cuts he had throb in their own individual and very personal ways.

'But why you? Why can't someone else go?'

She was sitting on the bed next to him, bathing his forehead – for all the good it was doing.

'Because I know Ambrosius and he'll listen to me and … well, because *Bruenor* knows I'll come back.'

And there, *there* was the irony, because after so many attempts at excluding himself permanently from Llangollen, coming back really was what he intended to do. Bruenor wasn't going to let Ceridwen and/or Griff leave with Llew, which was exactly how the king could be sure the scribe would return. And if Llew wanted anyone alive at the end of the whole adventure, he'd have to return with both items on this very short shopping list:

Northern Land Of The Picts – things to get:
General Ambrosius (1)
Big Army (1)

It wasn't a mental list either. He'd actually written it down, though he didn't really know why. It wasn't likely he was going to get there and forget what he came for.

Well, this was it, he mused dryly – the next peak in the high-flying career of the boy from a small but not insignificant little clan in southern Powys. Once again on the move, only this time to the wildest of the wilderlands. And there somehow, in that vast expanse, he was expected to find one man and his army, knowing only that his was the direction they were heading in when he last heard. Of course, it was possible they hadn't even left the south-east yet, but supposing he went all the way down there only to find that they *had*? What was he supposed to do then? No, it wasn't worth the risk. By the time he'd finally got north from there, the siege of Llangollen would be totally over and everybody would be …

… he decided to leave the thought unfinished.

Of course, the chances of *that* happening anyway were still pretty … well, he didn't want to think about it. In itself, going *north* was a ridiculous undertaking, but it was – to use an over-used phrase – the only chance they'd got.

'All right,' he said to her earnestly, trying not to make his bruises throb even more, 'this is what we're doing. When I come back and the huge army that I've managed to pick up on the way has lifted the siege and defeated the Scotti, you, me and Griff are out of here and on a boat, understand?' I don't care what the situation is, I don't care who needs us to stay, or why, we are all going!'

She nodded and tried to smile. This failed and so she ended up with a wistful, almost regretful expression on her face. Aha, he thought, I know that look! She's thinking maybe we should have left when I first suggested it! That maybe I was right! Ha! Fine time to come round to my way of thinking! Typical! That makes me so – … Ow! Ow! Owie! Ow! Ruddy Nora!

As it happened, he could not leave straight away, much to Bruenor's annoyance. A series of bright, cloudless days and very bright moonlit nights made it impossible for him to leave Langollen without being seen. He'd insisted on taking a *horse*-drawn cart – again, to Bruenor's disapproval, because horses were useful in war and valuable with it … but Llew had pointed out that he didn't ride well and that ox-drawn wagons were far too slow if he was seriously going to make a break for it.

Griff had protested vociferously when he heard Llew was to travel without at least one armed man to guard him – the chances of the scribe being attacked en route were more than likely, but Bruenor had insisted that no one else could be spared. Every man who could stand would almost certainly be needed on the hill fort's walls. This was actually why Llew *could* be spared – because he *couldn't* stand very well.

'Oh well,' he said grimly, 'at least I'll have the sword.'

Griffith was loading it onto the cart for him. Llew was sitting on a little bench outside the hut, watching him.

'Don't knock it,' said Griff, 'I watched you shatter a siege ladder with that thing. And don't get me wrong … you might be the greatest warrior in all the world underneath for all I know … but I never heard of anyone being able to do that. Not in all my years of soldiering, honest I haven't. And, of course, now Ceridwen's told me the rumours … about Horsa and that … well, who knows what this thing is? That's all I'm saying …'

Llew sighed, exasperated.

'I told her to keep quiet about that.'

'She only told me!' said Griffith, immediately rushing to Ceridwen's defence as he always did. 'And we was alone in the hut and everything.'

'Yes, well, look how much good *that* did us with Thomas!' Llew winced… one of his ribs was really playing up this morning. 'Look, you two are going to have to be really careful … I'm not going to be here to talk you out of trouble.'

'Oh yeah, and you always do a *fine* job of that!' said Griffith, amused, 'Mr Three Crack Legions!'

'Kept me alive, didn't it?'

'More by luck than cunning,' Griff snorted. 'And anyway, don't you worry – I'll look after her.'

'Griff …'

The sudden hollowness of Llew's voice made Griff stop and look round.

'If they do break through – the Scotti, I mean.'

'They won't get within an inch of either of us,' said Griff, looking directly into Llew's eyes, so that they both understood perfectly. Then lightly Griff said, 'Now what do you want doing with these?'

He was gesturing to a pile of sacks that had been stored virtually since they arrived on the stationary wagon. A pile that had been added to with more sacks and then covered over with a specially made portable roof of wood and thatch to keep it from getting wet. Every one of the sacks was stuffed full to bursting with Llew's parchments.

'Well, he's not going to need them where he's going, is he?' said Ceridwen, bustling out of the hut, 'so they can be here for him when he gets back, can't they, Llew?'

Llew tried to keep the expression on his face in 'casual'. The thing was, the thing *was* … well, there was a chance, wasn't there, that he *wasn't* going to make it back … that something might happen to him … and well, if that happened, well then, he wasn't bringing Ambrosius, chances were … and if that happened, then Llangollen would be taken by the Scotti and the parchments would be destroyed along with … everything else. So … *so* … worse-case scenario here … perhaps it was better to get the parchments out of there so that if *something were to happen to him* … maybe they could be taken to a monastery or something and looked after.

What he couldn't explain was how important those parchments were to him.

'Oh,' she said, 'okay.'

And her expression didn't change either.

So, the wagon was loaded. Llew'd had a couple of days rest and now he could just about hobble around slowly without passing out. All they had to do was wait for some natural camouflage – a darkened moonless night, for instance – for the little wagon to sneak out from the main gate and past the Scotti soldiers that patrolled constantly between the surrounding encampments. Or if not Dark Of The Moon, Gwynedd was famous for its eerie and extremely thick mists, often known by the locals as the 'breath of the dragon'. Just one of these would have been enough to give him cover.

However, disguise came in the only way he could have expected one night in the form of pouring, drenching, dense sheets of icy cold rain and high north winds. Not only was it raining so hard Llew could barely see his hand stretched out in front of him, he knew he would have the advantage that every enemy patrolman would have either his hood or his helmet firmly pulled over his eyes and his head down into his chest with his cloak wrapped tight around him as he tried to stay dry. Llew barely had time to kiss Ceridwen goodbye before the gates were opened and he was spurring his horse on, fast as it would go, out towards the mountain roads, the bumping of the cart playing havoc with his bruised ribs as it jogged at speed over the rocky track, and hoping against hope the horse had a vague idea of where it was going.

Meanwhile, Griff had the guard on the gates doubled and the patrols on the perimeter walls were told to keep a sharp eye out. He didn't want to risk anyone – of, say, a spying persuasion – being able to sneak out of Llangollen towards the Scotti camp. Later, he went back to Llew's hut and gave Ceridwen a bit of cloth to blow her nose on and wipe her eyes with. And he tried to think of something to say, but couldn't. Which was pretty unusual for Griffith, especially when he was uncomfortable.

No one could watch Llew fade off into the distance, because there wasn't a distance to watch him fade off into; just sheets of driving rain, which, as omens go for last hopes, wasn't considered good.

Ambrosius trotted along on his horse as the sergeant trying to ride the smaller and less manageable pony attempted to keep up. The sergeant wasn't used to riding, let alone this fast, but these days it had become a necessity.

'You see, Sergeant? All it takes is a little persuasion! People want this to work! With King Ceneu on-side, we now have all the kings of northern Prydein in our alliance.'

'Yes, sir!'

The movement of a trotting pony prevented the sergeant from arguing with the Old Man. Not that he'd have argued anyway, because everyone knew that

Ambrosius was good at heart and no one wanted to disillusion him by telling him the facts. However, the facts were that the kings of Elmet, Rheged and the other northern nations had become part of the new alliance in name only. They hadn't committed any soldiers or gold. They had, of course, agreed to resist any attack by the Picts or even the Saxons, but they would have done that anyway.

'So, what news, Sergeant? I assume that messenger had something of import to say.'

'Yes, sir. It's as we feared. The Angles are now spreading far up the eastern coast and the Saxons are moving on Londinium. If we don't do something fast they'll have overwhelmed the South-East … that's what the reports say sir – ow!'

The pony had just stumbled on a bump.

'Anyway, the chieftains are urging you to get back there now, sir. Oh, and there's a rebellion against your authority in Gwent again, sir. You'll need to deal with that as well!'

So far, the campaign could be said to have been going well. A couple of small skirmishes with a few tribes just south of Hadrian's Wall had been pretty successful, if short. The real tough stuff would come when they headed into the territory of tribes like the Votadini.

'But dammit, Sergeant, we're just about to deal with the Picts!'

'Don't blame me, sir, I'm only the messenger. Actually, I'm only telling you what the messenger said, so I'm only the *messenger* of the messenger, if you see what I mean –'

'Yes, thank you, Sergeant.'

'What I mean is, sir, that we need to go back.'

Ambrosius was thinking to himself as they trotted along. Well, by getting the Northern kings on-side and pushing back the smaller Pictish tribes, they *had* strengthened the northern defences somewhat, but dammit all! This one was going to be the big one! Destroy the Votadini – or at least severely deplete their strength – and secure the north. On the other hand, they did sound rather desperate in the south. And then there was Gwent (which, of all the luck, had to be west, didn't it? Why couldn't these things ever happen in the one place?) … what was he going to do about that?

'I think you'll find I don't know how to reverse, Sergeant.'

'No, sir?'

'No.'

There was a pause while Ambrosius thought some more.

'I do, however, know the way to do a pretty sharp U-turn. Inform the captains we're returning south.'

'Very good, sir.'

Llew's journey through the Northern kingdoms was relatively uneventful. He was lucky enough to avoid any bandits or scavengers, possibly because once again he'd donned his old monk's cowl – the one that Nascien had given him – and it was possible that again this may have put off potential thieves on the grounds of holy men generally having no money (unless, of course, they were Bishop Derfel of Elmet, who everyone said was richer than all the kings put together) and retribution in the afterlife. He did occasionally pick up a temporary travelling companion to share the journey for part of the way.

… There was the young man in full armour that was plainly a girl, putting on a ridiculous 'gruff voice', looking for the Rhegedian army, because she said she was planning on joining up. At night, she would sob and sing laments to her soldier boyfriend when she thought Llew was asleep.

… There was the old gypsy with one tooth who sat next to Llew on the wagon and kept trying to force a handful of long grass at him, saying, 'cross my palm with silver for a little lucky heather, good sir'.

… There was a man claiming to be a druid, but when questioned further didn't seem to know what one was.

… And finally there was the blacksmith's wife of a certain age and ample bosom on the way to a wedding who kept putting her hand on Llew's knee and saying things like, 'Oh you are a saucy one, Sir Monk! 'Tis a good job for thee thou art holy! Lumme and 'Strewth!'

After this, Llew stopped picking up hitchers. It was getting into full-blown Autumn now and the land was full of colour – reds and browns. After a brief week in which he had found the terrain becoming flat, he now found he was having to climb hills once again and, the further north he got, the more treacherous the hill paths became. He had passed through a number of cities on the way, trying to find out the whereabouts of Ambrosius and the army. No one seemed to know, although most seemed to agree this: that Ambrosius was in the North somewhere, or that then again he might not be … which was a fat load of use. His attempts at intelligence gathering, however, nearly got him into trouble when he was travelling through the city of York. After asking the usual questions in the market, some of the traders started looking at him suspiciously and then, when he went back to the inn where he'd been lodging, he heard that some soldiers were on the lookout for a monk who might be a spy or a Peleganist or both. This, had he not been hastily shoving his things into the back of his wagon and then urging the horse quickly along the city's cobbled streets, might have made him think wryly of Thomas. But it didn't, because he was a bit busy to 'do' wry.

Finally, he came upon a hilly land of heather and bracken and knew he was coming to the edge of Ynys Prydein – or at least what he thought of as the civilised part of it ' to the land that even the Romans had been unable or unwilling to conquer. A farmer had told him that the most feared tribe nearest the wall was called the Votadini and they lived in a country known as the

Mountains of Blood. Llew figured that this would be the tribe Ambrosius would try to tame or break first, so he was heading toward the area their territory was supposed to be in. One evening, as the horse trudged along, he saw something looming against the setting sun. Some sort of structure – solid and regular in shape ... not part of the landscape ' the brightness of the sunset made it impossible to see it properly. He thought it might be a row of houses at first and it wasn't until he was almost upon it that he was able to see it clearly.

A wall. *The* wall.

It wasn't its height that impressed him ' about fifteen feet in all ... he'd seen many higher temples and buildings in Aquae Sulis, Londinium and other places ... but its length. It just seemed to go on forever in both directions. It was an impressive sight, although where once patrols had marched along its ramparts, it was completely deserted and the wind whistled around it eerily as if to emphasise that, now, it was literally useless. He stepped down from the wagon to take a closer look, running his hand along the stones. It was as solid as the day it was built and probably would remain so for thousands of years to come. Llew's fingers came upon some letters carved into the stone. They too had been there for a long time and it was hard for Llew to make them out in the dusk. He peered a little closer.

'Romans Rule.'

It was written in Cymru. Was it done by a Celticised Roman when they *did*? Or by a Cymru when they'd *gone*?

Either way, it was pretty ironic.

In his mind's ear, he fancied he could hear drums, the clanking of ironmongery, the tramping of Roman army sandals, the shouting of orders in Latin. Quite frankly, it gave him the willies, so he climbed back on the wagon and spurred the horse on, along the path and through a large and once-fortified gateway in the wall. The great iron gates that had hung there at one time had now long gone. Probably taken, melted down and now re-made in the form of several hundred Pictish swords.

Llew shivered and decided he would be out of sight of the wall before he made camp as the little wagon slowly journeyed into the wild lands of the North.

He was in a wood; well, a forest really. He'd been in it for several days and it wasn't easy going, because the path was becoming less and less path-like and becoming more and more dense wood-like. Often, he'd had to get off and push from the back as the horse struggled forward – not easy, because he still wasn't in brilliant physical shape. He'd fallen a few times doing this, adding more cuts and bruises to the ones already in existence, and tearing his now pretty threadbare cowl. In fact, so threadbare and torn was this robe that certain bits of him not necessarily meant for the rest of the world to see were rather visible and he was thinking he would have to change back into his proper clothing, or even his armour, because anyone who saw him was going to think that if he *was* a monk he was also some sort of flasher. Besides, it was getting cooler. Winter plainly came early to these parts of the world. However, his more pressing problem was moving forward. The path here plainly ended. There was a clearing in which to turn the wagon round, but no way of moving forward that he could see. This was a problem. Okay, he didn't know where he was, but he knew he was going vaguely in the right direction for the Votadini clan and going back would mean travelling several days to the beginning of the forest and trying to find a way round. And a couple of days may not make a huge difference in the grand scheme of things, but he knew the longer he left it, the more chance that Llangollen would fall.

If it hadn't fallen already, of course.

He tried not to think of this. There was a chance that, any day now, he would find Ambrosius and, if he did, he knew he would be able to persuade him to take the army south-west to Gwynedd. After all, if Ambrosius knew that, in actual fact, he *didn't* owe anything to Bruenor for the death of Horsa and consequently the great victory at Egelesprep,[77] then he must know that he owed *Llew*. And, also, it was in Ambrosius's interests to keep the Scotti out of Gwynedd. They were like the Saxons: once they got a foothold, there was no getting rid of them; not, er … not that the Saxons *had* got a foothold was anyone's fault, of course. Ahem.

So, going back was not the preferred option.

He tied the horse to a tree, deciding to do a little reconnaissance. It was just possible that the path started again a little further ahead and, if that was the case, maybe a bit of work with the rusty sword might clear enough of the way ahead to get to it.

Llew climbed up a steep bank to see if there was a better view from higher up, although after a while he realised the flora and fauna disguised the fact that the 'steep bank' was actually more of a cliff and, by the time he'd climbed up a few feet to see if he was any nearer the top, he found he'd gone too far to get down and was going to have to keep going anyway and find another way back to the wagon. This was not turning into a good day. Struggling, grazing himself and tearing his robe even more on tree branches and sharp rocks, he finally managed to get to a plateau of sorts, tree- and scrub-covered, but with a rough path running downward and apparently north. Great – all he needed to do was work out a way to get a wagon and horse up the cliff. Then he turned to the right and saw what the path led to going the other way … a cave, and it had the skull of a horse outside it. Now the skull was broken, grimy and the horse had obviously been dead a good long time, but that *didn't* mean there weren't fresher more recently stripped bones inside the cave. Llew had heard that there were still bears in the

---

[77] Oops!

woods of the north and he had no desire to meet one. This was a pity because it appeared that a growling noise was approaching from inside.

'Rrrrrrrrrrrrrrrrrrrrrrr ...'

Llew slowly started to back away down the path. His instinct was to turn and run forwards quickly, but his head was saying, 'No, you'll never outrun a bear ... see what it does first ... it might not be interested in you. In fact, it's probably *more* afraid of you than *you* are of –'

Wrong again. Wrong every time. A hairy creature over six feet high came bounding out of the cave, roaring. It bounded at Llew, who tripped over backwards as the creature leapt, landing on top of him – and it sat on his chest. Then it stopped roaring.

'Llew? Is it ... thee, my brother?' it said, astonished. 'I knew thee wouldst come.'

Llew was pretty astonished himself.

'Nascien?'

Later, they were sitting in Nascien's cave; a fire was going, which the monk was using to roast a couple of wood pigeon on.

'Yea, they did cast me out and said I would burn, be stoned or burn at the stake if any found me, so I took to the hills and wandered the earth. As thou canst see, I did divest myself of all worldly garments!'

Oh, indeed he had. Nascien was as naked as the day he was born, except for the fact on that particular day he wouldn't have had the huge beard that had grown so long he could wrap it round himself.

'And so it was that I came here to this cave ...'

'What happened to Britu?' asked Llew curiously.

'The younger Vortigern did wander with me for a time. He did find this cave with me and stayed with me through one Winter. We lived but on the nuts and berries of the forest, for the Lord doth provide.'

'And then what?'

Nascien shifted a little uncomfortably.

'Well ... the Lord doth not quite provide quite so much in the nut and berry line when Winter goes to its darkest.'

'So he died? He starved to death?'

'We do not die, brother! Our bodies die, yea, but our spirits do enter the kingdom of the Lord!'

'Ah. And you buried him?'

Nascien looked a little uncomfortable.

'Hmm,' he said, ambiguously.

Llew, for a brief few seconds, wondered just how a naked Nascien had managed to survive on nuts and berries for a whole Winter and then decided it was perhaps best if he never knew.

' 'Twas about this time that I began to have the visions,' Nascien said brightly.

'Oh? What visions?'

'Visions of you, my brother. I knew you would come here. A creature called Myrddin did come to me in my dreams and told me of your coming. He said thou wast looking for an army and that thou wouldst find one, but not the one thou looked for.'

Llew wasn't sure how to take this news. Myrddin was the name in the old language for guess who? It meant that Merlin was interfering again, trying to nudge him in a certain direction for reasons of his own and right now Llew didn't have time for all that. He certainly didn't have time to try and fathom out what the hell it meant.

'He sayeth that –'

Llew held up his hand for Nascien to stop.

'I don't care! Anything that little sod Merlin says and I'm going to try and do the opposite, okay? So you may as well not tell me.'

'But he says he doth control your destiny … and that in yours are all of ours entwined.'

'Yes, well, this time he's wrong. I've got bigger things to worry about than him! There are lives at stake. Now, do you know if there's a tribe near here called the Votadini?'

Nascien told him that the Votadini were about two days walk from the cave if you followed the river. He hadn't, however, heard of any Cymru attack on them and he was sure he would have if it had happened.

'How?'

'My visions would have told me!' he said earnestly and wide eyed.

'Oh good. Right, looks as if I'm going to have to look for Ambrosius elsewhere then.'

This was a blow.

'No, no, thou must go to the Votadini! My vision … Myrddin –'

'Yes, yes, yes. Well, like I said, I don't do what the likes of Merlin tells me any more because every time I do, I end up at the point of death and quite frankly that's not a point I enjoy!'

'But Myrddin did prophecy thou wouldst go there!'

'Yeah? You know what Merlin can do with his prophecy –?'

'The woman is there! Ygrain. She was taken prisoner there some years ago!'

'I don't know anyone called Ygrain!'

'No, for you know her as Megan!'

Llew stopped. A name he had not heard or thought of for a very, very long was suddenly entering his mind and to his utter fury and dismay made his heart do a little 'ooh yeah!!!' Her? Megan? Here? He'd even passed through Elmet on his way north and learned that a king Mor (as opposed to Pelinore) was on the throne, but so set on his task was he that he'd never really given it much thought. And now he cursed himself for the fool that he was, because he knew he could not just leave Megan in the clutches of the Votadini. Somehow, he must at least try to formulate a plan of rescue.

By the next day, he'd come up with one … well, the nearest thing to a plan without it being one. A sort of plan-ette. He would leave the horse and wagon with Nascien – on the understanding that no matter how cold it got, Nascien would look after the horse, feed it and under no circumstances eat it. He would sneak into the Votadini country, passing himself of as a … wandering itinerant monk scribe (which they would think was harmless, of course)! He would find where Megan was kept, break her out, sneak her away under cover of darkness, make his way back here to the wagon and then take the way he'd come, back through the forest, where he would search for Ambrosius, who plainly hadn't got this far North yet. Then, when he'd found the army, they would all travel together back to Gwynedd where hopefully the siege was still going on and rescue everyone. And that would, with luck, show *her* that actually he was a *real* hero not just some handsome thicko like Pelinore and he could tell her all about his exploits on the way – like … the battle and Horsa and the treaty and the siege ladder and everything. Oh, and she could meet Ceridwen. And *then* she'd see who'd married the right who. Oh yes.

Deep down, he knew it wasn't terribly healthy to think like this.

He'd decided to take one bag of his parchments with him as part of the disguise and he had kept the raggedy cowl on, although he'd slipped on some trews underneath – firstly for modesty (although real monks didn't wear them) and secondly for warmth, because it really was starting to get chilly. He did, however, leave the sword behind, which he did so with great regret because it was useful in certain difficult situations, but the truth was that, however rusty looking, it was a warrior's sword and a monk-scribe who walked into a strange camp wearing trews and a sword under his cowl might look like a monk-scribe who was in fact *not* a monk-scribe! Which, in fact, he was. Or wasn't. Either way, he didn't want his would-be hosts to know it.

Two days later he came out of the woods, following the river as Nascien had instructed and come into a glen where ahead of him were three huge mountains, all apparently crimson in colour.

Ah, these must be the Mountains of Blood, he thought to himself as he hobbled down the hill. He had to admit they looked quite impressive. He could see the mountainsides dotted with little settlements, each with its own small plumes of smoke making horizontal lines towards the east because of the wind.

'Good day, good day!' he said in a cheery sing-song voice as he passed a shepherd, sitting on a nearby rock, minding his sheep, 'no need to worry, just a passing itinerant monk-scribe is all I am. Hey ho.'

The shepherd just stared at him. Llew hoped this was going to work. Perhaps the 'hey ho' wasn't a fantastic touch. He continued hobbling along (one of his legs was still bad) towards the foothills of the first mountain. The river was narrower here. There was a woman drawing water in a big wooden bucket. She stood up and began to stare at him too.

'Hello, hello, fair maiden, hey ho,' he said in the same sing-song fashion, 'just a wandering monk-scribe from far away passing through on the way to … see King Lot in Orkney … no need to panic –'

Blimey, she really was staring at him, wide-eyed and open-mouthed. He had just about reached her by now.

'No need to panic, although I know you're not used to strangers in these parts. I – **RUDDY NORA!!!**'

He had realised who she was.

'That's good,' she said through clenched teeth, 'a monk who swears, but badly! What the hell are you doing here?'

He looked round to make sure nobody was watching. Nobody was.

'I've come to rescue you!' he hissed.

'Oh,' she said, 'that's interesting.'

It was, as reunion exchanges go, a bit of a disappointment. He had rather hoped at a little more joy at a) his appearing here, of all places, out of nowhere and b) the learning of his mission, particularly as he'd come there out of the goodness of his heart. And to be fair to Megan, perhaps if she had not been otherwise distracted, she might have shown a little more enthusiasm. However, her pregnancy aside, she had other things to worry about.

For trouble had been brewing in the Mountains of Blood.

It had begun, as it often does where families are concerned, with the talk of who was to inherit what. There is nothing so likely to set brother against brother, or brother against sister, or father against son, or sister against father, or all three of them against mother, as the subject of who will get that carriage clock – the one that *everybody* thinks is really quite ugly but that has been in the family for generations and therefore has managed to attain the mysterious rank of 'heirloom'. The family that was as loving, caring and supportive as it was possible to be, the Christmas-card family, the family that makes the average angel look a little bit cynical, can turn on one another in the most bitter, bloody and treacherous fashion. Imagine, then, the consequences if the heirloom is not a carriage clock but a kingdom, and the family is not from a Christmas card, but a fifth-century feudal warrior caste dynasty in an area that was considered barbaric and violent, even for the times, each member of whom has their own warrior band.

The result, I am sure you will agree, is not likely to be a pretty sight.

For it was generally starting to be muttered that if Gorlois was not exactly in his dotage, he was not exactly in his prime either, and his sons had started demanding to know who was going to get what. Was one of them going to get the whole kingdom, or was he going to divide it up and give one son a mountain each (in the great narrative tradition of all things, Gorlois had three sons, although where life was less like a story was in the fact the each one was big, strong and extremely stupid, especially the youngest)? Gorlois had replied that he hadn't decided and that he planned on living a good while yet, so the question was irrelevant. However, being wise enough to see that they were serious and needed throwing a bone once in a while,[78] the king added that he would relinquish Prince Uther of his client ruling duties and they could fight each other for mountain number three.

And there it might have ended. Uther might have stepped down, been made to marry Morag The Fair and, as he himself had envisaged, also been forced into allying himself with one of the sons, hopefully the winning one. However, the one thing that nobody, not even Uther, had bothered to consider was the People.

Oh yes, them.

It is often the way of kings and princes to intrigue about kingdoms, lands, palaces and such-like, because of the wealth and power they represent, whilst at the same time forgetting that, without the farmers and soldiers and mothers and shepherds and milkmaids and carpenters and blacksmiths and tanners and drapers and prostitutes and, yes, even thieves ... well, there wouldn't be any wealth or power in the first place. So, whilst Uther was contemplating the fifth-century prince's equivalent of clearing his desk and wondering what he was going to do next, he started getting reports from some of his lower ranking chieftains ... the ones with their ears closest to the ground. They said *they'd* been getting reports that a lot of people – ordinary people – were complaining about the impending change in management. The thing was, that of the three Mountains Of Blood, Uther's was generally known to be the most profitable and the most comfortable. These people were looking over from their hovels and huts onto the other two mountainsides and they were seeing Gorlois' men running riot whenever the mood took them; they were seeing Gorlois himself point at something (farm, horse, woman), saying 'that's mine' and demanding he be allowed to take possession immediately. They were seeing crops fail because of a lack of organisation and occasionally they were seeing their cousins across the way go hungry because of it, or over high taxation (all of which seemed to be spent on more feasts for Gorlois and not protection from invasive soldiers/bandits or monsters/bears). The truth was, they knew that Uther was better at ruling because he had 'something upstairs', as it were; whereas Gorlois' sons were very empty in the attic department. And they didn't like the idea of the walking unfurnished loft conversions taking over. The word that was coming from the lower orders was that they would do anything rather than see Uther step down, and then his chieftains were adding that they too preferred working for him rather than, say, a certifiable maniac; so did their men, when it came to it.

---

[78] Obviously a man who respected his sons.

Uther began to realise that, although he'd never really wanted to be king, just resigning was going to leave a lot of these people not very happy. And didn't .... well, didn't people deserve to be happy sometimes? This life was hard enough, was it not, without expecting the man who'd looked after you and provided protection for you over time to simply abandon you so that someone's kids could have a new toy to fight over?

So he'd sent a messenger to Gorlois. The messenger was to say that Prince Uther was grateful for the offer of early retirement, *but* he'd rather stay in his old job if it was all the same to Gorlois. In reply, Gorlois had sent the messenger's head back in a bucket.

From Gorlois' point of view, Uther was just someone who he'd put in charge of his property. That mountain belonged to Gorlois and as far as he was concerned it was up to him whether or not Uther stayed there. Now he'd decided to give the mountain back to his sons, so what on earth was his nephew playing at?

There was a stand-off. Patrols from both sides were posted at the borders of each territory – something that had never been done before. It was also apparent by the size of these patrols that Gorlois' men outnumbered Uther's three to one.

'... and, on top of it all, I'm pregnant!'

Megan had taken Llew to a spare hut, got a fire going and given him some bread-like things to eat. Llew was grateful for this as the roast woodpigeon Nascien had served seemed a long time ago.

'Oh,' said Llew, a tad too carelessly, 'congratulations.'

It seemed a sort of logical thing to say. Although, once again, he felt the stirring of deep feelings of an envious nature, which he tried and failed to suppress. He didn't know why he should feel jealous – was it because *he'd* like to have been the father of this particular Happy Event? Or was it because – and this seemed more likely – he'd wanted to be the first of the pair of them ... first to be married, first to have a Happy Family, if just so he could thumb his nose at Megan and go 'Nyerr nyerr ne nyerr nyerr!'. In his head, of course. He knew that he obviously did have a Happy Family. Of sorts. He had a kind of wife and a kind of daft old uncle back in Llangollen, and the truth was that children could not have been on the cards because Ceridwen, like many members of her (former) profession, had certain herbs that she took to stop what she called 'accidents'[79] happening and had told Llew she wasn't going to stop taking them until things were a bit less hectic.

' "Congratulations"? Are you out of your mind?' exclaimed Megan. Then she lowered her voice to a hiss, 'The father's not my husband!'

'Ooh,' was all Llew could think to add.

---

[79] Although, why becoming unexpectedly pregnant is compared to ... say, spilling a glass of milk, or indeed being knocked over by an out-of-control horse, is anybody's guess.

'So …,' said Megan, 'rescue. You've come to rescue me?'

Llew started to explain about Llangollen and Ambrosius and Nascien. He decided to leave out the part about the fate of Britu. It probably wasn't a good time to tell a pregnant woman that her brother had almost certainly been eaten by an evangelical hermit that Llew had introduced him to. Then again, when was?

'Great!' said Megan enthusiastically, 'Uther can come too! What's the plan?'

'Uther?'

'Yes. He doesn't want to be a prince here and he's terribly good in battle, so your Ambrosius friend should want him on-side to help rescue Llangollen –'

'And I expect he's "terribly" handsome as well …,' muttered Llew to himself.

'Well? What if he is? It's not a crime, you know! Anyway, what's the plan?'

'Plan?'

Megan looked at him quizzically.

'Yes. *Plan!* The plan to escape!'

'Oh, well, when there's a chance, we sneak out under cover of dark and head for the forest, where Nascien's got the cart. Then we head south out of the forest and join up with Ambrosius' army.'

'Which is where, exactly?' asked Megan.

Llew flapped his hands around in some sort of vague directional gesture.

'In the north,' he said vaguely.

'Just "the north",' she said sarcastically. 'Don't know if you noticed, but we're in the north *here*! This is a pretty big bloody country … thingummy …'

Llew grimly realised she couldn't remember his name.

'… so just how do you know where they are?'

What's more, he was getting annoyed with her attitude.

'Because Ambrosius wants to keeps the Picts from invading us and currently the most aggressive Pictish tribe is you lot! He'll be looking for the Votadini, which means he can't be far.'

'So we sneak out, the three of us, somehow, being miraculously faster than the pursuing Votadini soldiers – and believe me they will pursue us – on a horse-drawn wagon and hope we run into your friend's army, who may or may not be somewhere in an area you call the North?'

Llew had no choice but sheepishly and rather quietly reply 'yes'.

Megan was quiet for a few seconds, evidently deep in thought. Finally, she said,

'Well, I suppose it's all we've got. We better go and talk to Uther.'

That was going to be less easy than it sounded. Uther was all the way over on his mountain and, since the little stand-off between Uther's people and Gorlois' people, Uther had not done much sneaking over to see Megan of late. In fact, he hadn't sneaked over at all. In *fact*, the Big News Megan had was still waiting impatiently to wend[80] its merry way to Uther's ears. Therefore, it was just possible that this was going to turn out to be a fairly lively meeting, when and if it happened.

There was another problem. Llew had been seen arriving. It may have only been by old Jock, the sleepy shepherd who sat upon his rock day in day out, never moving, allowing his dogs to do all the real work, but, gossip being gossip, the fact that Princess Ygrain had met a wandering itinerant priest and was currently entertaining him in her hut would be all over the Mountains Of Blood by now. So, his cover needed to look legitimate.

'You'd better go and talk to Andrew. Exchange priestly greetings or whatever one monk does when another one's in the area.'

Llew wrinkled his forehead.

'You wouldn't know what that would happen to be?'

'Of course I don't!' said Megan, exasperated, 'No one ever comes here. Okay, we've had a couple of wandering bards, collecting stories and trying to come up with pretty verses about the heather, but that's it! We're one step away from the end of the world!'

She propelled him to the doorway of the hut, pointed him in the direction Andrew would be and told him to make it look realistic. He was not to return until dark. As he walked through the settlement, he observed the people going about their daily business. They looked very similar to Cymru people going about their daily business ... a swineherd tending to his animals, some tradesmen haggling over prices ... a few warriors practising swordplay. These last he found most interesting. He remembered the tales of the fiendish Pictish warriors his grandmother had told by the fire. Half-warrior, half-demon, she'd said. It was good to know they weren't. On the other hand, they didn't look like slouches either. They were well equipped and it didn't take long for him to see they were good with their weapons.

Actually, he was doing Ambrosius a favour getting him to change direction, because this lot would be no pushover. Whereas the Irish over in Llangollen: well, they were just bandits and deserters. They wouldn't have been half as successful if it hadn't been for Bruenor's meanness. Ambrosius and a professional army should make short work of them ... if they got to Llangollen before it was too late, of course. He shivered, remembering that he'd left Llangollen what seemed like an awful long time ago. He hoped they were all right there. Except for Bruenor, of course. With a bit of luck, Bruenor had copped a couple of stray arrows by now.

It wasn't long before he arrived at the ramshackle hut that Andrew was using as a chapel. He found Andrew trying to chop up firewood with what

---

[80] In the Dark Ages people/things really wended. They don't wend any more. It's a non-wend world we live in.

appeared to be an almost completely blunt axe. Firewood was a good idea, Llew thought. It would snow tonight; he could feel it.

'Bugger bugger buggery bollocks!'

Llew wasn't sure this was monk-appropriate language. He coughed surreptitiously.

'Ahem. Erm, greetings, brother. God give you welcome.'

Andrew looked up and eyed him suspiciously.

'You're not a monk,' he said finally.

Llew was taken aback.

'What? Yes I am!'

'No you're not. I can tell. All monks can. *Real* monks, that is! You don't ... walk right. Or stand right. And that "greetings, brother" crap. No one talks like that ... well, except those mad Peleganists, and they're all dead. And "God give you welcome". Where d'you get that one from? A bard? And, in any case, *I'm* supposed to say that, not you! You're the guest! This is *my* home! If anyone was going to say "God give you welcome", it'd be me! Oh, don't worry ...,' he added quickly before Llew could pitch in with another protest, 'I'm not going to blow your cover. What do I care? Unless ... here, you're not an assassin in disguise, are you, come to do away with the king?'

'No!'

'Hmm. Pity.'

Andrew, apparently disappointed, turned and went back to trying to chop the firewood.

'Word has it you've been talking to the princess. Come to rescue her, have you?'

Llew gawped. This man appeared to know everything.

'Better do it quick, before that baby's born, 'cause if his nibs finds out who the father is ...'

The axe came down and, probably through the sheer force of the blow, caused the log Andrew was working on finally to split. Llew's eyes were even wider than they had been before!

'But how do you –?'

'Oh, *everybody* knows!' said Andrew, irritated, continuing with his work. 'Everybody except Gorlois, of course. And, as a monk, may I say that fornication is of course a sin under God blah blah blah ... you know how it goes. Anyway, you can't keep things quiet in a place like this, you know. I heard about you coming here before you'd even left the forest. One of our hunters saw you yesterday morning. You didn't see him, mind.'

Yesterday. Inwardly, Llew sighed with relief; the fact that Andrew hadn't mentioned it would mean they probably didn't know about Nascien and the wagon. Nevertheless, things were obviously pretty urgent. As soon as it was dark, he was going to have to get Megan and Uther out of there.

'Absolutely not. I cannot leave!'

It was plain to see things were not going according to plan. It was a shame really, because Llew had quite taken to Uther. Sneaking past the patrols on the borders between mountains Two and Three in the blizzard and pitch dark had been fairly unpleasant, but then when they'd got inside Uther's hall – all light and warmth – he'd been met by this large and hearty man, who clasped him to his chest and – when Megan had told him why Llew had come to their mountains – he'd been clasped to the big man's chest again.

'You're a good man, Llew! I like you!' he'd said, and Llew had found himself blushing with pride in the same way that he'd done when he'd incurred Ambrosius' pleasure. 'But, as you can see, she doesnae need rescuin', do you darlin', eh, eh?'

He phycially picked up Megan and whirled her round, causing her to laugh hysterically and Llew to look at his feet. He really hoped they weren't going to be like this all the way to Llangollen. If they were, they could find some other wagon to travel in.

Then there'd been the business of telling Uther the Big News. He'd been eating a leg of lamb at the time and taking a drink from an ale bowl. It took several minutes to stop him from choking. *Then* there'd been the business of telling both of them *Andrew's* Big News, ie the News that everybody else knew. It had taken several minutes to bring Megan round.

So then Llew could explain why Uther and Megan should leave with him tonight. What had followed was Uther's reaction.

'So, you're going to think about it?' he tried to say lightly. Uther gave him a look which said 'no', but in a much more forthright and unpleasant way.

'But *why*?' said Megan.

'Because I've got people … women, children, men … soldiers … Livestock … *everything* here to look after. I've got responsibilities! I'm not just gonnae *abandon* them so I can go and join some Cymru army! Especially not one bent on attacking my own land. Not that they're coming anyway!'

It occurred to Llew that Uther would get on very well with Griffith.

'But don't you see, if you stay – … what?' The last sentence had just kicked in.

'Ambrosius. He's not coming,' said Uther matter of factly. 'I've had spies following him and that rabble for months. They turned round weeks ago.'

Llew could feel the blood draining from his face. He just about managed to frame the word 'why'.

'Saxons, apparently. Or Angles. Or somesuch. Both, probably. Aye they were on their way here. Planning to attack us, as I understand it, so you *were* heading in the right direction when you came to find us. Anyway, it's a good job for us they did turn round, 'cause if they'd arrived just after we'd fought a civil war, I don't reckon we'd have been in much of a state to – … oh, someone pick him up and put his head between his knees.'

So that was it. He'd failed. After all that. Oh well. It'd been pretty hopeless anyway. Why should he be surprised? It was the story of his life.

Try and do some good. Fail.

And at least this time it wasn't his fault. At least they couldn't say, or rather *he* couldn't say, it was all down to him when Llangollen finally fell. And fall it would. He tried to keep his mind off the subject of what would happen to Ceridwen and Griff once the Irish finally managed to break down the hill fort's gates. Tried to keep his mind off the screams of terror and of pain, of the flames, the steel and the splintering and crackling wood. Tried and failed quite badly. Well, whatever happened, army or no army, he was going back there. He wasn't waiting around here for this lot to start killing each other; if he was going to die it was going to be in a place of his own choosing. And that place was going to be Llangollen with his family-of-sorts. Ironic really, seeing as he'd spent most of his life trying *not* to die there. Now he was going back to do just that. There was no time to follow Ambrosius south and even if he did catch up with him there was no way Ambrosius was going to lend even *part* of his army to Llew if he was engaged in fighting the Saxons. So, a one-man scribe army was going to Llangollen.

While he was thinking all this, Uther and Megan had been arguing about what to do next. Uther was in no doubt. There was going to be civil war whatever happened, so Megan may as well not sneak back to Gorlois' mountain that night. The truth would come out the next day and Gorlois and his sons and their armies would probably attack. Then there'd be an end to it. Megan's argument was that Uther was hopelessly outnumbered and they'd all die, so wouldn't it be better if they just ... left quietly. The people would be left without a prince and one of Gorlois' sons could just take over. However, Uther was unmoveable. He didn't ask for the job he'd got, but one of the conditions of taking it was that you weren't allowed to resign. Llew heard this and thought ... try telling that to Bruenor.

Which got him thinking – in itself quite difficult because Uther and Megan were shouting at each other now. She was calling him 'pigheaded' and he was calling her 'naive' and when that kind of thing happens it usually means that the argument has stopped being an argument and has become a slanging match. Finally, when the slanging match had evolved again – now morphing into sulky silence – he coughed tentatively and looked at Uther.

'My Lord ... is there any chance that, before the Votadini butcher one another and make the name of this place a little too literal for anybody's taste, is there any chance of parleying with the other side?'

Uther looked at him carefully and then motioned to one of his guards.

It was not a meeting that was easy to arrange. First, there had been the business of telling Gorlois the truth about Megan. This had fallen to Andrew the Monk, now possibly the only person in the whole kingdom given access to wander from one part of it to another. He didn't want to be the one to do it, but it was thought that, being a man of God, Gorlois was less likely to jump up and kill him immediately, which was small comfort to him.

Gorlois, it is fair to say, had not taken it well that his wife had been having an affair with his nephew and was about to have his child. It's probably understandable that he went what later might be described as 'a bit mental' and smashed up quite a lot of furniture – such as it was – as well as hitting anybody who happened to be standing at arm's length at around the time he was told. Then he calmed down a little, grunted that he'd got bored of her anyway and when he'd destroyed Uther's army – which he would – it'd be cliff top time. There was that tall one … the one who was always digging holes with her feet. Wasn't it about her turn?[81] Then Llew was brought in to Gorlois' hall, because Andrew had said that it was bad enough him having to tell the king the bad news, but he was damned if he was going to try and set up a meeting with Uther – the man who'd well … you know … with the king's wife – as well.

The fact that Gorlois hadn't a clue who Llew was helped because he was confused for the first few seconds of the conversation, by which time Llew had managed to come out with the main basic request. Gorlois was puzzled. Why should he, a man dishonoured and with the biggest army, want to talk to his nephew?

'Because I believe I have found a way so that you both may avoid bloodshed, Lord King,' said Llew. 'Uther would come here to your hall. Will you not let him?'

The truth was that Gorlois did not, in truth, want to fight with Uther. Yes, his army outnumbered Uther's three to one and so, yes, Uther's men would be defeated in any battle. However, Uther had not been given the title 'Dragon Head' because he was good at hopscotch and Gorlois knew that in any battle Uther would slaughter his way through the throng to get to the leader of whoever he was fighting. Which would mean that Gorlois would have to fight him. Which would mean that Gorlois would probably lose. And die. Which would be okay because honour would be satisfied and one of his sons would kill Uther and become king. But he'd still be dead. And Gorlois didn't really want to be dead if he could avoid it.

Besides, if it could be seen that he'd tried to negotiate before the inevitable but bloody battle, maybe those stubborn sods in Uther's kingdom who'd put him up to rebelling in the first place – those nasty little farmers and blacksmiths and the like – maybe they'd see that he, Gorlois, wasn't such a tyrant and bend to his will a bit less belligerently.

However, he had to back down without seeming to do so and Gorlois, who was not a man of subtleties, was thinking hard about how. Luckily, Llew was and could see how hard indeed the king was thinking by the fact that Gorlois was grimacing. He decided to risk all and make a suggestion.

---

[81] Proving he wasn't as stupid as he looked.

'Shall I tell Lord Uther you will grudgingly let him come and negotiate a quick death on the battlefield, Lord, when you have annihilated him utterly?'

There were a few encouraging noises from the chiefs gathered around the king. This guy was good.

Gorlois nodded.

And so it was that Llew found himself, later that day, back in Gorlois' hall. He was standing in the centre of the big room. On one side of him, a few feet off, sat Gorlois, flanked by his sons, his chieftains and some of his more important warriors. On the other side, again a few feet off, sat Uther and his retinue, the only difference being that next to Uther sat a woman. Megan. Everyone, Megan and Llew accepted, was armed to the teeth, and Llew knew full well that if he got this wrong, they'd simply march out, round up each other's armies and destroy each other. And not in a shy way. On the other hand, if he got it right …

'My lords and lady, I expect you're wondering why I've called you here.'

He didn't know why he'd said that, or indeed why he'd said it in a 'comedy' voice; he just knew that, deep down in his soul, something primal made him. As it was, the 'joke' fell flat and they all looked at him,[82] not so much blankly, more as if he'd just arrived from another planet. And then defecated in front of them.

Tough crowd.

He decided to plough on regardless. He had to make this work. He had to, for Griff and for Ceridwen and everyone in Llangollen;[83] but not only for them, for everyone in the Mountains of Blood. And possibly, if they went for it, it could buy the whole of Ynys Prydein some time.

'I propose Prince Uther take his army and any of his people that want to travel with him and leave these mountains to the country of Gwynedd.'

This was, of course, a cue for various occupants in the room to start muttering to one another until Llew held up his hand for silence. However, life rarely follows narrative tradition and he had to shout 'shut up!' loudly to get their attention again. Both Uther and Gorlois had remained stony-faced and silent throughout. It was Uther who spoke first.

'And who is to say that the people of Gwynedd will not object to my bringing an army with its people and settling there?'

'They will not, Lord. Even as we speak, the seat of Gwynedd, Llangollen, is under siege. Lift that siege and your army will be most welcome.'

More muttering, more calls for silence. The next question was from Gorlois. Treacherous Uther had refused to hand over his country when the king had requested it and now he had taken Gorlois' wife. How could he be trusted to leave and not come back? Uther, Gorlois said, wanted to be a king. If he was successful in Gwynedd, he would return to the Mountains of Blood with more men and he would attack Gorlois. Uther was a traitor!

---

[82] That one always does. Try it. I had a friend who tried that joke in a men's toilet once. Boy, was that a silence to behold.

[83] Except Bruenor.

There were shouts of anger from Uther's people. They didn't mean it, of course. It was all part of the ritual. One of them even stood up and shook his fist. Had there been a table, one of them might have gone 'grooooaaaahghghgg' and turned it over. But there wasn't, so they didn't. Uther, of course, still remained silent.

Llew had used the uproar to think on his feet. It was one objection he hadn't thought of. Of course it was. It was the objection of someone who was negotiating without wanting to find a solution. Gorlois may as well have said, 'I will not agree to your terms because you never have enough spoons'. However, it was an objection that had to be overcome and the only solution Llew could think of was one that was not going to be popular. With a certain person, anyway. Oh well, with a bit of luck that person was dead.

'The Lord Uther will stay in Gwynedd because he will be king there.'

Once again muttering; this time the tone was disbelieving. Even Megan was looking at him with an 'are you out of your mind?' expression. Gorlois wanted to know why they should believe this to be true. After all, who was Llew to give away kingdoms? And for once Llew was lost for words. Something kicked him in the back of his mind. He knew it was feeble, but it was the only thing he could think of.

'I am Llew Ap Gwyddno, scribe to Marcus Artorius and the emissary of Rome,' he said weakly, which was technically true at least. No one had actually *sacked* him. 'I gave Gwyrangon to the Saxons, which is where King Hengist rules as we speak. Is that not proof enough?'

Please don't ask me to prove that I'm not lying, he thought to himself desperately, because I can't. There was a surge of impressed muttering and clapping. The 'R' word had obviously impressed them. Truth was, the Votadini had always respected the Romans and things had gone downhill badly after the Romans had left. Gorlois stood up. He would accept these terms, he shouted, on one condition. And everyone quietened down to see what it was.

He pointed at Megan.

'She stays. He tries to return, she dies. If he leaves with his people for good, she will come to no harm.'

It was Megan who eventually persuaded Uther to accept the deal. The meeting had broken up in uproar with Uther refusing point blank to even consider it. Gorlois had said it was his final offer – the woman was his property and there was no way Uther was leaving with her. Gorlois would even guarantee her safety – swearing an oath to any God they chose – but she stayed in the mountains. If Uther couldn't accept that, then their two armies should meet on the big plain at the bottom of Mountain One at dawn.

That night she told him he had no choice. If he went into battle here, they'd all die.

'We might all die in Gwynedd,' he'd pointed out.

'Not according to Llew. He says they're just Irish pirates down there. The only reason they've been so successful is because Bruenor let his army desert him. And you'll have a kingdom!'

'I can't go without you!' he said emphatically.

Llew was present at this debate, which took place back in Uther's hall. To be honest, he was more than a little uncomfortable and not only because he seemed to have been sitting on the same wooden bench now for hours. The word 'gooseberry' kept coming into his head. However, it was freezing outside and he'd finished packing over an hour ago. It was, he reflected, time to leave, whatever they decided. He was not going to hang around here to watch a massacre in the snow ... he could just as well go and do that at Llangollen. *However*, if by staying for a few extra hours there was a chance of travelling back with a large-ish Pictish horde (always assuming they allowed him to stop off and pick up his cart and parchments on the way), then that's what he would do. But Megan and Uther argued – always the same argument ... always going round and round in circles and getting louder and crosser all the time. Which was running out. Dawn was coming ever closer. It was particularly sad to see how torn Uther was. He had a duty to his people, yes, but he wasn't going to leave behind the woman he loved, but then he had a duty to his people; yes, he could see that, but then he wasn't going to ... and so on.

Actually, after a while, it was starting to make Llew yawn a little bit.

He must have tuned out for a few minutes, because suddenly he noticed that it had gone quiet in the room and they were both looking at him.

'Er ... did I miss something?' he said.

'The choice is yours, Llew,' said Uther.

'What is? What choice?'

'Whatever happens I will go with my army. You can come with me as I'm sure you want to. I'll take you to Llangollen, I'll try to help your people and then, at the end of it, if I am king there ... you and your family can stay in high honour, or go wherever you like in the world. I promise I will help you, whatever you decide.'

Okay, thought Llew, blinking; nice. That seems like quite a nice choice. More than nice. Great! Not one I have to make right now, obviously. It'll depend what happens about the siege and such-like. But, I expect, if everybody's .... you know, alive, and if we can find a boat, we'll be off to the continent finally.

And that would be it. Everything he'd ever wanted. Right there on a plate. So, his quest it seemed would finally come to an end. And this time he knew it really would. There would be no slips between cup and lip. He'd go to Llangollen with an army behind him and a mighty warrior king beside him. That really would be it!!

Then he realised there was more. The choice hadn't actually been laid out before him yet.

'Or …?' he asked nervously.

'Or you can stay here for a wee while and help Megan escape as soon as an opportunity presents itself, while I go off and save your people.'

Llew blinked again. Megan looked at him, pleadingly.

'I am asking you, as a friend,' said Uther.

Inwardly, Llew thought, 'oh … oh, crap'.

Marcus had said, all those years ago, 'we are none of us here for long'. Llew had decided to amend it to 'we are none of us *where we want to be* for long' and would have added '*although we end up where we **don't** want to be for bloody ages*!!!', but he felt that, as a personal motto, it was probably lacking in catchiness.

Chapter 16 – Fire And Sword

The sky was one big sheet of dark, heavy-looking grey, as the snow fell in drifts. There was no wind. The warriors saddled their horses in silence. The families packing up ox-drawn carts did the same.[84] From a little way off, crowds of people had come to the river to watch the exodus. This was less a gesture of farewell and more a question of being the first to bag the best of the newly abandoned huts, although not everyone from the mountain was leaving with Uther. Things are never black and white in situations like this. For instance, it is almost certain that, when Moses led the Hebrews out of Egypt, there was at least one patriarch saying, 'follow that bearded lunatic into the desert? When we're safe and comfortable here? Are you out your **mind**?'[85] Such it was on Uther's mountain. There was a sizeable-ish pro-Gorlois faction in Uther's land … people who said that yes, Gorlois was a murderous tyrant, a slave driver and little more than a mountain bandit, but at least you knew where you were with him. And look at those manacles – quality workmanship… none of your rubbish.

And Llew was staying. With Megan. Of course he was staying, he reflected bitterly. Somehow he'd become the type of person who thinks of others before himself, or his own. When did *that* happen?

Megan and Uther had said a last goodbye and it hadn't gone well. They'd argued about the baby's name. Uther had absolutely insisted the baby be called Arth if it was a boy. Megan had told him he was insane – Arth sounded like something a dog did if someone made it eat cabbage. Uther said that it meant 'bear' in the old language and he wanted to honour the one that the wizard had saved them from. He wanted his son to be able to fight like that bear one day. Megan said that if they gave him that name, then he'd be bullied by all the other kids … which would make the name even more stupid. She wanted to call the child Owain and Uther said that sounded like a druid Cymru name and there was no way his son was going to wander round eating herbs and talking to trees. The only thing they hadn't argued about was the fact that it was going to be a boy. Somehow they both knew.

---

[84] Although not quite as silently as the warriors – families being what they are.

[85] And considering the Hebrews were to spend the next **forty years** wandering around in said desert when the Promised Land was only a couple of hundred miles north, he might have had a point.

And then it'd been time to go.

Megan was, of course, sobbing her heart out. Llew stood next to her, feeling and looking awkward despite being not particularly well disposed towards her right now. He should have been going with the newly exiled, back to Llangollen or whatever was left of it. Instead, he was stuck here. He *could* look on the bright side – if he hadn't stopped off here, he'd still be out in the northern wilderness looking for Ambrosius. At least, coming to the Mountains of Blood, he'd found an army he could send back home. Oh yes, he *could* make the best of it. However, it was snowing, he was colder than he'd ever been in his life[86] and quite frankly he didn't really *want* to. Even if he and Megan did get away – and that was still Llew's plan – and *even* if they made it to Llangollen, how was he going to explain Megan to Ceridwen?

'Hi, yes, this is the girl I told you about. Yes, I did have a bit of thing for her and yes, she's pregnant now, but all I did was rescue her. Honest. How've things been here? How was the siege? Oh dear, that sounds nasty. Still, least said soonest mended, eh?'

This would be doubly worse if and when Uther made it there and Ceridwen asked where Llew was.

'The scribe? Oh, he stayed behind to rescue my woman. I understand he had a bit of a thing for her at one time. She's pregnant.'

It made it all the more urgent for him to get Megan out as quickly as possible, which was difficult if not impossible. They would be watching her like a hawk. He didn't give much for Gorlois' guarantee of safety either. Oh, he had sworn that the princess would come to no harm, sworn on a bible and sworn on a pagan symbol some of the Votadini still worshipped while Andrew tutted and pretended to disapprove, but Llew was pretty sure that, as soon as Uther was out of sight, Gorlois would do exactly what he wanted. Uther, however, had seemed convinced enough by Gorlois' oath, although he had muttered to Llew before he saddled up, 'He's promised she'll come to no harm. He's sworn! He won't break it if you're still around. Or Andrew for that matter. Gorlois still thinks you're a monk and that you're staying to oversee the girl's safety. He believes in God. Or the Gods. One or the other. Either way, he thinks monks have power.'

'He ... he does?'

'Course. Why d'you think he does all that business with the wives? If he didn't think God had bolts of lightning to throw at him, he wouldnae bother, would he? Anyway, he won't make a promise like this lightly if he thinks you have direct communication with ...'

He pointed upwards.

'... Don't let him find out you're not holy.'

'Yes, Lord, but you made a promise that Megan wouldn't try to escape.'

---

[86] Which, as we know, was pretty cold.

'I never said *I* believed that load of nonsense, did I? If lightning comes from the sky, my friend, it's because of something more logical than some kind of wizardry, mark my words.'

Llew had, but he still wasn't so sure. He'd seen it being done once.

The warriors and people were now all packed and mounted up. Uther rode his horse to the front of the long column of horses and wagons, and then he wheeled round to take a last look at his old home. His face was granite, not betraying a single emotion – which said it all really ... because Uther was, certainly when it came to Megan, quite an emotional man.

It spoke volumes that he couldn't bring himself to look at her.

He turned his horse around and waved the column forward. Slowly but surely, to the sound of hoof beats on snow and the creaking of wooden wheels, the great caravan started to move off towards the forest. Megan fell to her knees sobbing copiously and Llew awkwardly tried putting a comforting hand on her shoulder, just stopping himself from saying something like 'there there' or 'don't worry, it'll be all right', because deep down he didn't think it would.

Within seconds of the last wagon disappearing into the woodland beyond the mountains, there was a rush of people trying to stake a claim on anything that had been vacated or left behind. Fights broke out as families tried to move into empty huts or halls, newly ownerless cattle and pigs were sent stampeding as crowds of budding livestock owners chased after them, knocking over abandoned gates and fences as they did so. Into this chaos rode Gorlois' three sons, each of them pretending to simply be observing it all, pretending that they didn't care, when actually each of them was thinking 'soon this'll be mine'. Llew could see that Uther's mountain was about to become a very dangerous place indeed. A civil war zone, in fact.[87] And, presumably, Gorlois would stand on top of one of his two mountains and laugh.

Or not.

It appeared Gorlois was not in a laughing mood. He was in a 'taking care of outstanding business' mood. And the first thing he did as soon as Uther was out of the way was send some soldiers to arrest Megan. She was put under guard and told she would not be hurt for the present. It was the 'for the present' that worried her (and Llew), because the present is more often than not followed by the future[88] and there'd been no guarantees about that.

Llew had immediately plucked up his courage and, still keeping in character as the 'itinerant monk-scribe and emissary of Rome', he went to plead Megan's case before the king, knowing that if they were to escape, it couldn't be done while she was chained and watched by soldiers. He found the king in his hall, surrounded by his usual retinue of chieftains, soldiers,

---

[87] Interesting because there is nothing 'civil' about war.
[88] And if it isn't, that's just as bad.

wives and general hangers-on. He was also surprised to find Andrew there, looking shifty. All eyes turned to Llew as he walked in. Silence descended on the room. Gorlois looked rather amused to see him. He grunted to one of his chiefs, who said, 'His Majesty is pleased you have come here, monk.'

'Monk.' 'Scribe.' Why, why, *why* was it impossible for these people to use his *name*? If they didn't know it, they only had to ask! He was utterly fed up with being a one-syllable object to people who considered themselves his betters. On the other hand, he was a stranger in the court of a very powerful king. The 'little turd' speech he had used on Bruenor would probably not be appropriate in this instance. Actually, it hadn't really been appropriate in *that* instance, and he still had some of the bruises and the gaps in his teeth to prove it.

'I thank his majesty. I have come to ask why the Princess Meg–'

'Ahem!!' coughed Andrew.

'... Ygrain has been chained and imprisoned? His majesty swore an oath that the princess would come to no harm.'

The king grinned even more widely and nodded at the chieftain, who also grinned.

'We rather think that the Prince Uther may have inadvertently misinterpreted a word in the agreement ...'

Llew had a sinking feeling that something bad was coming – a moment where it was all to go horribly wrong. He had experienced such moments before and they nearly always involved the enemy grinning just beforehand.

'What word would that be?' he said, trying to sound as casual and cheerful as possible. 'Did his Majesty not promise that the Princess Ygrain would come to no harm?'

He was frantically trying to figure out what the get-out clause would be. What word could be misinterpreted? Was it something to do with the real name of the princess, or the fact that there were about twenty princess Ygrains? Was Gorlois going to say that he meant some other Princess Ygrain would come to no harm, whereas Princess *Megan* ...? If Llew could just get a handle on this he might be able to mount some kind of defence (this was, he had realised pretty much as soon as he had walked in, going to be a trial of sorts) or counter argument. Gorlois, even with the help of that spokes-chieftain he was currently employing, surely wasn't going to be able to come up with anything clever. Was he?

'What his Majesty *meant* was, that the Princess Megan should come to *know* harm.'

Oh yes. He was.

'Do you see?' the chieftain was giggling, 'Prince Uther may have thought the princess would come to *no* harm, but actually the king was promising she would come to *know* harm, do you see?'

'Yes, yes!' muttered Llew deliberately, 'spelt differently, obviously.'

'Is it?' said the chieftain, now laughing out loud, 'we, Votadini, rather like you Cymru, rarely write things down.'

By now all the men in the room were laughing heartily, except for Andrew, who was looking awkward until Gorlois turned to look at him and then he pretended to laugh as well. A little too loudly. Oddly, the women didn't laugh at all. They just looked at their feet forlornly. Broken. They were pretty sure how this would end and then later, another of them – probably Dioneta – would be the next to suffer the same fate. It was only a matter of time.

Llew meanwhile was cursing himself – get it in writing! He should have known! He realised the audience had not come to an end. As Gorlois himself stopped guffawing, the rest of the court gradually stopped laughing too.

'Punishment!' he grunted.

Now it was Andrew's turn to speak.

'Majesty, once again I must protest,' he said wearily. 'Throwing a woman off a cliff for sinning is not the Christian way!'

Gorlois turned to his chieftain, who had apparently been given the role of Grand Inquisitor.

'His Majesty had thought you'd say something of this sort, Brother Andrew,' said the chieftain, 'and therefore your king had decided to grant clemency. The princess will not be thrown off the cliff.'

Now here was a turn-up for the books.

'He has seen the light, his Majesty, he has decided that he will renounce the old gods and become a true Christian, taking but one wife and forsaking all others, which he will be able to do once he has become a widower.'

Llew knew it was useless, but he decided to step in anyway.

'How can his Majesty be a widower when his wife is living?'

The chieftain turned back to Andrew.

'Brother Andrew, what does the mother church advocate as the punishment for adultery?'

Andrew floundered. Goodness knows why – he knew the answer well enough.

'Currently … well, I … believe it's stoning, or for royalty … erm … burning. At the … erm, at the stake.'

The chieftain turned back to Llew.

'That is how his Majesty can be a widower, *brother* Llewelyn,' he said, smirking. 'We will burn her.'

Later, it occured to Llew that, in a warped way, Gorlois was the most flexible and modern-thinking of all the kings he'd known – half-pagan, half-Christian … getting the best of both worlds. However, now it suited him he was embracing the modern world wholeheartedly. And he was also using the subtleties of words to help him break an unwanted oath. Even Vortigern wouldn't have thought of that.

It's just that he was a brutal tyrant with it.

Llew was thinking about this as he sneaked from hut to hut in the darkness, dodging the patrols and ignoring the sounds of quaffing, singing and generally making merry in the king's hall.

He knew this was hopeless. He knew he was going to get caught, but he had to try.

He had thought about leaving, just slipping out of the territory and making his way back to Nascien's cave, where hopefully his horse was still whole. They probably wouldn't chase him – what did they need him for? He could be on his horse and cart and off to Llangollen that night. And if he made it there and if Uther was king, he'd just have to say, 'sorry, I couldn't get her out' or, more likely, he could sneak in, get Ceridwen and Griffith and sneak out again and then go to the coast and get that boat he'd always been talking about.

Whatever. He could go. He'd seriously considered it.

But he knew he couldn't.

He'd promised Uther. He'd promised he'd get her out. Uther had left to help Llew's people on the basis of that promise, so he'd got no choice. Especially as he didn't believe in finding a clever way of using words to break it, not that he *could* have thought of one anyway. Besides, annoying as she'd become to him, he didn't like the idea of her ... well, it wasn't the pleasantest of ways to go. You had to hand it to the management at the Mother Church, they sure as hell knew how to make you scream.

He was nearly at the hut where she was being kept. Two guards stood outside. How was he going to get in?

Well, here's one way, he thought. You go up to the guards, you say something along the lines of, 'let me in to see the prisoner', and when they ask why, you say, 'I would look into the eyes of one who is to die'; or, remembering the cowl, 'I would comfort the prisoner with prayers'; or, 'I would spit on the most despised woman in all the Votadini lands'. Then, when they've let you in (after laughing evilly in agreement with you, of course) – presumably unaccompanied – you ... slip a knife to her so she can secretly undo her bonds and tunnel out the back when you've left her, then hoot like an owl so that she knows the coast's clear ... or you can shout 'Guard! Guard! Help! The prisoner is sick!', and when each one comes in you hit them over the back of the head with the frying pan, which will of course knock them out for ages so you can get away without them raising the alarm.

A number of options, any one of which could work, he was sure. Llew strode up to the hut.

'Let me in to see the prisoner!' he demanded.

The guards looked at one another, then turned to Llew.

'at for?' said one.

so good.

'ok into the eyes of one who is to die!'

There was a pause as both guards took this in.

'Why?' said the other guard.

Ah.

'Well ... well ...' – thinking on feet time again – 'it's something you do with condemned prisoners ...'

'Is it?' The first guard was looking extraordinarily puzzled.

'Yes! You know – the eyes being the window of the soul and that,' Llew bungled on, 'oh, yes ... that and praying with them. I am, after all, a monk.'

He felt he was now back on track.

'Sorry,' said the first guard, 'no one in for prayers except Brother Andrew. King's orders.'

'Oh.' Llew was disappointed, but he knew he had to keep trying. He adopted a conspiratorial tone to the first guard: '... What I want really is to spit on the most despised woman in the Votadini lands.'

'You what?' Now the first guard was appalled. 'You think I'd let you in there so you can spit on the poor girl? Don't you think her lot's bad enough right now?'

'But ... why on this *earth* would you want to look into her eyes?' This from the second guard, who was still very puzzled by all this.

'I mean, you do know she's being burned at the stake tomorrow?' The first guard was getting quite angry. '... And you think I'd let you in to spit on her? What kind of monster are you?'

Llew realised that he'd fallen at the first fence. He also knew, to his mortification, that Megan was inside the hut right now *hearing* him fall at the first fence.

'Actually,' he said, starting to turn away, 'maybe I won't bother.'

'Too right you won't bother!' shouted the first guard, picking up a chunk of ice and throwing it at Llew as he turned and walked away. 'Go on, get out of it!!! Pervert!!'

'But ... what would it *achieve*?' the other guard was saying, totally nonplussed, 'eyes are just eyes, aren't they?'

Llew waited until he was out of their range of vision before he slipped behind a barn and slumped against its wooden walls. This needed thinking about. Okay, he couldn't get past the guards, but maybe he could get them to go away, thus leaving him clear to sneak in and rescue Megan. A distraction! That was it. Supposing he were to start a fire nearby ... say in this barn ... then surely the guards would rush to the river with buckets to help put out the blaze. If it was big enough, there'd be enough of a distraction for him and Megan to get away entirely. It seemed like a good plan. So the next thing would be to locate the nearest naked flame.

A couple of torches blazed on poles at the door of one of the huts a few yards off. Inside he could hear the voices of a few men chatting and laughing whilst playing a Nine Men's game, the details of their conversation muffled from the outside. He crept over to the hut's entrance and gingerly lifted one of the torches from its pole. Then he returned to the barn and sneaked inside. It was empty, save for some straw on the ground for whatever farm animals it had once housed and the odd bit of timber. And it was dry. The thatched roof had easily kept the snow out … it was as well built a barn as you could want.

Which was a shame, because he was now about to burn it to the ground.

He extended his arm downwards, pointing the torch towards the floor. The straw started to smoulder, little licks of flame began spreading slowly outwards as gradually the fire started to take. He backed away as the flames started to spread further and grow higher, nipped out through the barn door and crept off to hide behind the hut he'd taken the torch from. He waited. Soon the flames would start to burn the timber in the barn, then the timber would set light to the wooden walls. They'd get fiercer and higher, but with a bit of luck no one would notice anything was amiss until they were high enough to take the thatched roof … which was covered in snow. This would fall onto the fire as the roof collapsed, but wouldn't be near enough to put it out. It would, however, make a lot of noise. Steam hissing. And that would alert people – if the flames hadn't done so already – and by then the blaze would be huge. Everyone would be running from all directions to put the damn thing out, which would of course take ages.

He drew his cloak around him and hugged himself. He was freezing (as usual). Still, not to worry, soon there'd be a big barn on fire to keep him warm while he rescued Megan …

… He woke with a start, even colder than he had been before. The conversation from inside the hut had long stopped. Everyone must have gone to sleep. How had be managed to doze off, sitting outside in this weather? You don't sleep in snow like this, not without a fire beside you or a roof over your head. You do and you'll die. He knew that. Everyone knew that. And … what was that barn doing? Surely by now he should be hearing a few people shouting things like 'fire!', 'water!', or preferably both. He got up and peaked round the side of the hut. The barn stood there as it had done not long before, a big black and above all whole shape in the dark. He crept over again and opened the door.

The straw was gone. All burned up and black. Some of the timber was too, but not much of it. Everything else was pretty much as it was – the walls … the roof. The bloody fire must have gone out! Damn it! He'd have to go and nick another torch now. He turned round in frustration and almost bumped into the second of Megan's guards.

'You've got to be the worst arsonist I've ever seen,' he said, before he hit Llew over the head with his sword. Interestingly enough, Llew was knocked out cold as quickly and for as long as he'd hoped the guards would be in one of his escape plans.

The next day.

They were raising the stake. They'd chopped a tree down, stripped it of branches and were now inserting the bass of it into a hole they'd dug in the ground. From Andrew's chapel – where they were keeping Llew tied up – he could hear complaints. There'd been a load of dry straw and timber in one of the barns. They'd wanted to put it around the base of the stake because it would burn quicker. Unfortunately, it wasn't there any more, so they were going to have to collect firewood from the forest at the foot of the mountains. Finding wood that wasn't damp in this weather would be a miracle, which would mean that it would burn more slowly, which would mean a more drawn out and painful death for the princess.

Nice one, Llew.

'You have to help me!' Llew hissed at Andrew, who was busying himself with a broom, trying to get rid of non-existent dust and cobwebs.

'You have to untie me and let me go!'

Andrew did the interesting thing of answering while at the same time pretending not to hear what was being said to him.

'I have to help him? That's what he says, is it? Interesting. Wonder how he came to *that* little conclusion.'

He swept a little more vigorously in a corner he'd cleaned not five minutes before for the fifth time.

'Because if you don't they're going to burn her alive!'

'Does he have any idea, really any idea what it's like to be me! Stuck up in a god-forsaken place at Rome's behest!'

'Erm … yes I do, actually. I used to be a Roman representative!'

'I meant the Pope, not his stupid emperor! You can't run away from God, you know!'

Pretty hard to run away from *anyone* in my experience, thought Llew.

'Every day! Every *day*, I have to live with the fact that *madman* will probably have me killed! And while it was less likely when there was someone like Uther to keep Gorlois in check,' Andrew's voice was getting higher now, 'it isn't less likely any more now! And it's probably been made worse now that loony-features is embracing *Christian brotherly love*!!'

Frustrated, Llew struggled madly against his ropes, to no avail.

'What kind of monk are you?' he breathed angrily.

'More of a monk than he'll ever be!' Andrew snapped back, whilst still not actually talking directly to Llew. 'A monk that didn't give him away and also … and also made sure she's not going to be stoned to death, which is much nastier than the stake, believe me … for which I notice I'm not getting any credit!!!'

'You're the only one who can help now!!!' Llew was shouting at him, trying to blink back the tears. 'You have to listen! You have to let me go!'

Andrew leaned the broom against the wall.

'I'm going for a walk now,' he said, to no one in particular, and walked out of the chapel, closing the door behind him.

Well, fire wasn't going to save Megan like it had saved Llew in a similar situation and now, it seemed, neither was the love of God.

Llew grunted desperately as he struggled in vain with his bonds. This was not how it was supposed to go. For a start, one of his rescue attempts should have been at least partially successful. And he'd only had two! He should have been able to have a third go. He didn't know why, he just knew that was how it was supposed to be. He wasn't supposed to be hit over the head just after the second one! And the second one was at least supposed to fail a little more spectacularly – not with the bloody fire just happening to go out! Where was the point in that? And now, his last hope, the stupid monk, who's *supposed* to be cowardly, *but* is persuaded to come through and against his nature be brave at the end ... was walking out without being any help whatsoever. And the ropes weren't coming undone either ... surely they should have loosened a *bit*. ... Nascien! Maybe he could get a message to Nascien! 'How, stupid?' his inner critic asked, 'telepathy?' And then he realised that now he'd thought of it, it was never going to happen. It would have only happened if he hadn't thought of it, because Nascien coming to the rescue had to be a surprise.

Why was he thinking like this? Like it was supposed to be a tale told by a bard! Who *thought* like that?

Megan used to. Which was why he was here in the bloody first place. Ironic.

The door of the chapel burst open.

At last!

Two guards came in and pulled him to his feet.

'You ...,' he said, breathless, '... you're going to untie me, right? You're going to help!'

They were guards from last night! And they'd shown compassion to Megan. They hadn't wanted him to spit on her! One of them had thought it weird that Llew had wanted to gloat. This was it. They'd take him and Megan to the edge of the settlement and he'd ask why they were doing it and they'd say, 'because we knew someone like you once and there was no one there to help' ... that sort of thing.

'You what?' said the first guard, looking at him nonplussed. 'No, we're taking you to watch the burning. It's sunset.'

Bugger!

'Gorlois says everyone has to be there,' added the second.

It had been erected by the river, where the ground was saturated and slushy. The snow went brown almost at the same moment it settled there. The tree they had cut down from the forest and stripped was green oak – it doesn't so much burn as steam. At the base of the stake were such kindling and timbers as people had been able to find, or spare. At this time of year, that was not much.

It must have been tempting to say, 'look, the damn thing won't light properly and quite frankly we need the wood for ourselves. And Night's coming down. Why not postpone? Why don't we all meet here again in, say ... Spring?' However, *despite* the temptation, no one said it. Llew found he was being dragged along as part of a crowd. He could just make out lines of torches as they came down from all three mountains. As Gorlois had said, everyone had to be there.

What was terrifying to him now, for the first time ever, was not that he had to face his own death. He was going to have to face the death of someone he did not want to die. Everything was running against his expectations – he'd expected to be able to escape, he'd expected to be able to rescue Megan. He knew in his heart that he still expected Megan in some way to be rescued, which almost certainly meant that it wasn't going to happen and he would have to watch her burn alive.

The guard pulled the end of the rope taut and shoved him face-forward onto a tree, tying him tightly so that he could barely move. He was just able to turn his head towards the stake, where he could see people starting to mingle near the base of the stake, forming a circular clearing a few feet away from the piles of kindling.

A drum started beating, slowly, loudly. On the edge of his hearing, Llew could just make out some of the women chanting. An old chant ... in the old language ... he could barely understand it, but he knew it had something to do with blood and bone.

Just in front, a dais had been set with a chair on the top for Gorlois. The old king was now making his way towards it, with his bodyguard and his chieftains, laughing and chatting with members of the crowd.

Surely Andrew would help. In the end. The monk would come through, surely. He must.

The Ygrains were now gathering, just in front of the dais. They bowed to the king and then took their place at the edge of the circle. Llew could see that one of them, Dioneta, was also mumbling the chant to herself as the drum beat continued. The other wives were starting to join in and, as they did so, the chant got gradually louder.

This, he reflected, for Gorlois' final conversion was not looking terribly Christian. And where was Andrew anyway? Ah, there he was, holding a flaming torch – in charge of lighting the fire – so, it really wasn't looking like Andrew was going to do any rescuing any time soon.

Gorlois' three sons now entered the clearing. They too bowed to the king and took their place at the edge of the circle. The drum beat on.

But then something changed. Or maybe not *changed* as such; there just seemd to be a new perception of reality as it stood. Things were obviously not going to plan. Gorlois was looking unnerved, he was glancing around him, not apparently liking what he was hearing. The chanting was increasing in volume still, becoming shriller and quite disturbing. He shouted for silence, but his voice was lost in the sound of the women and the drum. Gorlois looked to Andrew for some advice, but the monk, just as puzzled as he was, could only shrug. Gorlois called to his guards and his chieftains, but they just seemed to ignore him. The men now joined in … chanting, chanting, chanting … blood and bone.

'It started with the women, apparently …,' hissed a familiar voice in his ear.

Llew could just make out a hooded figure next to him.

'Megan?' he whispered.

'They've been plotting against him for ages. They've persuaded the sons to rebel, but there's going to be a huge fight. Then they're going to kill him. Apparently, no one wanted to become Christian.'

Llew could feel a knife sawing the ropes behind him. This didn't fit either – he was being rescued by the woman he was supposed to be rescuing.

'Erm … when did you get away?'

'When you were making an utter arse of yourself trying to burn that barn down. I sneaked out of the hut. The guards have been looking for me ever since. Only they obviously haven't told the king because they're in on the plot. It'd all be working out beautifully if it weren't for one thing …'

Llew could feel the ropes loosening and a bad feeling about the 'one thing'. There always was 'one thing' in matters where things should all have worked out beautifully.

'Which is?'

'All of the sons have decided that *I'm* going to be their queen afterwards. There's going to be one heck of a fight for *me* as well! So I think, while everybody's distracted with the business of killing and burning Gorlois, we ought to make ourselves scarce, don't you?'

The last of the rope fell away.

'Good idea. We'll follow the river through the woods.'

As they sneaked away in the dark, Llew couldn't help thinking that this was a bit of history he was missing out on. Behind him, hundreds of hands started to grab and claw at a terrified Gorlois and a monk was wielding a flaming torch trying to stop them doing the same to him …

They still tell tales of the Votadini in that part of the country, about how a mighty king was brought down by the women of the tribe and that a war started between each of his sons over who would be king after him and as to who would be that king's queen. And the fight was to be all the worse because the one chosen to be the queen had been stolen away by a thief disguised as an itinerant monk-scribe … and the sons sent a band of men on horseback to find the thief and the woman, to kill him and bring her back. The plan had been to fight each other for her, but the woman and the monk-scribe fell to their deaths while they were being chased. That's the tale they still tell.

... so Llew was actually wrong. He *was* part of history again, only he wasn't there to witness it – well, not all of it anyway.

But Gorlois burned at the stake nevertheless and the Mountains Of Blood became true to their name, because the country was plunged into civil war and everybody said it would never have happened if Uther Dragon Head had been around to run things. However, this internal strife meant that no raiding parties were sent south of the border for an awful long time. So it's just possible that, by accident, a certain person managed to do something right for a change. Or so his father would have said.

It was almost impossible making their escape through the forest on the wintry moonless night. The only guide they had was the river, which was frozen over, so they walked, or rather slid along it, discovering on the way that it wasn't frozen over completely and that every now and again one of them was able to prove that it was a river they were following with the words, 'Ow! Bloody hell, that's cold!' It was also as slippery as ... well, ice ... which made the going even slower.

'... You see, there was this time when I'd said aloud to Gorlois that all this business of killing off his wives and then picking another prime one from the herd was, well ... a bit demeaning to women ...'

Demeaning certainly was one way of putting it, Llew had to admit to himself as they slid along the new icy path. A wind blew, an icy wind.

'.... And it got them all thinking, apparently. So they started planning – you know, a word in one ear here, a word in another there. I mean, I didn't know of course, but that was *why* no one ever said anything to Gorlois about me and Uther ...'

Uther and *I*, surely, Llew thought irritably – she'd really lost a few of her airs and graces since she'd come up here. Less of the princess about her. He wasn't sure he liked it. In her, anyway. Of course, he'd have *hated* Ceridwen to be all royal. Ceridwen. Maybe, just maybe, he was going to get home to her, find she was okay, that Griff was okay and that Uther was now king.

That would be sweet.

'... So when Gorlois decided to kill me and become a full-time Christian, well, that was when the sons decided to act, because all three of them wanted to marry me ...,' she said.

Yes, thought Llew darkly, it's only about the *fifth* time you've told me that.

'I mean, I had no idea! Really! What is it about men falling in love with me? How come I never notice –?'

'Do you think we can concentrate on getting out of Votadini country as fast as possible?' he said, trying not to sound as irritated as he actually was; 'only, as soon as they discover we're missing, they're going to come after us.'

He couldn't see her expression in the dark, but he could hear her perfectly well and her next words were positively laced with an undertone of 'don't-get-snotty-with-me-I'm- the-princess-who-just-rescued-you'.

'They won't be able to track us. Not on ice. They'll use hunting hounds and hunting hounds can't even cross water. *Everyone* knows that.'

He decided to say nothing. At this rate, if they travelled all night, they might just make it to Nascien's cave by dawn; then they could be on the cart and that would give them some speed and also some cover. As far as the Votadini knew, they'd escaped *on foot. Then* they might widen to two people on horseback – assuming (wrongly) that's what the fugitives would choose to travel by next. If he could get rid of his monk's cowl and find some other clothes, they could perhaps disguise themselves as a peasant couple. Monk's cowl ... something made him remember his rescue. She'd hooded herself ... obviously so as not show her face ... but the hood was connected to some sort of robe ...

'Where on earth did you get a monk's cowl from?'

'That monk, of course!' she said, puzzled.

'What, Andrew?'

'No ... the weird one. The one that made poor Britu go all funny.'

'Nascien?'

'Yes. He turned up with poor Britu in Elmet when I was married to Pelinore. I found this in the chapel where we let them stay after they'd left. Always knew it would come in handy. I had it washed, of course – it was awfully ... you know ... pungent.'

She wrinkled her nose.

'Nascien, who we're going to meet now?' he said aghast.

'Are we? Oh good. I can ask him what he chose to wear instead.'

She found out the next day.

Nascien, good as his word, had kept their transport in fine condition during the time Llew had been away. He'd even been on scouting expeditions to local homesteads so as to obtain food for the horse.

'People did giveth freely with my barely asking,' he said to Llew earnestly.

Llew wasn't surprised. There was something earnestly innocent about Nascien. Saying no to him would be like kicking a puppy. Add that to the fact that he was also completely naked – which might make you want him to leave your hearth, sooner rather than later – and Llew could bet that Nascien had got all the food he wanted.

' 'Tis true,' continued Nascien, ' 'is what Tolly and I have both supped upon since the snows fell.'

Tolly was the name Nascien had given to the horse.

Megan, seeing Nascien's naked state, was within minutes mastering the new skill of looking at someone while averting her eyes at the same time. It was, she reflected, particularly lucky he had the beard. Meanwhile, Llew was hurriedly hitching up Tolly to the cart and preparing for travel.

'I'God's truth,' said Nascien, 'there hath been precious little else to eat this winter. I pray 'twill not be like the last …'

Llew looked at the half-starved hermit and shivered. It didn't bear thinking about how cold Nascien must be. He was practically blue, which is not a healthy colour for anyone.

'Don't you think you'd better come with us?' he said.

'I am a holy man! The Lord will provide! I will live on *love*!'

'Nascien, last winter you barely survived. All you had was nuts and berries.'

'And bear meat. And also …,' he looked towards Megan, significantly, having recently learned that this was Vortigern Britu's sister, '… well, thou knowest.'

'Exactly, neither of those two particular foodstuffs are likely to present themselves again, are they? Stay here and you'll die.'

'Thou hast a point,' Nascien admitted, sagely.

'Can I have a word with you, please, Llew?'

Megan had approached and was standing next to the wagon with a tight-lipped smile. She turned and walked away, urgently indicating for Llew to follow her. Llew left Nascien doing up Tolly's harness and joined her where she'd stopped a few feet off.

'What?' he said bluntly.

'I am not sitting up on the wagon with a … naked man,' she hissed.

'He's not naked. That beard and hair pretty much covers everything,' Llew hissed back. 'Anyway, if Nascien travels with us it'll improve the disguise! They'll be looking for two people travelling on foot, not three on a wagon.'

'I told you they won't be coming after us. They're in the middle of the civil war and they can't track us over ice!'

'Well, I'm sorry, but Nascien is coming with us.'

'It's not seemly for a princess to be seen –'

'Seemly'? 'Princess'? Not lost *that* many of her airs and graces then.

'Well, listen, *Princess*,' he said through clenched teeth, 'you want "seemly"? Just turn round and go back the way we've come. There's three nice young princes who'll happily give you a right royal welcome when you get back there. You always wanted to be queen? Well, go be queen of the Votadini!'

'I rescued you, remember?' she fired at him.

Llew drummed up every inch of irony and sarcasm he had from the depths of his being and decided to use it in what he said next.

'Oh dear, I'm sorry,' he offered, 'maybe I'll get a chance to do something for *you* one day.'

He trudged back towards the cart. There was, he reflected, two other reasons he wanted Nascien with them. The first was that, just like Ceridwen and Griff and, in a strange way, even Megan ... Nascien had become his family. You didn't necessarily like all of them, but you did things for each other unquestioningly. You sure as hell didn't leave them behind in a snow-covered forest to starve to death. Well, not unless they really got on your nerves. Just like she was doing right now. This, as far as Llew was concerned, was the *second* reason Nascien was coming.

Llew was pleased also to learn that all his sacks of parchment had remained in good condition while he'd been away. Nascien had moved them up to the cave to keep them out of the damp – no small feat to get them all up that cliff. And as it turned out no small feat to get them down again when it was time to load up and leave. It delayed them for over an hour, which Llew regretted, despite Megan's bravado, because he wouldn't be happy until they were out of the northern lands and south of the wall.

However, now as they trotted through the snow-covered paths with nothing to do but watch steam rising from their nostrils and mouths ... Llew and Nascien sitting in front, Megan in the back complaining that she couldn't be comfortable amongst all these sacks of parchment and asking were they there yet ... *now* it seemed as if they might just make it.

By the end of the day, they were out of the forest with still no sign of their pursuers. That night they risked a campfire as they stopped and rested. Llew couldn't help noticing that far, *far* away in the distance he could see a tiny orange dot. So what? So someone *else* had a campfire too. Could be anyone.

Next day, the spot seemed to be a little closer.

They were going through very mountainous country now. Difficult for a horse and wagon at the best of times. Even more difficult through snow. And out in the open, without the shelter of the trees, the snow had become much deeper. It was not long before both Llew and Nascien were having to push from the back, up hill while Megan drove the horse from the front. At one point, Llew had muttered something about pushing being unseemly for a princess and Megan had jumped down from the wagon and dramatically announced her intention to do her share, but Nascien – naked, emaciated Nascien – had intervened.

'Art thou mad?!' he had shouted. 'Thou has a loaf in the oven. Thou wilt pop any day soon!'

And Megan had meekly got back on the cart without a word.

Meantime, that strange campfire got nearer.

And it was cold. Terribly cold. And the wind whipped across their faces, making it feel colder. Even Nascien decided to forsake the hermetical life for a few days and wear some animal skins he'd brought along. None of them could remember it being so cold.

The day before Llew was sure they were in reach of Hadrian's Wall, they saw them on the horizon just behind them at sunset. Riders. About a hundred.

He knew … they *all* knew, the riders were Votadini … it would have been nice to pretend to themselves that they were just some other warriors who happened to be travelling a few miles behind them in the same direction. Or bandits who wouldn't really be interested in robbing them. Or something. But they knew they were the horsemen of the Votadini, riding to take Megan back and to kill Llew. Nascien was probably going to be all right, but this didn't give any of them much comfort.

Llew urged the horses into a trot. The horsemen had started to dip below the horizon. When they surfaced again, they were much closer.

'Oh, they can't possibly track us,' he said, mimicking Megan.

An hour later, it was almost completely dark. Llew glanced behind and could see that the riders were gaining on them – it was a matter of maybe ten or fifteen yards. Each rider carried a flaming torch. Llew urged the horse to go faster – it whinnied in complaint, but obeyed, nevertheless. The left side of the wagon rose in the air as they rounded a sudden bend, causing Megan to scream.

Dangerous to ride a wagon at speed – you didn't know what might be on the road to tip you over. Besides, this was a mountain road – every now and then you looked either right or left to see a sheer drop. You couldn't see the bottom, of course, not in the dark. Actually, for a lot of them you couldn't see the bottom in the day. Nevertheless, Llew slapped the reins again. If they could just get past the wall … it was unlikely Gorlois' sons would want to cross the border out of the Pict lands into Elmet. They might be well armed enough to capture an escaping wagon, but not to start a war.

Not much to hope for, but anything was better than nothing. He urged the horse onwards, making the wagon go even faster; they were galloping now, the wagon occasionally lifting in the air as they went over bumps. The first of the horsemen were in plain sight now, flaming torch in one hand, spear in the other. They spurred their steeds on, each anxious to be the one to win the coveted prize – doubtless the sons of Gorlois had put a very high price on the capture of these fugitives.

'They're coming!' Megan screamed. 'Can't we go any faster?'

There was no time for a sarcastic reply of the 'oh yes, I just love a chase that's all' kind, because the first of the riders was now level and aiming a spear, poised and ready to throw. Suddenly, as the rider jerked his arm forward, Nascien reached over and grabbed the end of the weapon, pulling it towards him. This was not something the rider had expected. He lost his balance and toppled sideways off his horse, screaming as he went under the wheels of the cart.

'Ooh. Look what I have got!' said Nascien, amazed. He was holding both the warrior's flaming torch and the spear.

'Throw it!!!' yelled Llew; 'the spear. Chuck it at him!'

Nascien chucked the spear at the second rider, who was now level with them on the other side. Not being a warrior, Nascien's throw fell short, but it shot under the horse's front legs, causing it to trip up and somersault forwards, screaming and taking its rider down with it.

There were three more riders now, a little further back – and, glancing behind him, Llew could see the torch lights line of the rest of the war band streaming off into the black horizon.

'They're getting closer!' screamed Megan.

'Take the reins!' Llew shouted at Nascien and then leapt into the back of the wagon, frantically searching through sacks of parchment for the other of his prized possessions. He found it soon enough. The old rusty sword. This time, there was no fight to get it out of the scabbard. The sword plainly knew this was not the hour to be mucking around. Llew drew the sword and swung it just as the first of the three warriors was about to throw his torch into the back of the wagon.

The only thing that was left of the warrior and the horse afterwards was the flaming torch, which seemed to hang in the air briefly before dropping to the ground; although, later that night, when everything was over, some wolves approached the area and reflected that they'd never had their food freshly minced for them before.

The wagon turned sharply to the right, almost tipping over and righting itself again. The lights of the warriors were briefly invisible, before coming into view again behind them.

The other two front riders hung back a little, evidently (and after seeing the sword in action, wisely) waiting for more of their comrades to catch up before they attacked again. This time they'd do it in a big rush. Llew turned to see that Megan was about to throw away the flaming torch Nascien had acquired from one of them.

'Megan! No!' he shouted over the noise of the wind and the wagon.

She turned to look at him, affronted.

'Don't order me about!' she shouted back. 'It's dark! If I chuck this they won't be able to see us!'

'I've got an idea!'

It had come to him as he saw the line of flame-lit riders stretching back into the dark. No, the riders had not used hounds. They'd followed them by watching out for every time they'd started a fire at night and heading towards it.

He just had to wait for the right bit in the road.

He looked back. More of the war band was getting closer and closer. If he was going to do this, it would have to be soon. If enough of them got close enough, they could all attack at once and then, sword or no, the three of them would be dead meat. But he needed just enough distance between him and them so that they could see the wagon and the light and not much else.

The wagon swerved sharply to the left, causing Llew to swing out dizzily over the edge before he forced himself back in.

He sheathed the sword, tied the belt round his waist, then snatched the torch from Megan.

'Hey!'

'When the time comes, hold on and don't let go! Stay with Nascien! Go home to Llangollen! Don't stop until you get there!'

'What are you talking about?'

He made his way back down to the front of the wagon, sat down next to Nascien and took the reins from him. With a crack, he urged the horse into a full, hard gallop, fast as it could go.

'Art thou mad? We can but hardly see the road …'

'Get on the horse. When I say, you pull the reins in whichever direction I tell you! Understand?'

'But … what –'

'Just do it! And don't make any noise!'

There was now just about the distance Llew needed. Gingerly, Nascien eased himself down on to the horse below.

'What the bloody hell is he doing?' Megan shouted incredulously as she made her way onto the wagon seat next to Llew.

'Now you! Get on behind him!'

'I will not! It's far too –'

He'd been ready for this. He'd grabbed the back of her robe and hurled her, screaming, onto the horse in front. She grabbed wildly in the dark and the only thing she found to hang on to caused Nascien to scream louder than he ever had when preaching the Peleganist gospel back in Londinium.

'My beard! My beard! Thou hast me by the beard, woman!'

'You're lucky it was just the beard, you nude lunatic!' she screamed back. 'Just help me!!'

Nascien reached down and swung her up and over onto the horse in front of him.

'What the hell's going on?' she screamed. 'I hope you realise this isn't good for the baby!'

It was amazing what women could think of at times like this. He refrained from pointing out that being chased by a band of painted Votadini warriors wasn't good for any of them should they get caught – mainly because of the noise of the hooves and the wind and the clatter of the wheels on the rough track … but also because he needed to concentrate. It was very dark now. With the speed they were going, the time to act would come upon them very suddenly. No hesitation – he'd have to just do it and hope for the best …

There it was: a fork in the road!

'To the right!!! Pull the reins to the right!!!!' he shouted.

He knew it would be the last thing he shouted to them for a long while, but there was no time for goodbyes. At the same moment, he let the reins go. Still holding the torch aloft, he reached downward and, using every ounce of his strength, pulled out the pin connecting the wagon to the horse. Nascien jerked the harness to the right. Wagon and horse separated, speeding up as they did so, Llew forcing all his weight to the left of the wagon.

The last he saw was of them galloping off into the night on the rightward path.

He was now freewheeling downhill at speed on the left fork with the torch held high. He turned to look behind him: hundreds of torches, little specks like fireflies bouncing on behind him in the night. They were going his way! This part of the plan had worked!

The problem with the next part of the plan was that it didn't as yet exist. The trick was, what to do next? He had no way of stopping the wagon, which was still going downhill and speeding up all the time. The positive side was that he could keep them following him for as long as there was a path, but … well, he needed to get off and escape … and what about his papers? And when should he get rid of the torch? He had to admit to himself that he hadn't really thought this through … then he realised something was bothering him … what was it? Oh yes. Lack of noise. No clattering of the wheels, although the wind was whistling quite a lot. And lack of movement. No bump bump bump as the wagon went over the rough, rocky track …

And then the wagon began to dip violently and it was at this point he realised he'd gone off a cliff.

And then there was an awful splintering.

When Llew awoke, he found he was lying in the snow. Deep, freezing snow, and getting deeper all the time, because flakes of it were falling from the sky. He was (unsurprisingly) shivering. He couldn't see much, although miraculously the torch was a few feet away from him, lying on its side and still burning. Groaning, he tried to move towards it, forcing himself first onto his elbows. Okay. Then, pressing his hands on the ground, he pulled himself onto one knee. Okay. Then – and a little more tentatively, because something was telling him he shouldn't be doing it – he tried to get onto the other knee …

And felt a screaming, white-hot shaft of pain greater than he ever had in his whole life shoot through his whole body.

He collapsed onto his side, breathing deeply in the vain hope that this would make the pain go away. Which it didn't, although after a while it did subside a little.

Oh good. A broken leg. Helpful.

Lying there, he found he was becoming aware of voices, far far above him. An argument. Something about not climbing down a place called Morag's Tooth Crag in the dark and are you out of your mind, they're dead anyway, no one could have survived that fall. This was followed by horses' hooves. Horses' hooves going away.

And then there was silence.

His eyes were getting used to the dark now as the torchlight was slowly going out, becoming not much more than a flicker. He could make out bits of shattered wagon and wooden wheels spread all over the place. He could see his sacks of scrolls, which seemed to have landed in a pile together; a couple of them had split open, spilling their contents on the snow. Other than that, nothing. Just rocks. Maybe a few tufts of grass. It looked as if he'd landed on a ledge of some sort. A wide one. If he'd been going any faster, the momentum of the wagon would have pushed him further *out* and he would have fallen further *down*.

So he had to be thankful for small mercies, really.

He knew lying there wasn't going to do him any good. It was freezing. If he just lay still, he'd eventually get sleepy and then he'd pass out and die. If nothing else, he must get hold of the torch before it went out. He must make a fire. He rolled back onto his stomach and tried to pull himself along, crawling hand over hand through the snow towards the flickering object. Every movement sent an intense spasm of pain through his body, so any hopes of him perhaps limping to safety or shelter somewhere were dying as fast as the flames were on the torch. Knowing he wasn't going to make it in time, he stretched as far and as hard as he could, this too causing him to sweat and shake with the pain, so that he was just able to grab the handle and lift the torch upright before it went out entirely.

And then it went out entirely. Llew lay face downwards in despair.

'Noooo!!!'

It sprang back into life, a mushroom of red and orange.

'How the hell did that –?'

'Greetings, Llewellyn Ap Gwyddno.'

Llew recognised the old man/young man voice even before he looked up into the burning blue eyes. There was Merlin, a man now – it had been many years since their last meeting ... last face-to-face meeting anyway. He was wearing long dark robes decorated with symbols Llew didn't recognise and carried a staff. His beard and hair were also long and black, but he had his forehead tonsured like a druid.

'Oh yes, I've been watching you. I've been watching your progress since the day we met ...,' said Merlin, apparently reading his thoughts. 'Where is Caliburn?'

The name rang a bell, but he wasn't really in the mood to try and remember ... what with the intense pain and all.

'What?'

Merlin turned away and went to the remains of the wagon, searching through the pile of sacks and parchment.

'Why?' Llew managed to croak, 'why have you been watching me?'

'Because things do not happen by themselves,' said Merlin without looking round; 'people must be in their proper places. For cause and effect.'

'What do you mean? What things?'

'The one who is to come! A king. A great king – the bear warrior – who will rid the world of all our foes and will restore this land to its former glory! Island Of The Mighty. His deeds will become the stuff of legend.'

Llew winced.

'Frankly,' he whispered with effort, 'that sounds like a ridiculous load of bard's cobblers.'

Merlin smiled and picked up what he was looking for. The sword. He held it up and admired it in the torchlight.

'You were a necessary piece on the board, Llewellyn Ap Gwyddno. Be thankful you have played your part well enough. That part is now over –'

It was about this moment that Merlin noticed the torch had been dropped on the ground again, still burning, just before Llew hit him hard on the nose, knocking him over. The superhuman anger that had welled up in Llew and caused him to ignore the terrible pain he was in then dissipated enough for Llew to collapse on the ground again. Blood spurted from Merlin's nose, which he tried unsuccessfully to stem with one hand.

'Ow!! Oww!' he moaned. 'What did you do that for?'

The mysterious voice had gone now.

'You can talk normally then?' winced Llew, trying to put his leg in a position that didn't make him want to vomit.

'Of course I can! I just use the voice to scare people! Not much point in being a prophet if you can't scare people! They'd think you were mad! Oooh gods, that hurts!!! Why did you hit me?'

The tone was as much offended as painful.

'Because my whole life you've been shaping what I do, you weird sod!' Llew's anger rose again, 'and then you just dismiss it! "Sorry, mate, nothing to do with you – you're just a piece in a board game"?!! And I'm just supposed to accept it?! *I want you to tell me what this is all about!!!!*'

Merlin tried to wipe his nose on his robe.

'I don't know, do I? I do what the gods tell me! They want this king to come, they want him to have the sword and they want me to make it happen! I needed you to do some of the things necessary – like looking after the sword and the woman.'

'The woman … Megan?'

'Ygrain, yes – she's to be the king's mother. They told me to get you to do it and I did! You don't question the gods!'

'And that's it? That's all I'm getting!'

'That's more than most people get their whole lives! You're not the only one involved in this, you know!'

Merlin wiped his nose once more and looked at him, darkly.

'I was going to rescue you,' he sniffed, 'but sod that! Not any more!'

He stood up, retrieving the sword and his staff from the ground.

'I only came for this anyway.'

The name 'Caliburn' suddenly registered with Llew.

'Is it really Caliburn, the sword of Rhydderch?!' Llew asked desperately.

'I'm not telling you!'

Merlin started to walk away towards what seemed to be a narrow path heading downwards.

'You can't leave me here!' shouted Llew after him.

'Oh I can't, eh?' Merlin shouted back, 'just watch me!'

'It's freezing! I'll die! You can't let me die here in the cold.' Llew could hear the desperation and pain in his voice, making it rise, fall and break at strange chromatic intervals.

'There's a shepherd lives in the valley. He usually comes out of his cave and looks for his lost sheep at dawn. You better hope he does so when this one comes, hadn't you?'

Merlin turned back to him. He was now just a grey shadow in the distance.

'You have the torch, Llewellyn Ap Gwyddno,' and now the strange magical voice was back, 'make a fire.'

'What with! There's only rocks and grass here! Merlin! *Merlin!!*' he screamed, '**Merlin**!!!'

But the shadow was gone.

Llew forced himself to sit up and pick up the torch, breathing heavily and shivering. He knew he must get warm if he was to survive the night ... but what to burn? The remains of the cart? Impossible. It was all big thick planks of wood – it wouldn't catch light without kindling, a lot of kindling ... like dry twigs or ... or ...

His eye fell on one of the split parchment sacks. Flakes of snow were falling now. It wouldn't be long before the sacks were completely covered ... Unless ...

Unless they were on fire – the thought came to him less like a revelation and more like a ... fast-acting germ, because it was not a pleasant thought, it was a thought that made him physically sick – on fire and keeping him warm. Some might survive, he thought, but not many – parchment burns quickly and there were a good few hours till dawn, he was sure.

It wasn't, he had to admit, much of a choice.

Slowly and very painfully, tears beginning to stream from his eyes, holding the torch high in one hand, he began to crawl towards the sacks.

It hurt so much, he was seeing things – hallucinating – he was remembering his childhood, back in the village, huddling round the fire, an iron cauldron boiling in front of him while his grandmother told stories of the Old Ones ... then Aquae Sulis, in those big buildings full of heat, so many rooms full of heat ... Aquae Sulis on the mighty river ... water flowing to the sea ... to the hot lands. Water ... water flowing ... heat ... cauldron ... supposing ... supposing you could put a hot iron cauldron in every room of a big house, join them together ... pump the hot water around it and to and from each one ... that'd be better than the hypocaust ... you could seal it ... stop the water from turning to steam ... if you made the cauldron *flat*, you could put it against the wall and it wouldn't take up so much room ... a house full of flat iron cauldrons all pumping hot water from one to another ... keeping the whole place warm ... it was a really good idea. A new kind of magic.

Visions. Magic. A prophet now, too.

If he survived the night he'd have to write all this down.

Epilogue

In 1160, a monk called Robert De Guillaume, a contemporary of Geoffrey of Monmouth (arguably the first Arthurian biographer), claimed to have found a fragment of an ancient page of manuscript, referring to the siege of Llangollen. Geoffrey himself had dismissed it, believing the page to be a forgery, and told Robert to destroy it. Before doing so, Robert copied down the writing in his private journal. This journal now resides in the British Library. The page itself, written in Latin, appears to be a verbatim account by a veteran of the siege to an unknown recorder, many years after the event itself.

According to Robert, the fragment read:

'... for the old man did sayeth unto me, "So we was starving for many months and much hunger was had and I thought Ceridwen would waste away, but Prince Uther Pen Dragon came with his mighty army and laid waste to the rascals in a great battle and no one knew what happened to Matholwch but I hope he lost his arm like I had once lost mine or worse and there was much rejoicing and the gates was opened and Uther was welcomed in by King Bruenor and there was much feasting and then two days after Princess Megan did return unto us what I had not seen for many years with the great hairy man of the Lord – him that I had also seen with Vortigern Britu – who was so shocking in his raiment that Ceridwen and the other ladies did turn away and scream and there was more rejoicing for Megan was to be married to Prince Uther by the hairy man and she was to have a baby which was to be called Arth, but we all called him Arthur; but anyway the King Bruenor held counsel with Uther Pen Dragon and not much could be heard of what they said except that Bruenor much cursing from him came and shouting "he did promise you what? That little –"'

At this point, Robert writes that the page was torn.

THE END

Printed in the United States
97250LV00001B/150/A